# Chloe Marr

## A. A. Milne

This edition published in 2023 by Farrago,
an imprint of Duckworth Books Ltd
1 Golden Court, Richmond, TW9 1EU, United Kingdom

www.farragobooks.com

First published in 1946 by Methuen & Co. Ltd.

This book is a work of fiction. Names, characters, businesses, organisations,
places and events other than those clearly in the public domain, are either the
product of the author's imagination or are used fictitiously. Any resemblance
to actual persons, living or dead, events or locales is entirely coincidental.

A catalogue record for this book is available from the British Library.

Paperback ISBN: 978-1-78842-457-8
eISBN: 978-1-78842-458-5

Cover design and illustration by Emanuel Santos

# Have you read them all?

Treat yourself to the *Marvellous Milne* series —

### Mr Pim
One of Milne's most popular novels – a warm, funny,
comedy of manners with a happy ending

### Two People
A gentle novel considering how a relationship can work when those
concerned have less in common than they once thought.

### Four Days' Wonder
A hilarious spoof on the detective novel.

Turn to the end of this book for a full list of the series.

# Chapter One

## 1

As the clock struck twelve on this late June morning, Miss Chloe Marr, fragrant and newly-powdered, came like a goddess from the bath, girdled herself with Ellen's help, and stepped into her knickers unaided. A telephone bell rang.

'See who it is,' said Chloe, wrapping a dressing-gown round her. 'Slippers.'

Ellen placed slippers at Miss Marr's feet, and padded to the telephone. 'All right, all right,' she grumbled to its ringing.

'If it's Mr Denham, I've gone out, and won't be back till this evening.'

'Anybody else you won't be back till this evening for? What about Mr Hinge, or whatever he calls himself?'

'Well, see who it is, don't stand there talking.'

'Hallo,' said Ellen down the telephone. She listened, put the mouthpiece against her stomach, and said, 'Mr Lancing is downstairs.'

'Oh!' said Chloe. 'Ask him— No, I'll speak to him.'

'Miss Marr will speak to Mr Lancing,' said Ellen to the telephone, and handed it over to Chloe.

'Hallo, darling,' said Chloe. 'What are you doing here at this time of day? . . . Well, it's a very poor excuse. You must think of a better one next time.' She laughed and said, 'Well, just five minutes. And Claude! Are you there? Darling, count a hundred first. I'm only

1

just out of bed . . . No, *not* like that. Like this: One—Two—Three, lunging alternately to the right and left . . . I leave that to you, darling. Inhale through anything you like, as long as you make it a good, honest hundred. Till then.'

She came to the dressing-table, saying, 'It's Mr Lancing.'

'I told you,' said Ellen. 'You won't have time to make your face up while he counts a hundred. More like a thousand'

'Mr Lancing is a painter. Paint means nothing to him. Except for the lips, this is a study in the nude.' She gazed at herself in the glass. 'Try and make the bed look a little less like a bed; Mr Lancing is very young.'

'He goes on as if he was ninety.'

'When you are my age, Ellen, you will realize that that is one of the signs of extreme youth.'

Ellen, pulling the eiderdown over the bed and patting out the pillows, laughed cynically.

'When I'm twice your age, more like.'

'I was being polite,' explained Miss Marr severely. She painted her mouth with a loving finger; and, seeing Ellen in the mirror, said 'Don't overdo it. We don't want him to think I spent the night in somebody else's bed.'

'What *do* we want him to think?' grumbled Ellen.

'That I slept like an innocent child from dusk to dawn, and glided out of my couch at dawn like a—My good Ellen, what the hell do we care *what* he thinks? There's the other telephone. See who it is.'

Ellen listened, and said down the telephone, 'Just a moment, Lord Sheppey.' Chloe frowned violently into the mirror, and pointed a thumb over her shoulder at the bathroom. After a suitable pause Ellen said, 'Miss Marr says can you leave a message, or shall she ring you later, she's in her bath . . . Very good, Lord Sheppey. We have your number. I'll tell her. Good-bye.' As she hung the receiver up, the bell rang again surprisingly. She listened, and said, 'Oh, I'm sorry, Mr Denham, Miss Marr has just gone out . . . Yes, she had to be out early to-day . . . I'll tell her, yes. Yes, as soon as she comes in. We have your number. Good-bye.'

2

'Well, that's got rid of two of them for the day,' said Miss Marr complacently. 'Listen, there's Mr Lancing.' She pulled her dressing-gown more tightly round her and tied its sash. 'He's in love with me, Ellen, did you know?'

'You say that of all of them.'

'Well, they all are, aren't they?'

'More fools they.'

'Oh, well, now you're opening up an entirely new subject.' She gave herself a last look. 'Right, I'm ready.' She stood up.

Claude Lancing came into the sitting-room. He was small and dark and neat, with an odd air of being both alert and imperturbable. His movements were quick, but made without any appearance of hurry. If you were told that he was a first-class boxer, you would believe it, and it would be true. If you were told that he was a first-class painter, it would not be true, but he believed that it was going to be. After all, he was only twenty-three.

'Darling!' called Chloe from her bedroom. 'Come in!'

As he came, she leant towards him, holding out her cheek for his kiss. His hand made to go round her waist, but she was quick too, and had had much more practice. She caught the hand in hers, giving it a loving squeeze and returning it to him. His kiss came no nearer to her mouth than she had intended. She went back to her dressing-table. 'You can sit there and watch me do my face,' she said, as she tied up her hair.

'Must you? I was wondering why you looked so lovely.'

'"And I'd always thought she was so plain," you'd been saying to yourself. Ellen, I think Mr Lancing must want a drink. Sit down, Ellen will get it.'

'What about *you*?'

'I'll have just a sip of yours. I shall be drinking like a mad thing in about half an hour. So you think I look better without my little make-up?'

'Yes. Of course, you can't help being beautiful with a face that shape—'

'And eyes like stars, and teeth like pearls, and a nose like a scimitar—go on,' scoffed Chloe.

'Not stars. Wet violets with the sun on them.'

'Yes, I've heard *that* said before.'

'I'll tell you one thing about you.'

'Do. I know nothing of the subject.'

'You're the only woman I've ever met who doesn't get a kick out of being told she's beautiful.'

'And you're twenty-three, and you've met your mother and your old nurse and your sister Claudia. Fancy!'

'Well, you're rather overstating the case. My mother died when I was two. I may have said "Pitty Mummy," but I wouldn't know her reactions.'

'Oh, darling, I'm sorry.' She put an impulsive hand out to him, and he held it. 'I don't mean about your mother dying, because I expect you've got over it by now, or about being a little lost orphan, but—' She took her hand away, and said, 'Ellen, why did I say I was sorry? What am I sorry for? I can't imagine. Is that Mr Lancing's drink?'

Ellen came to them with the incomparable Chloe Cocktail.

'Give it to me,' ordered Chloe. She sipped it, leaving a kiss within the cup, and bestowed it on Claude as it were a decoration. 'There, darling. And I'll only put a very little make-up on to-day, if you like me best like that.'

'Bless you,' said Claude, looking into her eyes, and drinking to her.

Chloe gave him all her heart in her eyes, or what he thought was her heart, and returned to the mirror. 'How's Claudia?' she asked brightly. 'Getting on nicely?'

'I don't know what she's like at the Academy, but she's terribly like an actress at home.'

'There was a time when *I* thought of being an actress, but Ellen said I was one already, and the urge left me.'

'That I never did, Miss Marr,' said Ellen indignantly.

'Then I must be thinking of somebody else. Or something else. Enjoying your drink, darling?'

Claude nodded. He had a wonderful feeling of well-being. He could see himself sitting there: at ease in Chloe Marr's bedroom: the Beautiful and Notorious Miss Marr. And then another picture came

4

suddenly into his head: of Venus and her Mirror: a modern Venus, all curves and litheness, seated at her dressing-table, and, reflected in the mirror far away and small, a very old gentleman sitting up stiffly, in a very stiff collar, on a very stiff chair, holding a top-hat stiffly on his knees. It would be an allegory of— of something. Or perhaps leave out the man, and the mirror too if it came to that, and just put poor old Ellen in. Or Ellen's face in the mirror. Two women, showing what beauty must come to. Yes, that would be good. But of course he'd seen it first as a very small old gentleman in a top-hat, so perhaps—

'What are you thinking about, darling?' said Chloe to the mirror.

'My art,' said Claude, with one of his rare smiles.

'So am I.' She looked at herself more closely. 'Well?' she said, turning round. 'What's the verdict?'

Claude took a deep breath.

'You were right,' he said. 'You couldn't be more beautiful than that.'

Chloe laughed triumphantly, and the telephone bell rang. 'Darling, you'll have to leave me now. I must dress.'

# 2

As Barnaby had often told her, she was the loveliest, sweetest, truest, kindest, most generous girl in the world. Always, afterwards, he had realized that she was none of these things. Except loveliest. Hers was not a benignant beauty, a beauty that comforted, a spiritual beauty which illumed and made more beautiful the beauty which hid it. Her beauty was beauty triumphant; alive, challenging, insistent; a brilliant attack on the sex of every man. Was it a cold, deliberate attack? When he was away from her, he wondered. When he was with her, he surrendered. It was happiness just to look at her. So he looked at her once a week . . . and thought about her for the rest of the week.

Barnaby was thirty-something; with an honest, blunt-nosed, ugly, handsome face, and friendly grey eyes under upward-pointing eyebrows. As he took those eyes off her to look at the bill, she said, 'Are we being good, darling?'

Chloe liked going to the expensive places to lunch, and Barnaby liked taking her to them; but they had an understanding that the bill was never to be more than twenty-four shillings. Once, a long time ago, it had been twenty-four shillings, and she had said, 'Now, let's never go beyond that.' When they didn't go beyond it, they were good.

'Fairly good,' he said.

She withdrew her eyes from her little mirror, glanced at the bill, and said, 'Oh, *darling*!'

'We had an extra cocktail,' he explained.

'So we did,' she said, relieved, and went back to her mirror. 'We're really *quite* good now, aren't we?'

'I don't know about good,' said Barnaby. 'I'm just sensible. And if you think I'd rather lunch for a shilling by myself at some beastly tea-shop than lunch with you here for thirty shillings, you're just an idiot.'

'Darling!' She gave him that lovely, quick, tender smile which she had given, he knew, to a hundred men, but which remained always a private benediction. 'Do I cost you *very* much?'

'Not a penny too much, sweetheart.'

'Well, it isn't *really*, is it? We have lunch or something once a week, when we're both in London, which makes it a good deal less than once a week, and if it's only just over a pound each time—'

'I thought a perfect lady never went into all this.'

'Darling, I'm never a perfect lady with *you*. Haven't you discovered that yet?'

'Not as completely as I should like.'

Again that smile, with a hint of laughter this time, intimate and loving. Even if all the others had had it, he didn't mind.

'I always feel different with *you*. You know it.'

'Good heavens, yes. I'm practically the only nice man you've ever met.'

'Well, you're the only one I can say what I like to.'

'What would you like to say?'

Her hand found his, and stayed there. 'What I was going to say—'

6

'—lady or no lady—'

'—was that it only comes to fifty pounds a year, and we do get a lot of happiness for that, don't we, darling?'

'We do. It's worth three times the money.'

This was as well, because that was what it was: about a hundred and fifty, one way and another. However, he lived on the other four-fifty as happily as he could have lived away from Chloe on anything.

She began to look for her gloves. Generally they went back to look for them, or she took another pair from her bag, and said, 'Never mind, darling. I can ring up.'

'When do we meet again, sweetie?'

'When you like,' said Barnaby. 'Couldn't we have a day in the country together?'

'What about the stuffy old office?'

'I'm taking a week's holiday next week. To fit in with one of these family men.'

'Darling, how exciting! Why didn't you tell me? Where are you going?'

'I'm waiting for you to say. Is next Thursday all right?'

'Don't be silly, ducky. Aren't you going away properly?'

'No. I'd go away improperly, if you'd come. We'd go to Brittany. I know a village.'

Again that quick look, that quick intimate smile. But different. No one had ever had it like that before. Except— Well, what did it matter, anyway?

Chloe sighed and put on her gloves.

'Why don't we?' she asked.

'God knows.'

'I don't love you enough, my darling.'

'So I suppose.'

'You wouldn't like it if I wasn't really loving you.'

'Yes, I should.'

She laughed happily.

'Oh, darling, I'm glad you said that. I should have hated you if you'd gone all Tennyson suddenly.'

'Try hating me for a change. Anything to be different from the others. As a matter of fact, I shouldn't like it.'

'I think you would. I think you would.'

'No. If you did it for me, you would do it for all the others. I should hate that.' Chloe flashed a look at him, and drooped her head to her gloves. 'Let's stick to England. Thursday? If you don't feel like the country, we could take a hamper to Lord's. Gentlemen and Players.'

'All right, darling. And we'll go to Brittany *one* day.'

'We will.'

'I absolutely promise.'

'So do I. I may be ninety at the time, but I'll make the crossing somehow.'

'We'll come on deck in our bath-chairs, and have them side by side.'

'I hope it will be calm. It wants to be calm for bath-chairs.'

'They've got brakes they put on them now so that they don't roll backwards down the Leas at Folkestone. They used to lose a lot of old ladies at one time.'

'I'll inquire into all that,' said Barnaby.

'Oh, darling, I do love you,' cried Chloe, and it sounded to him like a sudden cry from the heart, but meaning, 'Oh, darling, I *wish* I loved you!'

In the taxi he said, 'Take off your gloves till we get to Antoine's.'

'Darling . . . Will you take the taxi on?'

'I think I'd better, or I shall be late. Where shall we go on Thursday?'

'We'll see how we feel, darling. Ring me up on Tuesday, and we'll talk it over.'

'Right.'

Even if he were married to Chloe, even if Chloe were his own for ever, he would have to leave her now. He couldn't sit holding her hand for an hour and a half while she had her hair set. It would look so strange.

'Good-bye, my darling, my Chloe.'

'Good-bye, dear one. Thank you for my lovely lunch. And you'll ring up on Tuesday. Eleven o'clock.'

A quick light kiss on his mouth, and she was gone. 'Prossers,' said Barnaby savagely to the driver. 'At the top of Chancery Lane.'

# 3

Miss Marr, her hair newly set and looking, which was one of its charms, as if it had been set yesterday, was sitting on the divan with the Duke of St Ives. Many a woman had found that this was a dangerous thing to do, but not Chloe. She had met him a fortnight ago. She knew all about the Duchess and faithful Freddy Winter; she knew all about the Duke and as many glamour girls as had names to identify them. When he said, with a conquering smile, could he come to see her and perhaps they might go out somewhere (what?), she asked him to tea. She let him in herself; they were obviously alone in the flat. He must have thought that this was too easy. Chloe must have thought so too. He went away with a bewildered look on his face, and an invitation, for which he had thanked her humbly, to come to tea again some time. To show the purity of his intentions this time, he had brought a game called Reversi with him. ('Any sort of game,' he had said at Hamleys. 'Isn't there something called Ludo or something? Or anything.') They sat on the divan together, but the Reversi board was between them. It was their fifth game and what made it very exciting was that they had each won two.

'Go on, Tommy, I can hardly bear it.'

Chloe was as excited as a child. If the Duke didn't do anything about it, and he didn't see what he could do about it, two whole rows of his black counters were going to be red. 'Is it my turn, is it my turn?' she said impatiently.

'Damn,' said the Duke gloomily. 'It looks as if you're going to win.'

'Do you give me best? Do you own that I'm a better Reversi player than you? Because if so, you can have a drink.'

'I do,' said the Duke. 'And I want a drink like hell.'

Chloe swept the counters triumphantly into their box, in case he changed his mind, and busied herself with bottles.

'Your flowers do look so lovely,' she said. 'It was sweet of you.'

'It needn't always be flowers, you know.'

'Well, well, aren't we lucky?'

'Damn it, you have birthdays, don't you?'

'Every now and then. Every year, to come out into the open.'

'When?'

'Yes, I think I'd better tell you when it's closer. I'll write it down, so that there will be no mistake.'

'How old are you, Chloe?'

'Twenty-eight.'

'I'm forty-three.'

'What do I say now?'

'Thirteen years ago—'

'Don't tell me. I can do it. You would have been thirty, and I should have been fifteen.'

'Yes. Too young. You'd have been too young. Henrietta was twenty-two.'

'This sounds like a near-proposal. If Things had been Different.'

'Supposing they had been?'

Chloe looked at him thoughtfully, the shaker in one hand, a glass in the other. Under her silent, passionless valuation he began to feel uncomfortable.

'I'm not much to look at,' he admitted with an uneasy laugh. But it was the first time he had ever thought so.

'Good enough,' she said absently. And then, making up her mind, 'Well, we'd have got engaged, anyway.' She poured out his drink.

'You know, you're utterly unlike any other woman I've ever met.'

Any other woman would have asked 'How many women have you said that to?' but Chloe didn't. She gave the impression that there weren't any other women. She smiled an acknowledgment of her uniqueness.

'Now drink that up like a good little boy and then you must go.' She gave him his cocktail. 'Because I must have my bath.'

'I'd give a thousand pounds to see you,' he burst out.

'I'm sure you would.'

'I'm sorry. I oughtn't to have said that. Not to you.'

'Say anything once, Tommy. I'll let you know when you ring the bell. Or hit the marker.'

'You know, I'd got quite the wrong idea about you.'

'You're not the only one. It leads to a lot of disappointment.'

The Duke nodded, a little gloomily.

'May I bring Henrietta to see you one day?' he asked; and seemed to be listening to himself with surprise.

'Of course.'

'Dammit,' he laughed, 'I've never made *that* offer to a woman before. But then—'

'I'm different,' smiled Chloe.

'My God, you are.' He finished his drink and stood up.

'Like it?'

'What's it called?'

'Chloe's Delight.'

'I'd have drunk it more slowly if I'd known.'

'Now that's really a nice thing to say, Tommy.'

'I'm sorry about the other day.'

'That isn't. It's silly. Of course you took a chance. Why shouldn't you? I'm glad you did. Now we know where we are.'

'I suppose in a way,' said the Duke, looking on the bright side, 'it *was* a sort of compliment.'

Chloe laughed, shaking her head at him.

'It's a compliment which leaps to the mind very easily. You'd be surprised.' She held out her hand. 'Good-bye.'

He took her hand in his, and said, 'Could we go out one night, do you think?'

'Well, I think now, don't you?' He realized that she meant 'Now that we know where we are.'

'Thank you. I'll ring up. What are you smiling at?'

'Shan't tell you.'

'Oh, all right. Good-bye, lovely Chloe.' He bent and kissed her hand.

'Good-bye, darling. You're rather sweet.'

# 4

It was possibly the thought of Ellen which had made Chloe smile.

Ellen called Miss Marr's friends by their names: Mr Lancing, Lord Sheppey, Mrs Clavering, and so forth. It was a point of pride with her to hold herself above the 'Sir' and 'Madam' class of servant. Some of these friends believed that Ellen was an old theatrical dresser whom Miss Marr had found destitute and taken on out of pity. Others, who were not so sure that Miss Marr did things out of pity, thought that Ellen was her old nurse. Nobody asked Chloe. This was partly because, when one knew her well enough to ask her, one knew that the answer would be appropriate rather than authentic; partly because, by the time one knew her as well as that, Ellen had no separate existence apart from Chloe, and Chloe (sometimes it seemed) no separate existence apart from her.

'You know, my dear,' said Sir Everard one day, 'when you get married, Ellen will go on your honeymoon with you, and you'll make up a little bed for her in the corner of your room; and then, if any difficulties arise—and they say that the honeymoon is a difficult time—she can be appealed to with perfect confidence. "We never do, do we, Ellen?"'

'Did you find them arise much, Everard?'

Sir Everard, who had been married three times, and still was, smiled, and said:

'I was going to add—and you shan't put me off—that it is the difficulty of making love to you and Ellen simultaneously which has prevented you receiving any offers of marriage so far. Get rid of Ellen, and it may be that a Chartered Accountant would ask for your hand.'

'Goody, goody,' said Chloe gleefully. 'A real Chartered Accountant. They're swell at figures,' she explained. 'Like me.'

Ellen, then, would have to talk to the Duke of St Ives on the telephone, and she wouldn't say 'Your Grace' and she could hardly say 'Duke'. So what? 'Yes, Duke of St. Ives, I'll tell her, we have your number.' Very awkward for her. But as she helped Miss Marr into the black dress that evening, all she knew was that the Duke had been to tea again, and that the orchids which had just come were from somebody called Tommy.

'Or the blue after all?' said Chloe, a mirror in her hand, her back to the long glass.

'I don't think Mr Walsh notices,' said Ellen wearily. The blue had been on twice already.

'We shan't be alone at the Berkeley, you know. There are always one or two other people there. And at the Four Hundred.'

'You wore the blue at the Four Hundred last week,' said Ellen, fastening on to the cue so luckily given to her. The telephone bell rang. 'That'll be Mr Walsh.'

'And, as you say, he doesn't notice. Ask him to come up.' She held an orchid against her breast at different angles, liking herself. 'You were quite right, Ellen. The blue would have been terrible.'

None of Miss Marr's friends ever ceased to wonder how she could go about with the others, and to all but himself Percy Walsh offered the most constant field of surprised speculation. He was nearly forty; good-looking in what is called (in peace-time) the military style; tall and heavily-built, with an inclination to actual stoutness; slow, deliberate of speech, sure that what he said was worth listening to, that what he had done was worth recounting. So, when he spoke, he never coloured his words, nor tried to make them more interesting; for the fact that it was he who was saying them was surely enough. His slow, lazy, self-assured voice would have given equal value to the regrettable news that he had just shot the Chancellor of the Exchequer by mistake, and to the good news that he had been wearing a pair of Digby and Lawson's shooting boots when doing it.

'Good evening, darling,' called Chloe through the door.

''Evening, old girl.'

'Shan't be a moment. Help yourself.'

'Thanks.' He helped himself and settled down comfortably. 'I met a feller once who knew a feller whose governor made potato-crisps, when I say made them, I mean that was what he made.'

'I follow you, darling. (No, just a little higher, Ellen.)'

'Struck me as damn strange, making potato-crisps all day and all night, don't know what you think about it.'

'Damn strange, darling. (Key in the bag, Ellen?) Still, somebody must make them.'

'Point is it wasn't a side-line with this feller, he just made potato-crisps. If you'd asked him what he was, he'd have had to say he was the potato-crisp feller. Well, that strikes me as a damned unlikely thing to be.'

'If you'd seen it in a picture, you wouldn't have believed it was true.'

'What's that?'

'Don't say another word. I am now about to burst upon your vision.' She came through the door triumphantly, very tall on her high heels, every inch of her crying, childlike, 'Look at *me*!'

Percy looked at her, getting slowly to his feet.

'Well?'

'Don't hurry me, there's a word I'm trying to think of; what it comes to is, if I were one of these poets you hear about, that's the word I'd use.'

'I simply can't wait. I suppose it's no good suggesting some?'

'Radiant. That's it, radiant.'

'Darling, you don't have to be a poet to think of a long word like that.'

'It's just a word I happened to see, and I said to myself, "That's how the old girl looks sometimes." Well, let's have a kiss.'

He put an arm round her waist, and kissed her.

'Has anybody ever fallen down when you've done that?' asked Chloe. 'One of your smaller girl-friends? Or do you warn them to get the back foot up against something?' She took her drink from the table, glancing at her face in the mirror above it. She was intact.

'Leaving all that on one side and going back to what I was saying, it struck me as more than a bit surprising if you asked a feller what his son was going to do, talking about his son and wondering, well, not really giving a damn of course, but just for something to talk about, and he said he was going to make potato-crisps. Well, it's just how it strikes you.'

'Could I have the last little one, do you think?'

'Oh, sorry.' He held out the dish, so nearly empty.

'I always wondered who ate them,' said Chloe, nibbling delicately, 'but I do see now that there must be a very impressive sale for them.' She sat down on the arm of his chair. 'Where are we going? I think the Berkeley, and the Paul Muni.'

'Right. I did explain to you, didn't I, how it was about supper? This feller Chater. George Chater.'

'Is she pretty? (Ellen, ring up the Berkeley and ask for a sofa-table for Mr Walsh.) Dark or fair?'

'Who?'

'This girl you've thrown me over for.'

'I don't know what you're talking about. I'm talking about George Chater. He lives down at Woking, don't ask me why, but there it is, that's where he lives, and he's coming up from Woking and giving this party. His uncle left him a very tidy tea-business in the City, and when he's not there, he's down at Woking, and he's throwing this party at the Embassy for a niece of his who's just got engaged—by a very odd coincidence, at least it strikes me as odd—to this feller I was telling you about whose governor makes potato-crisps. So it all looks as though I shall meet him to-night. Hanson his name is, I ought to have told you that before. You've heard of Hanson's Potato-Crisps?'

'After to-night, darling, I shall be able to say truthfully that I have. Did you keep your taxi?'

A sudden light came into Percy's eyes.

'That's a damn strange thing,' he said. 'I never thought of that before. How would it be if I rang up this feller Chater, and asked him if I might bring you along to the party? I don't suppose he'd mind.'

'I don't suppose he would, darling, but his niece might.'

'Why?'

Chloe smiled and stood up, and looked down at herself, and sighed, and said, 'I don't know.'

'It's just that I don't like to think of you beating up for home at the very moment when things are beginning to hot up, as you might say.'

'Oh, Percy, don't be so stupid,' said Chloe impatiently. 'I'm supping at the Savoy with Everard, and we're going on to the Four Hundred. My cloak, Ellen.'

# 5

Sir Everard Hale had once declared his feelings for Chloe to be those of an incestuous uncle. 'However,' he added, 'luckily I am not your uncle.'

Chloe gave him an amused smile, and said that he might as well finish the sentence.

'The end is not yet; I am still hoping,' said Everard firmly. 'What I am trying to explain now is that Conscience, who has an absurd reputation for being well-informed, never says to me behind her hand, 'Remember you have a wife', but 'Remember she is your niece'. Why is that?'

They were at the Savoy to-night; in the corner of the window which Chloe loved, for it put the whole Grill Room in front of her, and yet left her private. Everard was fifty-something. He looked like a well-preserved actor who was still looking fifty-something when he was really sixty-something. He was very proud of Chloe; and it was partly the realization of this which made him think of himself as her uncle, or some one responsible for her. He liked to believe that Chloe had come out, or, anyhow, bloomed under his auspices.

He enjoyed introducing important people to her, and seeing them fall, as instantly as had he, to her compelling conjunction of beauty and wit. So proud, so complacent might a Sultan feel displaying his latest purchase, or a newly-married husband still sure of his young wife. It made him, as Barnaby had cried to be made, 'different from the others', when in fact he was as much her slave as all of them. But a slave who wore his fetters lightly, with an air of tolerant amusement.

'Had a good day?' he asked, putting up an unnecessary eye-glass through which to study the *menu.*

'Lovely, thank you, Everard.'

They ordered supper, while the champagne, ordered in advance, was uncorked and poured out. Everard raised his glass, and said with as much feeling as his nature allowed him to express, 'Always.'

'Always, darling,' said Chloe, in her cool, velvet voice, touching her glass against his.

'Well, what's come over the tape to-day? Any new quotations?'

Chloe laughed, and said that Hales Preferred had gone up a point.

'Not they. I'm steady in the market at 78, and you know it. What of that new young fellow? Claude, isn't it?'

'Claude Lancing?'

'May be. He comes to the mind as Claude. Being new he should be quoted at ninety. I shall have the intense satisfaction of watching him drop, point by point.'

'Don't be so absurd, Everard. He's only twenty-three. I mean age. Well—every way.'

'It's a wonderful age to be,' said Everard wistfully. 'If I were twenty-three, I should ask you to wait five years until I had caught you up, and then marry me. Has he done that yet?'

'He has asked me to marry him. Of course.'

'And so as to be sure of losing neither him nor yourself you said, "Let's go on as we are, and see how we feel."'

'I told him,' mocked Chloe, 'that he must ask my Uncle Everard.'

'To which he replied: "I will live in thy heart, die in thy lap, and be buried in thy eyes; and, moreover, I will go with thee to thy uncle's."'

'Claude, poor darling, would have to go by himself to *his* uncle's, before he could even buy a licence.'

'You ignore the supreme aptness of my quotation, probably because you didn't recognize it as one. How like a woman.'

'Dearest, dearest Everard, I played Benedick at school, and barely recognized it because you said it so badly. Listen.' She clasped both hands to her heart, leaning towards him. You felt that Benedick was down on his knees at Beatrice's feet. 'I will live in thy heart'— the lovely voice throbbed with emotion—'die in thy lap'—the ecstasy of dying so!—'and be buried in thy eyes'—ah! the peace of it! Whereupon Benedick rose, dusted his knees, and added in a bright, cheerful voice: *'And,* moreover, I will go with thee to thy uncle's.'

'Darling, darling, marry me,' urged Everard, quite carried away. 'You're heaven. I can't do without you.'

'What about your wife? You'd have to do without *her.'*

'We've gone into all that. She'd divorce me, and be glad to.'

'As you say, darling,' said Chloe gently, 'we've gone into all that.'

'Sorry. I'm a fool.' He drank deeply, wiped his mouth, and said with a wink, 'Stopped being a fool.'

'You're very sweet,' said Chloe, smiling fondly at him. 'I couldn't do without *you.'*

'Good. To return to your incredible schooldays: I suppose they made you play Benedick because even then you despised matrimony.'

'I was a great big girl.'

'Then you can't have looked much like Benedick. All the same, I wish I'd known you then.'

'You're the second man who's said that to-day. I must look up a photograph.'

'Who's the other?' asked Everard jealously. 'Not young Claude? He'd have been in his rompers.'

'Tommy.'

'St. Ives? Yes, I was afraid it was coming. Be gentle with him. He can't help being a Duke.'

'Don't you trust me, darling?'

'Shall I give you another quotation?'

'Oh, do you know another one?'

Everard laughed, and quoted:

*'If all the harm that's been done by men*
  *Were doubled and doubled and doubled again, And melted*
  *and fused into vapour, and then Were squared and raised*
  *to the power of ten, It wouldn't be nearly enough, not near,*
  *To keep a small girl for the tenth of a year.'*

'And don't tell me,' he added,' that you recited *that* on Speech Day before all the Old Girls and Governesses, Like it?'

'Yes,' said Chloe thoughtfully. 'I wonder if it's true.'

On their way back from the Four Hundred, Chloe said:

'I am alone in my little service flat, and it is three o'clock in the morning, but if you'd like to come up for a drink, ducky, you can.'

Everard, who knew that he would get nothing more than a drink, said that he wouldn't keep her up, and he'd take the taxi on.

'Then good-night, my darling, and thank you for a lovely, lovely time.'

He put his arms round her as she lifted up her mouth, and held her there.

'God bless you, my sweet,' he said, as he let her go.

She jumped lightly out, cried his address to the driver, and was gone.

'And it didn't mean a damn thing to her,' thought Everard, as he wiped the lipstick away.

# Chapter Two

## 1

When Claudia Lancing writes her reminiscences, she will probably omit to say that her first inspiration to the stage came from her father, Henry Lancing, whose anecdotes of Civil Service life made it so essential that she should get away from home and do something. Any art is, in a sense, an escape from life, but hers was uniquely an escape from Henry's life. Claude was coming to London, anyhow; he, obviously, had to 'do' something. Claudia, fearing to be left alone with her father, looked round for her life-work, and decided that it was acting. She would come to London too, and attend the Royal Academy of Dramatic Art. She and Claude would live together on their mother's money; little enough, but enough. For the moment Claude saw only the advantages of this arrangement: a housekeeper and a model.

'Right,' said Claude.

Henry went more fully into the matter.

'I cannot contest your decision, Claudia,' he said. 'I remember Sir Laurence telling me once how when he was at the cross-roads—'

'Yes, you told us, Father,' said Claudia.

This might have put off another father, but not Henry.

'Ah,' he said, 'then you remember how *his* father said to him—' And so on.

Both Claude and Claudia remembered this well. Over Claudia's bed was a highly-coloured and highly-imaginative picture by Claude, entitled 'Sir Laurence at the Cross-Roads'. By Millais out of Tennyson, as he explained.

They lived in a studio on the Fulham Road; and Claude had the bed behind the screen and Claudia had the cupboard. It was very uncomfortable, but it was a studio, and almost Chelsea. Of the two of them Claudia drew the greater satisfaction from this fact.

'All right,' said Claude, 'you can let the expression go for a bit. I'll tell you when I want it again. It's only that the expression—I mean the idea—helps to get the body right.'

How much of man's achievement in the arts has been inspired by woman. It was only since meeting Chloe that Claude had felt the urge for expressing himself in the comic papers, and acknowledging cheques from them at the end of the month. A side-line, he told himself, to which he could devote his evenings; but a necessary side-line for anybody who wanted to take anybody to the Savoy.

Claudia smiled rather stiffly and let the expression go. She also put the tennis-racket down.

'Mind my talking?' she asked.

'Not if you don't mind my not listening,' said Claude, busy on his drawing.

'You know, this is really rather good practice for me. I mean getting the expression. Let's see how quickly I can do it. Amused Contempt— no, that's not very good. Amused Contempt—that's better. Now then quickly: Amused Contempt—Surprise— Innocence—'. She contorted her pretty, well-meaning, little face into the positions which are now accepted as expressing these emotions.

'I should have thought,' said Claude, not looking at her, 'that it was very *bad* practice for you.'

'Why?' said Claudia, still experimenting with Innocence, which she seemed to find elusive; perhaps because the usual adjective for it is 'wide-eyed', and her deep-set, eager little black eyes couldn't do the work. 'Innocence' she murmured to herself again, and decided to defend it instead, crossing her hands over her breast.

'The proper way to express an emotion is to feel the emotion first.'

'You can't always on the stage,' said Claudia, who now knew all about it. 'Well, suppose I'm listening to the heroine telling about the hand that came out in the night and clutched at her. Well, naturally I express horror, don't I?'

'I should,' said Claude.

'Well, but the author might have written it badly, or the actress might be playing it badly, and it mightn't sound at all horrible. But I could *help* the audience by showing in my face how horrible it was. What we call playing up to each other. I mean it all *helps* to create the feeling of horror.' She added 'Horror', and showed him what she meant.

Claude took one glance at it, and said that it wouldn't help him at all.

'Well, of course the lighting's all wrong. I mean, all that comes in, too. The *ensemble.*'

'The what?'

'What I said,' snapped Claudia, a little annoyed. 'Considering I rehearse dud scenes from the French classics two days a week, on the off chance that the author knows a couple of French words and wants to get them into his next play—'

'Talking of the classics, did I ever tell you what Sir Laurence said to me once about Catullus?' began Claude. This was a sure way of restoring good humour. Claudia laughed and said 'Never, darling, I've often wanted to know. Was it at the cross-roads?' Claude grunted, feeling that Claudia always just carried a thing too far. How different from Chloe. Chloe would never have said, 'Was it at the cross-roads?'

'I think the racket now, if you don't mind. In front of the body in two hands. No, not that. You've just stepped into a musical comedy saying your only line "Well, girls, who's for a game?" and the only girl who doesn't go flat after two notes says "Oh, to be playing again that game of love with Harry at Trouville": Song "The Game of Love": and there you are, standing around while she sings, with your racket in two hands, and—*that's* what I mean. Good.'

Claudia was silent for a little, and then said, 'Well, I mean, take laughing. That's one of the things we have to do.'

Claude, who wasn't interested, asked why.

'In case one of the characters says something funny. Use your brains, darling.'

'Sorry, I'm trying to draw, you know.' Relaxing for a moment, he said, 'Are you any good at it?'

'Well, not bad. Say something, and I'll show you.'

'When is a door not a door?'

Claudia, who was really rather good at it and had been told so that morning, gave him a ripple of delighted laughter.

'That one went pretty well,' said Claude, looking thoughtfully at his drawing. 'I must think seriously about becoming a dramatist.'

'Now I'll show you Dora. Just give it me again, will you?'

'Do what?'

'Say the joke again.'

This time Claudia gave a prolonged nervous giggle, and explained that that was Dora.

'Who's Dora?'

'One of the girls at the Academy.'

'Was that like her?'

'It was. Really.'

Claude held his drawing out at arm's length, and said, 'Hopeful girl, Dora.'

'Her father makes bicycles or something. I mean she's all *right*. I mean for money.'

'I wish Henry made bicycles. Henry would make superb bicycles. They would go on and on and on and round and round and round and never never stop.'

'Oh, do you?' said Claudia. 'I think it's rather fun like this. We've got just enough to live on, but not enough to spoil our art.'

'It would take a devil of a lot to spoil *my* art,' said Claude, wondering with whom Chloe was dining this Sunday night.

'Is it as bad as that, darling?' said Claudia brightly.

'Don't you believe all that rubbish about independent means spoiling an artist. If I had independent means, I shouldn't be doing this stuff.'

'What's wrong with it, anyhow? It doesn't do you any harm, does it, learning how to draw? It doesn't do an actress any harm going into musical comedy. She can always learn *something* from it. Stage-sense or timing, or something. It only hurts you if you let it hurt you.'

'Well done, Brighteyes. My God, the girl's intelligent. Takes after her brother. All right, and now you can give us the famous expression again. Sort of contemptuous amusement—here, where is the damned thing?' His left hand fluttered round the table and lighted on a piece of paper. '"*She*—that's you—*to latest profiteer*: Don't you *love* Borotra? *He*: Yes, I always stay with the Governor."'

Claudia, forgetting that she was an actress, gave the nervous laugh of one who had expected the climax later.

'Thank you very much,' said Claude. He added a line to the joke, and read, '"*He, under the impression that Borotra is a tropical island*: Yes, I always stay with the Governor," Now we shall *all* see it.'

There was no mistake about Claudia's laugh this time. It was the genuine thing.

'That's rather good, Claude. Did you make that up yourself?'

'Like Hell I did. God, I sweated blood over that.'

'It's rather good.' She was thoughtful for a little, and then said, 'Of course, you *could* ask a man if he loved Borotra without having a tennis racket in your hand.'

'Not,' said Claude firmly, 'in a comic paper.'

It had never been a good joke, but somehow it seemed better now that Claudia hadn't seen it; worthy, almost, of Chloe's intelligence. That was what was so wonderful about Chloe. She never let you down. There was no flaw in her body, no flaw in her mind. Think of all those girls one met in May Week. All looking very pretty and well-dressed; all gay and charming; and then you sit close up to one and talk to her, and it's all no good. Something's wrong. She was all right from the front, and now she reminds you horribly of somebody else; or there's a bit of superfluous hair about; or there's a

24

spot coming on the corner of her mouth; or she's perspiring; or her hands are ugly; or you try one of the three best jokes in the world on her, and she laughs mechanically. Something. But you were safe with Chloe. No matter how close you were to her, she would never let you down.

'I've just thought of something,' said Claudia. 'Shall I tell you?'

'I don't see why not.'

'Well, when I say "Don't you love Borotra?" I'm all interested, and thinking of him, and loving him myself; and it's only when I hear the answer that I'm contemptuous. Well, if the action of the drawing takes some moments, which moment is it that you're catching? Is it always the last?'

'Don't ask me. I hate this sort of joke, anyway. As a matter of fact, she isn't looking contemptuous any more. Just eager and excited.'

'Like this?' said Claudia eagerly—and excitedly.

Claude looked at her, and looked beyond her at Chloe, and thought how different, and said 'More or less'.

Five minutes later Claudia was standing at his shoulder and saying indignantly that it wasn't a bit like her.

'It wasn't meant to be,' said Claude.

'All the same, she reminds me of somebody.'

'Vaguely like a woman?' suggested Claude.

'*I* know! That girl you're always seeing in the *Sketch* and the *Tatler,* the one who's supposed to be living with Sir Everard Hale. *You* know! Chloe Marr!'

In a cold voice, which she hardly recognized, Claude asked her *who* supposed it; and she knew at once that he knew Chloe Marr and was in love with her. And she knew that, if she were not careful, she would lose him.

'You know what people are,' she said quickly. 'They say *anything* of *anybody.* I suppose they once had lunch together or something. Besides, if you're as beautiful as that, people always take it for granted that you're living with somebody.'

'And who do they say *you're* living with?' asked Claude, his voice friendly again.

Claudia kissed his ear and said, 'My clever little brother. But then I'm not beautiful. Like her.'

The telephone rang, and she said 'I'll go, darling'; but Claude in his unhurried way was there before she had finished saying it.

# 2

The General's wife was staying on with the Claverings for a few days, but the General had to be at work on the Monday; so Chloe had offered to drive him up on the Sunday evening after dinner. The week-end had been like all other week-ends at Croxton. She encouraged her host, who made what would have been outrageous love to her if it hadn't so obviously been humorous; she played with the twins; she was kind to an average selection of young men, and friendly to the young women. None of them took up very much of her time. The greater part of this week-end, as of all others at Croxton, was spent with Kitty Clavering, once known on the stage as Kitty Kelso. They sat in the garden, or in Kitty's bedroom, and reviewed the world, told each other stories, and made each other laugh. Kitty, after forty adventurous years, still looked exactly as she must have looked at twelve, with all that wide-eyed innocence which Claudia found so hard to reproduce.

'I didn't know you went in for Generals,' said Chloe, when she was having the guests explained to her. They were sitting in the walled-in garden, eating strawberries.

'Oh, my sweet, this isn't Generals. This is *the* General, the one I ran away with. Cecil. Didn't I ever tell you about him?'

'No, darling. Make it up as you go along.'

Kitty, not really needing the invitation, slapped Chloe's hand and said, 'It was when I ran away from my first husband, Ernest. I pinned a note on the bed-spread. No sooner had I left the house, and gone to have my hair set before joining Cecil at Victoria Station than Ernest comes creeping into my bedroom and pins a note on my pin-cushion. That, darling, is what I call irony. The two notes, so near to each

26

other, yet so far. Each with an irrevocable message to communicate, yet irrevocably prohibited from communicating it. Do you mind all these long words?'

'I'm keeping up splendidly,' said Chloe. 'He was running away too?'

'Yes. I suppose so. I never heard who she was. He just said, vulgarly and rather crudely, "Good-bye, Kitty, I cannot bear it any longer."'

'And what did yours say?'

'Mine said with infinite pathos, "Good-bye, *Ernest*, I cannot bear it any longer."'

'*Much* more dignified, darling.'

'That's what I thought. Fortunately Elise kept her head. As soon as she found the notes, she rang up my hairdresser, and I returned at once and consulted my solicitor. On his instructions I wrote another little note, saying, "*Come back*, Ernest, I cannot bear it any longer."'

'What about Cecil? Or is he still at Victoria?'

'Don't be silly, darling. He's just round the corner. Perhaps I had better lower my voice a little.' She pitched it a note or two higher, and went on: 'All would have been well if Ernest, who was a very literal-minded man, hadn't immediately come back to me; and we didn't part until six months later, by which time Cecil had got tired of waiting, married somebody else, and was sent to some station abroad.'

'He seems fond of stations. Is this the wife?'

'Yes. Don't laugh, darling, but her name is Victoria. It's impossible to say that there is no Design in Life.'

From the moment it was suggested to him, the General had looked forward to that evening drive with Miss Marr, and he was naturally a little disappointed when he discovered that Ellen was included in the party. He had hoped to hold Chloe's hand most of the way, but now he didn't; either because he felt he didn't know her well enough, or because he felt he didn't know Ellen well enough. In fact, neither of them would have thought anything of it. And since an invitation to supper, if it were to be worth while, would have to exclude Ellen, and he was beginning to think that this was impossible, he did not suggest supper, nor ask her in for a drink on arriving at Eaton Place, but merely kissed her hand, as any General might, and decided to order a few roses next morning on his way to the War House. So Chloe came to her own little flat in South Audley Street, to find herself alone in London on a Sunday night at the ridiculous hour of ten. She promptly rang up Barnaby. Hearing that Barnaby was in the country, and wouldn't be back till Monday evening, she rang up Claude.

# 3

Claude had wondered whether to kiss her. He thought that he would like his sister to see him kissing Miss Chloe Marr, and he thought that he would like it to be a secret between him and Chloe, and he thought that Chloe mightn't like Claudia to know that he kissed her, and he thought that Chloe might be annoyed if a secret were made of anything so simple as a kiss. All this would have made it difficult for him, if Chloe had not made it so easy. The arm which she held out was uncompromisingly straight, and the smile said anything which he liked to believe. He shook hands and introduced her to Claudia.

'I hope you didn't mind me wishing myself on you,' Chloe said to her, with the warm friendliness which radiated from her so naturally at a first meeting. 'I'm a very good listener, and having heard everything about you, except the one thing that matters, I felt I must come and see you. And, to be quite frank, I was all alone, and very bored.'

'Of course not,' said Claudia eagerly. 'It's lovely to see you.'

Claude gave his sister an approving smile for this, and asked Chloe what was the one thing that mattered.

'Well, naturally, what a woman looks like. I guessed you were pretty, but not nearly as pretty as this. Of course I only had Claude to go by,' she added, with a mocking smile for him.

Claudia coloured charmingly, as she could never have done if told to at the Academy, and said that brothers didn't notice their sisters' faces. Claude said she didn't mean notice, she meant saying

28

complimentary things about it every day, which got boring after about twenty years. Then, the instinctive host, he said, 'We've got nothing to eat or drink. I did warn you, didn't I?'

'Yes, we have,' said Claudia quickly, 'we've got the cherries.'

The look on Claude's face, which cried contemptuously 'Cherries for a woman who should be bathed in champagne and caviare!' had barely time to form. Chloe said eagerly:

'In a paper bag?'

'Yes. Look!' Claudia pushed them triumphantly along the table. 'I'm sorry,' said Chloe, taking her gloves off, 'I'm going to eat them all. I'll leave my bracelet in exchange, I'll give you a reference to my banker, I'll sign the pledge never to smoke, drink, or swear again, but I'm going to eat them all. Where do we flick the stones? The "we",' she added, 'is purely conventional.'

Claude opened a window close to the table.

'Is that the sort of little alley I came up?'

'Yes. It's quite safe.'

Chloe put a cherry in her mouth, munched, removed the stone, flicked it neatly out of the window, and said, 'No, I can't do it alone. It's no fun. Have a cherry?' She held out the bag to Claudia. 'This isn't unselfishness, it's just that I like competition.'

They munched and flicked. Claudia thought: She's lovely. What a silly little schoolgirl I seem. She's so complete. She's got everything. *I* shall be like that one day. When I'm playing leading parts. In a year or two. Well, in two or three years. Of course I'm small, but men like small girls. It makes them feel more protective. I wonder if it's true about Sir Everard—and all the others. Well, why shouldn't she?

'Did either of you ever discover,' said Chloe, still eating, '*why* Life was just a bowl of cherries? I used to lie awake and wonder. It kept me awake for years. Then I decided that it wasn't, and went to sleep again.'

'What did it rhyme with?' asked Claude.

'That's the profoundest thing that has ever been said on the subject. Or, indeed, on any subject.' She felt in the bag, and announced that alas! Life had come to its predestined end. 'So let's turn to Art.'

It was Claudia who insisted on showing Chloe the drawing, the artist saying, but not very convincingly, 'Oh no, dammit.' Chloe looked down at it for a long time, and her eyes came slowly, sidelong, up to Claude's, and sent a message to them; and he read in it a loving acknowledgment of her presence in his picture, and a pledge that it would always be so between them.

'It's a little like *you,* don't you think?' said Claudia.

This time it was a smile which flashed to Claude, as Chloe said: 'Is it? Then what am I supposed to be saying?'

'It's just a stupid joke,' said Claude.

'It isn't, Claude, it's very good. If you don't tell her, I will.'

'Hurry up, one of you, I can't wait.'

'Oh, all right. *She* says, "Don't you love Borotra?" and *he* says, "Yes, I always stay with the Governor."' It seemed more unfunny to him now than ever before.

Perhaps it wouldn't have seemed very funny to Chloe, but Claudia said quickly, 'It does sound so *exactly* like a tropical island, doesn't it?' and her desire to help was so obvious that Chloe added to a quick look of understanding which would have thrilled a lover a delighted laugh which would have reassured the most self-depreciative author.

'Oh, but this is wonderful!' she said. 'You must have a series. Next week she says, "Don't you adore Perry?" and he says, "I always drink cider." The week after—'

'Please don't think that I like this sort of joke.'

'Don't stop me. The week after, she says, "What do you think of Austin?" and he says, "I prefer a Morris," and she says, "What about Lacoste?" and he says, "It's just as cheap"—in fact, be of good comfort, Master Ridley, we have this day lit such a candle by God's grace as I trust shall never be put out.'

'If you're not careful, darling, *you'll* be put out.'

With one half of his mind he was hoping that Claudia had noticed the 'darling', with the other half he was hoping that she hadn't. But Claudia was already thinking 'What fun if they got married. I should be a bridesmaid, of course. I don't believe any of those stories. Wasn't she a great friend of Wilson Kelly's? Well, I mean, if she's my sister-in-law, and knows Wilson Kelly, I mean she could hardly help mentioning me to him, and if I went to see him—' She wondered what time of the year this would be, and what she would be wearing, so that Wilson Kelly would say, after she had laughed once or twice, 'You're just the young actress I've been looking for, Miss Lancing—' Of course, it would be Claudia after they had been rehearsing for a day or two, he wasn't so old really, just right, and of course there was nothing in those stories about him and Chloe, well, there couldn't be or she wouldn't be marrying Claude.

The young married couple were walking round the studio, looking at Claude's drawings pinned on the walls for decoration. They came to Sir Laurence at the Cross-Roads; and Chloe, hearing the explanation of it, said absently, 'Do you know anything about potato-crisps?'

'I know that you eat them.'

'I meant socially. Their private lives. I heard a great deal of their inner history the other day from a friend. What one might call the Whole Story. Luckily I haven't remembered any of it.'

'And your friend's name *wasn't* Henry Lancing?'

'No,' she said, with an appreciative smile for his quickness. 'But it made me think of the cross-roads in a potato's life.'

She said her good-byes, calling them Claude and Claudia, and wished good luck to the drawing. 'Oh, and, Claudia, if, when you know it all, you want an introduction to any particular person, and I happen to have met him—'

'Oh, you *are* sweet,' cried Claudia; and then, wonderingly, 'Didn't *you* ever want to go on the stage?'

Chloe cleared her throat in an introductory manner, and said: 'All the world's a stage, and all the men and women in it players. They have their exits and their entrances. Which is one of the reasons why I am now leaving you. Good-bye, darlings.'

'I'll see you into a taxi, shall I?'

'Oh, do, Claude, that will be lovely.'

It was also lovely to kiss her again.

# 4

There was the usual hurry in the morning when Miss Rattigan arrived, Claudia having overslept herself, as she so often did. Miss Rattigan 'did' for them, artists being her speciality. She was a bulky but not beautiful young woman; indeed, not so young now; and for more years than she liked to remember, she had been afraid that one of her artists would suddenly insist on her posing for him in the nude. Even John Heron, who so far had only painted bowls of flowers on a polished mahogany table, was not above suspicion of working up to Miss Rattigan. Fortunately her mother had told her what to say. 'Quite quietly, Maude, looking him squarely in the face: "If it's just me you want, as I might be having tea with a friend, that's one thing; but I don't take my clothes off for the King himself in all his glory." He'll see at once the sort of girl you are.' Miss Rattigan was still waiting for an opportunity to show him the sort of girl she was.

She tapped on Claude's screen and said: 'Miss Lancing's out of the bath, Mr Lancing, and the water's on the boil.'

'Thanks,' said Claude. He swung himself out of bed, and began to feel for his slippers. 'What's the weather like?'

'Nice, bright morning, this morning. I see by the paper there's been another horrible murder down Maidstone way.'

'Well, *I* didn't do it.'

'I see by the paper they found a clergyman's collar in the vicinity.'

'Was there a clergyman inside it?'

'Just the collar, Mr Lancing. In the vicinity. I always say, if a girl can't trust herself with a Reverend, who *can* she trust herself with?'

'You're right, Miss Rattigan, it's a hard life for us women.' He came from behind the screen in his dressing-gown.

'You're right there, Mr Lancing. Look at me. I oughtn't to be doing this really.'

'Now I think *you're* right again.'

'Well, I don't do it really. I mean it's more to oblige, as I told you at the time.' She raised her voice and said, 'I'm going now, Miss Lancing.'

'Right,' called Claudia.

'I'm going now, Mr Lancing, if there's nothing else you want.'

'Right,' said Claude.

She went. Claude shaved. 'Make the tea, darling, I'm frantically late,' shouted Claudia. He made it, and retired to the other cupboard, which was the bathroom . . .

Claudia rushed in, book in hand. She poured herself a cup of tea, propped the book against the teapot, and muttered to herself. Then she closed her eyes and said aloud:

*'Cesario, by the roses of the spring*
*By maidhood, honour, truth and everything—*

'Thank God, I needn't draw at breakfast,' said Claude, coming into the room. He scratched the back of Claudia's neck, said 'Good morning, Brighteyes,' and sat down. She took no notice, but went on:

*'I love thee so that, maugre all thy pride,*
*Nor wit, nor reason, can my passion hide.*
*Do not extort my reasons for this clause—*
*For that I woo, thou therefore hast no cause.'*

'A great man Shakespeare, I always say,' said Claude. 'Would he mind if I had the teapot for a moment?'

Claudia waved him into silence, and went on:

*'But rather reason thus with reason fetter,*
*Love sought is good, but given unsought is better.'*

'It was,' said Claude, 'Burbage's insistent demand for exit lines which drove Shakespeare back to Stratford at the comparatively early age of forty-five.'

'It's all right,' said Claudia, shutting the book, 'I know it.' She poured out her brother's tea. 'There's a tomato if you want it.'

'Thanks. I gather that you are playing the part of Olivia. How Olivia do you feel in the early morning? I feel very.'

'Thank heaven I can learn words. Some of the girls are hopeless. Of course, the men are worse. Dora's terrible. Of course, it doesn't matter in a modern play, you can always say *something*, but if you dry up in Shakespeare, you're done.'

'Not at all. Why? Historical play. Henry the Ninth, Part Six. There has been a slight hitch in the proceedings, and you and Dora are left alone and wordless on the stage. Is a Lancing to be left wordless? Never. You carry on.' He sucked at his tomato. 'Er—yes. Like this:

*'Go tell our cousin, Earl of Westmorland, Hengist and Horsa, Dukes of Buckingham, And Longbow, Strongbow, Wrongbow and the rest That these their charges lie upon our hearts Most dearly, making that which came before As naught compared with that which comes hereafter*

—at which point Richard the Third finds his horse and gallops on. Easy.'

'That's rather good. I mean it's rather like.'

'I told you last night I ought to have been a dramatist.'

'Wasn't last night fun? She is a dear, isn't she? I think she's sweet. I think it was sweet of her to say she would introduce me to anybody who—' Her eye lighted on her wrist-watch, and she jumped up saying, 'Damn, I shall be late again.' She vanished into the bathroom.

There was an anatomy class for Claude this morning. Just before he left for it he rang up Chloe. After a little delay Ellen informed him that Miss Marr was in her bath, and asked if he would leave a message. Failing to improvise anything more transmissible than Hallo darling, he said that Oh, well, it didn't matter, and came gloomily into the Fulham Road.

At three o'clock a large basket of cherries was delivered at the studio by Messrs Fortnum and Mason. It was addressed to 'Mr and Miss

Lancing', and the card within said, 'Just a slice of life with love from Chloe.' Claudia thought it was perfectly sweet of her. Luckily she was going to dinner with Dora, and then to a play, so that Claude had the studio and the evening to himself. He wrote to thank Chloe: a long letter covered with little drawings, including one of a potato at the cross-roads. She could hardly fail to ring him up and say how amused she was.

# Chapter Three

## I

The 'Prossers' to which Barnaby had driven after leaving Chloe was established in 1870, as it announced in gold lettering on its windows. This seemed to Barnaby to proclaim Prossers not so much an old-established firm as an old-fashioned one. If one could not go back further than 1870, one should be silent about one's age.

It was Dr Alvin Strange Prosser who was responsible for the windows. In 1868 he had a care of souls in a Midland town; together with a doctorate of divinity of uncertain origin, and a passion for writing. He began his literary career by interpreting the Bible 'for students and others' in a series of broad-minded volumes. His first book (not unnaturally) was *Genesis Interpreted* by Dr Alvin Strange Prosser. This was followed six months later by *Exodus Interpreted* by Dr Alvin Strange Prosser, author of *Genesis Interpreted*. Realizing by the time he got to Deuteronomy that it was the middleman who took the money, he bought back the rights in his earlier books, turned his collar round, and started publishing for himself. It was now the aim of Prossers not only to interpret the Bible, but to bring it right into the homes of the people. A new series was begun, the first of many 'under the personal editorship of Dr Alvin Strange Prosser'. Two of its earliest and most successful volumes were *If David Lived in Dulwich* and *Joseph in Jermyn Street*; but there was an immediate sale even for the last one (published while the Editor was Holidaying in Antioch, and subsequently withdrawn) called *Ham at Hampstead*. By 1890 Alvin Strange Prosser was sufficiently established in the homes of the people to be identifiable as Prosser. *Prosser on the Parables* followed *Prosser on the Miracles*, and preceded *Prosser on the Plagues*. All this was leading up to the great work to which the author subsequently supposed he had been dedicated in infancy: *Prosser's Midnight Talks with the Dead*. The talks were quite informal. 'Tell me, Ezekiel,' Dr Prosser would say, and Ezekiel would keep in character as much as possible by replying 'Hearken, O Prosser. Unfortunately, in the middle of a conversation with Shadrach, Meshach and Abednego, in which, though outnumbered, he was more than holding his own, Dr Prosser was attacked by vertigo; and though he recovered sufficiently to announce that he was the original Scarlet Woman, and to make a will leaving everything to a Mr Gladstone who had died some years earlier, he was never quite himself again. His death six months later came as a relief to his nephew, and brought certain changes in the policy of the firm.

The changes, however, were made gradually and sensibly. The nephew was no hypocrite and no fool. The personal editorship of Dr Alvin Strange Prosser was now lost to the firm: moreover, the great man's only posthumous work, some disordered notes for a Midnight Talk with Rahab, was hardly suitable for publication. Yet the name of Prosser still meant something to the public and its goodwill was not lightly to be thrown away. Money was to be made in the publishing business, not only by sensational fiction; but equally it was not only to be made by free-and-easy religion. The future watchword of Prossers should be Education: education in all branches of knowledge.

So now, with Barnaby's help, Prossers, from the top of Chancery Lane, brought knowledge to the fireside.

Stainer, the managing director, came into Barnaby's room, and said, 'Do you ever go to Wimbledon, Rush?'

'When I can get tickets. It's not worth standing in a *queue.*'

'Dolly has a couple for next week. She wondered if you'd take her. You said you were staying in London, didn't you?'

'Yes. I should love to. What day?'

He had had dinner with the Stainers from time to time. Dolly was small and fair and fluffy and well-rounded, and looked twenty years younger than her husband. In *Do's and Don't's for Wives* (Prosser, 2*s*. 6*d*.) it is written: 'Never let your husband take you for granted. Show him that his men friends are attractive to you, and he will realize that he must make himself attractive too.' It was not for Dolly to question a Prosser book. She made it clear to her husband that Barnaby was attractive to her; and Stainer, guessing that Barnaby was in love with somebody else, made it clear to her that he wasn't in the least jealous. This was disappointing for Dolly, but it gave their friendship a sort of humorous licence which both of them enjoyed.

'Thursday,' said Stainer. 'That all right?'

'Oh! What a pity.'

'Engaged?'

'Yes. Damn. The one day.'

'Couldn't alter it, I suppose?'

Could he? Should he? Barnaby thought quickly. It was the sort of thing Chloe did to him, and he had never done to her. An arrangement made with her was sacred to him. They had definitely arranged to spend Thursday together, it was already in his engagement-book. To alter it now would mean ringing up, and getting no answer, and ringing up again and getting that damned engaged signal, and then getting through and she not being sure, and she wanting to know who he was going with, and what Dolly was like, and Dolly kept waiting, and unable to find somebody else . . . no, all too difficult. And what did it matter so long as he had Thursday with Chloe?

'No. No, I'm afraid not. Too complicated. Damn, I should have loved it. Tell her so, will you, and how sorry I am.'

'She'll be sorry too. Well, she'll have to get somebody else. I'll tell her how it was.'

'And give her my love.'

'I will.'

Barnaby had been at Prossers for five years. He had intended to be an architect, had, in fact, been an architect; and, on the authority of the books of reference, was still an architect. But it is no good just sitting in an office and being an architect, unless there is a demand for your services by somebody willing to pay for them. There was no demand for Barnaby's services. To while away the first four years of waiting he read the *Encyclopaedia Britannica;* to amuse himself in the last year he wrote a little book called *How to be an Architect.* The acceptance of the latter by Prossers (when the jokes had been taken out) introduced him to Stainer, and initiated the 'Your Boy' series. I. *Your Boy as Architect* by Barnaby Rush. It happened that Cardew's monumental work in six volumes, *Architecture Through the Ages,* was just going through the press, and Barnaby, very much out of work in the sense that he had never been in it, offered to help with the proofs. The offer was gratefully accepted. Gradually it came to be understood in the office that Mr Rush had a valuable store, or what seemed so to the ignorant, of highly specialized knowledge on a variety of subjects. 'Is Mr Rush in the office to-day?' Stainer would say. 'Then ask *him.* He might know.' And so, from being in the Autumn List 'Barnaby Rush, A.R.I.B.A., the well-known architect', he became by the Spring the firm's Mr Rush and General Editor of the 'Your Boy' series.

Three years ago one of Prossers' most distinguished and deco-rated authors had summoned Stainer to Berkshire for the week-end, to discuss what he described as a project of great importance in the world of science. Stainer, with no knowledge of what was or what wasn't important in the world of science, and a tenderness for his own garden at week-ends, told Rush to go. Barnaby went.

Chloe was there.

(So, of course, was Ellen.)

Chloe drove him back to London on the Sunday evening, mostly with one hand, and they had supper together . . .

That was three years ago. He was now thirty-five.

# 2

The Duke rang up on Monday. Ellen was quite equal to him.

'Just a moment,' she said, and then, mouthpiece to stomach, 'The Duke of something.' Chloe stretched out a hand for the telephone.

'Hallo, Tommy. Good morning, and how *are* you? ... Wimbledon? Yes, I should love to. What day? . . . Oh! Well, when will you be sure? . . . Oh, no, we must go *one* day . . . All right, darling, ring me up to-morrow. Better make it seven, and then I'm sure to be in. No, I can't promise, but I'll keep both days free till then if I can. . . Well, we can arrange that when we meet. Good-bye, darling.'

She hung the receiver up and said, 'The Duke of St. Ives.'

'Cornwall or somewhere, isn't it?' said Ellen.

'Let me have my book.'

'You've got a fitting on Friday.'

'I know.' She opened the engagement-book and sat up in bed, tapping her teeth with a pencil. 'I think you'd better ring up some time to-day and say that I may want to come on Thursday instead, and will that be all right. Oh, damn, no, I don't want to do that, and I don't suppose they'd be ready, anyhow. We might try early Saturday morning—when am I starting?'

'Isn't it in the book?'

'I shouldn't ask you if it were. Ring up Mr Walsh, and ask him what time he's calling for me on Saturday, and then ring up— No, *wait*! No, don't. Oh, hell, I can't *think*. I didn't *sleep* till six o'clock this morning, and then that damned man rang up at nine—'

'Lord Sheppey again?'

'Yes. Oh, Ellen, I'm so unhappy.'

'What's the matter, Miss Marr?'

'Nothing. Everything. I'll have my bath.'

# 3

Barnaby had spent the week-end in the country. He had been asked to stay until Tuesday, but there was no convenient train which would get him to London before eleven, when he had arranged to ring up Chloe. So he came back on Monday evening.

At eleven o'clock on Tuesday he rang up Chloe, and got the engaged signal. All Chloe's correspondence was conducted by telephone. It was initiated by her correspondents, and the engaged signal was part of the pattern of their daily lives. Barnaby heard it at intervals for the next three-quarters of an hour.

At 11.45 a very sleepy voice said 'Hallo!' and then 'Oh, it's you'.

'You sound as if you'd only just woken up,' said Barnaby.

'Well, I have. Couldn't you have rung a little later? I didn't get to sleep till six. What's the time now?'

'Quarter to twelve.'

'Gracious, I must get up. *Ellen!*' And then to Barnaby, 'I thought you were going to ring at eleven.'

'I did. You were engaged.'

'Well, really, Barnaby, you might have tried again.'

'I tried ten more times. You were very busy.'

'I told you I was asleep. Oh, I remember now. I took the receiver off when I went to bed. People ring up at simply any time of the morning.'

'I know. Sometimes even at the time they've arranged to.'

'*Ellen!* Darling, I *must* get up now. Could you ring up in a quarter of an hour? Would you mind very much?'

'Right.'

'Till then, sweetie.'

Barnaby had been going to Lord's. Play had begun at eleven, and Hammond would have been batting. 'Why the devil,' he thought, 'couldn't we have arranged it all last Thursday; just as Dolly and I would have arranged it if we had been going to Wimbledon? Why all this perpetual ringing up?'

He gave her twenty minutes. Ellen answered, and asked him to hold on, Miss Marr was just coming. She came five minutes later.

'Hallo, sweetheart, how are you? I was in my bath.'

'Are you out now, or going back again?'

'Out. Aren't we, Ellen? No, not those.'

'Well,' said Barnaby, 'what about it?'

'What about what, darling?'

'Thursday.'

'Oh! Oh, yes. I was just going to ring you up about that, wasn't I, Ellen? Ducky, it *might* have to be Friday instead. Would you mind *very* much?'

'When would you know for certain?'

'To-morrow. It's just that I *may* have to have a fitting on Thursday afternoon at three, and we were going to have the *whole* day, weren't we? You did want to, didn't you?'

'Yes.'

'We could have lunch *only* on Thursday, or the whole day on Friday, whichever you liked, sweetie.'

'Of course, I'd much rather have the whole day.'

'That's what I thought. So I'm trying to get the fitting postponed till Friday, and, if I can, then Thursday is *our* day, and if not, Friday. Is that all right, darling?'

'Couldn't we definitely say Friday now, and then it's all fixed, and you needn't bother about altering anything?'

'Oh, darling, Friday's such a long way off! Besides, I *have* already asked them—you rang up, didn't you, Ellen? —and I thought you'd rather it was Thursday, because of the cricket. Will that be all right, darling?'

'Of course.'

'I'll let you know to-morrow. When will you ring up? Eleven?'

'If you don't leave the receiver off.'

'Oh, darling, I'm sorry about that. I promise I won't to-morrow, and I'll be a good-tempered girl.'

'All right, darling. Eleven o'clock.'

'That will be lovely. How are you, darling?'

'Oh, all right.'

'What are you doing to-day?'

'I thought of going to Lord's.'

'You'll be late, won't you?'

Barnaby took a deep breath, counted five, and said, 'A little.'

'Well, enjoy yourself, baby. And be sure to ring me up to-morrow. I simply *must* get dressed now. Good-bye, darling.'

'Good-bye, darling,' said Barnaby.

He had meant to ring up Peter and suggest golf for to-morrow. Peter had a car, and would only play at Sunningdale. That meant starting at ten. Now he was tied to London until eleven. I am a damned fool, he thought. What do I get out of it? He went to Lord's. There was loud applause as he came into the ground, and Hammond walked back to the pavilion.

By 11.20 on Wednesday he was talking to Chloe again.

'Oh, darling,' she said, 'I'm terribly sorry, but to-morrow's no good. I've got this fitting at three—'

'Couldn't they alter it?'

'No. That's just it. They couldn't.'

'Never mind, darling. Friday will be just as good.'

'Oh, ducky, I can't on *Friday*! Friday I'm lunching with Tommy. Well, if you call it lunching, a drink and a nibble. We've got to be at Wimbledon by two. I thought it was Thursday you said. Didn't *you*, Ellen? It was always *Thursday*, sweetie—I remember your saying—'

'Yes, but you said yesterday when I rang you up—'

'Just a moment.' A murmured conversation. Then, 'Sorry, darling, I had to sign for something. Darling, couldn't we have a day *next* week— Oh, but I suppose your holiday will be over?'

'Yes. Oh, well, let's just have lunch to-morrow.'

'*Ellen*! . . . Hold on a moment, darling.' There was a long pause. 'Are you there, sweetie? I was just looking at my book, seeing if we could manage just lunch, but I don't think it would be very nice, darling. I'm having a hair-set in the morning, and I doubt if I should be out before quarter to two. And I see now my fitting is 2.30, so that gives us such a very little time. And I must go and see about some shoes, so I probably shan't have any lunch at all. *Ellen*! Darling, I simply must have my bath. What will you do to-morrow? Play golf or something? . . . I might give you a ring.'

'I'm not sure. I may go into the country.'

'Anybody I know, or by yourself?'

'Just a moment.' Barnaby was learning the technique. He put the receiver down, leant out of the window, and said '*Damn* you' several times. He came back and said, "Sorry, darling, a man at the door. I simply *must go* now. I'll ring you in a day or two, and we'll arrange something for next week or the week after. If you feel like it. Good-bye.'

As he had often told himself, she was the most treacherous, unfaithful, unscrupulous, egotistical liar in the whole world.

He filled a pipe. He didn't want to smoke, but he had to do something. Women (he thought) have an amazing reserve of stupidity. She promised to spend Thursday with me; yet, according to her own specially prepared story, with the whole library of truth and fiction to choose from, she tells me that, after making this promise, she deliberately arranged with a hairdresser to occupy her morning and a dressmaker to occupy her afternoon. Probably it's a lie. Probably these things were all arranged for Friday, and now she wants to go to Wimbledon with Tommy on Thursday. (Who on earth is Tommy? Never heard of him before, and she always tells me.) And she doesn't understand that it's much more insulting to throw me over deliberately for a couple of tradesmen than to throw me over, in special circumstances, for another man. Of course she goes about with other men. Of course she's fond of them. If Tommy is something new, then naturally she wants to accept his first invitation. Particularly to Wimbledon—who wouldn't? If she had asked me, of course I would have changed the day. But how can she pretend to be fond of me in the very least, if she can destroy our only day, our only possible day together, for silly little things like hair-sets and dress-fittings? How much would *she* like it, with much less reason for taking it to heart, if I broke a date with her in order to get my hair cut, or buy a pair of trousers?

What should he do now? Too late for golf. Go to Lord's again, and play golf to-morrow? Lord's was a good place to which to take an aching heart. The seats had a sort of comforting hardness, and the cricket played a melancholy accompaniment to one's thoughts. Then, at some flashing stroke, some beautiful co-ordination of mind and body, one realized suddenly that women didn't matter. It was a man's world. Once, walking away from Twickenham after the most thrilling Rugger match of the year, Barnaby had come face to face with a poster of a lovely girl, as scantily dressed as the London County Council would permit, advertising a leg-show at some theatre. 'You poor fool,' he thought. 'Who cares?' But that was before he met Chloe.

The telephone bell rang as he got to the door. He felt inclined to leave it, but it might be somebody suggesting golf, somebody who knew he wasn't at the office. Cricket or golf, anything in the open air, and leave the women to their little puss-in-the-corner parlour games.

'Hallo,' he said.

'Oh, darling, you're still there. I was so afraid you would have gone out.'

'Oh, hallo!' (How nearly he had missed her!)

'Sweetie, I've been thinking. Are you doing anything *very* special to-night?'

'No.'

'Then why don't we have a lovely evening together? We always seem to have been lunching lately.'

'Well, why don't we?'

'Well, let's. Where shall we go? Oh, *I* know. What about the show at the Hippodrome, or would that bore you?'

'No. Perfect.'

'Or is there anywhere else you'd like?'

'No. I'm all for the Hippodrome.'

'Well, if *you'd* like it, darling, let's go. And we could have supper afterwards, could we? Just as you like, of course, darling—'

'Good heavens, of course we will.'

'And perhaps go on somewhere and dance. Would that be nice?'

'Lovely.'

'Oh, darling, I *am* glad. And you're not angry with me for inviting myself like this?'

'Sweetheart. When shall I call for you?'

'Well, let me think. I don't think dinner, do you? Why don't you come here at half-past seven, or just a second earlier, and we'll have a drink and a crisp together.'

'A drink and a what?'

Chloe laughed.

'No, darling, not what you think, just something to eat. A potato-crisp. Just lately they've come into my life in a big way.' She laughed again. 'I feel much happier now than I did ten minutes ago. Do you?'

'Ever so much.'

'Hooray!'

'Hooray! How swell are you going to be?'

'Oh, very. I've got a new dress specially for you, darling. I hope you won't think it's improper.'

'I shall be very disappointed if I don't.'

A happy laugh, and 'Oh, darling, I do like going out with *vous.*'

'So do I.'

'Black tie for you, sweetie, because I love you like that.'

'Right.'

'Darling, I simply must have my bath.'

'All right, ducky. Seven-twenty-five.'

'Goody, goody, goody. What are you going to do now?'

'Lord's, I think.'

'Enjoy yourself, sweetie. Give my love to both the umpires, and say I'm terribly happy because I'm going out with my best boy to-night. Will you promise to do that?'

'I was going to, anyhow. I thought at the luncheon interval. *Not* interrupt the game.'

'Just as you like, darling. Is Grace playing?'

'He's dead.'

'Oh, yes, you told me. Well, give my love to Bradman. Is *he* playing?'

'He's in Australia.'

'Well, send him a cable, and tell him I'm going out with my best boy to-night.'

'I will.'

'What about Hobbs? Is *he* playing?'

'He's retired from the game.'

'Nobody seems to be playing. It is eleven a side, isn't it?'

'Sweetheart, I'm playing and you're playing, and what does it matter about any one else?'

'Who said it did? Darling, I love you. At least, that's what you think I said, but I shall deny it in Court. Anything I say to-night under the influence of drink cannot be used in evidence against me. I just adore you—or am I thinking of somebody else? Darling, I *must* have my bath. You keep on stopping me. You don't seem to want me to be clean. *Ellen!* Good-bye, angel. Seven-thirty prompt.'

'Seven twenty-five. Good-bye, my darling.'

'Seven twenty-four. Bless you, ducky.'

'Seven twenty-three. Good-bye, sweet.'

'Going at seven twenty-three, going, going—good-bye, Mr Rush—gone!'

But she wasn't. The telephone-bell rang again while he was still thinking how sweet she was.

'Hallo, darling! I find I have a moment to myself while Ellen looks for the soap. I know we had it last week, because I remember using it. What are you doing to-night? Anything interesting?'

'Just staying quietly at home and reading *The Wealth of Nations*.'

'Oh, is that good?'

'Very.'

'Is that the one where the girl thinks she's in love with another man, but the other man is in love with another girl, so they don't?'

'You're thinking of *The Origin of Species*.'

'So I am. I think of it a lot. I think of nothing else.'

'Darling, I meant to say before—what about orchids?'

'Oh, you *are* sweet! But really, darling, I don't quite see how there'd be room for them, I mean above the waist.'

'Good. But you could wear them on your bag or your cloak—'

'No, really not, sweetie. You're too good to me as it is. Just yourself, please.'

'All right, darling.'

'I shall now leave you. Why don't we have a nice talk on the telephone sometimes? Life is such a rush, Mr Rush. No sooner here than there. Good-bye, pet.'

'Good-bye, Chloe sweet.'

This time she was gone.

On his way to Lord's Barnaby thought: I am a very ordinary man, in a very ordinary office, earning a very ordinary salary. Chloe is the One Woman, with all London at her feet. There isn't a Duke or a Millionaire, a Genius or a Cabinet Minister, who wouldn't marry her to-morrow if he were free, or get divorced for her if he weren't. If she marries, and she must one day, she will marry a man like that, not a nonentity with £600 a year . . . Hair-sets and dress-fittings are to Chloe what golf and watching cricket are to me: part of the fabric of life. Going out with people, with the right people to the right places at the right time, and at the right intervals between those times, so that she sees neither too much nor too little of the right man, looking, herself, always exactly right: this is her work, her business, just as a man's is what it is, and mine is selling books. There are only seven days in the week; and yet I take it for granted that, as soon as I demand one of them from her, all the complicated arrangements which make up her life have to be so co-ordinated that I get my day put aside for me, ringed off, and regarded as absolutely sacred. All because I am the utterly unimportant Barnaby Rush, who has nothing whatever to offer her.

He had a happy day at Lord's, watching the Gentlemen bat with one half of his mind, and thinking of Chloe with the other. When he got home, in plenty of time to dress, there was a little box waiting for him. It was from a florist's. Inside was a red carnation, and the words 'For you, my darling, from your Chloe'.

As he had often told her, she was the loveliest, sweetest, truest, kindest, most generous girl in the world. No wonder that he loved her.

# Chapter Four

## 1

Contemplating our present exalted position, and looking back on the life which brought us there, we find that there is rarely a moment in it of which we can say: This happened then. It was then that the decision was made, the career was founded, the battle was won. The decisive moment happens more often in fiction than in real life; which is not strange, for the decisive moment is also the picturesque moment.

So it is impossible to say when Percy Walsh decided that he was engaged to Chloe. Had he proposed to her in the customary way, and she accepted him, then he could have noted in his diary that at 2.35 a.m. on June 5th at the Embassy he said, 'What about it, old girl?' and she said, 'Oh, all right'; this being, for a few weeks anyhow, a decisive moment in his life. But, in fact, he did not ask her to marry him. He merely let the conviction grow on him that she was going to; assuming by degrees, or, more accurately, assuming that he was assuming, the proprietary rights which are considered to be the perquisite of the engaged man. None of Chloe's other friends was deceived, for each one knew (or thought he knew) his Chloe. And though one of them might think, 'She couldn't possibly fall for a man like Walsh', and another might think, 'She couldn't marry Percy, if she won't even marry me', it was Everard who knew (or thought he knew) the real answer: which was simply that the last man to whom Chloe would ever concede rights was the man who had the right to them. If she let Percy give himself the airs of an engaged man, she couldn't be engaged to him. She was just amused by him.

To-day Percy was going through the traditional ceremony of presenting the 'little woman' to his 'people'. Superb Chloe was the little woman; the 'people' were Aunt Essie and the Vicar of Much Hadingham.

'I told you how it was about this fella,' said Percy, not untruthfully. 'He's no relation, if you know what I mean, but he's the fella who christened me.'

'Does he live with your aunt?' asked Chloe. 'I mean, of course, in a nice way.'

'No, I told you, he's the fella who christened me.'

'But you must have been very young then, darling. You wouldn't be talking about the old christening days years after, and saying, "Do you remember how cold the water was?" and "Do you remember—"'

'Sorry. Did that frighten you?'

'No.'

'The damn fella cut right across me. A Red by the look of him. There's a lot of that going about this side of London. That's the worst of living in Essex. Well, as I was saying, when a fella christens you, and goes so far as to write a long letter to you at school when you're being confirmed, a fella you've known all your life, mark you, and played for Essex, well, naturally, there he is. And when my people went down in the *Titanic*, and it was touch and go whether I went to Rugby or Harrow, and there was this fella Alfred Winghampton, practically on Aunt Essie's doorstep, and my whole future, as you might say, tottering in the balance, well, naturally Aunt Essie turned to him and said, "What about it?" and by the mercy of God he was an old Harrovian, otherwise I might have gone to Rugby.'

'I see, darling. How providential all round. It was just that I didn't realize that he and Aunt Essie had brought you up together.'

'Well, you might put it like that, but you can't get away from the central fact that he was the fella who christened me. By the way, you'd better call her Aunt Essie straight off, I think. I mean, don't feel that you have to wait till she asks you to, because she probably never will.'

'Do I call him Uncle Alfred straight off?'

'Well, that's a point,' said Percy, and for a mile or two he gave his mind to it.

'What do *you* call him?' asked Chloe, trying to help.

'I call him Wing, if you get me. Short for Winghampton,' he explained, in case she didn't.

'I might call him Hampton,' said Chloe.

After another mile Percy said that perhaps, taking it all in all, she had better call him Mr Winghampton.

'I think so too, darling,' said Chloe comfortingly.

# 2

'Well, my dear Essie,' said the Vicar of Much Hadingham, throwing his hat to the grass and settling himself in a deck-chair next to her, 'have you discovered the solution to your problem?'

'What problem is that, Alfred?'

'Whether they are actually engaged.'

'Not from anything which Percy has written. I shall know as soon as I see her.'

'There has been nothing in the paper.'

'No.'

'Perhaps the boy wished for your approval of the lady before announcing it.'

'It is not for me to approve or disapprove. He is old enough to make up his own mind.'

'Yes. It is hard to realize that he is nearly forty.'

'Only when you think of him. Not when you look at him.'

'True,' chuckled the Vicar. 'May I have one of your cigarettes?'

'Don't be silly.'

As he lit one, he said, 'One has heard of her, of course. I am told that her photograph is often in the *Tatler*.'

'I don't see the *Tatler*.'

'Nor I. She is not, I understand, an actress.'

'Nor, I believe, is Percy an actor.'

'No, no, quite so. Well, we shall know better when we see her.'

'What are you trying to say, Alfred?'

'Nothing, Essie, nothing. I was just thinking aloud.'

'You've been told something. Personally I never believe anything I am told.'

'Then it's no use my telling you,' smiled the Vicar, 'that you're a very wise woman.'

'I suppose she has a past.'

'A present was also implied.'

'Then if the present is not Percy, they are not engaged, and it is no concern of ours.'

'How very true. May I help myself to a drink, or would it be more polite to wait until they arrive? You know all these things.'

'It would be more polite to offer me one first. And then pour one for yourself. It will mellow you, so that you don't click your tongue when you see her, and say, "Tut-tut, a woman of Belial".'

'Really, Essie! I don't know which I resent most: the suggestion that I would do any such thing, or the implication that I should not wish to help you before I helped myself.'

'Dear Alfred.' She put out a hand which he raised gently to his lips.

'Dear Essie.' He drank his sherry with the air of one who was giving it his whole attention.

'Don't you sometimes wish,' said Miss Walsh suddenly, 'that *you* had a past?'

'At my age, my dear, a past is all that I can hope to have—in this world.'

'All the more reason for wishing that it were worth looking back on. When I was twenty, I had a proposal of marriage from a man who was reputed to be a heavy drinker. Yet we loved each other dearly.'

'And you refused him for the reason that he drank?'

'Yes. How right I was. In five years he had drunk himself into his grave.'

'How you must have rejoiced at your escape, dear Essie.'

'I did. But doubtless I should have rejoiced still more, had I been married to him. And for thirty-five years I have been denied the happiness of living again the ecstatic moments of those five years . . . and the happiness of not living again the agony of them. Makes you think, young Alfred.'

'Life,' said the Vicar, putting his hat on, and then impatiently pulling it off, and sending it with a backhand flick of the wrist twenty yards across the lawn, 'life is very difficult. I have always thought so, and always contended so. Wherefore I merely record now that my vocation has not permitted me to build up a past of rich and exotic colouring, and that, if it had, my conscience would never have stopped saying in a reproachful voice, "How *could* you?"'

'For every woman of my age who says to herself, "How could I *ever*!" there are ten who say, "Why did I never?"'

'I must admit that in such (as I hold them to be) uncanonical confessions from your sex as have come my way, remorse for lost or wasted opportunities has sometimes seemed to express itself in ambiguous terms. I gather from you, however, that they were not ambiguous.'

There was another short silence, broken only by the sound of the Vicar pouring himself out a second glass of sherry.

'On an Hellenic Tour one Spring,' he began suddenly— and was either lost in the memory of it, or decided that he wouldn't tell that one after all; for the story ended there, and he began again: 'When I was a young man of twenty, and had not yet given up all idea of entering my father's tannery, there was a girl—' Again he was silent; and then sighed, and said, as if he had told both stories, 'All this, of course, was before I married Agnes.'

'Naturally,' said Miss Walsh.

# 3

One of Percy's longer stories, if any of them may be so picked out, tells of an occasion in his boyhood, when a domestic crisis, which arose on a Sunday afternoon, demanded from him a piece of constructive work in the sanitary engineering line, of which the local expert, arriving after the crisis was over, declared that it couldn't have been done better if the young gentleman had been a natural-born plumber himself. Perhaps this is what he should have been. As it was, he spent five days a week on the Stock Exchange, and the greater part of his week-ends on the odd jobs which Aunt Essie had put by for him. 'Leave it for Mr Walsh,' she would say to the handy-man or the cook, 'he will be down on Saturday.' So firmly was his reputation now established.

It was perhaps fortunate, then, that there was something the matter with the boiler to-day.

'Do you mind, old girl?' said Percy, when the symptoms had been given to him at lunch. 'I'll just give it the once over, while you and Aunt Essie have a heart to heart.'

'I shall be resting this afternoon,' said Miss Walsh. 'I want Alfred to show Miss Marr the garden, if he will.'

'I oughtn't to, but I most certainly will,' said the Vicar firmly.

By the time Percy had got into his boiler suit, and Miss Walsh into a wrapper, Chloe and the Vicar were in the rose-garden.

'Let's sit down, shall we?' said Chloe. 'I get a lot of roses sent me, and they all have very long stalks, and there is only one rose on each stalk. Of course it's fun opening the boxes, and wondering who they are from, and arranging them, but they never seem to come from a garden, only from a friend. So it's nice sitting here, where they grow together as they please and I only have to arrange myself in order to enjoy them.'

'You must have been in many rose-gardens before, Miss Marr, for I suppose you are always out of London at week-ends.'

'Yes, but I've never put it quite like that before,' said Chloe, flashing a smile at him.

'No, no,' protested the Vicar, 'please don't suppose that I was doubting your sincerity. I just wondered—' He took off his hat, and rubbed his silver head; and then, wrinkling up a puzzled face, said, almost in surprise, 'Or was I doubting it? I suppose I was. Dear me! How quickly a thought flashes and dies, leaving a train of speech behind it; and by the time we have spoken, we have lost touch with the thought, and claim, in good faith, some other origin for our words. If you were insincere for a moment, Miss Marr, so, it seems, was I. Both my manners and my morals need your forgiveness.'

'Now listen,' said Chloe, putting her hand gently on his. 'That was a very pretty speech, rather elaborately worded, rather, as it seemed, self-conscious. Well, prettiness never did anybody any harm, and some of the most delightful men I know have elaborate minds, and one way or another we are all self-conscious. So I don't criticize it, I just record it as a clue to the sort of man you are. Well,' said Chloe, and now she was holding his brown, wrinkled hand in her firm, cool, young one, 'are you getting to know me from what I say, what I do, how I look; or are you just keeping an eye on me to see that I don't hide from you the character you had already imagined for me? *Now* be sincere, Mr Winghampton.' She gave his hand a friendly pressure, and left it.

'Miss Marr,' said the Vicar of Much Hadingham. He looked at the hand which she had held, and the brackets at the sides of his mouth deepened for a moment, but he didn't seem to be getting nearer to words. 'Miss Marr,' he tried again, and again stopped. 'Miss Marr,' he said finally. He put his hat firmly on his head, pulled it off, and whirled it across the grass. Chloe waited.

'I don't know what to say.'

'Try saying Chloe.'

'What a good idea! What a brilliant idea!' He leant back in the seat, looking at her, and pulling at his chin. 'I think you've found the solution. Chloe!' And then, wonderingly, 'Chloe!'

'Like it?'

'Yes . . . I suppose—no, that's absurd. No, it wouldn't do.'

'Why not, Alfred?'

He laughed, shaking his head at her.

'Well, privately,' said Chloe. 'Or, say, at Christmas.'

'Very well, at Christmas. You will be here at Christmas, no doubt. Percy always comes . . . No!' he shouted suddenly. 'You're not engaged to Percy! That was what put me wrong. Of course! How could you possibly be!'

'They all say that,' said Chloe. 'Sooner or later.'

'Well, now I shall be sincere. I *had* formed some thought of you in my mind. A very dear friend of mine was saying that when elderly women expressed remorse for their past lives, they were regretting, not the worldly, or possibly illicit, pleasures which they had wilfully enjoyed, but those which they had heedlessly missed. I had assumed, Chloe, without any warrant, that when you were old, you would look back and find—shall I say?—little to regret.'

'Very nicely said, Alfred.' She patted his hand.

'No, no, you mustn't. You are *not* engaged to Percy?'

'Of course not.'

'Sensible girl. Well?'

'I wonder. Shall I perhaps regret that I didn't confess my sins to a clergyman, with whom I once sat in a rose-garden?'

'No. I shall do as you asked me to do—judge you as you seem to be. Look at the roses. I sit here and thank God with all my heart for their beauty. Suppose I could also overhear them, talking to each other, saying in their velvet voices wise and lively and understanding things. Then I should thank God for a still more blessed miracle. So now I sit here, Chloe, and look at you and listen to you, and roses are all round me, and I thank God that there is so much beauty in the world.'

'But if there were blight on the roses, you would want to spray them.'

'Not these. They are not in my charge. I should wait until the owner of them asked me to.'

'Yes.' She sighed, and gave herself a little shake; and gave him a little laugh, and said, 'We are very serious for a summer day. Do you ever come up to London to buy yourself a new surplice?'

'Sometimes.'

'Shall we have lunch next time you come? I'll drive you down to Hampton Court, and we'll have lunch there. Would that be nice?'

'For me, yes. But for you—why should you waste your time on an old gentleman?'

The smile she gave him seemed both to mock and to caress him.

'I never waste any time,' she said.

# 4

The Vicar returned to the vicarage after tea, possibly to revise his sermon, but was back again for dinner. In the dining-room, after the ladies had left, Percy said:

'Well, as I was telling you, George Chater rang me up that morning. He'd got the Freddy Watsons and one or two other people coming out to dinner that night, and he wanted to know if I was free. Well, I don't mind telling you that that struck me as a damn strange thing to do, because George Chater is not the sort of fella to ask a fella to dinner in the morning, and expect him to turn up in a white tie and tails the same evening. Well, it came out that Freddy Watson had taken a damn bad toss the day before—well, naturally, when you hear that a fella has taken a damn bad toss, you take it for granted that that's what he's taken, and I said, "Well, he's been asking for it for the last two seasons," but apparently he'd fallen off the top of a step-ladder, trying to paint the bathroom ceiling green. Damn strange thing to do, it seems to me, when your missus has £10,000 a year of her own. However, there it was, that's what he'd done. The point was, would I take Freddy's place, and keep the numbers right? Well, as a matter of fact, George Chater has done me one or two damn good turns. I've never told Aunt Essie this, but there was a time when it was all Regent Street to a raspberry ice—'

The Vicar was leaning over the deck-rail in the early morning sunlight, as the islands rose one by one from the sea—what was her name? Not Chloe . . . She was neither dark nor fair, but between, and she had violet eyes —no, that was Chloe—and he held her hand, and he thought, 'Now I have held her hand, I shall have to ask her to marry me,' because in those days—

'Well, to cut a long story short, I didn't do anything. The port was just going round again, and a fella called Carruthers was telling us a damn funny story—get me to tell you that another time, damn funny story it was about a fella he knew in the F.M.S. who was calling on the wife of a fella—oh, well, perhaps not, I was forgetting for the moment—funny thing, I was telling this story only the other day to a woman I know, and as luck would have it, I just pulled myself up in time, and I said, "Look here, old girl, I can't *tell you,* but if you like to remind me to tell your husband next time I see him, and he cares to pass it on to you, that's *his* look-out." Well, to get back to what I was saying, I don't know how it strikes *you,* but it always seems to me a damned uncivil thing to use another fellow's telephone for a trunk-call. But passing all that for the moment—'

The Vicar was thirty. No, then he would have been in orders. Twenty-five, or was that too young? She must be nearly thirty herself. Very well, then, he's thirty-two, and in the Army . . . just going into Parliament . . . his first play just coming on . . . just succeeded to the title, Lord Winghampton . . . Oh, to be young again! No, no, he was happy to be old. It was less disturbing to be old . . .

'Well, one way and another, time went on, and by the time we'd joined the ladies, and had a round or two, and Chater had shown us a Dutch bed his missus had picked up—damned unpatriotic, I call it, damn strange thing to do, but that's the Bolshy side of her coming out—well, what with one thing and another—'

The Vicar, one hand in his pocket, one hand twisting the stem of his empty glass, stretched at full length in his chair, smiled happily at the ceiling.

# 5

In the drawing-room Miss Walsh stitched and said:

'I always wonder who Percy will marry. I try to see her in my mind, but it's difficult. Have you known him long?'

'It seems a long time.'

'Yes, it would do that. That is a very beautiful dress you're wearing.'

'I wondered if I was overdoing it in such a quiet, happy house, in such a quiet, happy country. I didn't really mean to wear it, but then I suddenly felt I'd like you to see it.'

'I'm very glad you did, my dear. I hope Maggie was helpful. Or shall I say, not unhelpful.'

'Oh, very, thank you.'

'I expect you usually bring your own maid.'

'Yes, but she isn't called Suzette. She is a dear old thing called Ellen, and has been with me for some years. We both get a little tired of each other at times, but we manage to make it up.'

'Maggie is only a country girl, of course, but she's clever with her fingers, and is very teachable. Do you like the country?'

'No.'

'How nice to hear somebody say that. "No" is such a difficult single word for the modern generation, which always has to excuse it with an "actually" or an "as a matter of fact".'

'Perhaps I'm not quite the modern generation.'

Miss Walsh looked at her, and said, 'I don't think you're any generation, my dear.' She went on with her work again. 'Why don't you like the country?'

'It makes me unhappy. I feel that I'm missing something.' 'Why do you walk through the fields in gloves, missing so much and so much?' quoted Miss Walsh to herself.

'I shouldn't do that,' smiled Chloe. 'Not unless we were going to Church. I should always wear the right things. That's what I mean by missing. There are other things than the right things, but I'm too busy to think about them in London. In the country there is more time to think, and I feel that I want something which I'm not getting.'

'Would you like to go to church to-morrow?'

As soon as she had said it, Miss Walsh looked up apologetically, and caught Chloe's laughing eye; and they laughed together.

'No, no,' said Miss Walsh. 'I didn't mean "Would you like to see a clergyman, dear?"'

'I should like to hear a clergyman; to hear this particular one. His wife is dead, I suppose.'

'Yes. Fifteen years ago. And all his family is abroad. Where so many poor clergymen's sons end up. Empire building. So, in a quiet, friendly way, we keep each other company.'

'I can't help envying you both,' said Chloe.

'Don't you think that when we envy other people their qualities, their lives, their possessions—we don't mean "I wish I were you", but "I wish I had some of the things *you've* got in addition to all I've got"?'

'I think I generally mean: "I'd like to be you every Tuesday afternoon, just for a change"; and, when Tuesday came, I'd be so busy being myself, I'd say, "Let's make it Wednesday this week, if you don't mind".'

'I should like to be you,' said Miss Walsh suddenly, 'for one glorious year, and then come back to myself, and think about it for the rest of my life.'

'I think you would find a year too long.'

'I'd risk it. When you're getting on for sixty, you would risk anything.'

'I hope I shan't live to sixty. I should be so terribly bad at it.'

'Not you. You'll be a very happy, very wise, old grandmother,' said Miss Walsh, but she didn't say it as if she believed it. Chloe laughed derisively, and came across to the sofa.

'May I look?'

'Just putting an E on a handkerchief.'

'Is Essie short for Esther?'

'Esmeralda,' said Miss Walsh, getting a little colour into her cheeks.

'Oh, how lovely!' cried Chloe. 'Esmeralda! You ought to flaunt it, and dress up to it.'

'Who for, my dear?'

'Esmeralda Walsh, of course. Who else?'

'It's a little late now. You should have said all this thirty years ago.'

'I meant to, but I forgot. Now listen, Esmeralda. Where do you get your clothes? Don't say Chelmsford.'

'Colchester.'

'Well, you didn't say Chelmsford. But why not try London? Big place. Lots of shops.'

'Wouldn't know which was which.'

'We'll go together. We'll get you all Esmeralda for the Harvest Festival. It will be a secret from Mr Winghampton until he sees you suddenly in church between two vegetable marrows. What fun! Darling, say you will?'

Chloe's arms were round her suddenly. Miss Walsh found herself saying that she would.

# 6

As soon as the car turned into the road, Chloe said:

'How are you, darling, and what have you been doing with yourself over the week-end?'

Percy gave her a long and literal account of what he had been doing with himself over the week-end.

'So that's how it was, old girl. First the boiler, and then the garden shears, and then the egg-whisk. Coming on the top of each other like that, and the egg-whisk being absolutely virgin ground as far as I was concerned, well, it meant leaving you to the old people for longer than I liked. But there it was. How did you get on with them? They're not very lively at the best of times, I grant you, and I have a shrewd suspicion that Wing is losing his sense of humour, so if you want an apology, old girl, you can have it.'

'No apology needed, darling. I just wondered where you'd been staying.'

The Vicar, who had come to see them off, stood with Aunt Essie in the doorway waving good-bye. As soon as the car had turned into the road, he said:

'Well, she is not marrying him.'

'It wouldn't matter,' said Aunt Essie. 'No man will ever hold her.'

'She is very lovely.'

'She is very clever,' said Aunt Essie. 'But I don't mind.'

# Chapter Five

## 1

Back in the office after his week's holiday, Barnaby was drawing up a prospectus of *Prosser's Encyclopaedia;* or, as it might come to be called, *Prosser's Handy Knowall.*

The original idea for this original publication had come from Miss Lynette Silver, Stainer's secretary. At four o'clock each afternoon a cup of tea, with an Osborne biscuit in the saucer, was followed into Barnaby's room by a mass of tumbled fair hair, prominent blue eyes, irreproachable legs, and a nose a little too long. To the eye of the beholder it gave the effect of a pleasing design for a pretty girl which had never quite worked itself out. When on duty Miss Silver wore glasses with white shell rims, and these, somehow, made her look prettier, or perhaps gave more strongly the impression that prettiness would have been within her reach if she had not been too absorbed in her work to bother about it. She had a friend called Humby, presumed to be short for Humbert, of whom the office knew almost as much as she did. Barnaby liked her, because she was so obviously and so happily in love.

'Your tea, Mr Rush, and it's Monday.'

'Thanks, Silvie. Here you are.' He handed over a shilling.

'Thank you, Mr Rush. Don't mind my sitting on your desk, do you? I got an idea.' She perched on the corner of his desk, smiling happily at him and swinging her beautiful legs.

'Would a cigarette help it?'

'Well, I won't say it wouldn't.' He gave her one, and lit it for her. 'Thanks a lot. First time my Humby gave me a cig he said, "Have a cig," and I said, "Ta," and he just took no notice, and lit one for himself, and I thought, "Well, if that isn't rude," and as soon as it was going properly he took it out of his mouth and put it into mine, so there I was and no trouble at all. And now he always does it. Surprises my friends sometimes; they say, "Well!" Of course, I wouldn't take it from anybody but my Humby, it wouldn't be natural, would it, but when two people love each other—'

'Absolutely, Silvie. Everything's all right then. Well, what's the idea?'

'Well, it just came to me. Humby and I were lying out on the Heath yesterday doing a crossword, and one of the clues was "Planet", well, of course, Humby said "Venus" and gave me a look, and when I'd thought of Mars—for him, because of being in the Territorials— well, we still hadn't got one of six letters, so we let that go, and tried one of the cross ones, and it was "Dickens schoolmaster", and Humby said Squeers because he'd read *Pickwick Papers*. He's read ever such a lot, and it fitted beautifully, but it was wrong, because it had to end with "e", well, I mean you can't read all through Dickens looking for a schoolmaster ending in "e", so Humby said, "Why isn't there a sort of special crossword encyclopaedia, cheap, where you could look everything up quickly, because thousands and thousands of people do crosswords," so I thought, "Well, that's an idea," and I mentioned it to Mr Stainer, and he said, "Run along and talk to Mr Rush about it, and see what *he* thinks." So here I am.' She gave him her happy smile.

'You're quite right, Silvie, it's an idea.'

'You could call it *Prosser's Crossword Encyclopaedia.*'

'Well, I'm not sure about that. A lot of people don't do crosswords, and a good many of the regulars like to pretend that they never look things up. Same as Rhyming Dictionaries. I daresay Tennyson had one, but he wouldn't have liked Browning to see him buying one.'

'My Humby's grand-dad promised Humby five shillings if he read *Paradise Lost* right through when he was twelve, I mean he began when he was twelve, it didn't matter when he finished, and

Humby got half-way through in about six weeks, and thought well that's half a crown, and then somehow he sort of lost interest until he was eighteen and saving up for his bike and he said it took him a long time to find where he'd left off, almost as long as reading it all over again, because he didn't want to cheat, and then just as he finished, his grand-dad died, so in a kind of way he'd read it for nothing, except that Humby says it's a wonderful poem and he must be the only man in England who's read it right through, and probably all the middle part twice.'

'I expect he is. I congratulate him.'

'Your talking about the Rhyming Dictionary made me think of it. Well, but Mr Rush, if you don't call it a Crossword Encyclopaedia, then it isn't Humby's idea at all. I mean, is it?'

'It's Humby's idea, whatever we call it. What we want to do is to give the title a universal appeal, and then advertise it as the Crossword-Solvers' Companion, or Indispensable to Crossword Solvers, or something like that. It's funny that we've never published an encyclopaedia before.'

'There's *Prosser's Biblical Vade-mecum*, Mr Rush.'

'Yes, there's that.'

'My Humby doesn't believe in the Book of Genesis,' said Miss Silver with loving pride.

All this had happened a month ago, and now Barnaby was trying to get the idea into some sort of shape. There was no doubt of the shape. Section I: Chloe. Section II: Chloe. Section III: Chloe. She overran his mind. He could still feel her physical presence in his arms; he could close his eyes, and take oath that she was there.

Carnation in button-hole, he had called for her, laughed with her, supped with her, danced with her, driven her home. 'Come up for a drink, darling,' she had said, and he had come up. They sat in her little sitting-room, facing each other, their feet on a tuffet between them, a drink by the side of each chair; the time and the place alike meaningless to Chloe. Or so it seemed. She might, thought Barnaby, be one of those unsophisticated mid-Victorian maidens, whose innocence moved even transpontine villains to mercy; she might be entirely sexless; she might be a sadist, practising a special form of tantalization. Yet he knew, or thought he knew, that she was none of these things. Perhaps, like a princess in a fairy-book, she had devised a series of tests for her lovers. First test: Self control. That seemed absurd, too.

'You still haven't told me about Tommy,' he said.

'Tommy, darling?'

'The man you're deserting me for to-morrow. The snake in the grass who whispered Wimbledon in your ear.'

'Oh! Well, we came out to-night instead. Haven't you liked it, darling?'

'You know I have, sweetheart. Adored.'

'Then you mustn't complain.'

'I've never felt less like complaining. Who's Tommy?'

'The Duke of St. Ives.'

'Oh!'

'You needn't say "Oh" like that. He doesn't mean a thing to me.'

'I didn't get the intonation right. "*Oh!*" No, that's not much better. But it wasn't a jealous "Oh", darling.'

'Oh, wasn't it?' said Chloe quickly. 'Then I must see if I can't make you jealous.'

'Stop it!' said Barnaby.

She laughed, and blew him a kiss. Three o'clock in the morning, thought Barnaby, and we've had a bottle of champagne each, and danced to all her favourite tunes, and she's blowing kisses.

'You're a ridiculous woman,' he said. 'You want everything both ways.'

'That's not being ridiculous, it's just being a woman.'

'I suppose it is. You know, sometimes I think you're absolutely detestable, and sometimes I get a sort of glimmering notion that it isn't altogether your fault.'

'Why am I detestable?' said Chloe with interest.

'You tell such lies for one thing.'

'Women are brought up to tell lies. As soon as they begin to grow up, girls are taught not to be frank about themselves. You hadn't thought of that.'

'I told you I had an idea it wasn't altogether your fault.'

'Tell me a single lie I've ever told you.'

Barnaby laughed.

'No, you don't.'

'What don't I, darling?'

'Two years ago come Michaelmas, or whenever it was, you gave me that very same challenge, and like a fool I took it on.'

'Who won?'

'You, of course. I gave you six perfect examples, and you just told them all over again.'

'Well, there you are.'

'There I was. Humbled, crushed, absolutely in the right, and apologizing like billy-o. Not again, my lovely.'

'It was at Quinto's,' said Chloe lazily. 'The first time we went there. Yes, just about two years ago.'

'Oh, my darling, do you really remember?'

'You had that tie I told you never to wear again. *Have* you ever worn it again?'

'Those were my school house-colours.'

'Then you ought to have grown out of them by now, ducky. I don't wear my school gym-suit.'

'Darling, you know perfectly well you never had a gym-suit. On your first day at school you sent for the headmistress and told her that you had decided to abolish gym-suits, and that you wouldn't be in to lunch, as the drawing-master was taking you to the Metropole.'

Chloe laughed and said, 'What are you doing to-morrow, sweetie?'

'I'll tell you what I was asked to do.'

'What?'

'Go to Wimbledon.'

'Aren't you going?'

'No.'

'Why not, darling? We could have waved to each other.'

'I didn't know that, not at the time. I thought I had something better to do.'

'Oh!' Chloe was silent for a little, and then said, 'Is she very nice?'

'She's rather fun. I like her.'

'As much as you like me?'

'Ten times more.'

Chloe laughed happily. 'Who is she?'

'Shan't tell you. You wouldn't tell me who Tommy was until I'd asked you six times.'

'Who is she, who is she, who is she, who is she, who is she? How many times is that?'

'Five.'

'Who *is* the damned woman? Six.'

'Our managing director's wife.'

'Oh, darling, don't get mixed up with a married woman.'

'I'm not. I'm mixed up with a single woman.'

'Sweetheart! Is she in love with you?'

Barnaby laughed.

'Of course not.'

'I don't see why not. I am.'

'But then you're a very intelligent woman.'

'Isn't she?'

'My standards are rather high, darling. She's all right. If there were no Chloes in the world, I could probably pretend I was in love with her.'

'You do only love me, don't you, darling?'

'Yes.'

'I only love you.'

'Bless you, my lovely,' said Barnaby, not believing that it was true. She stood up suddenly.

'I must go to bed.'

'So must I,' he said, getting up reluctantly. The evening over. From the very beginning this moment had never been out of his mind; the moment when it was over.

'You needn't go yet, darling. Stay in here, and make yourself another drink, and I'll come in and say good-night to you when I'm undressed.'

His heart was in his throat. With difficulty he swallowed it down, and said 'Right'. He filled his glass with soda-water, and drank. Oh, that time could stay still, now, for ever . . .

'Darling?' she called.

'Yes?'

She meant, Are you there, are you ready for me, are you ready to go? She came in.

She was in his arms, held tight against him, he had kissed her, she was gone.

'Good-night, dearest one,' she called from behind her door.

'Good-night, my lovely,' he tried to say.

Then he was outside. And the days went on, and it was Monday. And he could still feel her body pressing against his heart, as he drew up his plans for that compendium of knowledge, *Prosser's Encyclopaedia*.

# 2

But the title was still uncertain, and was to remain so until the following week. Then Stainer sent for Rush, and said, 'What about calling it *Prosser's Power Box?*'

Barnaby looked surprised. It had never occurred to him to call it this.

'And you put in brackets under the title "*Knowledge is Power*",' said Stainer. 'Marshall's idea. I think it's good.'

'Distinctive and alliterative,' said Marshall, enjoying the long words. He looked at Barnaby over his spectacles and thought, I haven't had your education, young man, and I dare say I'm not what you call a gentleman, but I'm a better man than you for all that, and I've forgotten more about publishing than you'll ever learn. He smoothed down his grizzled, tobacco-stained moustache, and said, 'Alliterative *and* suggestive.'

'What do you think, Rush?'

'Y-yes,' said Barnaby, 'it's not bad.'

'You don't like it?'

'I think it sounds better now than it will when it's on the market. If you wrote a novel, whose motive was the value of knowledge or something of that sort, *The Power Box* would be an excellent title for it. Suggestive and all that, as Marshall says, which is just what you want for a novel. But for an easy-going Encyclopaedia it seems a little—pompous. I can't quite see anyone who wants a handy book of reference going into a bookseller's and asking for *Prosser's Power Box.*'

'Marshall?'

'What Mr Rush means is that he can't see Mr Rush going into a bookseller's and asking for *Prosser's Power Box.*'

'Well, I do, yes. And I think I'm a fairly average sort of person.'

'No, Mr Rush, you're not. That's where you make your mistake. That's where all your class make their mistake. It isn't so much a mistake as a deliberate falsification of values.' He looked at Barnaby over the top of his glasses, rubbing down his moustache and saying to himself, 'Put that in your pipe, young man, and see how you like it.'

Stainer glanced across at Barnaby, and finding that no offence was being taken, said, 'Just how, Marshall?'

'Well, if Mr Rush and I were to go up into Oxford Street, and take a note of the first hundred men that went by, how many of 'em would have had Mr Rush's education, how many of 'em would think as he thinks, and want what he wants? Well, there's your average man. If I asked Mr Rush what he thought about God or the Trade Union movement or Love, or dog-racing or the best brand of champagne, and then held my hand up as he was about to answer' (said Marshall, holding up his hand as if to stop the traffic), 'and said, "No, I'll ask the next man who comes by, and *he'll* tell me what you think about it", would Mr Rush agree? And as for the first hundred women, is Mr Rush going to speak for *them* too?' (And that's for you, young man.)

'Yes, I don't know that women go in for encyclopaedias very much,' said Stainer.

'Not for themselves, but they'll buy a nice cheap one as a Christmas present for the husband, and will *they* mind asking for

*Prosser's Power Box*? Why, they don't even mind asking a young man in a chemist's shop for toilet-paper.' He turned his head and said, 'Do they, Miss Silver?'

Barnaby gasped, Stainer laughed, and Miss Silver smiled happily at all of them, and said, 'Well, really, Mr Marshall, I don't see how we'd ever get it if we did mind.'

Marshall chuckled in appreciation of himself, and looked up at Barnaby to see if Barnaby was appreciating him too, his aptness, his knowledge of women; and, seeing all this in Barnaby's eyes, thought you aren't a bad young fellow, and when you've been here as long as I have, p'r'aps you'll begin to know something about publishing.

'There's another thing, Rush,' said Stainer. 'Take *Who's Who*. What would you have made of that, when it was first suggested? *Black's Dictionary of Contemporary Biography*, or something. *Who's Who* would just have seemed vulgar and facetious. But now it doesn't seem anything. *Who's Who* is just a noise you make when you want a large red book. Nobody thinks of it as anything else. Well, Silvie, you look as though you'd got a laugh coming. What is it? After all, it's your book.'

'Well, it was really my Humby's, Mr Stainer.'

'Same thing.'

Silvie went pink with happiness and said, 'Well, it was only a silly thing Humby said, but it made me laugh thinking of it just now, well it made us both laugh, but I couldn't tell you really, it's so silly.'

'Come on, never waste a good laugh.'

'Well, it was just talking about the funny things books were called, and Humby said it would be funny if one of those funny books was called *A Kick in the Pants* and you said to the shopman, "I want a Kick in the Pants". Well, that's all, Mr Stainer, and I'm really ashamed, it's so silly,' but she gurgled with laughter as she thought of it again, and made everybody else laugh.

'Silvie, you're heavenly,' said Barnaby, smiling at her. Lucky Humby, he thought, to be in love with somebody so young, so happy, and so much in love with him.

'All right, then,' Stainer went on. 'We're agreed that knowledge is power, I don't know who said it first, Shakespeare probably—'

'Bacon,' said Marshall surprisingly.

'Hallo, I didn't know you were a Baconian.'

'I'm nothing so daft, Mr Stainer. I'm telling you Bacon said it. The first book I read when I started educating myself was Bacon's Essays. It's no bad beginning, Mr Rush.'

'Evidently not,' smiled Barnaby. 'I must try.'

'Well, all right. Bacon said it. We provide a book of knowledge, and instead of calling it a Knowledge Box we call it a Power Box. What's wrong with that?'

'It's the sort of knowledge we're providing. Take motor-cars. If we were to tell the reader how to make a car, we might be telling him how to become Lord Nuffield, and that's power. But what we *are* going to tell him is just the names of the different makes and the names of the different parts, and there's no power to be got out of that sort of knowledge. I'm just afraid that the title may mislead.'

'Yes. Yes,' said Stainer thoughtfully. 'There's something in that. What do you think, Marshall?'

Marshall smoothed down his moustache and said, 'I didn't think anything of your other objections, Mr Rush, but there's force in what you're saying now. Maybe I was thinking too much of the ordinary Encyclopaedia.' He sighed and added, 'Maybe I was.' He shook his head at Barnaby and thought, you've got me this time, young man, but you won't get me next time.

'Yes, well, now we're back where we started. Any ideas, Rush?'

'One or two.' He took a piece of paper from his pocket, and said, 'I keep putting them down, and crossing them off. Oh, not so bad. Four survivors.'

'Well, let's have 'em.'

'They're all rather on the same lines, but I think they're the right lines. *Facts You'd Forgotten.*'

'Quite good.'

*'Can I Help?'*

'Yes, I like that. I rather think it's better.'

*'Ask Me Another.'*

Stainer grunted doubtfully. 'That's what you say when you can't answer the first one, isn't it? Hardly do.'

'No. I wondered. And the last is *Any More Questions?'*

'That's the one, Mr Rush,' said Marshall. 'That's the one. That's a good one.'

Stainer looked at his watch.

'I agree. All right, Rush, we'll fix it at that. Leave out the question-mark. I don't like question-marks in titles. We must have it out by Christmas, of course. There's no copyright in facts, it's just a matter of collection. There are plenty of the regulars available for that sort of work. But it's got to be planned. You've been doing that, I suppose?'

'On very broad lines. But they divide and sub-divide endlessly. It will be a whole-time job for somebody, if we're to be in time for the Christmas sales. My God, it will.'

'Got anybody in your eye?'

'One or two. I was going to ask you about them.'

'Right. I've got a suggestion of my own.' He stood up. 'Thanks for coming, Marshall. I think we'd better work backwards. Fix the price now at five shillings, settle on the paper and binding, and then you can give Mr Rush an idea of the number of pages. Double column, of course. First edition, say ten thousand. That's conservative. After all, Rush, there's no limit to facts either way. You can make the book as long or as short as you like.'

'Quite.'

'Royalty, Mr Stainer?'

'The editor will have to have one, and there will be fees. Say ten per cent, for the editor, and five per cent., that's £125, for fees. You can get a lot of work out of five women at £2 5 apiece. Eh, Silvie? Well, I think that's all.' And, as Marshall went, he added, 'Wait a moment, Rush. You'd better get the letters off, Silvie.'

When the two of them were alone, he said, 'Cigarette?'

'Thanks.'

'Dolly insists that you come to dinner on Friday. Can you manage it?'

'I should love it.'

'She saw you at the Hippodrome the other night, and was madly jealous. Hence the demand for your company.'

Barnaby laughed, not knowing whether to feel complacent or annoyed. He wanted to be seen with Chloe, the envy of all, and yet to keep his friendship with her secret.

'I didn't see her,' he said.

'I gather that you had something far more exciting to look at. In any case she was in the circle. It just occurred to me, Rush—why don't *you* edit this thing, in your spare time? Or haven't you got any spare time?'

'Most of the evenings. I don't go out much.'

'Well. Think it over. And there's always a certain amount of spare time in the office, we won't be too strict about that. It's worth the royalty to us if you make a good job of it, and it'll be worth something to you.'

'It's terribly good of you. I'm almost certain the answer is Yes.'

'Tell me to-morrow. You want to look at it all round.'

'Right,' said Barnaby.

# 3

'Hallo, darling,' called Chloe from her bedroom. 'Pour yourself out a drink.'

'What about you?'

'And me. I'll be with you in a moment. How are you?'

'Very well.'

'So am I. Aren't I, Ellen? I haven't sworn once this morning. Neither has Ellen. Oh, yes, she has. She said "Damn all Rooshians, Prooshians and pin-cushions".'

'That I didn't, Miss Marr. I never said anything of the sort.'

'She says she didn't. I misunderstood her. I shan't be a moment, ducky.'

'Right.'

It was Friday. They had not met since that night, more than two weeks ago. She had found it difficult to fix a day, and even now he was having no more than a drink with her before she went out to lunch. But it was still only quarter to one, and her lunch wasn't until half-past; three quarters of an hour here with her—or with her and Ellen. Surely she could have dressed and got rid of Ellen before he came; or, if she couldn't be completely dressed by then, surely she could have dressed herself just for once? How different from the last time they were here together!

She came in, complete except for her hat, closing the bedroom-door behind her as she came. Well, Ellen was that far away. He stood up to kiss her. She turned her face away from him.

'Just my peach-like cheek, darling. I've a ravishing lipstick on which has got to see me through lunch.'

Why? he thought angrily. Why not put it on after they had kissed—a half an hour afterwards if she liked?

He touched her cheek with his lips, and said, 'Here's your drink,' thinking, The only thing that matters in the world is one's work. Thank God I've got some work to do. Thank God I can give myself up to work for the next three months, and forget her. As she has forgotten that night. If I reminded her of it, she wouldn't know what I was talking about.

'Thank you,' said Chloe, and seemed to be waiting for something. He knew that he was on trial. He knew that it was childish of him to be sulky and resentful without apparent reason; to have followed his own thoughts to resentment, and left her, gay as she evidently was this morning, to hers. He made a sudden effort to save himself, saying, 'You're looking lovely, darling. What they used to call a sight for sore eyes. How do you get sore eyes?'

'By looking at a lot of eye-sores, probably. Any more questions, ladies and gentlemen?'

His face lit up as he laughed and said, 'Bless you, sweetheart. And if that doesn't bring me luck, nothing will.'

'Have I said something?' asked Chloe, looking surprised.

'Yes. It's a long story. Will it bore you if I tell you?'

'Listen, darling. You may not be a film-star for looks, though I love your funny, knobbly face and your funny faun's eyebrows, and your conversation may not be a cascade of brilliant epigram (thank God), but you've never come within a million miles of boring me, and that's more than I can say of any other man I've ever known. Now tell me all about it while I yawn my head off.'

She sat down on the sofa, and patted the place next to her. In another moment they were holding hands, and he was telling her all about *Prosser's Encyclopaedia*.

'Oh, ducky!' She pressed his hand. 'How many copies will you have to sell to be a millionaire?'

'Only forty million.'

'Nothing! We'll manage that in no time.'

'Will you marry me when I'm a millionaire?'

'Of course. Couldn't wait. Darling, I'll make *everybody* I know buy one. Now let's think what we can do. Goody, goody, goody! I *couldn't* be more excited. Where's your glass, sweetie?'

She filled it and her own, and holding hers up, said, 'Forty million copies!'

They stood, glasses raised, looking into each other's eyes; for a moment only; then the intimate silence was shattered by the loud insistence of the telephone bell. Chloe lowered her glass, and listened. Ellen's voice could be heard. Ellen came into the room, closing the door behind her.

'Duke of St. Ives.'

'Oh, hell! What did you say?'

'Said I thought you'd gone out to lunch, but I wasn't quite sure.'

'And now you're searching the west wing; while he holds on. Darling, do forgive me. He's a crashing bore, but I must just say a word to him. Go on with your drink, I shan't be a moment.'

She went into the bedroom, leaving the door open. Barnaby heard her say, '*Hallo*, darling! How *are* you,' and then, 'Wait a moment, sweetie, I can't hear properly.' The door was shut. No more words could be heard, but from time to time Chloe's happy laugh rang out. The blurred voice . . . and the laugh . . . on and on and on.

She came in at last with her hat and bag. 'Darling, I must absolutely fly.' She picked up her glass and drained it. We're drinking to forty million copies, thought Barnaby bitterly, and this is how we do it. He drank, thinking, She's forgotten all about that. 'Ellen, have you rung for a taxi? Can I drop you anywhere, ducky? I'm going to Claridge's.'

'No, I'll walk.'

'Where will you lunch?' They were in the lift together.

'I don't know. Sandwich in Fleet Street. I shan't have much time.'

'Ring me up on Tuesday, and let's arrange a proper lunch. Darling, I'm sorry about to-day. I wish we could have had longer.'

(We could have, if you hadn't talked to that damned man. On and on and on. Suppose I'd talked like that to some girl, when you'd come to *me* for a drink? How would *you* have liked it?)

'That's all right, darling.'

They stepped out of the lift, she gave him her cheek to kiss, she was in the taxi, she was gone.

After all, he had his work. Nobody could take *that* from him. He remembered suddenly with pleasure that he was dining with the Stainers to-night. Well, that was something. Dolly was fun. He liked looking at her, he liked laughing with her, he liked making love to her. It was stupid to think that Chloe was the only woman in the world.

# Chapter Six

## 1

There had been a day some years ago when the Parliamentary Correspondents of half a dozen papers simultaneously informed their unconcerned readers that Sir Everard Hale was generally regarded as 'one of the most promising of our younger politicians', who had 'long been marked out for promotion'. This was the day when he was appointed Assistant Parliamentary Secretary (unpaid) to Lord Stanisfield. His duties bore no relation to the minor office which he held; for there is as yet no official designation of one who acts as host at week-ends for those of the Cabinet who play squash: keeps the Minister in touch with modern usages of speech: and introduces foreign emissaries to the more public pleasures of London. The news of his appointment sent a few people to their *Who's Who*, where they read that he was the 12th Baronet, lived at Chanters Abbey and Bruton Street, was married, and had one son, Jonathan, aged seven.

Jonathan was eight when he came into the breakfast-room at Bruton Street one morning, on his way to his day-school. Everard was drinking coffee with one hand, and reading *The Times* with the other.

'Good morning, sir,' said Jonathan solemnly.

'Good morning, rascal.'

Jonathan laughed happily. This was the great joke for to-day. His bedtime story a few nights before had been in answer to the perennial 'Tell me about when *you* were a little boy', and had revealed the fact that Everard had always called his father 'Sir'. They did in those days. So Jonathan thought that he would try it to-day.

When he had kissed his father, he said, 'Did you know that the world was round?'

'Good heavens, you don't say so.'

'It is. Really. I would have told you before, only you were away. You think it's flat when you look at it, but it's really round like an orange.'

'When we're at Chanters,' said Everard, 'I think it's nobbly.'

Jonathan nodded.

'So do I. *Very* nobbly. But you might have nobbles on an orange, mightn't you?'

'Easily.'

'I thought you might. Well, it's round like an orange with nobbles on. And do you know why you don't fall off?'

'I was just going to ask you. Why?'

Jonathan thought for a long time.

'I've forgotten,' he said.

Everard looked disappointed.

'Well, I'll ask him again to-day, and let you know. Will that be all right?'

'Quite all right.'

'I suppose *he* remembers?'

'Sure to. Schoolmasters remember everything.'

'I should think it's rather nice being a schoolmaster. Did *you* ever want to be a schoolmaster, darling?'

'Never.'

'I don't think I want to be one.'

'No, I shouldn't.'

'I'm going to be a baronet one day.'

'When I'm dead.'

'Oh! Oh, well, I don't think I want to be a baronet.'

'All right, rubbish, let's hope you won't be for a long time.'

'If I ever am one, I shall be Sir Jonathan, shan't I?'

'Yes.'

'Like *your* father. What was *his* father called?'

'Sir Everard.'

'And *his* father?'

'Sir Jonathan. I've told you all this over and over again.'

'I know. But I'm thinking. Does it have to go like that?'

'It always does in our family. I don't know why.'

'I expect that was why I was called Jonathan.'

'Must have been.'

Jonathan put back his head and closed his eyes.

'Here!' said Everard, 'don't go to sleep! You're just off to school.'

'Not for another minute. I'm thinking of something important.'

'Can I help?'

'Well, it's this. If we had another son in our family, and his name was Lancelot and I died, then he'd be the eldest son, and if *you* died, he'd be Sir Lancelot. Wouldn't he?'

'Yes, but we haven't, and you won't. At least not to-day.'

'And *then*,' said Jonathan triumphantly, 'there wouldn't *be* a Sir Jonathan, and *all* your plans would have gone wrong. And so,' he took a deep breath, 'if you had a lot of sons, you'd have to call them *all* Jonathan so as to be safe, and *they'd* all have a lot of sons and have to call them *all* Everard so as to be safe, and *they'd* all have a lot of sons and have to call them *all* Jonathan so as to be safe, and *they'd* all have—'

'Stop it!'

Jonathan laughed happily, and said, 'I thought of that in bed last night, only it's rather difficult getting it unwound. *I* think it's funny.'

'Very.'

'Well, I'm going to school now. Good-bye, darling Sir.'

'Good-bye, darling rascal.'

That was the last word Everard said to him, the last time he saw his son alive. As Jonathan stepped off the pavement, he turned to wave in case anybody was looking, and was knocked down by a car; one more natural death in those so busy, so highly civilized days.

Jonathan's mother had not been motherly, for Jonathan had meant little to her. As a girl, she had never been drawn towards perambulators, as a young woman she had rather disliked children. She had a woman's ability to make everything which she did seem right to herself, and she was now assured that all mothers spoilt their children, and that it was her duty to hide the great love which naturally she felt for her only child. When Jonathan was a young man, they would be tremendous friends, and everybody would suppose them to be brother and sister, for she would have taken immense trouble to keep herself young and beautiful. Indeed, she could tell herself that it was for Jonathan's sake that she was spending now so many hours every week in the retention of beauty. And when Jonathan married, she would be like a beautiful elder sister to his wife also. That was the time when so many mothers failed; that was where she would be the perfect mother. In this way she told herself that she was already the perfect mother.

Everard didn't think so. He thought that she was the worst mother he had ever known. With one half of his mind he resented this, and with the other half he was glad of it, for it made Jonathan more completely his. He had been very much in love with her when he married her, and she, it had seemed, with him; but after Jonathan's birth she had taken less interest in what she was accustomed to describe as 'all that'. She still loved him of course, and was prepared to be as devoted a sister to him as she was going to be, later, to Jonathan and Jonathan's wife. What wife, or mother, she asked herself, could be more? And though Everard sometimes wished that she could have been definitely one or the other, if she couldn't be both, yet he was genuinely fond of her, still attracted by her, and with Jonathan and Chanters always there, an uncommonly happy man.

But, like all happy men, he would lie awake at night sometimes, imagining that disaster had fallen on him. Only one real disaster could fall; he might lose his son. Imagining this, he knew that with Jonathan would go Cecily. For they could never comfort each other. However sorry she felt, her sorrow would be only for him, because he was unhappy; and he would hate her for not feeling unhappy for herself. Gradually she would come to resent his unhappiness; feeling, if not saying, that, after all, he still had her; knowing that whatever she said, or didn't say, would be useless and wrong. And he would know that he could never talk about Jonathan to her. He could talk about him to a stranger or to one who loved him; but not to one who knew him, and should have loved him, but loved him not . . .

It happened just like that; perhaps the more certainly because he was ready for it to happen like that. Within six months she was divorcing him, and he was no longer marked out for promotion. Within eighteen months he had married again. Janet had been comforting, she had been loving, she had been understanding, she had been very sweet. And she and her son had died together on the day when he was born. The happy man he had once been seemed very far away.

At fifty he married for the third time. Chanters still wanted its Jonathan. But Lady Hale, it seemed, preferred men to babies; and younger men to older men. He knew now that, if she ever had a child, it would be an accidental one; and it would not be his.

He sat to-day on the terrace at Chanters, waiting for his guests. He looked over the lovely wooded nobbles of this lovely part of a world which was really round, and thought, as he so often thought, of Chloe's son: Jonathan.

# 2

The telephone bell rang. Ellen said 'Mrs Clavering'.

'Ask her to come up,' said Chloe from her dressing-table. After an unusually long interval Kitty came.

'Good morning, Ellen. Lovely day. Good morning, darling, may I come in, or are you adjusting your false bosom?'

'Nature has more than provided. Come in, ducky.'

'I used to have a pneumatic one,' said Kitty, coming into the bedroom. 'At a very tender moment in our lives, a young man, I forget his name, plucked and pinned a rose on my breast. There was a loud explosion, which I found it quite impossible to explain, and he sailed for South Africa next morning. Oh, is *that* where you put your lipstick?'

Chloe laughed and said: 'You're looking very smart. Where did you get that coat?'

'An old Jew pedlar who came to the door. You know how they do. Listen, darling, I've got the most fascinating little hamper, and we're lunching on the road. That's why I took such a long time coming up, because just as the lift got going, I remembered I hadn't told Mayfield to collect it, and I pressed the wrong button, and went right down to the basement, and as I'd never been there before, I thought I ought to look round a little.'

'Lovely, darling. I adore hampers.'

'You'll lie down and worship this one.' Chloe stood up, and let her wrapper fall. 'I wish I were made like you. I swell in all the right places, but there's so little open country in between. I once tried to add six inches to my height. You had to enclose half a crown. So I went into a post office and bought a postal order. Nothing further happened. That seemed to be all the treatment.'

'The stretching up to reach the top of the counter?' said Chloe, interested.

Kitty slapped her hand. 'Don't be silly, darling. What are you wearing? Not that it matters. Why do I always look like an actress, and you look like a well-dressed woman?'

'A little depressed about yourself this morning, sweetie? Have a drink? Drinks, Ellen.'

Kitty gave a sigh of relief.

'What a long time you've been saying that. I was just going to ask if I could go to your bathroom and drink out of your tooth glass, only you might have thought it was a lady-like way of concealing my real desires.'

'Sorry, darling. Your conversation was so enthralling, I couldn't get a drink in edgeways.'

'I *have* been told that I talk too much,' said Kitty, innocently surprised.

'Not by me, pet.'

Kitty sat down at Chloe's dressing-table and gazed at herself in the glass. 'By the Judge in my divorce case. He asked me to confine my answers as far as possible to simple affirmation or negation. I said that I hadn't driven a hundred miles to his police court, and bought a new hat, just to say Yes and No.' She sighed, and added, 'If my nose were only two inches longer, I should be quite, quite beautiful.'

Kitty had known Chloe for three years without really knowing her at all. They were great friends; they were constantly together, and always glad to be together; but all the confidences had come from Kitty. It was true that these confidences were often of imaginary episodes in her life, invented to suit the moment; but this was only because she had already told the true story, and still felt the need to talk. No relevant detail of her married lives had been withheld; from the full story of the birth of the twins to the particulars of Bill's income and her own settlement. The accounts might vary from time to time, but the truth had been there, and any woman of Chloe's intelligence would be able to identify it.

But Chloe revealed nothing. Inquisitive questions slid off her back as smoothly as (one may presume) the larger assumptions of the Athanasian Creed slide off the backs of choir-boys. Where did Chloe's money come from; with which of her friends was she having an affair?—Kitty longed for an answer to both questions. To the first, Chloe had said, 'The bank, darling,' and to the second, 'All, of course; don't be silly.' They had been talking their usual nonsense, and the questioner could no more take offence than the questioned; but Kitty knew that Chloe was saying, quite definitely if quite pleasantly, 'That's *my* business.' Fancy having an affair and not wanting to tell your best friend all about it! Most unfeminine! Perhaps, thought Kitty, it was this combination of tremendous sex appeal and little femininity behind it which made Chloe so irresistible.

They lunched on the hills above Winchester. Mayfield took himself, his sandwiches and his bottle of beer to a discreet distance, and left them the comfort of the car.

'There's something so sweetly primitive about a picnic in the open air,' said Kitty. She was sitting in the Rolls, unpacking a pot of caviare, while Chloe uncorked the hock. 'So romantic. That was how I became engaged to Ernest. We were on a little mound together having lunch, and he was just beginning to get attentive when I realized that things were not as they seemed. Have you ever sat on an ants' nest, darling?'

'Never, sweetie. I've hardly done anything.'

'By the time we were both comfortable again, there was no need for him to propose. We were as good as married. I mean, you can't have ants slapped to death on you for twenty minutes, and then say, "Oh, Mr Merryweather!"'

'Has it ever occurred to you,' said Chloe, smiling to herself, 'how surprised the clergyman would be, if instead of saying "I will" you said "I have"?'

'Of course it hasn't, darling. Otherwise I should have said it.'

They lunched and talked and laughed, and seemed like two children together. They were on their way to Chanters for the week-end. Lady Hale was understood to be at Le Touquet.

'In fact, I'm only invited as your chaperone,' said Kitty.

'What nonsense, ducky. There'll be lots of other people there.'

'I hope so. I don't want to knit in a corner by myself all the time, and say "I wonder where those two young people have got to." I meant that as a married woman and a mother I expect to provide the necessary domestic atmosphere.'

'How are the heavenly twins?'

'More saint-like than ever. And they sent you oceans of love. You know, Chloe, sometimes I can't believe they're really mine. If I were the father instead of the mother, I should consult my solicitor. As it is, I don't seem to have any real grounds for suspicion, but I still regard it as some sort of a miracle. Have you ever thought about the universe in a big way?'

'It's crazy,' said Chloe decisively.

'Well, I wouldn't say that. But if you think of caviare, you do feel that somebody took a lot of trouble for nothing.'

They drove down into Winchester, and bought photographs of the cathedral. Derek wanted picture-postcards of cathedrals taken from the north, and Diana wanted picture-postcards of cathedrals taken from the south. The joint collection was known as the Marr Collection, and was housed in the Marr Museum: the corner of the Croxton nursery beyond the stuffed woodcock. Under the terms of the endowment (five shillings), Derek was curator of the North Wing, and Diana curator of the South. No postcard was eligible for the collection unless *(a)* it had come through the post with a *6d.* stamp on it (to help pay off the National Debt), *(b)* had the words 'from the north' or 'from the south' printed on it, and *(c)* bore a declaration from two witnesses to say that they had compared the cathedral with the photograph, taken bearings, and satisfied themselves that the particulars as given were correct.

'Sometimes I wish you hadn't started this, darling,' said Kitty, as they came out of their fifth stationers. 'And we've still got to walk round the thing.'

'It was a very wet Sunday afternoon,' pleaded Chloe.

'I know. One's hand was forced. But if you'd just happened to say bishops instead of cathedrals, it would have made our end of it more interesting. Have you got the compass?'

They certified and sent off their postcards, and drove on to Chanters. 'We'll take Salisbury on the way home,' said Kitty.

# 3

Chloe found an old friend in the hall when she came down to dinner.

'Hallo, Wil,' she said.

'*Chloe!* My *angel!*' cried Wilson Kelly. He strode down stage with outstretched hands, leaving an apology over his shoulder to the woman he had been talking to. 'Is it really *true?*' He took both her hands in his, and raised them to his lips.

'Nice to see you again, ducky.'

'You must know each other, you must love each other!' said Kelly. 'My two dearest friends!' He made a parcel of Chloe's hands, and covered them with his own. 'Come!' Hands leading, he brought her up to the cocktails, where Kitty stood. 'How shall I introduce you? Formally? Miss Marr—Mrs Clavering? Impossible! Chloe!— Kitty! My friends'!'

Looking more innocent than ever, Kitty said that she had often heard of Miss Marr, and had longed to meet her. Chloe said that of course she had seen Miss Kelso on the stage, and had always liked her work.

'You remember her in *Fiddle strings*?' cried Kelly, shaker in hand. 'You were wonderful in that, Kitty. I always say that was your best performance. That wonderful scene in the Third Act—you remember it, Chloe?—where she lay dead on the sofa, with a bunch of wild flowers on her breast, and I tried to play my violin to her, but it was no good, my hands dropped to my sides, and then I began to speak—slowly at first, the words torn out of me, and then faster and faster, letting the audience see that it was her whom I had always loved.'

'You're thinking of *Hamlet*, aren't you, darling?' said Kitty. 'You wouldn't have wanted a fiddle for that.'

'No, no, no,' said Kelly. 'You know the play I mean, Chloe. My father had died, and I suspected that he had been murdered, and I used to wander about the country, playing my violin and pretending to be mad'—he tapped his head, either to indicate madness or to help his memory— 'I ought to remember, I was the author, at least I wrote it with that fellow—what the devil's his name?—'

'William Shakespeare,' said Kitty.

'Was it Shakespeare?' said Kelly doubtfully. He shook his head. 'No, no, it was a modern play—'

'You might have been playing Shakespeare in modern dress,' suggested Chloe. 'Had you got a bicycle?'

'Anyway, darling,' said Kitty, 'I've never played with you in any sort of dress, on or off a bicycle.'

'Why should I have had a bicycle, sweetheart?' asked Kelly, in the patient voice of a good-tempered governess.

'Getting about the country,' said Chloe cheerfully. 'Is that my drink?'

'Ah, yes.' He gave it to her. 'I remember I *did* wheel a bicycle on to the stage once, but that was a different play. *Young Man's Fancy*, you remember it? I wrote it one week-end with—Trubshaw, was it? It set the scene, I thought—this young man, in love with— now who was the girl? Not you, Kitty, this would be before your time —madly in love with her, and he'd ridden over on his bicycle, ten miles, it placed him at once, you see, his love and his poverty— long dusty ride—*no car*—one knew all about him, as soon as he came on to the stage.'

'They'd know that anyhow, darling,' said Chloe. 'They'd say "Coo! It's Wilson Kelly!" Even without the bicycle.'

'Why are we talking about bicycles?' asked Kitty.

'I have *no* idea,' said Chloe.

There were two distinctive features about the plays in which Wilson Kelly appeared; features which distinguished them, not from each other, but from the plays in which Wilson Kelly did not appear. The first was that Wilson Kelly was always billed as part-author; the second was that at some time in the unfolding of the drama he was either urged by another character, or felt a sudden private need, to play Hoffmann's *Barcarolle* on the violin. The connection between these two features is fairly clear. The author had not envisaged a violin-solo, and had made little preparation for it; the actor, therefore, with his greater experience, felt it necessary to collaborate. Nobody with Wilson Kelly's appreciation of stagecraft would be satisfied with the bare request ('Let's have a tune, dad') made of one who had hitherto given no evidence of a love of music or the possession of a musical instrument; a violin solo must be introduced more gradually and more subtly than that. A Shakespeare, writing alone, may startle us with the sudden stage direction '*Exit pursued by a bear*'; but 'The Winter's Tale by William Shakespeare and Wilson Kelly' would have made it clear in an earlier scene that a particular bear was in the neighbourhood. So, too, would it have shrunk from an unheralded '*Enter Leontes with violin*'. '*Re-enter Leontes with violin*', after the usual modest disclaimers, was much more convincing.

There was, of course, no insistence by the author (or authors) that any particular piece should be played. The character whom Wilson

Kelly was impersonating (or, as some thought, who was impersonating Wilson Kelly) winged his way down the Groves of Music, and lighted carelessly upon—yesterday this, to-morrow that—but, as it happened, to-day upon, let me see, ah, yes! the *Barcarolle*. It was not the only piece which Wilson Kelly could play, but it was probably the only piece which he could still play correctly.

That an actor who could play the violin should feel that it was a pity to waste a ready-made audience was natural enough. What made Kelly's performance slightly uncanny was his apparent conviction on each occasion that nothing like this had ever happened to an audience before. He was superbly unselfconscious about violins; whereas his friends in his company blushed at the first mention of the word. In appearance he was impressively dark and sinister, with a long sharp nose which was undesirable on its own merits, but caused no comment in such a well-known face as Wilson Kelly's.

He had advanced to the door to greet Everard and induct him to the drinks; forgetting, perhaps, that Everard was his host and had seen him to his room half an hour before. Chloe and Kitty giggled at each other, and moved away from the table.

'I'd forgotten that he was so heavenly,' murmured Chloe. 'Weren't you ever in a play with him?'

'Never. But he did once ask me to share his flat.'

'Why did you refuse, darling? No lift?'

Kitty, who was drinking, gave a sudden snort of laughter, said 'Pardon, Mrs Hopkins,' and felt for her handkerchief.

'You really want a towel,' said Chloe.

'Listen, darling,' said Kitty firmly. 'If this is to be a nice party, I mustn't get the giggles. So stop it.'

They went back to the others.

At dinner Everard said quietly to Chloe, 'I've been asked to go to South America.'

'Not by the police, darling?'

He smiled at her and said, 'No. A Parliamentary trade commission.'

'Is that much in your line, Everard?'

'Not much. But you want one or two extras who can wear an eyeglass, and make love to influential people's wives—the British milord tradition.'

'Darling, don't you dare to make love to hot-blooded Brazilians. I won't have it.'

'Well, I'm not certain that I shall go yet.'

'How long would it be, sweetie? I can't spare you for long.'

'Three months, anyway. We have a look round the States first. It would be a long time away from you, Chloe. Heaven knows what you'd be up to.'

'Nothing that I should be afraid of telling you.'

'Let's talk of it afterwards. Your neighbour has something urgent to communicate.'

She turned to a waiting Kelly.

'I forget if you know Bangkok well?' he began.

'Not really well,' said Chloe. 'I generally go to Bognor.'

'I was just telling Mrs Donnisthorne of an amusing experience I had there.'

'How did it go? I mean, was she amused?'

Kelly laughed suddenly, and in laughing became quite attractive.

'You're just the same, Chloe. I'd forgotten.'

'Well, darling, I don't take the end of other people's conversations. What were you doing at Bangkok?'

'Hadn't you heard? My Tour of Australia and the Far East?' Just so might Napoleon have said 'Hadn't you *heard* that I'd gone in for soldiering?'

'The talk of London, sweetie. Was it a great success?'

'Financially, so-so. Conditions are very difficult out there. Of course I had a guarantee. But artistically and socially it was a real triumph. Politically, too—I've been making a report to the authorities—they seem to be delighted. One can do a good deal, you know.'

'I'm *sure you* could, Wil.'

'I must have made something like thirty speeches— apart, of course, from those the audience insisted on after each performance— playing on the theme of Empire, the Motherland, ties of blood, what do they know of England. It was the most amazing sight, those spellbound audiences. It was a revelation to me. One was very proud to do something in one's humble way for one's country.'

'Darling, I want you to do something for *me*—if you're not too grand now.'

Kelly said quietly and unaffectedly, 'You know quite well, my dear, that you have only to ask.'

'It's just that I have a little friend at the Academy, quick, bright, pretty, as keen as can be. I'm not asking you to make her your leading lady, or even to let her understudy the girl who says "Your car is here, madam"; but will you come and have a drink with me, and meet her? She'll get a tremendous kick out of it, and it will be a real encourage-ment to her. You needn't think about her again. *She'll* do all that.'

'My dear, of course!' He whipped out a pocket diary, and poised a gold pencil over it. He didn't ask the company to stop eating and watch him make a note in his diary; he merely gave the impression that if it did, he would be supremely unconscious of the fact. 'What day shall we say? I could manage Friday.' He added doubtfully, 'I *think*,' in case he had forgotten an invitation from the Secretary of State for the Dominions.

'I'll give you a ring,' said Chloe. 'Is that my pencil?'

'Well, of *course* it is, darling!' He had come across it that morning when searching for the key of his dressing-case, and his voice was reproachful. 'It never leaves me.'

It left him now for a moment while she twisted it about and read 'Love from Chloe' in her own writing. How many years ago? He sighed sentimentally, indicating that he was ready for her to revive his tender memories of those days . . . She gave the pencil back to him.

'How's Helen?' she said brightly.

Wilson Kelly issued a cold but apparently favourable bulletin on the health of his wife.

# 4

Having bathed in the sea, Everard, Chloe, Kitty and a young man called Julian-something lay on the beach, bathing in the sun. Kitty had taken off the top of her two-piece ('Shut your eyes a moment, gents') and lay face downwards. It was her first hot day, she was covered with oil and was hoping for the best. Julian, who had been almost unnecessarily helpful with the oil, lay face downwards beside her in a pair of trunks. Chloe, in a white one-piece, a towel fallen across her knees, lay on her back, her face in the shade of a large umbrella, her eyes closed. Everard, in shirt and trousers, leaning on one elbow, let sand run between his fingers, and looked at Chloe.

*Julian-something thought:* She's the old man's, I suppose, one can't butt in. Wonder if she's expensive. Toby says he's going to Brazil for six months. Hell, she's not going to give a figure like that a six months' holiday. There's probably a waiting-list a mile long. Well, no harm in trying. This fat girl's all right. One could have a lot of fun with her. What about those twins she was talking about? Nine years old! Popping up on bicycles. Oh, no, damn it . . .

*Kitty thought:* The older I get, the more bloody I think men are. I mean they're so bloody single-minded. They ought just to be kept for the night. I'd sooner spend a day with Chloe than with any man in the world. Funny about her. She likes men, and doesn't want to marry them, and I hate them and can't live without them. I wonder if she *would* marry Everard. Poor darling, if only that bitch of a woman— Look at her now with her towel over her knees. My God, what a figure, but even she knows that knees are no good. Except for babies. Oh, please God, see that my babies aren't being run over to-day, and let me have a letter from them to-morrow, not that it's in the least likely, so I shan't blame you, but they did go on about the address and giggle when I told them, but it wouldn't get here in time, so it might be a telegram. Fancy Wil turning up again! Doesn't Everard know, or wasn't it true, or what? I don't know, *I* don't care. I'm going to sleep . . .

*Everard thought:* Three months, say four months there and back. And on the first day out I get a wireless saying that she's broken her neck, or, more likely, somebody's broken it for her. I have to go on, too late for the funeral anyway, *noblesse oblige* and all that. 'Much sympathy will be expressed for Sir Everard Hale, in the sudden tragic loss of his wife.' Tight probably. And in four months I'm back, and—give it six months for decency, two months later we're married. January. Cyprus? Oh, my God, why will nothing ever happen as one wants it to? I suppose if it did, every single one of us would fall down dead. Plenty of wives who want Chloe dead. I think I've been right about her, keeping in the background, but always there. Never being jealous—no, always being jealous, but never showing it. The more there are to be jealous of, the less there is to be jealous about—I'm glad I saw that. And gave her more and more lovers. Are they lovers? Not they. She's untouchable. The virgin goddess. Nobody else knows it, it's my secret. Is it true? I don't know, I don't care, I'm looking at her, she's mine while I can look at her . . .

Chloe opened lazy eyes, gave him a little friendly smile, formed her lovely mouth into the ghost of a kiss, and closed her eyes again . . . Everard lit a cigar. There was always that.

# Chapter Seven

## 1

Artists, in whatever medium, are traditionally assumed to be unworldly creatures. Claudia suited her temperament to the supposed requirements of her calling; it was the least she could do in preparation for it. She had, of course, as much to learn in this branch of her trade as in all the others. She did not know that actresses could eat more than any male manual worker, and habitually did; she did not know that they had, and had to have, the virtues of the prize schoolgirl: tidiness, method, punctuality and perseverance; her own virtues, in fact, which she had hoped to leave with Henry in Hampshire. She saw the profession as composed of careless, untidy, happy-go-lucky creatures, existing on the lightest possible meals at the most casual possible times. She lived, in consequence, in some discomfort of body, but in great comfort of soul, convinced that's how Mrs Siddons had lived. Perhaps she had made the mistake of thinking that acting was an art.

Claude, who was undoubtedly practising an art, had no wish to be anything but himself. He could not understand why, if you liked painting, you wanted to grow an orange-coloured beard; nor why (alternatively, for he was open-minded about it), if you liked growing an orange-coloured beard, you wanted to paint. So he remained what he had always been: immaculately neat, short-haired and methodical: looking as if he had stepped from a band-box, or, more probably, from a bank.

In fact, he was, at this moment, engaged with those columns of pounds, shillings and pence which are the lifeblood of men in banks. The Great Borotra Joke had been accepted, but not yet paid for. On the credit side one might put down—what? Say ten guineas. Well, leave that for the moment, and consider the debit side. He wrote at the head of the page '*Evening with Chloe*', and drew, for the hundredth time, her lovely head, and then, as an afterthought,

| 2 dinners | £150 |
| Champagne | 110 |
| Cocktails | 60 |
| Coffee | 20 |
| Waiter | 60 |
| Total | £300 |

Add, to be on the safe side, five shillings to the dinners, four shillings to the champagne, and a shilling to the cocktails, and you had £3 10s. It could hardly be more.

Next:

| Play (or film) and programme (*max.*) | |
| (Might be less. Where shall we go?) | £156 |
| 2 suppers (*min.*) | 170 |
| Champagne (again?) | 110 |
| Coffee | 202 |
| suppers *(max.)* | 220? |

Damn. This is getting difficult. Say £6 for dinner *and* supper. That's £7 5 s. 6d. *Taxis*: Me to Her, Us to Dinner, Dinner to Play, Play to Supper, Supper to Her, and I can walk home if necessary. Ten bob for the first four (*max.*) and five bob for the last, because of the time. All right, say £8 altogether. Easy if I get the ten guineas.

But shall I?

He drew Chloe full-face, and scrawled it out, nothing like her. It was that child-like certainty of her beauty which was so characteristic;

that 'Here I am, and wasn't it worth waiting for?'—a sort of (but it was blasphemy to think such a word of a goddess), a sort of cockiness, which was, in some magic way, so unaggressive as to be almost humility, as if she were dressing up and playing the Princess, and laughing at herself inside. No, that wasn't right— oh, hell, suppose he only got six guineas? Well, we might have cocktails and caviare sandwiches instead of dinner, because of going to a very early play and having supper afterwards. We could do that for a pound, and that would make six altogether. Damn it, I *must* get six guineas, it's absolute black-and-white slave traffic if I don't.

All right, then, he could afford it. What he couldn't afford was to wait until he got the money, for then it would be August, and Chloe, for certain, out of London. That didn't matter, he could borrow from himself; there was enough money in the bank to keep him until dividends were due in December. Now that he was certain of being able to repay, he could take six guineas out. Six guineas and Chloe out.

He put down his pencil and walked to the telephone . . . No. Number engaged, will you hold on, Miss Marr is out, Miss Marr is in her bath, Miss Marr will be in directly, Miss Marr will be out directly, will you leave a message—*No!* That might do for the others, but not for Claude Lancing. Not again. A letter, and leave the ringing up to her.

'Darling. You didn't answer my last letter telling you how happy I was at school, but since then I have had three letters from other people, so I don't mind. Do you remember coming here a year or two ago and seeing a so-called joke about a tennis player called something? It has just been accepted. There was once a man who took a joke round to an editor, and got half a crown for it, and he came back a little later, and said reproachfully, "That was a bad half-crown you gave me", and the editor said, "Well, it was a bad joke". Forgetting about him, and looking on the bright side, couldn't we celebrate my first earnings together by going out one night? Do, darling, thus proving that you take an interest in my career. Otherwise I shall become a house-painter, and our paths will lie on different levels. Even so

I shall wave to you when I can from scaffolding, and remain your elevated but always devoted Claude.'

He dropped the letter in the box, thinking, 'With any luck she'll ring up to-morrow'.

She did.

A voice said: 'Is Miss Lancing in? . . . Oh! . . . Is that Mr Lancing? Will you hold on a minute?' And then, after a pause, 'Miss Marr would like to speak to you, will you hold on?'

Claude had time to register his thanks that Claudia had made her hurried exit for the day; had time to think, and be a little ashamed of thinking, that he might have been more comfortable in London alone; had time to wonder why Chloe was awake so early this morning; and then she was there.

'Hallo, darling, how are you?'

'All right, darling, how are *you*?'

'As well as can be expected in the middle of breakfast. I'm eating—what's that stuff you give horses?'

'Oats?'

'Something like that. Ellen says it's good for me. Is Claudia off to school with her little satchel?'

'Just gone.'

'I had a delightful invitation for her.'

'Good. Does it include me?'

'You've got it wrong, darling. I had a delightful invitation *from* you.'

'Oh, did you get it? And will you?'

'I will. In Scotland you're married if you say "I will" in the presence of two witnesses. Did you know?'

'Couldn't we go to Scotland together one day?' In his pleasant baritone, in his quietly efficient way, he sang '*I'll take the high road*—'

'*And I'll take the low road,*' sang Chloe, '*And I'll be in Scotland afore ye.* And listen, Misterr Lancing, ye're no a guid Scotsman. It's "tak".'

'*My error. Try an English one.* Drink to me only wihith thine eye—eyes—'

'*And I—I will dri-ink with maine.* Sorry, darling, my drink was too long, that's always been my trouble, once I get anywhere near a drink— Are you still there, ducky, or have you blacked your face and joined your friends on the beach?'

'*Way down upon the Swanee River—*'

'I was afraid so. I had an invitation which I wished to extend to you and your sister, Miss Lancing, but I can always write to the Harbour Master. Darling, you do sing nicely.'

'So do you. You're heaven.'

'Does Claudia sing?'

'Yes. Gifted family.'

'I want her to meet Wilson Kelly. Can you bring her here for a drink on Friday, and you and I will get together in the bathroom or somewhere and arrange our little evening, while he tells her the story of his life, and how to act, and all that. Would that be nice?'

'Lovely. You *are* a sweet.'

'I think it's the grape-nuts or whatever they are. Friday about six?'

'Right.'

'And thank you for my invitation, darling, and your lovely letter, and I'm so glad about the joke. We'll think of some more on our evening.'

'Bless you. And thank you for coming, Chloe darling.'

'I must return to my oats. Good-bye, sweetie.'

'Good-bye, darling.'

He put the receiver up, and thought: 'Twice. I'm seeing her twice.' He tried to remember what he had said in his lovely letter.


# 2


Claudia, no less definitely than Claude, was beginning to feel that she would have been more comfortable in London without the family. It was so necessary, she saw now, for an actress to Live Her Own Life: to plumb the heights and depths of emotion: to widen the arch of experience so that she could view the world untrammelled: in short, not to have to have a late tea with Herbert Potter under the constant chaperonage of the Express Dairy Company, but to be able to take him home to the privacy of her own little flat. She saw the two of them before the fire (this, of course, would be in the autumn—'the first autumn fire, there's something about it, I always think'), each stretched out comfortably in an armchair, or, if the arch of experience happened to widen in that direction, the two of them in one chair, discussing endlessly their Art. And then a drink? She could afford a very cheap sherry— better than all those things you have to mix; and then a little dinner together, something daintily whipped up by her in one of those chafing-dishes—one would, of course, get a chafing-dish and learn how to whip up things daintily in it; and perhaps after dinner they would run through a little scene, experimenting in the technique which they had been discussing—a scene, as it might be, from Romeo and Juliet. And one day, who knows? One day they might find themselves writing a play together, as with their special knowledge of stagecraft they would be so competent to do. The Tree of Life by Herbert Potter and Claudia Lancing: Potter-and-Lancing might become as famous in theatrical history as Beaumont-and—

'Pardon,' said Beaumont, shifting a leg under the tea-table and catching Fletcher once again on the ankle.

'It's quite all right,' said Fletcher. But *how* much more untrammelled in her own little flat!

Herbert Potter was a large, moon-faced young man in spectacles, with an untidy scrub of upstanding fair hair and very little chin. It was understood, by those to whom he had confided, that as little more than a child he had sold newspapers in the streets of Coventry; that he had risen from this to the dignity of errand-boy on a box-tricycle; and had then become a waiter. But all through this apprenticeship to Life the Stage had called to him. It had been his constant ambition to save enough from his meagre earnings to afford himself the Academy fees and the freedom of London. Somehow or other, after years of struggle, he had achieved his ambition, and here he was. It was natural, then, that Claudia should find herself drawn towards him, for she too (she felt at times) had gone through much the same struggle in pursuit of the same ends; although, of course, she had not actually been a waitress.

Dora, more sceptical as befitted one whose father made bicycles, said that there were some very rich Potters in Coventry, and she wondered—

'So there are at Stoke-on-Trent,' snapped Claudia, 'but it doesn't follow that they're all relations.'

'Of course not, darling. I just wondered.'

'Wondered what?'

'Oh, nothing, darling.'

'I mean, why *shouldn't* it be true? Charles Laughton was a waiter, wasn't he? And Edgar Wallace sold papers in the streets. I don't see what there is to wonder about.'

'I was wondering who it was who rode the tricycle,' said Dora.

'*Stop* that chattering,' shouted an angry voice. 'I will *not* have— Now Miss Fairlight, once again, please.' And any answer which Claudia would have made was forgotten by the time she was free to make it.

This afternoon, as on other suitable afternoons, 'Potter on Stagecraft, by kind permission of the Express Dairy Company', was in Claudia's curriculum for the day. Another advantage of the little flat would be the absence of the numerous customers, not, so to speak, on the books, who shared with Claudia the privilege of audience. Herbert never seemed embarrassed, as Claudia was at first, by the range of his voice. He felt, and felt rightly, that the prime duty of an actor was audibility, and if he ever reached the dignity of the Open Air Theatre, his '*Soft, who comes here?*' would have told all Regent's Park that he, anyhow, was standing there.

'What we must always remember, Miss Lancing,' shouted Herbert, 'is that values on the stage are purely subjective.'

She would have asked him to call her Claudia, but felt that the Express Dairy Company knew quite enough about her already.

'Yes, aren't they?' she said. 'That's just it.'

'Our end—Shakespeare himself has said it—is to hold the mirror up to Nature. Now when you look in the mirror, Miss Lancing, what do you see?'

'Myself,' whispered Claudia, in the vague hope that some sort of average would now be struck, and the conversation reduced to a reasonable level of audibility.

'Pardon me, no. *That*,' he pointed out with a piece of buttered bun, 'is your left eye. But if you look in your mirror, it will appear to be your right eye. Try to-morrow when you get up.'

Herbert's idea that a woman only looked in a mirror when she got up seemed to Claudia strangely out-of-date. She took a compact from her bag, and powdered her nose. He went on:

'So, you see, if you wish the audience to whom you are holding up the mirror to think that you are, as you are now, powdering your nose with your *right* hand, you must in actual fact powder it with your *left*. Isn't it so?'

Claudia agreed under her breath that it was so.

'You see what I mean. What they call the "natural school of acting" seems unnatural simply because it's natural; but if it were unnatural, then it would seem natural on the other side of the footlights, because to *you* it was unnatural.'

An old gentleman six tables away shook his head sadly and went out. His hearing was all right, but his mental processes were evidently not what they were.

'Irving must have been wonderful,' said Claudia. 'And Kean, and all those. Don't you *wish* you'd seen Kean's Macbeth?'

Potter gave the impression that on the whole he rather wished that Kean could have seen his.

They walked towards Shaftesbury Avenue together, Potter holding her by the elbow and bending down to shout in her ear. Taxis drew up at their side, either in the certainty that they had been summoned, or in the hope that two people so close together would be looking for more privacy; they were marooned on islands for long periods, while Potter, still holding her elbow with one hand, sketched out large Shakespearian vistas with the other; and all the time Claudia said 'Yes, *isn't* it?' and 'I do so agree', until at last they came to a Number 14 'bus. Then, as her escort loosened his grip in order to take a solemn farewell of her, she darted inside, turning back on the step to wave to him, and saw him striding away with his head up and his hands flapping, as if it were their backward motion alone which propelled him through the air.

Waiting for her at the studio was the news of Chloe's invitation.

'Claude!' she cried. 'How marvellous! How wonderful of her!' Gone was the vision of the Potter-Lancing management, of that famous school of young actors whom the world would know later as old Potter-Lancingtonians. She was Wilson Kelly's leading lady. Perhaps she could persuade him to give Herbert Potter a small part. Well, of course she must. Dear old Herbert!

What was she to wear? First impressions were so important. He mustn't think her a silly little country schoolgirl. She went into her bedroom and reviewed her clothes, looking, as she told herself, for something smart and sophisticated, and knowing that the smartness and sophistication began and ended with the little black suit and the white frilly blouse. Well, no, it needn't end there; she could add an artificial buttonhole of white camellias, and—oh, damn, stockings. They wouldn't be right, they couldn't be right, they never were right. She emptied her stocking-drawer on to the bed, and sat down beside them. Which was the luckier way—to pick out the stockings which weren't laddered, and then hope that one pair was the right colour, or to pick out the just possible colours and hope that one of them was unladdered? It came to the same thing in the end, of course, and anyway she knew the answer. She had the one perfect pair, but it was just too light. That meant six-and-six, and half a crown for the buttonhole; they *must* have a taxi, but Claude could pay for that; thank God she had spent all that money on those lovely shoes, because a man like Wilson Kelly would look at your shoes at once, and if they had a taxi, and she sat down most of the time—well, that just shows, she thought, if they *hadn't* been too tight, I should have worn them out by now. I wish I were rich and could get a new hat. Why don't I *make* hats? She gave herself a moment in which to sell hats of her own exclusive design to the Queen, Lady Oxford and Miss Irene Vanbrugh, but returned to the stage at the urgent request of Miss Vanbrugh to play the second lead in her new play. Then she was back on the bed again, wondering if she could 'do something' to make a last year's very smart but ridiculous little black hat, which didn't suit her, look like a this year's very smart and not quite so ridiculous little black hat which did suit her. And then she put the hat and suit and stockings on, and the stockings, of course, *were* too light.

'May I come in?' called Claude, and came in. He said:

'With that intuitive sixth sense which has led to my being called The Watson of Cape Cod, I deduce that you are wondering how to ravish Wilson Kelly.'

'Well, naturally I want to look nice,' said Claudia at the mirror.

'Of course. I'm merely buying a Guards' tie, and hoping for the best, but then I don't want a job. You look very smart.'

She turned round eagerly.

'Oh, Claude, do you really think so? I must get another pair of stockings, of course, and I thought if I—'

'Very smart, and all wrong.'

'That's the stockings,' said Claudia quickly, and a little crossly. 'And I've got to do something to the hat. It isn't fair to come into a person's bedroom when she's trying effects, it's like having people commenting on a picture when you've just begun it, you know you'd hate it. I suppose you think I ought to be dressed like a little country girl.'

Claude sat down on the bed.

'When we left home on that winter's night,' said Claude, 'and walked out into the snow, I promised Henry that I would look after my little sister, as if she were my'—he thought for a moment—'my little sister. I pressed his hand, and said, "Henry, the little one is safe with me. I will guide her and protect her, in sickness and in health, just as if she were my—my little sister."'

'Don't be an idiot,' said Claudia, trying not to smile.

'So now I fulfil my promise. Listen, Brighteyes. And if it's nonsense, forget it. The only other woman there will be Chloe. *She* is twenty-eight, and she will not be dressed like a little country girl. *You* are sweet-and-twenty; very sweet and, if I may say so, very twenty. If this man wants to talk to a grown-up, perfectly dressed, woman-about-town, he can always talk to Chloe; and if he wants to engage a sophisticated, young actress to play a sophisticated, young part, he won't engage a very young, untried girl from your Academy, who has got herself up to *look* sophisticated. If you want to attract him, either as a man or as a manager, you must show him something which he's forgotten about, which he didn't believe existed any longer, and which is the absolute genuine thing—dewy youth, fragrant innocence, the Vicar's youngest daughter in her sunbonnet, maiden meditation underneath the wisteria—'

'Oh, shut up, Claude. You *are* an idiot.'

'Then let's both be sensible. And I still say that you can't be too young and too unsophisticated to catch the eye of a more than middle-aged actor-manager.'

'I see what you mean,' said Claudia, now a little shaken. 'The flowered cotton and the big hat.'

'Same as what you wore at the Talbots?—perfect. Everything that Tennyson loved. It is the miller's daughter, and she is grown so dear, so dear, that I would be the jewel that trembles in her ear. No ear-rings, though, that would be a mistake. Just a sweet girl-graduate in your golden hair, called early because you're Queen of the May, and saying "He cometh not". One of the rose-bud garden of girls, set with little wilful thorns, and sweet as English air could make you. And on her lover's arm she leant, and round her waist she felt it fold—'

'Of course, these stockings are just right with the flowered cotton,' said Claudia. 'Then I needn't get any new ones, and I could afford a little hanky.'

'I,' said Claude, now at full length on the bed, 'will give you a little hanky. Will it be more than two and nine-pence?'

'Half a crown. I'll just put it on now. Perhaps you won't like it as much as you think.' She took the cotton out of the wardrobe. 'Shut your eyes, darling, there's something about a blouse and knickers—'

'Tennyson said nothing about knickers,' protested Claude with his eyes shut. 'All he said was that he waited for the train at Coventry, and hung with grooms and porters on the bridge to watch the three tall spires, and there he shaped the city's ancient legend into this.'

'All right now, it was only the blouse.' She dropped the dress over her head and wriggled it down. 'It *is* pretty, you know. I do see what you mean.'

'I am but a landscape painter, and a village maiden she. It's charming. Will you sit for my next landscape, Miss Lancing?'

It was charming. Claude was right. She would wear it on Friday.

# 3

But Friday went wrong from the start. Actresses, Claudia remembered afterwards, were always superstitious about Friday, so perhaps that explained it. She gave their names to the porter, and, after a little telephoning, they were taken up to the flat. They were received by Ellen, who told them that she was expecting Miss Marr every minute. Claude looked round the room with the air of one who had seen it all before, and Claudia looked round it with the interest of one who hadn't; and she decided that when she had a little flat of her own, it would be just like this, only prettier. Claudia sat down at once, hoping that Chloe and Wilson Kelly would notice her shoes, because otherwise she was suffering for nothing. Claude hoped that Ellen would go soon, because otherwise he didn't see how he and Chloe could get together. He walked round the room, glancing at her books. There was a new one by a famous author lying on the table, and he opened it and read 'To my darling Chloe with all my love' above the author's initials. He picked up another one. It was dedicated 'To the Divine Chloe' with these lines written underneath:

*The author hopes his book will live,*
*But knows its worthlessness, and so he*
*Inscribes your name that* you *may give*
*It immortality, my Chloe.*

There were too many amorous authors about. A copy of *The Pilgrim's Progress* mollified him. Even if it had been given to her by

John Bunyan, it would have been given in a purely Christian spirit. He looked inside, and found that this time it was the illustrator who had forced it, and what he called his homage, on 'Lovely Chloe'. Claude decided to illustrate the Bible and give two copies to Dear Miss Marr. Claudia eased a foot out of a shoe, but realizing that it would never get back if it didn't go back at once, squeezed it in again.

A telephone bell sounded, and Ellen was heard answering it from the bedroom. In a little while the front-door bell rang. Ellen brought in a very large man and made a mumbled introduction, which left Claude and Claudia in no doubt that their name was Lancing, but gave them no further information. The large man said, 'Old girl not in yet. Well, what about a drink? What'll you have, Miss—er—'

'Lancing,' said Claudia. 'Hadn't we better—'

There was a rattle at the door, and Chloe came swiftly in. She wore a flowered cotton and a large hat, and looked incredibly lovely.

'Sorry, everybody. Ellen, take these.' And then to Claudia, '*How* are you, it *is* nice to see you. How are you, Claude? Percy, I don't know *what* you're doing here, but you can at least give Miss Lancing a drink.'

'Well, I'll tell you how it was, old girl,' said Percy.

'You must tell somebody else, I simply must telephone.' She gave Claudia a charming smile. 'Do forgive me.'

Claudia, who was now able to sit down again, wondered if she wouldn't have been better in the little black suit, but smiled as cheerfully as her feet would allow.

'You must try my special,' called out Chloe from the bedroom, and began dialling. 'That's it there, Mr Walsh,' said Ellen, returning from the hall. 'It only wants the ice.' She disappeared into the bedroom. Percy put in the ice and told them just how it was. It was a long story, involving reference to an episode in Oxford Street a few days before, when a damn colour-blind fella who looked as though he were just going cooking had the infernal impudence to say that Mr Walsh had run the lights, when everybody knew that the whole Police Force was simply riddled with Bolshevism, and a fella in the Board of Agriculture and Fisheries had told a fella he knew that the Civil Service was absolutely honeycombed with it, the result being that Mr Walsh sat on a damned hard seat for an hour and a half while the sergeant fella was lolling in an armchair doing the Crossword Puzzle in the *Police Gazette,* and pretending that he was getting through to somebody called George Chater to see how many whiskies Mr Walsh had had . . . Claudia, who had begun by listening with the intense interest of a promising young actress on the stage—('what we call playing-up to the other characters')—was lulled into unconsciousness, either by the monotony of Percy's voice or by the continuous accompaniment of rattles from the cocktail-shaker, and woke to what she supposed was a different story, since it involved a boar-hound called Agatha, a damn nice bitch. Claude seemed to be interested in neither story, being seated at the table with his back to Percy, turning the pages of *The Pilgrim's Progress.*

Chloe came in from the bedroom. Claude jumped to his feet, and had the shaker in his hand, while Percy from his armchair was still only sending preliminary ripples of movement through his frame. She sat on the sofa next to Claudia and said 'Yes, please, Claude,' and then 'Thank you, darling. Now then, Percy, I'm ready.' Claudia sent a wild appeal for help into the ether; Claude, who had put down the shaker, picked it up again and refilled his glass; Percy said, 'Well, I'll tell you how it was, old girl,' and a telephone bell rang. Ellen announced that Mr Kelly was on his way up.

Wilson Kelly didn't seem quite so glamorous off the stage; perhaps because he hadn't got his violin. Claudia had her hand decorously kissed, which she liked, and Chloe had her face emphatically kissed, which Claude didn't like. Then he and Percy had their hands shaken in a way which, if the Potter Theory were correct, would have seemed almost indecently natural across the footlights. Percy began his story again, but hadn't got far before it reminded Kelly of something which had happened to him when he was playing *Bill Travers* at Edinburgh. Nobody knew, nor was ever to know, whether *Bill Travers* was the name of the play or of the character assumed by Mr Kelly, but at least it was a different story from Percy's, and Claudia, as a fellow-Thespian, gave it eager attention; until she discovered that the fact that he was playing *Bill Travers* was only incidental to the main theme, which concerned the traffic lights of Edinburgh and the manners of its policemen. The conversation then became general, which meant that Percy went on with his story from the place where he had left off, with the words, 'Well, as I was saying, old girl,' putting his arm round Chloe's shoulders to keep her within hearing; and Kelly was reminded (by the fact that, as he reminded his hearers, it was a Friday) of an odd experience he had had one Thursday on his recent tour in Australia and the Far East, an experience which would seem the more odd to Claude and Claudia if they knew Bangkok well. Claudia, in agonies with her feet, said that she had never met him, and she didn't think Claude had, and Claude removed his eyes from Chloe, re-entered the conversation, and said that he had played golf with him once. Kelly said, 'I am speaking of Bangkok, the capital of Siam,' and Claudia, very red-faced, said, 'Oh, *Bangkok*!' and Claude added, 'Sorry, I thought you said Hancock.' He then joined Chloe and Percy. Chloe put an arm in his, squeezed it, and gave him her famous smile. Percy, who seemed to have come to the end of his story, said loudly, 'I say, old girl, who *is* the blighter?' and Chloe said, equally loudly, 'I don't know, he never signs his name,' and murmured to Claude, 'That's what we call tact.' Percy immediately became tactful, opening his mouth and jerking his head and eyes back over his left shoulder. Chloe whispered, 'Wilson Kelly,' and Percy said, 'Thought I'd seen that nose somewhere,' and went off to refill his glass.

'I'm sorry, darling,' said Chloe. 'It's that damned Percy.'

'Who is he?'

'Percy Walsh. God knows why Ellen let him up. He's spoilt everything.'

'Well, anyhow, what about our evening?'

'Our what? Oh, yes. How about next Friday, darling?'

'Lovely.'

'I'm going away for the week-end, and I *may* have to go on the Friday night, but I think I can arrange not to. So would you ring me up on Thursday morning? It's almost sure to be all right, but I can't be absolutely certain till then. Will you do that, darling?'

'Of course,' said Claude, with less enthusiasm than he would have liked to put into it.

Claudia, seeing a refreshed Percy coming their way; told Kelly that they would have to be going, she didn't know it was so late. With an immense effort she rose to her feet. 'Cramp,' she said brightly to an unnaturally alarmed Kelly. 'It's quite all right.' Chloe came to meet her, saying, 'Oh, must you really?' and Claude, seeing the look in his sister's eyes, let it be known that they had to go out to an early dinner. Chloe took them to the lift.

'It *has* been nice,' said Claudia. 'It *was* sweet of you to ask us.' Chloe looked remorsefully at Claude, giving the apology for Percy into his keeping. Out in the street Claudia said quickly, 'I *must* have a taxi.'

'Of course,' said her brother.

As the taxi left the kerb, she dropped her head on his shoulder, said, 'Oh, *Claude*! Oh, *Claude*!' and wept.

'Howl away, Brighteyes,' said Claude, putting an arm round her. 'Only kick your shoes off first.'

# 4

Claudia felt better after a bath and in her bedroom slippers, but still considered that she had much to forgive. This put Claude on a defensive which was the more dogged for being really half-hearted. He admitted to himself that Chloe was not to blame for the presence of Percy Walsh; that one couldn't do anything with Percy in a small flat except wish him dead; and that it was Percy who had really spoilt everything. But no, that was just it; not everything. It was not Percy who had chosen next Friday for their evening together; a day which gave her, not only a genuine reason for breaking the date, but, as he saw at once, the perfect excuse if she should wish to break it. Two hours ago he had been, in his more composed way, as eager in anticipation as Claudia. He had seen himself alone with Chloe, perhaps in her bedroom, perhaps going out with her on the excuse of getting cigarettes or a bottle of something; alone, and making sure and unalterable plans, she as eager as he, for their great evening.

It had not happened like that. Nothing had happened to give him any reassurance.

Yes, he might feel some resentment against Chloe. That was his privilege as her lover; but it was not a privilege he was prepared to share with Claudia.

'After all,' he said, 'what does the whole thing come to? Your shoes were too tight. I suppose you don't blame her for that.'

'If I hadn't been wearing that dress, I mightn't have been wearing the shoes, and if you'd let me wear what I wanted to wear, I should have been different from her, which was what you wanted me to be—'

'Oh, God. So now it's *my* fault. Anybody's but yours.'

'Well, why does she *know* a man like that Walsh man?'

'He wasn't the only bore there.'

'Naturally Wilson Kelly had to—I mean he—well, I think he was very interesting.'

'I was referring to the Lancings. They weren't exactly sparkling.'

'How you can expect anybody to sparkle when her feet—'

'There you are. Your shoes were too tight. That's what I said.'

'If I'd been wearing what I wanted to wear—'

'Then you would have been the life and soul of the party. I've often felt like that. If my sock suspender hadn't come down, I should have been marvellous.' He got up and put on his hat. 'I suggest that we now have some dinner. If you'll tell me where you are going to have yours, I'll have mine somewhere else. I hate quarrelling in public.'

'I don't want any dinner.'

'Then you can do that here quite comfortably. And to-morrow, when our feet hurt us less, we can decide whether we want to go on living together. I'm beginning to think that we don't, but let's be friendly about it.' He turned round at the door, and, seeing her so small and woeful, saw her suddenly as the child she had been in all their childish adventures together, and felt an ache of remembrance for those happy days. 'Cheer up, Brighteyes,' he said, 'you didn't look too bad. Walsh asked me who that damned pretty girl was, and I suppose he must have meant you.'

He went out, thinking, 'And may God forgive me for that one.'

Claudia, greatly revived, went into her bedroom, put on the flowered cotton and the big hat and looked at herself in the glass; trying to see herself as Mr Walsh must have seen her.

# 5

Left alone for a moment with Chloe, Wilson Kelly was saying it for Percy.

'Charming, charming. The perfect gypsy type. I see her in a striped petticoat with a tambourine. I wonder.' He wondered, rather noticeably. His new play, which was soon to go into rehearsal, was a modern comedy, but there was no reason why a gypsy girl shouldn't come to the French windows after dinner with her tambourine. Later he might pay a return visit on the gypsies with his violin; perhaps a new Third Act in the gypsy camp, coming back to the drawing-room later. All sorts of possibilities followed the entry into his mind of that magic word 'tambourine'.

'Can you take an engagement when you're at the Academy?' asked Chloe, apparently following him.

'She would hardly need to go back, would she? The training she would get on the stage—with me—the rough-and-tumble of the real thing—I have rather a way with these young girls, you know.'

'On the stage or off, Wil?' smiled Chloe.

If he heard it, he ignored it, and asked, 'How long has she been at the Academy?'

'Not long. A term or two.'

'I think I'll get her to come and dine with me one night.'

'Do, darling. She'd love it. That was her brother, you know.'

'Oh? What does *he* do?'

'Paints. He's devoted to her.' She looked at Kelly with her head on one side, and added: 'He got a blue for boxing.' She waited until Kelly's eyes met hers, and then said, 'Well, I must have my bath. Ellen! Give Mr Kelly Miss Lancing's telephone number.'

# Chapter Eight

## 1

It was August, and London was empty. To the seven million people still there it may have seemed full enough, as they fought their way into buses, swayed from straps on the Underground, or ate their lunches in crowded tea-shops surrounded by the abhorrent lunches of their neighbours; but to those of them who knew Chloe it was indeed empty, for she was at Biarritz, and even the familiar intimacy of the engaged signal was denied to them. However, one could write to her, though from a woman so accustomed to correspondence by telephone the prospect of a return letter seemed remote.

*Prossers. Thursday.*

My lovely,

If you had been in London, and hadn't turned me down for somebody else—I mean, if I hadn't turned you down for one of the many other, better, nobler, more lovely creatures whom I so rightly prefer—we might have been lunching together. Somehow I always think of Thursday as 'our' day, although, from time to time you have made every day of the week an oasis in the illimitable Strand. An oasis, as you probably know, is a place where you drink. For a list of the better-known oases see O in *Any More Questions.* A.M.Q., by the way, is hell. I keep on beginning again, which is my idea of hell, anyway, and it's a damnable book in any case, being a compendium of utterly useless knowledge. When I was an architect and waiting drearily for clients, I used to read the *Encyclopaedia Britannica* to keep myself from screaming, and I can tell you quite a bit about Albertus Magnus, Addison's Disease, and the Alps, all of which may be useful one day. But nothing in this damned book—oh, well, it's a job of work, and it may make money, and when I'm a millionaire you're going to marry me. Oh, darling, I wish I were richer or you loved me more, and of the two I would rather that you loved me more.

'My Humby' made a first appearance here yesterday. We all thought he was Humbert something, but Silvie introduced him proudly as Mr Spencer Humberson, a grave, young man in spectacles with a hobby of (you'll never guess what) inventing and making wire puzzles; you know the sort of thing—a ring and a key and a triangle inextricably locked, and you fiddle with them for three hours and suddenly they come to pieces in your hand, and you haven't the vaguest idea how you did it. He had his pockets stuffed with them, damn him, and left a couple behind, and I wasted the whole afternoon until Silvie came back with my tea and did them for me. She knows them all, of course, as a loving author's wife would know his books—backwards and in her sleep. He spends his working life making cardboard boxes, which seems all wrong, but at any moment he may invent a suspender which doesn't ladder, and then they will get married. It's to be called the Silvie, and I shall give you a review copy . . .

*Croxton,*

*Nr. Lewes.*

*Sunday.*

Thank you for the pattern, darling. I ought to have said this before—and I'm only saying it now because the Twins have asked me to ask you if there is a *Cathedral* at Biarritz— because if so you *won't* forget, will you, there's a pet. We have some *very* strange people with us this week-end—I don't know *what* they're doing here and whether they're Bill's friends or mine, I think one or two must have mistaken the house, there's one keeps calling me Lady Adela, *most* embarrassing— and at dinner last night, another one asked me how far it was to Hunstanton. I told him it was ten miles to Brighton and left him to work it out—I don't know *where* he thinks he is— he has a long drooping moustache and the Twins say they found him in a wood, but you know the way they talk . . .

*27 Harts Studios,*
*Fulham Road, S.W. 3.*

My Darling Chloe,

Even if you won't come out to dinner with me, or marry me, or do anything reasonable like that, I still adore you. Couldn't we have lunch together at an A.B.C. when I'm President of the Royal Academy, it would give me something to work for?

Meanwhile I must tell you the great news. Claudia dined with Wilson Kelly last night, and over the smoked salmon was offered the small part of a gypsy (or, as she would prefer, the part of a small gypsy) in his new play, Kelly's idea of a gypsy being of something in the Chorus of *Carmen* with a rose in its teeth, and quite unlike our Hampshire gypsies. He passed the next three courses in an interesting condition, having, so to speak, cancelled all his social engagements, and by the savoury was delivered triumphantly of the name of *Zella*. The studio is now littered with scraps of paper bearing the strange device, '*Zella* (a gypsy maid)—MISS CLAUDIA LANCING.' They go on tour at the end of September, which means that, if the play runs for more than a week (as Kelly seems to think it will) she leaves the Academy. This, I gather, serves the Academy right, for giving some end-of-term prize, scholarship or what not to a girl called Dora instead of to herself. It also means that she leaves me, which we had almost decided on, anyhow. So now I am a bachelor, and if you've got nothing else to do, will you marry me? . . .

*Whinnies,*
*Cromarty, N.B.*

Dear Miss Marr,

It gave me so much pleasure to meet you the other day, and it is understood, is it not, that you are to come to us for the week beginning September 2nd. That will be delightful. I am enclosing particulars of the route here, as it is cross-country and a little difficult for the new-comer. Looking forward so much to seeing you, I am,

Yours sincerely,
Henrietta St. Ives

*C/o George Chater Esq.,*
*Holmdene,*
*Woking.*

Well, old girl, I said I'd write, so I am; because I don't want you to think that I've let you down. I'm staying with old George for a few days, playing golf. I don't know if I told you about him, he lives down at Woking. He beat me this morning 3 and 2 but I pipped him in the afternoon, he was slicing all his drives. He's got a new Bentley, she does 80 without noticing it. How are you? Aunt Essie's writing to you, at least she said she was. It's been very hot lately so I expect you've been having it very hot. It's hotter where you are I expect. George Chater said he'd been to Biarritz once and it was damned hot, but that was before the war. I hope you're keeping fit, I had a bit of indigestion last week but it passed off. I met that young Lancing who I met in your flat, and he's coming to have a bite at the club when I get back and then I'm going to Wales. Well I think that's all as the drinks are just coming in, but I said I'd write so I have. Let's have a line, old girl, when you're not too busy, there's a kid in the house who collects stamps, old George's half nevew, his father married twice and this is his half nevew. Love and kisses and all that, cheerio and let me know as soon as you're back and we'll see what we can do.

Percy
*The Manor House,*
*Much Hadingham.*

My Dear Chloe,

I must thank you again for our happy day in London— no, I mean my happy day with you, for it cannot have been the delightful interlude for yourself that you made it for me. All the lovely things arrived together this morning, and what John Clayden, our postman, thought as he carried them up on his bicycle, I don't know, but he smiled as cheerily as ever, and I gave him a sixpence for his little girl, such a pretty even-tempered child, and a favourite of mine, but you can't spoil her luckily. So then I locked my door and dressed myself up, and—well, I wonder. I wish you had been here. It's Esmeralda, as you said, but she has been dead so long, I wonder if I am wise to resurrect her— as I know now I was wrong to let her die. Of course it is not she who has come to life in my mirror, but her grandmother, a well-preserved old lady with rather a Spanish taste in dress. I don't know what Alfred will think. But I shall dress myself up privately every day, and get myself used to this dashing Señora, and then perhaps I shall be able to carry her off. Oh, Chloe, my dear, you have given me a very exciting game to play, and I thought that I was done with exciting games.

What would make it perfect would be if you came down to me for that week-end—shall we say if you have *nowhere* else to go, and *hate* the idea of staying in London? I know, of course, my dear, that Alfred and I and our funny little lives in our funny little village are just things you glimpse out of a carriage window as the train goes by, and smile at, and forget; but if you did pull the communication-cord to see what happened (as you must often have wanted to) we would do our best to entertain you until the train went on again. But without that you have given us much happiness, and Alfred never stops telling me of his afternoon at Hampton Court.

Yours affectionately,
Esmeralda Walsh

*Green Room Club, W.C.2.*

Chloe, my darling, I am the bearer of grievous tidings. My poor, dear wife passed away suddenly two nights ago as the result of an accidental fall. Though we had not lived together for some years, the shock of her death is none the less crushing. My mind to-day goes back sadly to those earlier triumphs which we shared—I need only mention *Fiddle and I*, *The Green Cockade* and *Whither Do you Wander*. She was not, it must be admitted, a great actress, but she was a great trouper, a devoted comrade, and a constant inspiration, and it would be churlish not to admit that much of my success has been owed to her. *The Daily Telegraph* put this very well in a cutting which I enclose, and there are generous tributes in most of the other papers, several of them referring in a kindly way to the new romantic comedy which I am just putting into rehearsal. I have, of course, made it clear in a letter to the Press that, as always in the profession, personal feelings cannot be allowed to weigh against public duty, and we shall be opening at Culverhampton on the 19th of September as announced . . .

*The Vicarage,*
*Much Hadingham.*

My dear Chloe (you see how naturally it comes to me now!)—I have been thinking over what you said at Hampton Court, and I wish I could give you an answer to your problem. But the older I get, the less certainty I have about life, and of death I know only this: that it is the door which opens to us all Beauty and all Knowledge.

God has given you beauty, my dear, the most precious of all gifts; and you are right to guard it as if it were (which, indeed, it is) a sacred lamp in a world which holds so much that is ugly. I do not think that you would make a good charwoman, nor a good secretary of a Housing Committee, nor a good factory girl. Nor do I think that any of these by reason of her following is more to be praised than you. Earning a living is not the highest form of living; it is not what we were put into the world for; it is but a worldly means to a Divine end, the end being the development of God's spirit within us. And since that spirit is enlarged by the contemplation of beauty, a truly beautiful woman fulfils her destiny, unconsciously as it were, by becoming an inspiration to others.

But her responsibility does not end there. Beauty in a woman means power, and power is a terrible weapon, a weapon with which no one is safe who does not surrender himself to God. I think that your whole duty—to yourself, to your world, to your God—is to exercise that power beneficently. Throughout your years of glory you will be breaking many hearts; see to it that you do not break souls. If there are many who will say: 'For to see her was to love her, love but her, and love for ever,' let them also be able to say, 'To love her was a *spiritual* education.' Let it be in the noblest sense of the word *better* for them to have loved and lost than never to have loved at all.

Am I wasting your time? You are holiday-making, I suppose, and this letter will be sent on to you. I see you lying in the sun, reading it; will you smile to find that I took you so seriously? For perhaps you were just being kind to an elderly friend in the Church, giving him in your gracious way a theological problem to solve, as you would give another man a cross-word puzzle, or listen to a third man's domestic troubles. Even so, my dear Chloe, I shall not have wasted *my* time. It is a clergyman's business, I have discovered, to preach to those whose thoughts are eager to be elsewhere. As a friend of mine said: 'I expect watches to be looked at when I'm in the pulpit. But,' he added, 'not shaken and held to the ear.' . . .

*R.M.S. 'Aquitania.'*

My Dear One,

I believe that the right way to begin a letter in mid-ocean is to say, 'Well, here I am,' which is why I don't say it. We are an odd crowd, with most of whom I have a nodding acquaintance in the House. My only blood-brother is Sid Rowley, an ex-railway porter Labour Member, with a face like an interested monkey, an uninhibited laugh, a passion for boiled sweets, and a firm belief in a revolution in which he has promised to liquidate me. Meanwhile we talk the same language, which means that I can call him a damned fool, and he can call me a bloody one, without noticing it. I was in the Bar yesterday evening, and he came and leant affectionately against me, picked up and sipped the sherry which I had ordered for myself, said, 'Ah, it's the '74, I fancy, James,' drank it, and said, 'No, no, what am I thinking of, 73 and an 'arf.' He then handed me back the empty glass, saying, 'Now then, old man, it's your turn to stand *me* one.' Well, I like him.

I also like you, my darling. I wish I knew you better. Have you ever been in love? Do you know at all what it means? Sometimes I think of you as a very innocent, very sophisticated child, who knows it all but doesn't understand a word of it. You may smile and say, 'Just because I don't fall in love with *you*, darling, it doesn't mean that I can't fall in love with anybody.' Of course it doesn't, and it would be the maddest egotism to think so. But without being egotistic it is possible to know from a man's attitude to *your* dog, or horse or child or garden, however unattractive these may be, whether or not he is fond of dogs, and horses and children, or interested in gardens. You are interested in men, but—you aren't fond of them? You have the air of loving, but—you can't love? Outwardly you are so reckless and inwardly so reserved—my darling, what is your secret? . . .

*17 South Audley Mansions,*
*W.1.*

Dear Miss Marr,

I am sending on the letters in a big envelope as you said and Lord Sheppey rang up to ask for your address and I said you hadn't left one and no letters were being sent on. Yours truly—Ellen Maddick

# 2

These letters, and more letters like them, and letters from other people, and more letters like them, flowed in on Chloe. Some of the writers neither wished nor expected an answer; some wished, but did not expect. But there were some who calculated the earliest day on which it was possible for an answer to come, and from that day lived only from post to post.

Here is Chloe in reply.

*One telegram:*
My love and all my sympathetic understanding, Chloe.

*One letter:*

My Dearest Esmeralda,

Of *course* I am coming—try and stop me. Ought I to know when it is? Is it fixed like Christmas, movable like Easter, or different for each village like Vicars? I shall be very quiet and neat and respectful, I think I'll carry your prayer-book and say, 'Desearia, mi Señora, una manta sobre las rodillas?' That means, 'Would the gracious lady require a hassock for her knees?'—and you may think that a woman who can throw off the Spanish for hassock so carelessly could throw off anything—like a strip-tease dancer—but the truth is, darling, and I am nothing if not truthful sometimes, that I am writing this at full length on the Côte des Basques, and there is a very attentive *Basque sans Coat* (and most other things) sun-bathing next to me, and I wanted to take his mind off all he normally thinks about. He is now holding forth on the iniquities of the Spanish Church, which is at least a change. All the men here have one-way minds, and most of the women have two-way figures—coming and going—but some of the children are adorable, and so is the weather and the scenery, and all the things that help to fill up a picture-postcard. Hot, but I like it hot.

Darling, we are running down on the Spanish Church, and my boy friend wants a drink. Let me know the date as soon as possible. I shall be leaving here on the 26th and I am going to Scotland on the 2nd for a week, but I could cancel that if necessary, it isn't important. And of course I *could* leave before the 26th if the Harvest is early this year. So hurry, hurry, hurry and tell me *when*. And give my love to Alfred and thank him for his so wise, so kind, letter. I can't answer it here, he will guess why, but I'll be seeing him soon. Now for that drink.

Your loving
Chloe

The *Aquitania* reached New York, and Everard saw Sid Rowley safely into his first dinner jacket. Claude sidestepped his invitation to White's, and Percy went off to Wales. Aunt Essie told the Vicar of Much Hadingham that Chloe was coming to them for the Harvest Festival, and the Vicar hurled his hat across the lawn in delight. Wilson Kelly, wearing a black armlet of terrifying intensity, said 'No, no, darling, now watch *me*' to Claudia, and became in an instant a sulky gypsy girl with an imaginary tambourine. Barnaby, after an agony of indecision, found a formula for *Any More Questions* which kept him hard at work, but left his mind free to think of Chloe.

But what Chloe did, what Chloe thought of, none of them knew.

# Chapter Nine

## 1

Silvie was getting married in the autumn. Mrs Willoughby Prance, who managed the Juvenile Department and was herself responsible for *Prosser's Elementary Reader*, *The Nursery Mapmaker*, and *The Child's Introduction to Life*, had been elected chairwoman of the committee which was to organize Miss Silver's wedding-present. Mrs Prance combined the amplitude of an allegorical mother with the pince-nez of a high-school teacher and the Eton crop and cigarette-holder of a girl very much about town. Barnaby never felt quite at ease with her. Within a week of his coming into the office she had asked him to call her Prance, which, on any workable Victorian analogy, was a revelation of her affections demanding the chivalrous exchange, 'Won't you call me Rush?' She did. Presumably he was now licensed to smack her on some part of the back—but which? It was all a little difficult.

Prance called her committee together, and said in her business-like way that the first thing was to collect the money, and when that was done they would decide what to buy with it. It was no good wrangling about what make of car to give Silver and then finding they had just enough for a handkerchief case. She suggested that everybody be asked for a shilling, five shillings from heads of departments, and ten shillings from directors. No compulsion, nobody need give anything, probably some of them wouldn't feel they could afford it, but they all liked Silver, and she hoped there'd be a good rally. 'What's that, Fossett? Well, of course you can. That's why I said a shilling, so that any one who wants to give her a personal present can still subscribe to the general one. What's that, Luker? No, that's too difficult, must keep it simple—you agree, Wilkinson? Good, then we'll just put it to the vote, those in favour—carried—well, I must get on with my work, pass the word along, what's that, Fossett? Oh, tell 'em to bring it to *me,* if you can trust me, ha—ha!' She put another cigarette in her holder, and flicked a lighter at it. 'Same time next week, and see how much we've got. Cheerio.'

The committee drifted out, disappointed that so little time had been wasted. Rattling good fellows, all of 'em, thought Mrs Prance to herself, and settled down to work, feeling both popular and efficient. 'Silly old bitch,' said Miss Fossett to Mr Luker, on the other side of the door. 'Or what?' said Mr Luker darkly.

Silvie (Stainer was glad to hear) was not leaving Prosser's; not yet.

'Not till I have a baby, Mr Stainer, if that will be all right.'

'And when will that be?'

'Well, it will depend on Humby.'

'These things do, of course.'

Silvie gave her happy laugh, and said, I didn't mean that, I meant when he's making enough for the two of us.'

'The three of you, don't you mean?'

Silvie laughed again and said, 'Well, it might be four, Mr Stainer, if I had twins.'

'All right, call it twins. But don't go having 'em till you're ready for 'em.'

'Of *course* not, Mr Stainer!' said Silvie, almost shocked. 'As if Humby would!' But whether her confidence rested on the fact that he was just Humby, or that he was so good at wire puzzles, was not clear to Stainer.

The committee met again and decided on a tea-service. Barnaby, feeling that his five shillings did not express all the happiness which he wished for Silvie, added six pairs of silk stockings and hoped that they were the right size and colour.

'They're lovely,' cried Silvie, 'they're *exactly* right. Oh, Mr Rush, it *is* kind of you.'

'Well, I like seeing them on you,' said Barnaby. 'How many people have told you that you have the best legs in the publishing world?'

Sitting on his desk she held out the best legs in the publishing world, and smiled at them.

'Humby ever noticed them?'

She gave him a look which recognized his humour.

'First thing Humby said to me after we'd been introduced was to ask me if I'd gone up in the lift from South Ken about four o'clock one Sunday round about two months ago, because he'd seen a pair of legs going up and there couldn't be two pairs in the world, and really, Mr Rush, I had, but I don't say it was me, of course.'

'Nice to think it was.'

'Soon as we got engaged, we went to South Ken, and I got in the lift, and Humby stayed on the platform as if he was taking the next train, and I stood next to the gate, and as soon as he heard the lift starting, Humby came running up, and there it was just like the other time, and he says he *knows* it was me. So perhaps it was. Wasn't it funny?' She smiled happily at him and added, 'Legs get Humby down. I mean ugly ones. That's why it was, I expect, I mean him noticing like that.'

But three days later, when she brought in his tea, she had no smile for him.

'Hallo, Silvie, what's the matter?'

'Nothing, Mr Rush.'

'You've been crying.'

She shook her head, and shook the tears out of her eyes, and said, 'I'm just so silly, I can't stop unless I think of something else, and as soon as I stop working, it sort of comes again. I'm sorry, Mr Rush.'

'Is it Humby?'

She nodded, and burst out, 'He's got appendicitis— Oh; Mr Rush!' and gave way utterly.

Barnaby's relieved laugh shocked her into instant control of herself. She looked wonderingly at him.

'Is *that* all?' said Barnaby. 'Good heavens, what's appendicitis? I thought he'd run away with a Russian Princess or something. I thought you'd quarrelled, and parted for ever.'

'Quarrelled? *Me and Humby?*'

'Well, it was silly of me, but that's what I thought. Appendicitis? Pooh, nothing!'

'Have you had *yours* out?'

'Again and again. No, that's not true, but I've certainly had it out once. A very sensible thing to do just before getting married. Like having your hair cut.'

'Oh, Mr Rush, is it really like that? I can't help being frightened, I know it's silly.'

'When is it?'

'To-morrow morning. He went in this afternoon. St George's. Mr Stainer let me go with him. That's why I'm so late with the tea.'

'Hasn't he got any people in London?'

Silvie shook her head. 'His dad works in Leeds, he married again, so Humby doesn't see so much of him now.' 'Aren't you lucky, you've got him all to yourself?' She nodded. 'I'm to ring up to-morrow morning, and perhaps I may go and see him in the afternoon. Mr Stainer's ever so kind about it, he says that's all right for me. It *isn't* bad, appendicitis, is it, Mr Rush?'

'Of course not.' He put his hand out to his cup and then stopped. 'Have you had your own tea yet?'

'Of course not, Mr Rush, I've only just—'

'Well, drink that and listen to me'—he pushed his cup towards her—'go on, you can get me another afterwards . . . Finished? Now then: am I or am I not the editor of *Any More Questions?*'

'Yes, Mr Rush.'

'And do I or don't I know everything?'

'Yes, Mr Rush.'

'And have I or haven't I had my appendix out?'

'Yes, Mr Rush.'

'All right, then I know what I'm talking about. Silvie, *don't* go and see him to-morrow afternoon. It won't do *you* any good, because you'll think he's dying, and it won't do *him* any good, because he's just feeling deathly sick, and that isn't the time when you want company.'

'Yes, Mr Rush.'

'Where do you live? Fancy my not knowing after all these years.'

'Raynes Park way, my Aunt Minnie—'

'On the telephone?'

'Well, no, Mr Rush, Uncle Jim's funny like that, Auntie and I are always at him about it and he says it's just an excuse for gossiping and going without exercise. Of course, I *have* got a friend next door—'

'Right. Then you ring up to-morrow from here at lunch-time, and we'll leave together in the evening, and call in at the Hospital and find out how he is, but we won't go and see him. And you'll come home with me, I live just round the corner from the Hospital, we'll give them my telephone number, and you'll help me with the book, and we'll get some dinner sent in, and we'll go on doing the book, and there we are, all handy and in touch, and knowing the stop-press news, and you can catch the last train home. That all right?'

Silvie's eyes opened more and more widely, and tears began to come, and she said, 'It isn't because I'm unhappy, it's because you're so good to me.'

'Well, the point is, do you feel better now?'

She nodded. 'I can't *tell* you the difference, it's wonderful.'

'Then why the devil shouldn't *I* have a cup of tea?'

For the first time that day Silvie's happy laugh was heard in Prosser's.

# 2

It was not like having your hair cut.

They had been very kind, very sympathetic, at the Hospital. Barnaby had just managed to make them understand that Silvie was all that mattered; not the unknown Mr Humberson of Leeds. Funny, he thought, this insistence by hospitals on the next of kin. 'Will Mr Alfred Peabody, last heard of in Dewsbury sixteen years ago, go to St George's Hospital, London, where his brother lies seriously ill.' If he hadn't seen or written to his brother for sixteen years, would

Mr Alfred Peabody mind if he were dying now? Or was it simply that the Hospital didn't want a body on its hands, and was looking for somebody to whom it could say 'Yours' . . . if anything went wrong.

'If anything went wrong'—'if anything happened'. How impossible to say 'If he dies.'

Something had begun to go wrong; something had taken 'a very difficult turn'. Oh no, no, by no means, he had a good constitution, there was every hope—if nothing further went wrong. Perhaps Miss Silver had better be at hand—oh, that's good. And we have your telephone number.

Over his right shoulder he could just see Silvie where she lay on his sofa, her eyes closed. It was half-past eleven, and she had been tap-tapping her fears into the typewriter from seven o'clock, with the one little break for food. 'I couldn't eat, Mr Rush, I couldn't really, it would make me sick.'

'Ever eaten oysters?'

'I don't think I could.'

'It isn't a food, it's a medicine. No trouble to masticate. Just open the mouth and they go down. All the benefit of dinner without the hard work. A squeeze of lemon on each one, spear with fork, insert fork, swallow, and repeat twelve times. Brown bread and butter to taste. Liquid medicine on the right. Very good for you.'

'Oh, Mr Rush, it isn't champagne, is it? I don't think I ever.'

'Sparkling cough mixture. Try it.'

And then tap-tapping again, and Silvie thinking it will be all right if the next word begins with the first half of the alphabet, and Silvie thinking 'Of course it will be all right because it's Humby', and Silvie praying 'Oh God, let it be all right'. He could see her over his shoulder as he sat working at his desk. At any moment now the telephone might ring—Oh God, let it be all right. There isn't so much happiness in the world that you can kill it like this. There aren't so many people in the world loved as he is loved for you to say 'That love's wasted, I don't want it in my world. If it were Barnaby Rush it wouldn't matter, nobody would mind very much, they'd say 'It's sad about poor old Rush, very sudden coming like that', and Chloe would say 'Oh!' and be a little less gay at supper that night, and order beautiful flowers, and write on the card 'With all my love, darling'. But you mustn't kill 'my Humby'. It's just killing two people at once, and a cowardly way of doing it.

If he died, how much would Chloe mind? How much would he mind if Chloe died? A sorrow's crown of sorrow—remembrance of things past, remembering happiness in the past; but how much real happiness was there between a lover and one who loved not? She had got more happiness from their friendship than he. She had taken what she wanted from it. I can't go on like this, he thought. If she won't marry me, I must say good-bye. It will be hell for a little, and after that a strange new world and rather exciting. What shall I think about when I'm not thinking about Chloe any more? What used I to think about?

The telephone bell rang. Silvie, wide awake, terrified, was on her feet. 'All right, darling,' said Barnaby, taking off the receiver, 'it's going to be quite all right.'

'Hallo, sweetie.'

'Oh, hallo!' He turned round, shaking his head and his free hand at Silvie. 'How are you, darling?'

'Which one are you talking to, ducky?'

'Meaning how?'

'The beautiful young blonde stretched at full length on the sofa, or the middle-aged nondescript half a mile away?'

'What's all this, have you got a television set?'

'Darling, I believe you're being unfaithful to me. Don't say it's the manager's wife, I couldn't bear it.'

'You're talking nonsense, and you know it.' He couldn't help sounding unamused. He could feel Silvie at the back of him, saying, 'Oh, for God's sake stop! The Hospital may be trying to get on, saying it's all right, saying—Oh God, saying they want me.' If Silvie were out of the room, he could explain, but he couldn't say in front of her, 'I can't talk now, there's a man dying.'

'All right, darling, then if it's nonsense you can take me out to supper. I'm starving. All particulars when we meet.'

127

He knew that he couldn't; not for a moment was he in doubt of that. But it was strange to find that he wasn't even regretting that he couldn't. That would come later, perhaps. All his thoughts now were with Silvie.

How should he make Chloe understand?

'Darling, I'm very sorry. A friend of mine is having an operation, and we are waiting here for news. I'll ring up to-morrow, if I may. I must ring off now, because we're expecting a message from the Hospital at any moment.'

'Oh, I see. I'm sorry. I hope it will be all right. Good-night, darling.'

Her voice was subdued. Was it a little cool? But who wouldn't feel annoyed, annoyed with herself, at walking so gaily into tragedy? Perhaps he could have let her down more lightly, if— Oh, what the hell did it matter? Chloe had everything. In one terrible second Silvie might lose everything.

'Sorry, Silvie.'

'It's all right, Mr Rush, I couldn't help hearing. I hope you didn't mind, of course I'm frightfully in the way.'

'Rubbish. It was just a friend of mine.'

'Like me and Humby? Do you mind my asking?'

'Well—like one side of it,' he said with a little smile. 'You know, I've always thought Humby was the luckiest man in the world.'

'Do you mean she doesn't love you, Mr Rush?' said Silvie, shocked that love could be so wasted.

'Well, why should she?'

'You mean she loves somebody else?'

He shook his head.

'I don't think so. I think she would have told me. I think I should have known.'

'Oh! . . . Have you been in love with her a long time?'

'Three years.' With a little laugh at himself, he said, 'It's pretty hopeless, isn't it?'

Silvie looked at him with mournful eyes.

'I wish I could do something for you like they do in stories,' she said. 'So as to make it all come right. I keep thinking how I've been telling you about my Humby all these years—what you must have thought. Must have seemed sort of awfully selfish to you—sort of triumphing over you.'

He picked up her hand and kissed it.

'You're a dear, Silvie, I've loved knowing you were happy.'

'Oh!' She drew away from him. All the present came suddenly and terrifyingly back to her. Happy, he thought bitterly. What a word to choose!

He went back to his desk. 'I'll ring up, shall I? They ought to be able to tell us something by now.'

He dialled. She heard him speaking.

I'll count, thought Silvie. By the time I get to fifty I'll know. One, two, three, four, five, oh God, help me, six, seven, eight, now they're going to find out, I won't think of that, I'll just count, nine, ten . . . I'll shut my eyes and count, he'll tell me when he knows, thirty-one, thirty-two, I'll hear him hang up . . . Oh God, you can't, I can't . . . forty-five, forty-six, forty-seven—*Click!*

Mr Rush's face when he turned round! Oh, God! Oh, Humby, my darling! Oh, thank you, God!

'I'm going to cry,' choked Silvie. 'I don't care, I'm going to cry.' She began to laugh in a silly way. 'What did they say?'

'They're very pleased. It all seems quite straightforward now. What else? All like that—all ordinary now. Hair-cut. Oh, Silvie!'

She was crying now, no doubt about it. He became business-like.

'I think a drink, don't you? And then you can have a wash and brush-up, and then you can write him a little letter, and then I'll take you home in a taxi, more comfortable, and you can call in here in the morning, and we'll go round to the Hospital on the way to the office. After which,' he smiled at her, 'I shall hand you back to Humby and Mr Stainer. Here you are.' He gave her a glass. 'Humby!'

'Humby!' She drank, and looked at him, and then lifted her glass again. 'You!'

# 3

The fire was not quite out when he got back. He mixed himself a drink and sank into a chair. He felt tired and peaceful and happy.

It was one o'clock. Chloe was dancing. With whom, he wondered. He knew them all by name: Everard, Claude, Percy, Tommy, Julian (a new one), Colin, Arthur, and a dozen others. They had had surnames once, but he had forgotten most of them. Old names dropped out; new names took their place; here and there a 'regular' seemed immovable. He was one of the regulars—there were only three or four of them. Were they the ones she liked best, or the ones who loved her most? Or was it the same thing, their constancy making them the objects of her particular affection?

I ought to be feeling happy, he thought, because Silvie is happy again, but it isn't just that. It's because I'm horribly conscious of having done a kind thing. I'm really feeling rather smug. And the fact that I'm feeling smug now doesn't mean that I did a kind thing just in order to feel smug. But it does mean that, if I'm complacent over a very ordinary act of kindness, I don't do them very often. Perhaps I don't get the chance . . .

I *could* have taken her out to supper, it would have made no difference to Silvie, she could have gone back by train and been much too happy to notice the difference. Why didn't I? I just didn't want to. I wasn't in the mood. Chloe isn't real, that's what it is, she isn't real. She's something in a picture-book. She's two-dimensional. Has she got a heart? *Has* she got a heart? If not, what happened to it? Who killed it? When? When she was a child? Her first love-affair? Somebody broke it, or iced it up, or what? Supposing I said to her I've got two orphan children to look after ('No, darling, not mine'), they'd go to some horrible Charitable Home if I didn't, it means I shall be extremely hard up, and—I'm terribly sorry, darling, but we shan't be able to go to the Savoy, or the Ritz or the Berkeley any more. What would happen? Should we meet just as often? Would she understand and sympathize and approve? That's it, you see, I don't know; because we should be up against real life, and she doesn't belong to real life. That's why, compared with Silvie, she didn't matter just now.

(A little anxiously he glanced down the roll of his relations, wondering if any orphans were indeed likely to come his way . . . There seemed to be no immediate danger, thank God.)

That first time we met. At Allingham's. Pompous ass. We talked and laughed, I sat next to her at lunch, we wandered round the gardens together. That was all. And then she offered to drive me back to London, and we held hands all the way. We had supper together; I kissed her good-night. Well, what? What did she think when she was alone? Was she triumphant? 'One more captive to my bow and spear, one more feather in my cap?' Or was she disappointed? 'I thought he was going to be the one—but he isn't.' What does she want? What is she looking for? . . .

It was easy for those who didn't know her to think of her as Any Man's Mistress, or for those who knew her a little better than that to dismiss her as cold and heartless, taking all and giving nothing. Easy for a woman whose husband had been enchanted; easy for a man whose assurance had been disappointed. Barnaby recognized this, but was not troubled by it. They were wrong. There was some quality in her which put her outside such easy classification; a sort of detachment from the world; as if she came from nowhere and were going nowhere. As if she were not really interested in mortals, but had picked up the tricks and the language. Laugh at me, thought Barnaby. If I were twenty, you would be right. If I were in my second childhood, perhaps you would be right. But I'm thirty-five. And there's Everard Hale, who has been everywhere and met everybody; a man of the world if ever there was one. Are we all romantically in love, idealizing something worthless? It doesn't seem possible. Some of us must have grown up.

The fire had died down. Barnaby gathered himself out of his chair, and put his empty glass back on the table. Silvie was herself again; the book was nearly ready; he had finished with the dentist for another six months. A delightful world. And Chloe—the best company in it— always there. He would ring her up to-morrow. Heaven to be with her again. Chloe!

He went to bed.

# 4

It was Chloe who rang up.

'Hallo, darling,' she said, so quietly that he could hardly hear. 'I'm sorry about last night. Is it all right?'

'Thank God, yes. It was My Humby. Appendicitis, and looked rather bad for a moment. I was terrified.'

'Was that Silvie with you?'

'Yes. He was at St George's just round the corner, and she had nowhere to go. So she came and helped me with the book, while we waited for news.'

There was a little silence; and then she said, as if she were thinking of something else, 'You were going to show me those puzzles he makes. You never did.'

'I'm sorry, darling, I forgot all about it. I'll bring them next time. When will that be, sweetheart?'

'What are you doing this evening?'

His heart leaped; his brain raced over the possibilities, and rejected them doggedly.

'Silvie was coming back with me again, and we were going to try and finish off the book—and keep an eye on Humby.'

There was another silence.

'Are you there, darling?' asked Barnaby.

'I didn't sleep at all last night,' said Chloe's quiet voice, 'that's why I'm ringing up so early. When do you get to the office?'

'Ten normally. I was going to be there at half-past nine this morning.'

'Could you look in here for five minutes on the way? What are you doing now?'

'Middle of breakfast.'

'Oh, I'm sorry, darling. I'm always interrupting you.'

'Never. It's all the other things which are the interruption. May I have thirty seconds for silent calculation?'

'Go on with your breakfast while you're thinking. I'll hold on.'

Silvie again. Silvie was coming round this morning. She had to be at the office at nine-thirty, so she would be here not later than nine. They would look in at the hospital together. Well, that was all right, she could go on by herself, he needn't get there till ten.

'Hallo, darling?'

'Yes?'

'Calculations worked out and checked by cross-bearings. I shall be with you at nine-twenty to the dot. Will that be all right, darlingest?'

'Lovely. Good-bye till then, my dear one.'

What did it mean? What did she want?

He was still wondering as he sent up his name by the porter. The porter, Barnaby thought, must have wondered too, or perhaps he was past wondering.

The outer door was open. He rang and she called 'Come in, darling', and again 'Come in' from behind her bedroom door.

She was in bed. For the first time since he had known her he saw her face unadorned and thought that she had never looked so beautiful. It was a new beauty, gentler, more benignant than the beauty he had known. I wonder if her soul is like that too, he thought, beneath the worldly covering she shows. He dropped on his knees by the bed.

'You aren't ill, darling?'

'I don't think so. I didn't sleep, but I don't sometimes.'

'May I kiss you?'

'Put your arms round me and hold me tight.'

He held her close to him, and she said with a little sigh, 'I could go to sleep in your arms.'

'It's not I who am fighting against it, darling.'

'I know. You're very sweet. You will love me always, won't you?'

'I expect so. I shan't try, but I expect it will come like that.'

She said nothing for a little, and then, as if taking a great resolve, 'I will marry you, if you like.' There was just that emphasis on the 'will' which meant 'I don't want to, but I will'.

'If *you* like, darling, and when you like.'

'You do want to?'

'Terribly. I can't bear to think of it.'

'You sweet. We'll get married one day. Let's go on as we are for a little longer, and see how we feel about it. It needn't be just yet.' She gave a contented little sigh, and closed her eyes . . .

Barnaby realized suddenly his extreme physical discomfort. He realized too that this was the peak of Chloe's love for him: that she could never love him more than this, and would never want to marry him more than this. She was asleep in his arms, she had promised to be his wife; he should have been surrendering to the moment; but he remained horribly detached, feeling the strain on his arms and the back of his neck, wondering what the time was and when Ellen came; wishing that he hadn't left the outer door open. It's all no good, he thought. Three years is too long. Two years ago, even a year ago, I should have believed her and been wildly happy. But one can't go on loving a picture, a statue, a Princess in a fairy story, for three long years and expect it suddenly to come to life. This that is happening, this that she has said, isn't real. It means nothing by the standards of real life. We are just where we were three years ago. Nothing that she has said means anything. We shall go on as before, and I shall be as far away from her as ever. I was nearer to Silvie last night than I shall ever be to Chloe.

He tried very gently to release his left hand so that he could look at his wrist-watch.

'What is it, darling?' she murmured.

'This damned world. I must go. I've got to work.'

'Thank you for coming, dearest. I think I can sleep now.'

'Thank you for letting me see you like this. You look so lovely. Sleep, darling.'

Her eyes were still closed. He kissed them lightly. She turned over on her side, leaving his arms free. He stood up and stretched himself.

'Shall I take the receiver off?' he asked, but she did not answer. It seemed that she was asleep again.

He went out very quietly.

'It's an interlude,' he thought. 'It has no relation to anything which has happened or which is going to happen.' He signalled to a taxi. 'Prosser's, at the end of Chancery Lane.' As they jerked into movement, he thought, 'It might have been any of the others'.

# Chapter Ten

## 1

'Culverhampton,' wrote Mr Pope Ferrier, cigarette on lower lip, bottle in lap, 'is not often privileged to see the première of an entirely original play by such a noted author-actor-manager as Wilson Kelly, supported by his full London cast.' And he might have added that it would have had to forgo the privilege on this occasion if Kelly could have got an opening date at any more important town. But when the choice lies between Culverhampton and Peebles, and Culverhampton is chosen, one must make the best of it.

Mr Ferrier lacked personal attraction. He had the broad figure and shiny yellow face of a Japanese wrestler; his greased hair coalesced in dyed streaks which revealed an interstitial baldness; his fingers were rusty with nicotine, and he wore a black patch over one eye. But he was the best theatrical press-agent in the country—or so Wilson Kelly and Mr Ferrier believed. They had been together for nearly ten years, and had no respect for each other, but only professional admiration. They were together now. The cubby hole in which they sat was decorated with old posters, old properties, old programmes and old beer bottles; dusty pigeon-holes stuffed with old scripts; a large press which may have held ledgers once, but now handled a forgotten pair of trousers; a packing case on which Mr Ferrier sat, his feet on the trousers, his back against the wall; and a table on which stood a half-empty bottle of cough mixture, a chipped saucer of drawing-pins, a bicycle lamp, a paper-covered novel marked, with a distending tooth-pick, at the place where the last reader had broken down, and the all-necessary telephone. Mr Wilson Kelly was seated by, rather than at, the table, his chair being turned aside to catch such daylight as came through a reluctant window. He was reading what Our Theatrical Correspondent had said about him in to-day's issue of the *Culverhampton Courier*, knowing that Pope Ferrier had written it, but absorbing it with as much gratified surprise as if it had been an unsolicited tribute from an impartial and world-famous critic.

Offered to a distinguished member of any other profession or business, the hospitality of such an 'office' would have been rejected as an insult. Tucked away at the back of the Theatre Royal, Culverhampton, it was accepted by Kelly and Ferrier as a normal setting for their art.

'But,' wrote Ferrier, carrying on his opening sentence, 'Wilson Kelly has long had a tender corner in his heart for Culverhampton. For it was actually here that he first met the beautiful and talented Helen Brightman, that great artist who joined her life to his, and whose recent sad death left such a blank, not only in the theatrical world, but in the hearts of all who knew her. Moreover he is descended on his mother's side from a well-known Culverhampton family of the eighteenth century, and has in his possession an early and valuable print of the town which is not the least-prized rarity in his famous collection of *objets d'art*. It is not surprising, then, to hear that it had always been Mr Kelly's intention to signalize his connection with the town by the first presentation there of one of his London productions. But hitherto a malign Fate has stood in the way. Now at last . . . '

Ferrier tore the sheet off his pad and passed it to Kelly. 'Just to make sure I've got the facts right,' he said, and unscrewed the top of his bottle.

Appreciatively Kelly read and Ferrier drank.

'Very good, John, very good. Puts the facts out well.'

Ferrier lowered the bottle and wiped his mouth with the back of his hand.

'Ever see a print of that picture—First Meeting of Dante and Beatrice in Florence?' he asked.

'Yes, I suppose so. I know it. Why?'

'Just thinking. If we had had a companion picture painted: First meeting of Wilson and Helen in Llandudno, we should have wanted nine of 'em.'

'Oh, nonsense.'

'Margate, Nottingham, Eastbourne, Hull,' began Ferrier on his fingers, 'Llandudno, Sheffield—'

'I'm not responsible for all the silly stories you've put about,' said Kelly with a shrug. 'I could take you out now and show you the exact spot in King Street opposite the Post Office where I ran into her on my bicycle.'

'Definitely no, old man. Not bicycle. Show me the historic spot, and that's where your Rolls-Royce picked her up in the snow on that bloody cold night in Jan, and took her home to widowed mother. Clergyman's widow,' he announced, as he lifted the bottle to his lips, and, following up the picture in his mind, added, 'Hopeless Dawn.' He drank.

'I forget,' said Kelly impatiently. 'It was a long time ago. You made a note about the Lancing girl?'

Ferrier turned his pad round the other way, and read in a bland, monotonous voice: 'C.L.—recent discovery of K's—sister of well-known black-and-white artist and boxing blue—cross in brackets.—S.R.—recent discovery of K's—daughter of well-known consular official—question-mark. J.M.—recent discovery of K's—well-known Hampshire family—tick, five stars and three exclamation marks. I got carried away.' He looked up and said, 'That's Judy, the little girl with—'

'Yes, yes, yes, I asked you about Miss Lancing.'

'Well, now you know the answer. We keep all that, bar the private notes, till we open in London.' He went on reading. 'W.K. the well-known auth-act-man tells of an amusing adventure which befell him during his recent Empire tour black leopard query Singapore—now what the hell was that?'

'Singapore? I don't seem to remember—'

'No bloody reason why you should, old man. Something I read somewhere, happened to a missionary, wasted on a missionary, point was could it have happened in Singapore, if not where?'

'I don't remember a *black* leopard in Singapore,' murmured Kelly, making a serious effort to meet the story half-way.

'You will as soon as it comes back to me,' said Ferrier encouragingly. 'It was a tame one which brought up the morning tea or something. You'd have liked it.'

The company was going through a last week of rehearsals at Culverhampton. The manager of the musical-comedy company which should have preceded Kelly's had met his financial Waterloo among the fruit-machines of Blackpool; the Theatre Royal, unable to get a new booking in the time, was dark for a week; and Kelly gladly took advantage of this to bring his scenery in, and give his company an opportunity to get in the proper setting what he called its Culverhampton legs. The majority of the company did not much like this, preferring, not unnaturally, its own homes in London to lodgings in Culverhampton. But to Claudia theatrical lodgings in a provincial town, so familiar to her from all that she had imagined and read, were the beginning of romance.

From that moment at the Savoy Grill when Wilson Kelly had snapped his fingers and announced the birth of Zella a gypsy maid, life had become almost unbearably gratifying. Already she saw herself telling the younger generation the secret of success on the stage. Hard work, of course; that came above all. Luck? Yes, a little luck was necessary. She herself acknowledged that her very first engagement (*Zella a gypsy maid*) came to her through a chance meeting at a cocktail party. Mr Wilson Kelly, the famous author-actor-manager, had just completed his latest play, *Fortune's Wishbone*, and was looking for a young actress to create the part of Zella. Almost as soon as he entered the room his eye had singled her out, and he had said to himself, 'My gypsy maid!' Eagerly he had asked for an introduction; within five minutes he was telling her of his new play (*Fortune's Wishbone*); and at a little dinner at the Savoy that night, he formally asked her to join his company. Well, that was luck—good luck for her. But the point she wished to emphasize was this: that though luck might bring the opportunity, it was merit, and merit alone, which made the most of it. Don't let them ever—(she was now giving away prizes at the Academy)—don't let them ever think that a successful career owed itself to chance; and, still more important, don't let them ever think that chance could be given the responsibility for failure. 'Many of my colleagues on the stage,' she ended, warming to her theme, 'say that the profession is overcrowded, and they warn young aspirants to seek some other means of living. I do not share that view. Overcrowded, yes; but overcrowded with incompetence. There is room now, there will always be room, ample room, for genuine talent. Thank you all very much.' There were loud cheers; she dropped them an old-fashioned curtsey, and the proceedings ended.

Claudia had to admit to herself that *Zella* was not an outstanding character in the play. This, described hopefully by the authors, Carol Higgs and Wilson Kelly, as a 'new and original romantic comedy', concerned the love-affairs of *Betty Langton.* Already engaged to a fresh-faced young man, she was about to elope with a sallower one, when *Uncle Dudley* was called in. *Uncle Dudley* was the black sheep of the family, having refused to go into the family business on no better excuse than that he wished to join a Concert Party in the Far East. Thanks to the accidental discovery of a ruby mine in the neigh-bourhood of Bangkok, he had returned to England to find a warm welcome waiting for him at his sister-in-law's house. 'Oh, Dudley,' she implored, 'can't you do anything to bring Betty to her senses?' He did all that was possible; he played the Barcarolle to her. As the music died away, *Betty* rose from her chair, as if drawn by an irresistible magnet. *Dudley* put down his violin, and held out his arms . . . At this point young Mr Higgs, whose play it was, called attention to the fact that one of the things the Lord Chamberlain didn't much care about was incest. Annoyed, because he had forgotten about this, Kelly said that the right artistic ending to a play couldn't be allowed to fall down on a small matter like that. 'Uncle' was obviously a courtesy title. He was simply an old friend of *Betty's* mother, who had been in love with her at one time. Yes . . . yes . . . yes . . . they might have a little prologue, twenty years earlier, played well up-stage, perhaps through gauze . . . a tapestry hanging at the back of the Hall of Act I. Just a tender little love scene, at the end of which he hears that she loves another. *Betty's* father. And so he takes his breaking heart to the Far East. Act I. Twenty years later. She is a widow now. He returns to England. Mary! Dudley! And then the daughter comes in. This is my little Betty. 'Gradually we build up the suspense—will he marry the mother or the daughter? *Which?* You see the idea, Mr Higgs? Suspense.' Gradually Mr Higgs came to see this—and a good many other things.

It was at the end of Act II, while they were having coffee after dinner, that *Zella* came to the French windows, played an introductory chord on her guitar, and began to sing 'Santa Lucia'. 'Zella!' cried the sallow young man. 'What are *you* doing here?' This was what young Mr Higgs wanted to know. However, no explanation was offered to him. 'Never explain, Mr Higgs,' said Kelly, 'unless absolutely necessary. The audience will see at once— wait a moment. How would it be if she came on with a baby in her arms?' Young Mr Higgs said that it was almost impossible to play the guitar with a baby in the arms, you would be certain to drop one or other of them. Kelly covered his face with his hands. 'No, no, Mr Higgs,' came through his fingers, 'you must try to keep up with me. She is now singing a lullaby, a Spanish cradle song, to her babe, rocking it in her arms. I fling open the windows. "Zella!" cries Eustace. The audience sees at once that he is the father. He who aspires to the hand of Betty Langton, has seduced this little gypsy girl. Can it be that Betty will marry him? Suspense again, you see. From the other angle.' Kelly and Mr Higgs brooded over this for a little, and then Kelly said, 'Or how would it be if she came in after dinner and told our fortunes? Suppose she read a dark man in Betty's life—"You will link your life with a dark man". Eustace and I are dark, the other man is fair. You see? We could still have Eustace coming in and crying "Zella!" It leaves more to the imagination.'

With Zella still in this fluid state, Claudia attended the opening rehearsals of Act I. In addition to studying her own part, she was understudying the maid, played by Five Star Judy, so that she had some excuse for being there, and every excuse for feeling that she was now a real actress. It was a great moment when at last her own cue came, and a disappointing one when Kelly said 'Ah, yes. Yes. I'm afraid, my dear,' and he put an arm round her shoulders and removed her from the chalk line and two forms which represented the French windows, 'I'm afraid we shall have to leave this for the moment. Mr Higgs wants to make a little alteration. We feel that we want *more* from Zella. As Mr Higgs sees it now'— he turned down-stage and called to the empty spaces of the auditorium, 'you will let me have that by to-morrow, Mr Higgs?'— and then to Claudia, 'This is really one of the *big* moments of the play, and Mr Higgs feels that he hasn't *built it up* properly. I think, my dear, you'll like what he's writing for you. It *broadens* the part in a wonderful way. Straight on to Act III, Mr Simmons.'

During the next week Claudia stood at the chalk line, holding an imaginary guitar, an imaginary pack of cards, an imaginary tambourine or an imaginary baby, and waiting while Wilson Kelly with closed eyes visualized the tremendous possibilities. Then he would open his eyes, call to the empty auditorium, 'You see what I mean, Mr Higgs?' and to Simmons, 'We'll leave that for the moment. Act III, please.' It was not until their last day in London that Zella was finally stabilized. As follows:

*(A girl's voice is heard singing outside the French windows. Silence falls on the room, as they all listen to the first verse of 'Santa Lucia'. Then Dudley strides to the window and flings them open.)*

ZELLA *(a gypsy maid, carrying a guitar)*. You like my song, yes, no?
DUDLEY. Charming, my dear. *(To Mrs Langton.)* A girl from the gypsy camp in the village. I passed by it the other morning.
MRS LANGTON. How interesting! *(To Zella.)* Do sing us some more, dear.

BETTY
JOHN } Oh, do!

ZELLA *(holding out her hand)*. You cross my palm first, yes? It bring you luck.

DUDLEY *(with an amused laugh)*. Art for art's sake is no longer the fashion, I see. *(Giving Zella half a crown.)* Here you are, my dear.

ZELLA. Thank you. Now I sing.

*(She sings another verse. As she is in the middle of the third verse,*
Eustace *re-enters the room.)*

EUSTACE *(seeing Zella)*. Zella!
ZELLA. Eustace!

*(The guitar crashes to the ground, as they all stand transfixed.*
SLOW CURTAIN

It was on this day that Claudia lunched with young Mr Higgs at the *Moulin d'Or*. It was the first time that she had had an opportunity of speaking to him, and she took advantage of it to tell him how much she loved his play.

'My God!' said young Mr Higgs.

# 2

It was rather a bewildering lunch.

It began in the normal way, Claudia being asked what she would drink.

'I *think*,' said Claudia, screwing her little face up as if reviewing the cellar, 'I think a Gin and It.' She had no real liking for alcohol, but asking for a Gin and It always gave her a cosy feeling of sophistication; moreover, it was the only cocktail of whose name she was quite certain.

'A Gin and It and a Sidecar,' said young Mr Higgs to the waiter.

'Do you know, I think I'll change my mind and have a Sidecar too,' said Claudia. This also was normal. Any alternative, once she was sure of the name, was an occasion for hope.

'Two Sidecars. What shall we eat? Let's have oysters, shall we, or do you loathe them?'

'Oh, do let's. How lovely!'

Lunch was ordered. He looks about fifteen, thought Claudia, but I suppose he must be more.

'Now then, Miss Lancing,' said Higgs. 'By the way, may I call you Claudia? There seems to be a lot of that on the stage, and I was up at Cambridge with your brother. At least, I suppose it was your brother, Claude Lancing.'

'Yes, that's right. Fancy! Did you know each other? I used to come up for May Weeks, at least I did once. What fun if we'd met! Yes, do call me Claudia.'

'My name is Mr Higgs. At least it seems to be. You'd think, by now, Kelly could have called me Higgs. You can call me Carol if you like, but don't force it. Let it come.'

'Carol. Quite easy.'

'Good. No, I didn't know your brother. I was at Magdalene. I admired him from a distance. Why do you like this bloody play?'

Claudia, rather disconcerted, rather angry suddenly, tried to think of reasons for liking the play, or not liking the play; polite explanations or rude explanations why she had said she liked it when she didn't; and could think of nothing. The drinks coming, she lifted her glass and said snappily, 'All right, here's to its failure.'

A frown creased the fresh simplicity of young Mr Higgs's face. He held up a hand. 'Wait!' he said commandingly. 'We mustn't be in a hurry about this.'

'What's the matter?'

'If it's a failure, you're out of a job. Do you mind?'

'Of course I do!' To have thrown up the Academy for nothing! She realized for the first time how desperately important it was that the play should run. 'It *must* succeed! It *must*!'

'That settles it,' said Higgs. He raised his glass. 'Success!'

'Success!' said Claudia.

'And there's also the money, we mustn't forget that. But, oh God, what a bloody play.'

'Then why did you write it?'

'I didn't. Good Heavens, woman, do you realize that in the play which *I* wrote, Uncle Dudley was a comic character? I still think he's ineffably comic. I think that, given the right part, Wilson Kelly is our greatest comic actor. Everything he says and does makes me laugh. But he won't be playing for laughs on the night, and his technique is so good that he probably won't get them. He'll get a lot of cheers and a few internal groans. Mine will be the most heartfelt.'

'Well, why did you let your play be made all different? I mean made romantic instead of comic, if that's what you meant.'

Higgs slid an oyster into his mouth, swallowed, and said, 'Have you ever seen a rabbit with a snake?'

'Never, actually.'

'Neither have I. And I rather think I mean a ferret. Fascination, Claudia. That's the secret. The awful thing is that the rabbit likes it. He knows he's going to be eaten, and he just can't resist the novelty of it. That's me. Rabbit Higgs and Wilson Ferret.'

'Oh!' said Claudia. She looked a little unhappy.

'I see your point,' he said. 'Wilson Kelly is an old friend of yours, and you think I oughtn't to call him a ferret.'

'Well—'

'I could,' said young Mr Higgs, considering the point and deciding to be magnanimous, 'I *could* make it a weasel.'

'He's not an old friend of mine, but I'm grateful to him because he's given me my first chance, and I'm naturally grateful to him— and—and—'

'And you want to be a good trouper, and you've read somewhere that good troupers are always loyal to their chiefs.'

'Well, there *is* such a thing as loyalty—'

'I think I shall call him "Chief",' said young Mr Higgs thoughtfully. 'I knew there was something I was doing wrong, but I couldn't put a finger on it. "Yes, Chief." Sounds much better.'

Claudia looked round the room and said coldly, 'Is that John Gielgud over there?'

'Probably. Or Henry Irving.'

'I can't think why you asked me out to lunch,' she snapped, 'if you just want to make fun of my profession, and my part, and the play I'm in, which means so much to me.'

'Well, I can tell you why I asked you out to lunch. Hasn't anybody else ever told you?' Claudia's natural colour deepened suddenly. 'Yes, that's why. You really *are* rather sweet, you know. If an escaped lunatic buys the film rights of this play, and *The Times* says that I'm the greatest English dramatist since Ivor Novello, will you marry me?'

'You *are* an idiot,' laughed Claudia.

'Call me Mr Higgs.'

'Mr Higgs.'

'Heavenly,' he said, pressing his hand to his heart.

Claudia laughed again. It *was* fun being on the stage.

From time to time during that exciting week at Culverhampton, in dark and dusty corners of the theatre, or in the more cheerful anchorage of the Queen's Arms bar, Claudia would come across the two authors in earnest collaboration; and young Mr Higgs, conscious of her passing, would take no apparent notice of her, but put two fingers vertically up over each ear and waggle them, as reminder that he was playing his accustomed role. Every snatched meal between rehearsals was hurried down in the publicity of the Queen's Arms bar, local patrons listening stolidly to the bright chatter, and saying to each other behind hands, after giving the matter full consideration, 'Actors and Actresses'. Claudia loved those companionable moments. They were all brothers-in-arms, dependent on each other, engaged in a common assault on the public's emotions. The quarrels and the jealousies would come later. Meanwhile she drank delight of battle with her peers, and showed the delight so ingenuously, was so willing to do anybody else's work in addition to her own, that she was by way of becoming the mascot of the company, qualified for a smile from everybody and a friendly pat on the bottom from the more experienced men.

On the morning of the first dress-rehearsal, she was looking at attractive things in a shop-window in King Street when a voice behind her said, 'Yes, yes, pretty and pink, but *not* warm.'

She flashed round, coloured and said, 'Oh, it's you.'

'That Mr Higgs again. I love the way you blush. We shan't want those, not with the winter coming on.'

'You *are* ridiculous. I wasn't—I was just going to get some ribbon.'

> *Jenny would go in a domino*
> *Pretty and pink but warm,*
> *While I attended clad in a splendid*
> *Austrian uniform.*

'I thought it sounded familiar. Quotation from Rudyard Kipling and Wilson Kelly.'

'Mr Kelly wants me to have some ribbons on my guitar.'

'Of course, of course. Nice clean ones. Speaking as part-author I see Zella with red and yellow streamers. Her father was President of the M.C.C.—I should have told you this before, it would have helped you to build up the character—and her mother was the Romany Queen of Bognor Regis. She was playing the guitar outside the French windows of his house in Park Lane one night; a full moon hung low in the sky; and the only thing she remembered clearly afterwards was his red and yellow tie, and a voice saying "How's that?" Otherwise, she used to say, they all seemed much the same to her. That's why you have this passion for red and yellow.'

'Darling, you *have* got a nasty mind.'

How easily she had called him Darling!

'Would you say so?' He considered it—a little anxiously, it seemed.

'No, darling, of course not,' said Claudia quickly. She took his arm. 'Come in and help me buy the ribbon.' Giving his arm a little squeeze, she said, 'And don't be any different.'

It's I who am different, she thought. I don't know what's happening to me.

# 3

'How's Claudia?' said Chloe, as the waiter left to look for two champagne cocktails.

'Her first night to-night,' said Claude. And my first day, he thought. The first meal we've had alone together. I wish it hadn't been lunch.

'Why aren't you there, holding her hand?'

'Do you mean like this?' asked Claude, taking Chloe's from her lap.

She gave him a smile, and said, 'Yes, perhaps you're better in London.'

'We'll send her a telegram after lunch.'

'Two telegrams, darling. It's quantity not quality which counts in the theatre. Nobody reads them, you just pin them up on your screen, and get a mass effect. She's bound to be dressing with some other girl—'

'Ruby.'

'Very well then, we must beat Ruby's side of the screen. Would it be nice, darling, to drive round the post-offices of London together, and send her a whole series of telegrams, from John and Jack and Jill and Bill, sort of noncommittal names? And one or two difficult ones just to make her wonder. Would that be nice, darling?'

'It would be nice to drive round the post-offices of London together.'

She gave him her intimate smile again and said, 'All right, that's what we'll do.'

'And what would be still nicer would be if you came to the London first night with me.'

'I'm sorry, darling. I expect I shall be going with Everard. I generally do.'

'Who's Everard?'

'Everard Hale.'

'Oh! I thought he was in South America or somewhere.'

'He'll be back before then. They don't come to London till November. I had a letter from Wil.'

'Damn and Hell,' thought Claude, 'I won't be jealous, what's the good when there are so many?' He said, 'Did he tell you how she was getting on?'

'No, ducky, I don't suppose he wants to remember where he met her. He's getting ready to believe that he discovered her in a cabaret at Runcorn. I do hope the play isn't too terrible. It generally is.'

'Apparently the author was up at Cambridge with me.'

'That doesn't really help us, darling,' smiled Chloe. 'But it's nice to know that there were two of you there. How's Borotra?'

'My God, do you remember that?'

'Well, of course!' Chloe was surprised.

'Shall I tell you something?'

'You can tell me anything, darling. I'll stop you if I've heard it.'

'When I was waiting for you—'

'Wasn't I a punctual girl?'

'I suppose so. I got here early. I liked waiting for you, it's the best part really.'

'Oh, Claude!'

'And all the time I was waiting, I was wondering if you'd recognize me. I shouldn't have been a bit surprised if you hadn't. When you came in, I wanted to go up to you and say, "I am Claude Lancing".'

'Darling, what *do* you mean?'

'That's how you make me feel.' He looked away from her, he looked down at the tablecloth, and said in a low voice: 'You *don't* recognize me. I want to shake you, and say "Listen! I am Claude Lancing. I'm not Everard this, or Wil that or Percy the other. When you have lunch with somebody else to-morrow, I'm not just the man you had lunch with yesterday—same sort of lunch, same sort of talk, same sort of man. Even though you don't love me, I'm as different from other men for you, as you are different from every woman in the world for me." But you make me feel that I'm not. That, for you, I'm not Claude Lancing, but just Monday's man, who might so easily have been somebody else.'

Even as the words rushed from him, he was thinking, 'You fool, you bloody fool, you've spoilt everything. The happy lunch, the happy silly afternoon sending off telegrams, the kiss in the taxi. Now you've spoilt your only day, now you'll never get another.'

The waiter brought the drinks. Chloe said, 'Let's drink to Claudia, shall we?' She lifted her glass.

'Claudia,' said Claude. 'I'm sorry, darling. I expect I just wanted a drink.'

'Wasn't it clever of me to remember her name?'

'Oh, sweetheart,' he mumbled unhappily, 'I don't know why—do forgive me.'

'Why do you say things for which you have to be forgiven immediately after you've said them? If you think I'm just a head-hunter, trying to collect a string of men, and not caring anything about them, well, say so, and stick to it, you may be right. I'm sure you've read somewhere that women like being treated rough. Well, you would be the only man who'd ever been as rough with me as that, and perhaps I should admire you for it, who knows? But you want it both ways. You want to say the horrible things and let them rankle, and you want me to go on being as friendly as if they'd never been said. That's rather cowardly—Claude Lancing.'

'That's another thing about her,' he thought, 'she's so utterly clear-sighted, she sees exactly what I've done, what she says is absolutely true.' And at the same time he was thinking, 'And it's absolutely true what *I* said, only I said it badly'.

He looked at her suddenly with his rare, attractive smile. He said: 'You know, I can think of lots of things to say, and they are all quite hopeless.'

A smile glimmered at the corners of Chloe's mouth as she murmured, 'One of them mightn't be.'

'Well, I'll just give you some of the chapter headings. *One:* I'm not absolutely certain of this, but I *think* you look more beautiful when you're angry—'. He broke off and said, 'No, I haven't had enough experience, I shall have to let you know about that later. *Two:* You enjoy a quarrel, you're enjoying this thoroughly. *Three:* You're quite right, I oughtn't to have apologized. Apologizing was unforgivable. *Four:* What I said was true, and at least a dozen men have said it to you before. Only they didn't say it as clumsily as I did, and as completely out of the blue. What we're really all saying is, 'Oh, God, I wish you loved me.' *Five:* Thank Heaven, we're having lunch, so I've got another half-hour, anyway, before you say good-bye to me for ever. I do hope you're hungry, darling. You'll like the coffee here, it's wonderful. *Six:* What it comes to is that, when you're in love, you're defenceless. The other person can hit you how and when and where she likes. I resent this, and I had a sudden wild longing to get past your guard and hit you somewhere. At least I suppose that was it. But it's all very difficult. I feel more and more strongly that Life *isn't* just a bowl of cherries.'

'It isn't.'

'No, I thought not.'

Chloe said mournfully: 'I didn't ask you to love me, darling.'

'Liar.'

Chloe laughed appreciatively, as if accepting a compliment. Or so it seemed to Claude.

'You're a standing invitation to love. What you *don't* ask is that it should be laid out in front of you. It's like a man keeping on about the cigars he gave you at Christmas, when you only sent him a Christmas card. It makes you feel uncomfortable, and not quite so sure of yourself.'

'You sound very grown-up, darling. Are you really only twenty-three?'

'Unfortunately.'

'Oh, but why? It's a nice age to be.'

'Not when the girl you love is twenty-eight.'

'Twenty-seven, darling.'

He looked at her suspiciously.

'You told me that you were twenty-eight.'

'Ah, but I've had a birthday since then.'

Half sighing, half laughing, Claude said, 'Oh, God, I do love you. I do love talking to you. When was your birthday?'

'Quite lately. Look, darling, here's your little family of whitebait. Eat them up nicely.'

'I wish I'd known about your birthday. When was it, Chloe?' He put a forkful of fish into his mouth.

'And tuck the tails well in. That's better. When's *your* birthday, darling? I'll knit you a little bib.'

'I don't believe you've had a birthday.'

'Well, I haven't actually had it yet.'

'Well, when is it?'

'How you do go on. If you must know, I'm having it. It's to-day.'

'But—but—but—'

It was incredible! Incredible that she should have honoured *him* with her presence on this day, or, having so decided to honour him, not have let him know. Incredible that, being so honoured, he should have chosen this one day as the day on which to insult her.

'I can't believe it,' he said at last. 'I don't mean that I don't,' he added quickly, 'but—well, it's just that the King ought to be giving a party for you at Buckingham Palace, and you're lunching here with me.'

She gave him all her appreciation of this in her eyes, and said: 'You say very pretty things, darling. Tommy's giving me a little party to-night at Claridge's. So I thought it would be nice if you and I had a quiet little lunch together.'

'Who's Tommy?'

'Just Monday's man,' said Chloe with an innocent air. 'The man I'm having dinner with to-night.'

'Oh, Chloe!'

With the remorse which he felt came this other sudden feeling of loneliness as he thought of Chloe's party. Tommy and his friends, and her friends, boisterously gay together, and he so uncompromisingly outside their circle, outside all the many circles which had crossed the circle of Chloe's life. He hated to know that she had this freedom from him, not only on this night, but on so many days and nights, while he was never free from her. As if she were a disinterested party to whom he could put out a hand for sympathy, he asked, 'Have *you* ever been in love?'

It was not a question which seemed to need an answer, but in a low voice, as though to herself, Chloe answered it.

'Once,' said Chloe.

# 4

When the curtain went up for the tenth and last time, Wilson Kelly was taken completely by surprise. In fact, he had his back to the audience, and his violin was under his chin, some of the company having said (one supposes): 'Do give us that lovely thing again, Mr Kelly, I was in my dressing-room and couldn't hear it properly.' So, the play over, the audience, presumably, on its way out, Mr Kelly picks up his violin from the top of the piano and says, 'Oh, do you mean this?'—whereupon that damned fool Simmons rings up the curtain again. Luckily the company had made its request from the wings, so that Mr Kelly, the better able from his long experience to deal with these situations, was alone on the stage. He turned to the audience with a charming air of embarrassment; and since, to them as to all other audiences, the unexpected appearance of the theatre cat and a premature rising of the curtain were always the peak points of any play, they greeted him with affectionate laughter and a renewed outburst of applause. Once more there were loud cries of 'Speech!'

Wilson Kelly looked comically from his violin in one hand to the bow in the other, evidently wondering how they had come there and how he could get rid of them; and then decided, with a little shrug of resignation, to accept the informality of his position and do the best he could.

'Ladies and gentlemen,' he began. 'Or shall I say friends? No! Remembering my own associations, the associations of my forebears, with this beautiful and historic town, I shall take it upon myself to say—Fellow Citizens!'

In the wings young Mr Higgs said to Claudia, 'It's wonderful. Wonderful, wonderful and after that out of all whooping. Do you realize that this is going to happen in *every* town we go to? I shall never desert you, Mrs Micawber. I shall follow you around everywhere. For both your sakes.'

'Those were your flowers, weren't they?' whispered Claudia. 'Signed "Bunny"?'

'I wondered if you'd guess. You see, if I'd signed them "Mr Higgs", which is my real name, or even Carol, I couldn't have left out Ruby very well, or in fact any of the cast. Of course, if we get as far as London, I shall do the thing handsomely. Up here I thought that my two leading ladies would be enough—the stage one and the real one.'

'Carol, you *are* sweet.'

She was more happy than she had ever been. Carol's flowers, that wonderful *mass* of telegrams, from young men and girls she had almost forgotten—(who *was* Charmian? Someone at the Academy, she supposed, but surely she would have remembered the name?)—the sudden surprising applause given to her song, the relief of getting through without faltering, the knowledge that she had looked her prettiest, the surety of provincial success anyhow, Carol now at her side—how could she not be happy?

And how marvellous of Chloe to remember, and send her a telegram too! But perhaps Wilson Kelly had reminded her.

'To one who has just returned from the outposts of Empire in the Far East,' said Wilson Kelly, 'it is with a real sense of home-coming—'

Young Mr Higgs listened, rapt.

# Chapter Eleven

## 1

'You'd better call her Aunt Essie straight off,' said Percy. 'It's no good waiting for her to ask you, because she won't.'

'I see,' said Maisie. 'And I suppose I'd better call him Uncle Alfred, hadn't I?'

Percy swerved suddenly as one of those damned Bolshies who infest Romford cut across him.

'Sorry, old girl, did that frighten you?'

Maisie got her heart back in the right place and stammered, 'Not with you, darling. I should have been terribly frightened with anybody else.'

'Good girl,' said Percy, and squeezed her leg lovingly.

Once again Percy Walsh was going through the traditional ceremony of presenting the little woman to his people; but this time little was something more than a term of endearment. Maisie Good was blonde and tiny, with a corkscrew-curled head, a thought too big for her body; and in that head were two large adoring eyes for Percy, and on the third finger of Miss Maisie Good's left hand was Percy's idea of an engagement-ring, a gold half-hoop of alternate pearls and diamonds which Miss Good also adored, but rather for what it represented than for what it was. For it seemed wonderful to her that her great big Percy should love such a silly little girl as she was . . . and it was wonderful to know, on the authority of her brother in the City, that this great big man was pushing over something in the neighbourhood of £4,000 a year, *every* year.

They had been fellow-guests in Wales, and had been attracted to each other at once. A wet day, the first of many, found them, and left them, in the billiard-room together. She questioned him the story of his life, and, like Othello, he ran it through even from his boyish days to the very moment that she bade him tell it. He told her, if not of anthropophagi and men whose heads do grow beneath their shoulders (for he had never come across any of these), yet of George Chater and the fella who made potato-crisps. He also spoke of most disastrous chances at Newmarket; of moving accidents by flood and field, when it was all Regent Street to a raspberry ice that his putt would have gone down if the damn fella hadn't shifted just as he was playing; of hair-breadth 'scapes in the imminent deadly breach, and of being (at last) taken by the insolent foe and fined forty shillings. She thanked him and bade him, if he had a friend that loved her, but teach him how to tell his story, and that would win her. Upon this hint (if that is not too strong a word for it) he spake. All was well. She loved him for the Six Hearts he had passed, and he loved her that she'd have doubled them.

'Well, that's how it was. They'd run it up to six hearts, and there was I sitting pretty, right on top of the hearts with the King, Knave and three tiddlers, not to mention an ace of clubs. Well, Miss Good, what would *you* have done?'

'Doubled,' said Maisie, hoping that this was the answer.

Percy beamed at her.

'Just what old George would have done. He said, "Why the devil didn't you double, old man?" So I said to Bill Endacott—there's a good story about Bill and one of those tin-openers, things you open tins with, remind me to tell you that some time—I said to Bill, "What would *you* have done, Bill, if I'd doubled?" He said, "Switched to spades"; and there you are, we'd have been absolutely spun. Game, rubber and a fiver down apiece. As it was, we ran out next hand and came out a couple of quid up. All because I passed.'

Maisie nodded.

'I always say,' said Maisie, 'that it's just that sort of thing which makes the *really* good player—you know what I mean, the *first-class* player—so different from the ordinary player like me. Wasn't George—Mr Chater—awfully pleased?'

'Well, of course, I will say this for George, he never minds owning up when he's wrong. I remember once, we were at Deauville, I think it was Deauville, may have been Le Touquet, but that isn't the point, anyway we were sitting out on the terrace having a rouser—'

This only was the witchcraft Percy used.


# 2


It was, thought Miss Walsh, a little awkward that he should have chosen the week-end of Harvest Festival for Miss Good's visit. No, perhaps it was not fair to say that he had chosen it. Percy didn't choose awkwardnesses, they had a way of choosing him. It was natural that, as soon as he was engaged to Miss Good, he should wish to bring her to Bridglands; and it was inevitable that the week-end so fixed should be the one when Chloe was coming down. But would it not be a little embarrassing?

Mr Alfred Winghampton thought not.

'One of the charms of Percy, if that is the word I mean,' said the Vicar, 'is that the major portion of any embarrassment to be discerned in his neighbourhood is exhibited by his neighbours rather than by himself. I don't think our Percy will appreciate the need for embarrassment.'

'I was not thinking of Percy,' said Miss Walsh.

'Nor can I imagine Chloe either showing or causing embarrassment. What a word! Even to say it makes me feel embarrassed, and I keep on saying it.'

'I was not thinking of Chloe.'

'You feel that Miss Good— Need she know that her lover was once so foolish as to suppose that Chloe loved him?'

'Alfred, you are very stupid.'

'I am deeply conscious of it, my dear. It has been my constant endeavour—occasionally, I trust, rewarded—to hide it from my parishioners. Fortunately I have never been so stupid as to suppose I could hide it from you.'

'Stupid, but very dear.'

'I am as impervious to flattery as to insult,' said the Vicar grandly. 'Nothing shakes me from my indomitable purpose of knowing what is in your trivial, feminine mind. Out with it, Essie.'

'I have given Miss Good the Blue Room. Naturally. It is her first visit, and she is to be Percy's wife. Chloe will understand. But—'

'I also understand. My intelligence has been underrated. Will Miss Good, metaphorically speaking, find herself in the Blue Room all the time? With Chloe here, can Miss Good maintain herself as the centre of attraction which is her rightful place on this occasion? The answer is—' He pulled at his chin, and ended rather weakly, 'Well, it depends on—on a lot of things.'

'It depends chiefly on you, young Alfred,' said Miss Walsh, sternly.

'I shall have eyes for nobody but Miss Good,' said the Vicar of Much Hadingham.

Dear Alfred, thought Miss Walsh, with a very little smile for herself. How far he was from knowing, and now would never know, that it was neither Chloe nor Maisie who was to have been the star-turn of this week-end, but Esmeralda. The Esmeralda whom he had never really seen; whom, seeing now, he still would not see. Well, it was a joke which she would have to share with Chloe; a joke against them both really. I hope, she thought, Chloe gets here before they do, and then we can talk it over. Looks to me as though Esmeralda had better go back into her boxes. And stay there.

But Chloe wouldn't hear of any such nonsense.

She was the Bolshie who had cut across Percy at Romford, giving him a derisive hoot as she went past. When the first car drove up to the Manor House, and brought Essie and Alfred to the door, it was Chloe who delighted them by slipping out of it. She put her arms round Essie, disengaged herself, and held up a cheek to Alfred, saying, 'Come on, nobody's looking.' He kissed her in what he hoped was a fatherly way.

'They'll be another half-hour,' she said. 'Just time for you to tell me all about Miss Goody-Good. Are you excited? I am.' She gave Esmeralda her intimate smile, and added: 'For lots of reasons.'

Oh, it made you young to see her again, thought Essie. She had the magic of the first spring day; an alive beauty which put no questions and gave no answers; which was nothing but what it was—beauty. I think it's her voice as much as anything, her quick, lovely voice, her quickness.

When the dressing-cases were taken in and the car put away, Chloe said, 'I'll tidy up later if I may. I want to hear all about it from both of you before they come.'

'Then Chloe shall give us her opinion of the cocktail now, Alfred.' They went into the comfortable little square hall which Miss Walsh called her morning-room. 'I thought we wouldn't light the fire until this evening. It has kept so warm.'

'What they call an Indian summer,' said Alfred, 'though why, I do not know.' He filled a glass from the tray and presented it to Chloe. 'There you are.'

'Mrs Gosling got it from a book. She says it's a Blue Car. Is there such a thing?' 'There is now,' smiled Chloe.

'I thought that Miss Good—Maisie—would perhaps prefer a cocktail to sherry. These very young girls—'

'My dear, Percy has not even mentioned her age.'

Essie's eyes met Chloe's in a smiling exchange of certainties—and of gentle pity for Alfred. Of course she was very young.

'You must both drink too,' said Chloe. 'We stand or fall together.'

'The expert first.'

Chloe gave the comprehensive toast of Mrs Gosling, the Happy Pair, Essie and Alfred, Absent Friends, and Confusion to the King's Enemies. Then she drank, and closed her eyes in ecstasy.

'Heaven. Maisie will be under the table before she's got her gloves off.'

'It isn't too strong, dear?'

'Perfect, darling. Now tell me all about Maisie.'

The way she kept saying Maisie! and yet how else could she say it? Maisie! Was she a little—not jealous exactly, but offended that Percy could have shaken himself free so easily? Miss Walsh wondered, and hoped that she was not going to be naughty.

'You saw it in *The Times*, of course?'

Chloe nodded. 'But he wrote as well.'

'Oh!'

They said it together, Essie and Alfred. You could see them both trying to put that letter into words—Percy's words to the girl he had brought down to them three months before.

Chloe laughed at their outspoken faces.

'A nice letter. He didn't know what he was trying to say, but he did try to say it.'

'Apologetic?' suggested the Vicar.

'Very.'

'What had he got to apologize for?' demanded Miss Walsh, not quite sure whether she was defending Percy or Chloe.

'Nothing,' said Chloe. 'That is what made it so difficult for him.'

'Well, we must all give Miss Good a warm welcome, and show Percy that we approve his choice.'

'I'm sure we shall. What did he tell you about her?'

Wheels on the gravel. All on their feet. Miss Walsh, the assured hostess, advancing to the door, Chloe and the Vicar a little behind, Chloe catching his eye and giving him a mock-solemn look, and the Vicar shaking his head at her and trying not to smile; Chloe one of the family, one of the hostesses.

'Hallo-ullo-ullo,' called Percy. 'Tumble out, old girl, and introduce yourself.' He forced himself out on the other side, and went round the bonnet. 'Good God!'

'Hallo, Percy,' smiled Chloe.

He stared at her.

'Well, I'm damned.'

Aunt Essie was shaking hands with Maisie, and saying, 'We are so glad to see you, dear. Did you have a nice drive? This is

Mr Winghampton, Percy's guardian when he was a small boy. And Miss Marr.'

Maisie said 'How do you do' three times; and Percy kissed his aunt, said, 'Hallo, Wing, old man' to the Vicar, 'Fancy seeing you, old girl,' to Chloe, and in a general way 'Well, what about a drink?' They went inside.

'You'll have a cocktail, dear, or would you like to go upstairs first?'

'If you're wise, you'll have it now, old girl. While it's there.'

'It's got some ridiculous name, but Miss Marr says it's as it should be. Alfred!'

'On its way, my dear. There, Miss Good.'

'Oh, thank you,' said Maisie. 'Thank you. I'm sure it's lovely. But you will call me Maisie, won't you?'

'If I may,' bowed the Vicar. 'Thank you.'

'You recommend it, old girl?' said Percy to Chloe, and Maisie, unaware that there were two old girls, sipped and said, 'Oh, *yes*! It's lovely. Do try it, darling.'

'Never known Aunt Essie to go in for rousers before,' said Percy. He swallowed and gave an approving nod to Chloe. 'Your work, old girl?'

It was now clear to Maisie that there was another old girl in the room. She looked up and down Chloe, and decided to ask Percy all about her as soon as they were alone. One of those big women. Funny how she used to envy them. An old friend of the family, no doubt. Funny that Percy hadn't mentioned her.

'Mrs Gosling found it in a book,' explained Aunt Essie, 'and Chloe was our taster'—she turned to Maisie—'because, you see, Mr Winghampton and I haven't much experience of cocktails, being rather old-fashioned people, I daresay.'

'Not you, Aunt Essie,' said Percy, putting an arm round her shoulders. 'She's the gayest of the gay, darling. You'll see.' He held out his glass. 'I'll have another of those, Wing, old man.'

When Maisie was quite, quite sure that she wouldn't, she was taken up to the Blue Room, and Percy went out to put his car away. Chloe went with him, in case her own car wanted moving.

'Congratulations, darling,' she said as soon as they were alone. 'She's perfectly sweet.'

'She's a good kid,' said Percy coldly. 'When did *you* come down?'

'Half an hour ago. I'm quite an old friend of the family now.'

'Have you been down since we—since—'

'No, but I've seen them in London once or twice.'

'Yes, but dammit, old girl—I mean ask anybody. Ask a man of the world like old George—well, I mean you needn't ask *him*—'

'I wasn't going to, darling.'

'Well, what's the idea, coming down like this?'

'Naturally I wanted to see what your future wife was like. I think she's perfectly sweet. Just how I'd imagined her.'

Percy looked suspiciously at her. He wasn't quite sure whether this was a compliment to his beloved or not. On the whole he thought not.

'I don't care a damn how you imagined her,' he said sulkily. 'You can't get away from the central fact that when a fella brings an innocent young girl down to his family, a girl, mark you, that he proposes to marry, he doesn't expect to find—well, I mean naturally he's knocked about a bit, and he doesn't expect to find—well, anyhow, I think he ought to be consulted first.'

He looked up at Chloe when he had finished mumbling this, and was surprised to find that she was two inches taller, and the day not so warm as he had supposed.

'Tell me about this innocent young girl,' said a voice which he hardly recognized. 'It's such a long time since I was one myself that I've forgotten what they know. She knows your age, I suppose; she knows that you've been knocking about, as you put it, for twenty years—does she guess that in twenty years you've come in contact with an occasional woman, and taken her out to supper, and perhaps kissed her? Or is she just not sure whether you're one of the Little Brothers of Assisi or a Double Benedictine?'

Benedictines were a weakness of Percy's. Very unfair bringing them in like that.

'Of course she knows that I've—er—knocked about a bit.'

'Meaning by that that you've been to bed with one or two women in your time?'

Percy blew his nose loudly, and said through the handkerchief, 'Well, I mean, a fella isn't—I mean dammit—'

'Have you ever been to bed with *me*?'

He had to look into her eyes, they insisted so; and, looking, he felt again that she was beyond all women desirable, and knew that for him she had always been utterly untouchable.

'Good God, of course not.'

'Did you ever ask me to marry you?'

He couldn't remember. He supposed he had; but he seemed to read the answer in her eyes, and said 'No'.

'Did you ever think for a moment that I wanted you to?'

He knew the answer to that, the only answer a fella could make. 'Of course not,' he repeated.

She gave a little shrug as if saying 'There you are'. Suddenly she seemed her natural height again. It was almost as if she had been on the tips of her toes, ready to strike him with her lightning. She said in her ordinary voice:

'To-morrow, as you probably wouldn't know, is Harvest Festival. Essie and I have been seeing each other, and writing to each other, and she asked me some time ago, before you'd even met Miss Good, to come down for Harvest Festival Sunday. So that's why I'm here.'

Percy looked sheepish, and said Sorry, old girl, he'd been a damn fool.

'You have rather,' smiled Chloe, and suddenly he felt warm again. 'Now will you and Miss Good do something very nice for me, so that we can all be friends?'

'Of course, old girl, anything.' And when Chloe had explained about Esmeralda and the Great Surprise, and had told him how important it was that she should feel confident about herself, because that was half the secret of wearing clothes, and how helpful it would be if he and Miss Good—he could only say again, 'Well, of course, old girl.'

'I know it's bad luck on both of you, and particularly Miss Good with all her pretty dresses, to have come in for all this, but in a way it helps to make her one of the family, don't you think, darling? I mean being let straight into this little family joke that Essie and I have been preparing.' 'Well, of course, Maisie will be all for it. I say, it's damn good of you, old girl, to take all this trouble for Aunt Essie.'

'I've loved it. I shall always be grateful to you, Percy, for introducing me to two such dear people.'

'Well, they seem to have cottoned on to you all right. I say, call her Maisie, won't you? An old friend of the family and all that.'

'I will,' said Chloe, a little smile at the corners of her mouth.

So, as Maisie had guessed, that was what Miss Marr was. An old friend of the family.

# 3

Percy had rather a tricky piece of work waiting for him this week, in one of the attics. The gutter outside the window had broken away, and there was a peculiar smell in the corner by the cistern. It was not the sort of smell which would normally have been kept for Percy, being (if correctly diagnosed as coming from a dead rat under the boards) one of those which the passage of Time enhances rather than heals; but Miss Walsh had only noticed it that morning when going into the attic to see if the gutter could be reached from the window. For, if not, then a ladder must be put up in front of the house, and this might damage her beloved and still blooming Mermaid.

The first cold nights of early autumn had been more temperate than usual. The roses lingered on; even the dahlias were still a flame of glowing colour; nasturtiums sprawled over the steps, and mallows and marigolds and Michaelmas daisies were massed together in a last stand against the changing season. It was, perhaps, the garden's farewell week of glory. Now for six months it would have nothing to show but promise for the future.

So when Percy said, 'That's all right, Aunt Essie,' and then to Maisie, 'We'll see to that, won't we, old girl?' it was natural for Miss Walsh to feel that the garden, while still living, had the prior claim on Maisie's attention.

'You must both do as you please, dear; but I think, Percy, that whatever you find under the boards would be better found alone. I thought perhaps Maisie would just like to walk round the garden, and then she could join you when you were dealing with the gutter.'

Maisie expressed, as well as she could, her longing to go round the lovely garden, and, at the same time, her immunity from any sort of repulsion from anything in Percy's company; which would have left the position much as it was if Percy had not seen her suddenly as the little woman who looked to him for protection from the ugly realities of life. Feeling that a long-dead rat was one of these, and that old George wouldn't have hesitated in a similar crisis, he said firmly, 'You go with Aunt Essie, old girl. I'll give you a holler when I'm ready for you.'

She was just right for Percy, Aunt Essie decided as they walked round the garden together. Silly, but with her feet firmly on the ground. Silliness was the dress she displayed to charm the protective male; it suited those big round eyes in that little body, and made its sure appeal to the strong right arm and limited intelligence of a lover. Percy would protect his Maisie from the cruel world, and Maisie would see that he came to no harm in doing it.

'One is inclined to forget,' said the Vicar to Chloe, as they made their independent way to the rose-garden, 'that Percy is not only engaged to whoever it may be, but also wedded to his art. His Attic art in this case, if one might venture the play. Five thus becomes the perfect number, being divisible, possibly for the first time, into three pairs.'

'My husband has a wife in every attic,' murmured Chloe to herself, as if to see how it sounded.

'He has even mended the organ bellows. It is a wonderful gift. I wish I had it.'

'Who looks after the Vicarage for you?'

'Do you mean the domestic arrangements?'

'Yes.'

'I have a housekeeper. Very old, like the Vicarage. It —it's—I don't use so much of it now.'

'You live alone in three rooms, and the rest of it is just used for dusting?'

'Well, I suppose—'

'Alfred, you're crazy.'

'What can I do?'

'Stop being crazy.'

'Essie told me this morning that I was very stupid.'

'Crazy is the word she meant. Crackers.'

'I accept your verdict, my dear. I may say that I am the more inclined to agree with it, because you are a very intelligent young woman, and yet I haven't the least apprehension of what you are talking about.'

'Do you want it in words of one syllable?'

'It seems that I do.'

Chloe looked at him as if considering her next speech, and then sighed and shook her head. 'There are two words of two syllables. What shall we do about it?'

'Risk it,' smiled the Vicar.

'Right. Ready?'

'Yes.'

'Why don't you ask Essie to marry you?'

An extraordinary stillness came over the Vicar, a complete immobility. It was as though he were breathless with awe, incapable of movement, at a sudden vision of the past as it might have been, of the future as it might yet be. Chloe, equally still, equally silent, waited. The whole world waited . . . He gave a little sigh, and came back to life.

'You are quite right, dear girl,' he said gently; 'dear, dear girl. I have been crazy.'

Chloe patted his hand, saying nothing.

'Crazy not to have asked her years ago to marry me, not to have begged her to marry me. But I should be equally crazy to hope that she would marry me now, to suppose that I have anything left to offer her.'

'A great many people have asked me to marry them,' said Chloe. 'They have always given me the impression that they wanted something, not that they were offering anything. It's more flattering that way, really.'

'If I were just a little better off! Essie is a very well-to-do woman—'

'And you are a very mercenary man,' mocked Chloe. 'Well, you must pretend that you aren't after her money. Give a start of surprise when you hear that she has a bank account of her own. Say that you thought Percy sent her a postal order every week. You'll manage it somehow.'

The Vicar smiled at her and said, 'You don't think money matters?'

'Only to worldlings like me. Not to saints like you and Essie.'

'Essie, yes.' He looked across the rose-garden at the lovely old rose-covered house, and said 'Is it fair to ask her to leave all this?'

'Couldn't she make the Vicarage as beautiful?'

'Well—'

'There's more fun in the making, you know. Why, a woman even takes pleasure in moving a chair from one side of her fire-place to the other, and wondering if it's an improvement. What happiness you would be giving Essie.'

'You are very persuasive, my dear.' He patted her hand, and stood up. 'I shall now go home. I have some calls to make in the village.'

Chloe stood too, nearly as tall as he.

'You are not angry with me?'

'Angry? If it were customary, I would make, as they say, a day of it, and ask you to be my daughter.'

Chloe laughed happily, and they walked to the gate together. Behind them Percy could be heard hollering for his Maisie. Love lays strange duties upon its votaries, and in a little while Maisie would be crouched on the attic floor clinging to her Percy's feet, that time the upper half of him swayed outside the attic window and dammed a broken gutter. But Señorita Esmeralda and her maid would be in conference together in Miss Walsh's bedroom.

# 4

It was a golden Sunday afternoon. The lovers (to be romantic about Percy for a moment) were taking exercise somewhere; Chloe had withdrawn to her bedroom; two elderly people sat together under the cedar.

'I am, as you know, devoted to Chloe,' said the Vicar of Much Hadingham; 'Maisie seems quite a nice girl, and Percy is—well, I am used to Percy.' He took off his hat and flicked it over the lawn. Miss Walsh waited for the body of the statement to which this seemed to be the preamble, but the Vicar had no more to say.

'Is that all?' said Essie.

The Vicar came to himself with a start.

'All what?' he asked.

'You were just telling me that you had met Percy before somewhere.'

'Oh!' He thought back a little and said, 'It was only that I feel very happy to be with you, Essie. And only with you.'

'Thank you, Alfred.'

'The others come and go. They come and go.' He sighed.

Miss Walsh looked at him suspiciously.

'You aren't making a fool of yourself, are you, young Alfred?' 'No, my dear. Emphatically not. I have been a fool in the past, but not now. That is,' he added, 'if we are referring to the same thing.'

'I am referring to Chloe.'

'Chloe?' he asked uneasily.

'You aren't falling in love with Chloe?' said Miss Walsh.

He stared at her for a moment, and then began to laugh. There was no uneasiness in his laugh. It was all enjoyment.

'There's nothing men won't do,' said Miss Walsh defensively, 'whatever their age. And nothing a woman like Chloe can't make them do.'

The Vicar nodded, and said solemnly, 'I asked her yesterday to be my daughter.'

'Well, that's one way of beginning. And I suppose she said that she could only be a sister to you?'

'Dear Essie,' he laughed again. 'I am an old man of seventy.'

'You may be seventy, but you are not an old man, Alfred.'

'Do you mean that?'

The eagerness in his voice did not escape her. She said, 'I think that if Chloe ever marries she will marry a man much older than herself.'

'Possibly, my dear. But he will not be the seventy-year-old Vicar of a little Essex village.'

'I don't suppose he will. I imagine that he will have more respect for himself than to suggest it.'

The Vicar turned to her, and waited for her eyes to meet his, and held them there.

'Is it,' he said, 'disrespectful to oneself to ask a beautiful woman to marry one?'

Colouring a little, she didn't know why, a little at a loss, she didn't know why, Essie said, 'When it is quite obvious that she will laugh at him.'

'Will she laugh at him? Will she laugh at him when he tells her that for fifteen years he has been seeking her company, only happy in her company, always happy in her company, and yet so stupid that it never occurred to him to say, "Be with me always, for I am always in need of you"? She will be too kind to laugh, Essie; but she may say, yet feeling sorry for him, "It is too late now, I have made my life without you". She may say, "It was always too late. I have never felt the need of you". But she won't laugh at him'— he took her hand between his— 'will she, Essie?'

'Alfred, are you mad?'

'Crazy, darling Essie. Crackers. That is to say, I was. I am now, at last, wholly and beautifully sane.'

'At my age! After all these years! Ridiculous!'

'Just now, dear Essie, it was Chloe's age which was so ridiculous. You are a little arbitrary about age, my child.' Essie was silent, trying, but how difficult it was, to focus suddenly on a new undreamt-of world.

'I have lived here a long time,' she said at last. 'I am an old maid, set in my ways. Do I want to move into another house, and begin life all over again?'

'Yes,' said the Vicar promptly. 'You are longing to. You want to take all the things you love most out of this house, and put them into mine, and have the glorious fun of re-furnishing the whole house, and making the garden as beautiful as your own—which it could be under your care, Essie; and then you want to be able to tell Percy and Maisie that they can make their home here as soon as they are married, and you see how delightfully it all fits in.' He took both her hands in his, and leant towards her. 'Isn't that so, dearest?'

'Well,' said Miss Walsh, with a sudden deprecating smile, 'I will say that it does give a sort of *reason* for it all.' . . .

Half an hour later, as they walked towards the house, the Vicar said:

'You're looking uncommonly pretty to-day, my Essie. Is it a new dress or something? I don't think I've seen that dress before, have I?'

So much for Miss Esmeralda Walsh, thought Essie. She did not know whether to be glad or sorry. But she was glad that Chloe was in the house. She rather wanted to cry on someone's shoulder, and even then, she wouldn't know whether she were crying for unhappiness or for happiness. Perhaps Chloe would know.

# Chapter Twelve

## 1

Barnaby, being the editor of the *Your Boy* series, the compiler of *Any More Questions*, the manager of the Self Education Department, and, in fact, Prosser's Mr Rush, had, as was natural, an office to himself. Like most of the rooms at Prosser's, it was part of what had once been a larger room; in this case the Biblical Library, as it was called in the days of the founder. Dr Prosser had never despised the involuntary assistance of workers in the same field, and he liked to have them under his eye. His instinct was sound. If you are going to interpret Genesis, you will naturally call the Old Testament author in aid; and if the Old Testament is founded on such a rock of truth that there can only be one interpretation of that truth, the true one, then it is inevitable that other interpretations will follow the lines of yours, or, if theirs happen to come first, yours will follow the lines of theirs. It is clear, then, that, in the interests of truth, any theories or discoveries made by earlier writers, but overlooked by yourself, can and should be embodied in your own work with suitable acknowledgment. It is, of course, otiose to say, 'As the Rev. J. R. Hignett-Taylor has so well observed in his classic work *Light on Genesis*'; this is giving the man too much attention. All that is necessary is to rewrite the passage in your own words, with some such preamble as 'It has been frequently pointed out', or 'It is now a commonplace of criticism', or, perhaps best of all, 'As must have occurred to most earnest students of the text'; thus avoiding the distraction of parentheses and the irrelevance of footnotes.

The Biblical Library did not quite live up to its name. It contained a few hundred religious works, which formed presumably the cream of Biblical criticism; a circulating bookcase which was devoted to, and in some way supposed to typify, the travels of St. Paul; and certain well-guarded volumes of more general interest by French writers not, at the time of writing, within the canon. But it was a long room, and it gave Dr Prosser, who worked in it, opportunity for the occasional physical movement which exercises and clarifies the mind of an author. Hands jutting out behind the tails of his frock-coat, he would pace what he called the quarter-deck of his light-ship, revolving (to pursue the incongruous metaphor) shafts of guidance which his secretary could transform later into well-ordered prose.

With the passing of Dr Prosser passed the Biblical Library. Two walls of matchboarding re-created it as three rooms, of which the outside ones were now the offices of Barnaby and Mrs Prance, and the middle one was a storeroom of the firm's publications. This room served as a sound-proof cushion between the two outside rooms, so that the racket of Barnaby's typewriter and the boisterous voice of Mrs Prance bringing good cheer to a printer or a poetess spent themselves on the no-man's-land within.

But to-day a voice from the Library was coming through the matchboarding. Somebody was talking into a telephone. Barnaby, remembering that there had been a suggestion of cataloguing the firm's books, registered with something of a shock his first realization after all these years that there was a telephone in the store-room. This, then, was one of the girl-clerks from downstairs, or possibly some more experienced outsider with a real librarian's certificate, resting for a moment from her labours and sharing her leisure with an equally leisured friend.

'Yes?' the voice was saying, oh, so sweetly. 'Oh, well! . . . You must come and see . . . Do you?' A low laugh. 'Perhaps I will . . . I say perhaps I will.' An interrogative noise with closed lips . . . a little laugh with closed lips . . . 'Do you? . . . Well, that's a good thing . . .

*Oh*, no!' Another laugh, more mocking this time . . . 'M'm? . . . Oh, well, of course, if *that's* what you meant . . . What? . . . Oh, I see, I misunderstood you.' A ripple of laughter. 'What? . . . Oh, no, you must find out . . . Yes, I thought perhaps you would . . . Well, we'll see . . . You never know, do you?' . . .

A Princess talking down her bedside telephone to her lover, a housemaid talking down her mistress' telephone to her boy-friend (thought Barnaby) have but the one technique, the one language. They laugh in the same low-pitched provocative way; they make the same encouraging, interrogative, love-stirring indications of speech; with the same artifice they excite and caress and lead on and hold back the too hesitant, too eager male. It is the voice of Everywoman. I've never noticed it before, he thought, but now I know that I've heard it, or overheard it, a hundred times.

And with this knowledge came the sudden realization that he had never heard it from Chloe.

For a moment, wondering why he had never heard that voice from her, he gave himself the lover's answer that it was because she was different from, and superior to, all other women. Then, seeing that this was no answer, he decided that it was because she was so beautiful, so desirable, that she, alone among women, had no need of these feminine enticements. But this also was no answer, since to every lover the loved one was beautiful and desirable above all other women. Then he thought that he knew the true answer. Chloe was unique in that the pleasures of the chase meant nothing to her; her momentary and only satisfaction was in the kill.

What did that mean? Was it, as he had sometimes wondered and as often denied, that she was insatiable of conquest, looking ever for scalps to hang on her belt; reluctant to waste time in the killing? No, he would never believe that.

To the ordinary woman (he thought) the preliminaries to conquest: the beckoning, the flight, the hesitation, the advance, the mock-surrender, the surrender: were her farewell to youth. It was implanted, for some reason, in her subconscious mind that, when she married, she would automatically become a faithful wife, a devoted mother. No more invitations to love, no more withdrawals, no more pretty play in the spring-time. So, since her fixed intention was to get married, perhaps to get married to this very man, his love-making must be prolonged, until every least emotion, every last contrariety of her nature, had been exercised.

But to Chloe, it seemed, marriage was no desired haven, and she would only say farewell to youth when youth and beauty had left her. What benefit to prolong one man's pursuit when there were ten others ready to pursue, and she had no need of any of them? Indeed, if, as he had sometimes felt, it was her instinct to avoid all passion and to meet every man on a footing of friendship only, then she had reason for turning her batteries on him at the first encounter, hastening a surrender which was bound to come; so that, hearing her terms, he should not bother her with love again. But this did not mean that she would have any fixed objection to the constancy of her lovers, any sincere regret that she had won them. She was a woman.

She was a woman. Had she been, ridiculous as it must seem, jealous of Silvie? Not jealous in the common use of the word, but jealous suddenly for her own position in his life. Was her summons of him to her bedside just a feminine assertion of authority; her promise to marry him just a warning that he was hers to dispose of as she wished? 'You mustn't think of other people, darling, you must only think of me; and then perhaps I'll marry you one day.' Was that what she was saying? Not consciously saying it, but with the subconscious thought in her mind: Always up to now he has given up everything for me. Now for the first time he has given up me for another woman. Silvie was unhappy, she needed comforting; yes, I know, darling, it was sweet of you. But I am unhappy, I want comforting, too. Come to *me*. Yes, I *will* marry you, darling; and now that I have said it at last, now you must come to me always whenever I want you, and let *nothing* stand in the way.

Barnaby had a natural modesty which made it difficult for him to believe that he was of high importance to anybody else. If he thought that he was of importance to Chloe, it was just because he regarded himself as so unimportant to the rest of the world: no name, no money, no external advantages or unusual attributes: only because she had a particular regard for him could she give him so much of her time.

He had lunched with her twice since that morning. On the first occasion they had met at the Embassy Bar; and, as soon as they were in a corner together, drinks ordered, she had said brightly:

'How's my Humby?'

He didn't want to talk about Humby. He wanted to say, 'Do you remember the last time we were together?'

'Grand. How are *you,* darling?' (Last time you couldn't sleep. I held you in my arms until you slept.)

'Very well, thank you, Mr Rush. How are you?'

'Very well, thank you, Miss Marr. What do you think of the weather? Or don't you?'

'Not if I can help it. How's the book?'

'Finished.'

'How exciting. Are you pleased with it?'

'Fairly.'

'I *am* glad. Why are we talking like this? Do you know at all?' There was a coolness in her voice which seemed to say 'It's your fault, not mine'.

'I've got a vague idea.' The drinks came, and as he paid for them, he said, 'I'll tell you in a moment.' The barman gone, he raised his glass and murmured, 'I drink to you with my whole heart, my lovely.'

She acknowledged this with her eyes, but said nothing. He went on:

'You know, whenever we have been very close together one day, then I expect us to be not so close the next time we meet. Because it has so often happened like that. I know it has. I think that it has been your doing sometimes; and that means that at other times I've rather expected it, and been afraid of—of getting close to you, in case I was—I was held off. So at those times I've sort of held off myself, and then of course it has been *my* fault. I think that's what it is.'

'Whose fault is it to-day?' said Chloe coldly, so coldly.

'Mine, I suppose, but I feel that whatever I had said would have been wrong.'

'Why do you feel that?'

'Oh, hell, I don't know. I get depressed about myself at times, and feel that I'm just being a nuisance to you.'

Chloe relaxed at this and said: 'I'll let you know when you're a nuisance to me, darling.'

'Promise?'

'Absolutely.'

'Just write the word on a piece of packing-paper with a burnt stick, and send it to me in an unstamped envelope. I'll know who it's from, and I'll pay the postage.'

'May I say noosance? It's easier to spell. I'm not sure about the other.'

'I was coming to that. It's n-u-i. But make it noosance if it's easier. I shall answer on another piece of packing-paper "Noosance yourself", and then we needn't bother each other again. I may use blood—more dignified.'

'Oh, darling Barnaby,' cried Chloe, melting to him. 'I love you, I could never let you go!'

'Oh, darling Chloe. I love *you?*'

And on those terms they went up to lunch. But nothing was said about marriage.

It was a fortnight before they lunched again, and this time they went to a little restaurant in Greek Street. He had brought one of Humby's puzzles with him, and rather wished he hadn't, for it occupied her attention almost exclusively. Just at the end he interrupted her to say, 'We *are* getting married one day, aren't we?' wondering how she would answer; and she said, not lifting her eyes,

'Yes, darling, when I've done this.'

Which left things much as they were.

# 2

There was a loud knock at his door and Mrs Willoughby Prance came in, cigarette-holder in mouth.

'Rush, old man,' she said, 'I didn't think anything would ever come between us, but something has.' She jerked a thumb over her shoulder at the store-room. 'In there.'

'Can you hear her too?'

'*Hear* her? She's been revealing her whole love-life for the last hour. Makes what I tell the children about cowslips seem *very* silly. Who is she?'

'One of the girls from down below?'

'That she's not. I went in to tell her that I'd only been married twice and could I have the rest in a plain wrapper, and she just motioned me outside. I was so surprised, I went. If I go in again, I shall put her over my knee and smack her bottom, in which case she'll turn out to be Lady Ermyntrude and engaged to one of the Prosser boys. Be a good fellow, and see what you can do with her. Take her out to lunch, and tell her some of the other facts of life. Work, and how an office is run, and all that. I leave it to you, Rush. Cheerio.' She went out.

There was silence from the store-room. Barnaby lit a pipe, and told himself that if the voice began again, he would go in. Not that he had any personal complaint to make: he had only become aware of it in the last few minutes. But if it had been going on all morning, disturbing Prance—

Could she really have been married twice? Extraordinary. Two men looking round the world of women, and saying, 'I'll have that one.'

The door opened suddenly, and the Voice came in.

'I just wondered,' it said; '*are* you taking me out to lunch?'

'Oh, hallo!' said Barnaby.

'Hallo.'

They looked each other over. She was young, little more than twenty, with an odd air of assured authority; as if she were still Head Prefect and Tennis Captain, and the big world were her little world, and she had taken her rightful place in it. Not pretty, thought Barnaby at first, but curiously attractive, with high cheek-bones and Chinese-looking eyes in a beautifully held head. He tried to think of a word for her figure and general bearing, and decided that 'sturdy' didn't quite do it justice.

'Come right in. What's all this about lunch? Are you the girl next door?'

'Yes. Who are *you*?'

'I'm Barnaby Rush.'

She nodded. 'I'm Little Nell.'

'Rush, woman, Rush.'

'Sorry. Didn't your Father know about Dickens?'

'Not only knew about him, but knew him. You will be surprised, but I hope interested, to hear that I was actually registered as David Copperfield Rush. At the last moment, at my mother's earnest entreaty, I was christened Barnaby, thus keeping Dickens in the family, but not too obtrusively.'

'Most interesting. I'm Jill Morfrey.' *The* Jill Morfrey, she seemed to be saying. 'Was Dickens your godfather? What did he give you besides a signed copy of *Barnaby Budge*?'

'Just the signed copy of *Barnaby Budge*. My other godfather, Chaucer, gave me the *Canterbury Tales*. How old do you think I am?'

'I have no idea. And I don't know when Dickens died.' She leant back against his desk and took out her compact. 'Who is the person who was in here just now? I saw something for a moment, but it went away again.'

'Look here, Miss Morfrey, who are *you*, if it comes to that?'

'Do you mean pedigree, or why I'm here?'

'Both. Anything. Nothing. Tell me all that at lunch.' He looked at his watch and got up. 'A very good idea of yours.'

'Not mine. Hers. What makes her think that she's been married twice?'

'I say, did you hear *all* she said?' He tried to remember what she had said; and, more importantly, what he had said.

'Well, if you both heard what *I* said, talking down the telephone in a very low voice to—to—'

'Your uncle?'

She acknowledged this with the hint of a smile at the corners of those almond eyes, and went on, 'My uncle— well, naturally, I heard your friend shouting at the top of her voice through a megaphone. How a woman like that dares to talk about—well, let's have lunch.'

'Right. Her name, by the way, in case we wish to refer to her again, but I don't see why we should, is Mrs Willoughby Prance.'

'Also a friend of Dickens?'

'She is an esteemed colleague of mine who manages the Juvenile Department of Prosser's.'

'I shall buy my Book of Bunnies elsewhere in future,' said Miss Morfrey coldly.

They lunched, it was almost unavoidable, at the Savoy. Miss Morfrey didn't drink. Miss Morfrey didn't smoke.

'You do eat?' asked Barnaby a little anxiously. 'We want this thing to be a success.'

'I can eat anything. Order for yourself, and I'll have whatever you have.'

'Oh! . . . Well, translating rapidly into English, I shall have half a dozen oysters, and fillet of beef with trimmings. All right for you?'

'Yes, thank you. When you're manager of the Savoy, I'll give you a Thought for the Day.'

'Oh, do. One never knows.'

'Have two bills of fare, one with the prices and one without, and tell your waiters to give the host the pricelist and the guests the other. It's embarrassing enough choosing between so many different dishes; but when some are 3s. 6d. and some are 15 s. 6d., and one hasn't yet discovered what one's host's income is, it becomes still more embarrassing.'

Barnaby looked surprised.

'You don't mean to tell me,' he said, 'that every now and then you wonder if the fortunate man who is enjoying the privilege of entertaining you—oh, damn this sentence, it's getting much too long—anyway, you wonder if he is leaving himself enough to live on for the rest of the month?'

'Of course.'

'Miss Morfrey, it is indeed a privilege to be your host. If nothing else made you unique among women, this would. You're sure you won't help me out with a bottle of Chablis? It isn't "drink" in the most abandoned sense of the word.'

'Oh, I drink wine, of course. Have half a bottle, and I'll have half a glass. We've got to work afterwards.'

Barnaby gave the order, cleared his throat and said: 'This is where I do my stuff. Er—when you talk of "work", are we thinking of the same thing?'

Miss Morfrey looked at him. Miss Morfrey made it quite clear who was captain of the Tennis Six and who wasn't.

'Listen, Mr Rush,' she said kindly. 'I am not back at school, and I do not have to account for every minute of my time. In any case, as I get a fixed fee for the job I'm doing, it is my own time. Of course, if I had known that Prosser's was jerry-built, I shouldn't have used the telephone, and I should probably have breathed much more carefully. I have made a note that I owe Mr Stainer tuppence for the telephone-call.'

'Crushed,' said Barnaby. 'Never to look the world in the face again.'

'Sorry, that woman annoyed me.'

'She's an annoying woman. And if you ask me, I think that we've both treated you very rudely. Forget it, forgive it, and now let's talk about ourselves. Much more interesting.'

Her father, nobody quite knew why, was a clergyman: the Rev. Quentin Morfrey. He had a parish of a thousand souls in Warwickshire, a stable of half a dozen horses, three daughters and a herd of Jersey cows. His treasure, as therefore his heart, was in the stables. Of the daughters Jill was the youngest and set apart from her sisters. They, so much older than she, lived with the horses, and if ever they came out of a loose-box to put their heads into the schoolroom, it was to ask Miss Trigg if Jill were very busy. 'We have our Algebra,' Miss Trigg would say ridiculously, as if it could hold its own against the making of a poultice or the polishing of a bit; and Algebra would bow its head, or be taken at a run. In the afternoons, Jill's time was her own. She could spend it doing a boy's work on the farm or bicycling into the village with a message for somebody.

She liked riding well enough, but the Vicar could only afford to mount two of his daughters, so she made do with the old pony who still mowed the lawn. Mr Morfrey regarded Ptolemy and Titus as investments in the marriage market; if Beryl and Hermione were to marry, their opportunities would come through the exchanges of the hunting-field rather than of the dance floor or the tennis court. From the moment when their mother died he had had to think of these things. Jill could wait. By the time she was grown up she would probably have other assets than a good seat, a long stride, and an inability to talk about anything but horses. There were moments when she almost gave the promise of beauty. The two elder girls resembled Mr Morfrey; a catastrophe for which, a little unfairly, he had always held his wife responsible.

When Jill was fifteen, Miss Morfrey (Aunt Clara) decided to exercise her privilege as godmother.

'Why isn't that girl at school, Quentin?'

'My dear Clara, I cannot possibly afford it.'

This was true. The whole of his private income was devoted to the stables.

'You could get her into a school, I don't say it would be a select school, with what you pay Miss Trigg.'

'Miss Trigg is very useful in other ways.' So, he might have added, was Jill. Between them they ran the house.

Miss Morfrey came to a great decision.

'I shall take her for half-fees,' she said, with something of a sigh for the other half. Miss Morfrey's school was, and is, famous. The parents' entrance examination is the most exacting in the country.

'Very good of you, Clara, but you would still be well beyond my means.'

'You are not fair to the girl.'

'She is very happy.'

'That is quite irrelevant. Moreover, I very much doubt if it be true.' She struggled with herself in silence. The Vicar, back to the fire, flexed his knees, and thanked God once again for his constitution. How many men of his age—

'Quentin,' said Miss Morfrey firmly, 'I shall take her for nothing.'

A hush descended upon that part of Warwickshire. In the words of a forgotten poet, the general pulse of life stood still, and Nature made a pause . . .

'That is extremely good of you, my dear,' said the Vicar at last, awed to sincerity. 'After all,' he added, with the sudden twinkle which made you forgive him so much, 'you will be hearing my sermon to-morrow for nothing.'

Jill went to school. She knew that she was being educated for nothing, she resented it, and she was determined to give what she could in exchange. She sought knowledge, received knowledge, and imparted knowledge. You couldn't say that she was a pupil-teacher, that would not be fair to Miss Morfrey, but as a Prefect, as Captain of this and that, and, ultimately, as Head of the School, she paid her way. She did not ride; riding was an extra, and there were limits to Aunt Clara's generosity; but she was allowed to teach the children to ride.

She left school. She came back to the Vicar. Ptolemy and Titus had brought in a dividend at last, and her two sisters were married. A little surprisingly the Vicar announced his own engagement. Perhaps he had been waiting to get the elder girls out of the way, they called attention to his age so clearly. With a wife whose income was in itself sufficient for the stables, with two daughters paid off ('Bride's Father to Bride: Cheque and Horse') he could afford to be generous to Jill. At last he could mount her as a Morfrey should be mounted.

'I think I'd rather earn my living,' said Jill. 'Can you give me £200 a year?'

'Is that what you call earning your living?' chuckled the Vicar. He pulled back his elbows and expanded his chest. He was feeling tremendously fit this morning.

Jill explained patiently to the Lower Fourth that she had to qualify herself first, and that this would take both time and money. 'But make it a hundred if you like. I dare say I could manage.'

The Vicar resisted the temptation to toss her double or quits, and suggested splitting the difference.

'Thank you very much, Father,' said Jill. She had decided before she came into the harness-room that £150 was what she wanted.

So she came to London. She learnt typing and shorthand; she qualified as a librarian; she spent a year with a dress-designer; and she took lessons in German and Spanish. Her French was always good; French had not been an extra. Now she was ready to earn money, and she was still only twenty-one. With all her qualifications, with £150 a year settled on her, she felt very sure of herself . . .

This was her story. She gave Barnaby an outline of it in the Grill Room of the Savoy, between the oysters and the coffee.

'Thank you very much,' he said sincerely. 'It is delightful of you to make me feel such an old friend of the family.'

'Well, you asked for it.'

'I'm very glad I did. And now—how do you like it?'

'Like what?'

'Life.'

'Very much, thank you.'

'And how much of it are you going to spend at Prosser's?'

'I ought to be finished by Wednesday at latest.'

'And then we lose you?'

'Well, you've got on without me for a long time.'

'Can't think how we did.' He looked at his watch. 'I suppose we ought to be getting back.' He flicked his fingers for the bill. 'I've enjoyed my lunch, let me tell you.'

'So have I. Do you mind if I go and powder my nose? I'll meet you outside.'

'Right. It's upstairs, if you haven't—I mean, one hates—Oh, but you probably know.'

He stood up as she went, wondering if she had a sort of independence complex. She didn't want to know what her choice was costing him, she didn't want to see him pay the bill. That Aunt, he thought, must have been a brute.

He was still thinking of that strange life when a waiter came to his table with a folded piece of paper. But it was not the bill.

'From Miss Marr, Mr Rush. She has just gone.'

He realized with sudden discomfort that he had not thought of Chloe for an hour and a half.

'*Who is she, darling?*' (wrote Chloe). '*I'm frantically jealous.*'

# Chapter Thirteen

## 1

Chloe was up early next morning. She called out from the bathroom: 'Is that the post, Ellen? Anything exciting?'

'Lot o' bills,' said Ellen gloomily.

'We shall have to do something about that one day.'

'One from Mr Rush . . . That Mr Hinge again . . . There's a new one, would that be— Oh, there's one from Mrs Clavering.'

'Basil, probably. He's a poet, did I tell you?'

'Doesn't look like it, but I suppose he'd know. That car insurance—and we had the final notice last month.'

'Damn, write a cheque, will you? And bring me Mr Rush's letter. Leave the rest.'

Ellen brought the letter into the bathroom. 'You've got the water too hot again,' she said through the steam.

'Keep my fat down,' said Chloe, holding out an arm from the bath. 'Better ring down for breakfast. I shall be out in a minute.'

Darling One (wrote Barnaby),

She is a clergyman's daughter. Her name is Norval; on the Loamshire hills her father feeds his flock with honeyed texts that teach the rustic moralist to die in sober certainty of waking bliss. (Milton, Gray and Co. *Arr.* by B. Rush.) Now tell me about yours. And don't forget, my lovely, that we lunch next Thursday.

Your

Barnaby

She read it slowly, first smiling slightly, then frowning. She dropped it on the bathmat; went on with her bath; stretched out a wet hand for it, read it again, and dropped it again. While she was drying, she amused herself by picking it up with her toes, and placing it straight-legged, on the little medicine-cupboard. She did it in reverse with the other foot, which was more difficult; called out 'Ellen!' excitedly, and then 'Oh, never mind'; and returned it to the medicine-cupboard without an audience. Back in her bedroom she tore it up into very small pieces and fluttered them into the wastepaper basket.

'Breakfast coming up. I said an egg, do you good. You've got a long time to wait for lunch,' said Ellen. 'Did you call just now?'

'Could you pick up a piece of paper with your toes and put it on the little medicine-cupboard in the bathroom without bending your knee?' She was opening and reading her other letters.

'No,' said Ellen.

'I can.'

'You're younger than me. *And* longer legs.'

'Perhaps that's it. Just see what I'm doing on Thursday. Lunch.'

Ellen looked in the book and said 'Mr Rush'. Chloe seemed surprised.

'Where's that cheque? I'd better sign it. Put down Croxton for next Saturday, that's to-morrow week.'

She laid Kitty's letter on one side, and opened Basil's; skimmed over the delicate writing, and pushed it into a drawer of the dressing-table; glanced at the beginning and ending of the Hinge ephemeral, and dropped it into the basket.

'You'd better get dressed, hadn't you?' said Ellen. She turned a page of the book, took out the pencil, said, 'Cross on Sunday,' and waited, pencil poised.

'Damn, it's always coming. I believe you put them in anywhere.'

'Don't be so silly, Miss Marr.'

'The whole thing's silly if you ask me. Well I'd sooner Croxton than anywhere else. Put it down. Got the cheque?'

She was dressed, she had breakfasted, she was packed, her car was waiting down below. With a last warning from Ellen to go carefully because she wasn't insured 'or they'd say you weren't', and an 'All right, darling. I'll be good,' she drove off.

# 2

Everard Hale was reclining on 'A' deck, well wrapped up, drinking his mid-day soup, and talking to Mrs Pont-Padwick. He didn't particularly like the soup, but he liked the background which it gave to the subsequent cigar, and he liked the idle luxury of it. He didn't particularly like Mrs Pont-Padwick, but he liked the thought of Chloe which she brought to his mind. In a week he would turn his eyes, and Chloe would be there. He was feeling happier than he had felt for many years.

Mrs Dora Pont-Padwick was the widow of Padwick's Elasto-Bend Corsets. As a girl of eighteen it had been her privilege to display the Elasto-Bend 'in its many dainty varieties' to interested gatherings of her sex; and though she was supposed to be saying 'Look what the Elasto-Bend does for the figure', most of the spectators realized that they were looking at what Dora's figure was doing for the Elasto-Bend. To make these also Padwick-conscious a plump young woman shared the stage with Dora, embodying the principle of Stoutness Confined with such a smiling emphasis that hope returned to their bosoms; and for a moment Lily and Dora symbolized for them the Before and After between which all scientific research ranges.

One day there was a gentleman there. Dora came back into the dressing-room to change from Les Sylphides to Violette, giggling 'Oo, there's a gentleman there!' She felt that she ought to have been shocked, and found that she was pleasantly excited. Lily returned in Diane a few minutes later, saying dispiritedly, 'It's only old Padwick.' Mr Padwick had grey hair, a short chin beard, and a complete devotion to his business; but he was human. Violette convinced him that he had been a widower too long.

They lived comfortably but modestly in a small house in Sutton. When her husband died, Dora was surprised to find that she had an income for life of £2,000 a year. She called herself Mrs Pont-Padwick, substituted some other mode for the Elasto-Bend, and left Sutton.

'Don't think I'm snobbish about it, Sir Everard,' she had said, 'but I just felt I'd had enough of it.'

'My dear Mrs Pont-Padwick, I understand perfectly.'

'Same with the name. Now confess, Sir Everard, when I told you that I was Mrs Pont-Padwick, you never thought of the Elasto-Bend, now did you?'

'In the circumstances you won't mind my admitting that until to-day I had never heard of, nor, as far as I know, encountered the Elasto-Bend.'

Mrs Pont-Padwick seemed disappointed, and assured him that a great many ladies in Society wore it.

'They don't always confide in me to that extent,' smiled Sir Everard.

Their chairs were side by side. On the third day out she was making further confidences.

'Funny how I used to mind about things. My father was an analytical chemist. Well, he wasn't really, he was just a chemist. But I always said he was an analytical chemist. Now I don't seem to mind somehow.'

'Quite right. You have friends in America, I suppose?'

'Well, no. Not particularly. But Dad had a sea-sick remedy, invented it himself, Pont was the name, so he called it Pontine. Whenever we went to Margate or Southend as children, we'd go by the boat, and we'd try it, for the advertisement if you see what I mean, and we'd go on pleasure trips, what they call pleasure trips, only half the people are sick, but we never were, because of Pontine, at least the others never were, but I never was, anyway, so that's how I thought I must be a good sailor. So when Samuel died I went round the world and I wasn't sick once, so then I knew, and now when I've nothing else to do I just go to New York and back, it's better food than you get on land, and healthy, and you meet nice people, so why not, I say?'

Everard came as near to liking her then as he could ever come. Indeed, for a moment he thought that he liked her a good deal.

She was still very pretty, older than Chloe by five or six years, he judged, but well cared-for; and she was original enough to engage in the most monotonous form of travel for the simple reason that she wanted to do so. Why does a chicken cross the road? To get to the other side was always assumed to be the answer. To this extent it could fairly be said that Mrs Pont-Padwick was no chicken. She went in order to come back again, and wasn't afraid of saying so.

'You are the most sensible woman I have met for a long time,' said Sir Everard. 'If it were Chloe next to me,' he thought, 'and we were going round the world together'! He looked at his neighbour and thought, 'Who cares whether she is sensible or not, who cares, anyway?'

He had cabled to Chloe to say that he was landing at Southampton on Friday, was spending the week-end at Chanters, and would like Wednesday evening if she could possibly spare it. While Mrs Pont-Padwick was still fluttering under his compliment, a reply was brought to him from the wireless room.

*'Leaving for Southampton on Friday and by a strange coincidence spending the week-end at Chanters. I could give you a lift, all my love, Chloe.'*

'I beg your pardon,' he said, trying to focus on Dora. 'You were saying—'

'Not bad news, I hope?' said Dora. He looked so strange.

'No no. By no means. I must send a cable or two, but there's no immediate hurry.'

The horizon rose to meet the rail of the deck, and dipped again, and rose and dipped. Just to lie here and watch it— up, down, up, down, lazily, lazily—lie here and think of Chloe . . . God, how he hated this woman. Why had she ever left Sutton? But she would go soon, and then he would be alone with Chloe.

He was tall, and so was she. Their eyes met over the chattering crowd, and Everard's said, 'I love you, I love you, my darling,' and Chloe's eyes said, 'How lovely to see you, darling'; so much the same words, but so different. Extravagant affections filled the space between them. Passengers with no background became family men and women again, with welcoming mothers, husbands, wives, with children to be inquired after, wide-eyed children to greet; and in contact with these strange voices the personalities which one had known became subtly different, taking on a new colour, and classifying themselves in the reflection of their company. England had come home, and was resolving into her component parts; America had landed in a foreign country, and her diverse states were federated. Only Mrs Pont-Padwick remained what she had been. She was down below, waiting for the boat to turn round.

They smiled at each other, Chloe's smile saying, 'What a crowd! I can't move! How brown you are!'—his saying, 'I could stand here for ever looking at you. I shall never be as happy as tills again.' Indeed, they were more together then than they would be for some time after their first touch of hand. Not until final good-byes had been repeated, final arrangements unnecessarily confirmed, and all the formalities of leave-taking and arriving gone wearily through, were they able to talk to each other as more than acquaintances; not until they were alone in her car, and on the road to Chanters.

'Thank you for coming to meet me, Chloe.'

'Well, darling, I was on my way to Chanters, so it seemed silly not to.'

He laughed and shook his head at her, saying, 'There's no one there, you know.'

'Mrs Lambrick.'

'I was forgetting Mrs Lambrick.'

'She won't be shocked?'

'She certainly won't look it, and she certainly won't mention it. I can't swear to more than that.'

'Anything the young master does is right, is what I say.'

'Well, more or less, I suppose.'

'Darling, you aren't putting me off? You were glad to get my cable?'

'So glad that— Oh, that reminds me. You don't happen to be wearing a Padwick Elasto-Bend Corset?'

'No, darling. I'm wearing a little belt which I bought at a little belt shop called Elise. This is a very strange conversation, and we must wait to see how it develops. Go on, sweetie.'

Everard smiled at her contentedly, saying, 'It's a great pleasure to talk to you again. There was a woman on the boat—'

'Was that what she was wearing?'

'She used to be a mannequin for them. Then she married the inventor, and when he died she left off wearing them.'

'Tragic,' said Chloe. 'Or something. What does she wear now? Was she pretty? How old was she? Oh, and what about all those Brazilians?'

'There were only seven. Don't exaggerate.'

Chloe gave him her smile and slipped her left hand into his. She drove like this in silence for a little, and then said, 'You get arrested for this, and it all comes out in the papers. Do you mind?'

'Not a bit.'

After another silence she said, 'I wish things had been different.'

'They never are.'

'No. Who manages it all?'

'God, I suppose; but I don't know who he is.'

'Neither do I. I don't know what he's doing. I don't know what he's got to be proud of.'

'We can't blame it all on to him.'

'Oh, I don't want to blame anybody. I just want to know who's playing.'

He turned to look at her, but her eyes were fixed on the road in front, and in her lovely profile he could read nothing.

'What's worrying you, my dear?'

'General discontent. Ducky, I've got to change gear, do you mind?' She took her hand away, and put it back on the wheel. 'If my health weren't so perfect, I should have committed suicide long ago. What's your feeling about suicide?'

'There's always to-morrow.'

'That's just it. There's the damned day waiting for you, and it's just like any other day.'

'You can't be sure. You might meet somebody to-morrow, and fall in love with him.'

'Darling, I'm always doing that.'

'No.'

'What do you mean, No?'

'Want to hear?'

'Yes. No. All right, darling, tell me.'

'More than anything else you want to be happily married. You want a husband of your own and babies of your own— three—two boys and a girl. You want a house of your own to look after, a garden to make beautiful, children at school to write to and plan happiness for in the holidays, a dog to beg you for a walk each morning, old women in the village to talk to, and in the evening a husband to listen to the day's adventures, as you sit down to dinner together. I don't know if you would really be happy with that, and you don't know either, but you know that you must be very sure of the man first. Each new man whom you meet may hold the key to your—castle in the air. You encourage him to make love to you, you respond eagerly, and—no fires are lit. It is not that one, it will be the next one.'

Chloe was so silent that he thought that she hadn't heard, or, hearing, had been offended. After a little while she said:

'What's wrong with me?'

'Your Barnaby. I like the sound of him. What's wrong with *him*?'

'Nothing. He's sweet.'

'But you don't love him?'

'Only when I'm with him. That isn't love, is it?'

'No.'

'What you said just now—it was lovely. I nearly cried, I wanted it so. But suppose you were Elizabeth Barrett Browning or Jane Austen or Emily Bronte. It wouldn't do all the time, would it? You'd still want to write. You wouldn't want your writing to be a hole-and-corner business, in between taking the dog for a walk and mending the children's stockings. And if— Oh, darling, say it for me, you know what I want to say.'

Everard thought a little bitterly: 'If you're very beautiful, you don't want to waste it on a husband, a dog, and the old women in the

192

village.' Aloud he said: 'I know. You have your art too. But then that should content you. What does an artist want more than to-morrow?'

'I am an artist with something left out,' said Chloe decisively.

They drove on in silence. Two lines came into Everard's head.

*With every pleasing, every prudent part,*
*Say, what does Chloe want? She wants a heart.*

But he didn't say them aloud.

# 3

It was true that, if they were yours when they were alive then when they died you kept them for ever. Somebody had written like that to him when Jonathan was killed, and he had laughed, and put a notice in *The Times* thanking the many kind friends for their expressions of sympathy, and hoping to answer their letters personally in due course. But he had not answered; there was nothing to say. Now he realized that it was true. Jonathan, if he had lived, would have been grown-up by this time; any expression of love between them would have been bad form, even if there was love left to express. They would meet rarely, write as little as possible He would dislike his daughter-in-law, or she him. Father and son would differ in politics, in tastes, in creed. Son's career would be disappointing. There were so many barriers to unity. But now Jonathan had stayed unchanged through all these years; and still sometimes in the summer, when he walked down through the rolling wooded land to the edge of the sea, Jonathan's hand would be in his, and he would remember, not sadly now, happily, that first swim together.

'It *is* easier in the sea, isn't it?'

'Much easier.'

'It's because of the salt holding you up, and the salter it is, the easier it is.' An anxious little pause, and then: 'Is the sea *very* salt just here?'

'Very. People often make remarks about it.'

'If it were *all* salt, then you'd just sit on the top, wouldn't you?' At Everard's laugh Jonathan laughed too, an irresistible laugh, an *arpeggio* of pure happiness.

'You'll be all right. Any one who can swim the Bath Club can swim the Atlantic.'

'It isn't the swimming that's fearing, it's the enormousness. But I'm not really afraid, because if you're there, then it will be quite friendly.'

Would he ever see Jonathan again? Never; save in sudden re-livings of the past such as came to him at Chanters with all the vivid reality of a dream. Only here, not in any other world, could Jonathan be alive.

On this late October morning, while waiting for Chloe to come out, Jonathan had lived again for a moment, and brought him peace. Just as Barnaby had known on that morning in her bedroom, so Everard had known yesterday, with a certainty based on no admissible evidence, that Chloe would never be his. What she had said, what she had not said, driving in the car, had told him. She was lovely to look at, lovely to talk to, but she was not for him; nor, perhaps, for any man. From now on he was her guardian, her uncle, her adopted father. Chloe and Jonathan, his two children. He must think of her like that, if he thought of her at all. Better not to think of her.

Mrs Lambrick had prepared a bedroom for her in the visitor's wing, and, at Everard's suggestion, had installed Jessie in the dressing-room as her maid. Chloe had come down to him in the little panelled room which he used as a work-room, with that mocking smile on her face which he knew so well.

'All you want?'

'Yes, thank you, darling, except the ghost of Queen Elizabeth. I suppose she slept there once?'

'Either that, or King Charles hid there. We're not quite sure. You'll find out to-night.'

'Goody, goody. I hope it's Charles.'

'This is Charles I, you know, not Charles II.'

'Oh! Still, I'll see what I can do.'

'Thank God Jessie will be chaperoning you. We can't have any scandal about our blessed saint and martyr.'

Chloe looked at him, still with that mocking smile, and said, 'You're very sweet, Everard.'

'Thank you, my dear. Have a drink. We're dining here if you don't mind. More comfortable.'

It was difficult, sitting there together in the candle-light, not to wish for impossible things. My niece, he kept reminding himself, as the dinner went on. Just engaged to a charming fellow, and is telling me all about it. And I'm telling her about South America. My niece.

'I was there about six weeks. From now on I shall speak with authority. When I get up in the House, people will say, "This man knows what he's talking about. Why, my dear fellow, he's *been* there." I've lived in England for nearly sixty years, but when I talk about England, nobody says, "This man's an authority." They just say, "This man's a Conservative. Naturally he thinks like that."'

'Nobody's an authority on anything, darling. You'd expect a man who had spent all his life in the Law to be an authority on law. But in every law-suit both sides have taken counsel's opinion, and been told entirely opposite things. Silly. So what? Can I have a piece of your toast, sweetie? I seem to have eaten my own little rack.'

He pushed it across to her, saying, 'Enjoying your dinner?'

'M'm. I'm an authority on food. It's Heaven.'

They played billiards afterwards.

'Know anything about it?' asked Everard.

'A little.'

'Well, I'll give you 40 in 100, and we'll see how we get on.'

He saw as soon as she picked up the cue.

'I used to play a lot years and years ago,' she explained apologetically.

'When you were a babe-in-arms?'

'Little more.' She said it with a contemptuous shrug which forbade further questions: a momentary flash from that past of which he knew so little.

'It's an unfriendly game,' said Everard, when she was 75 to his 40, 'and I don't say that because I'm getting beaten. If you're in play, you don't want to talk, and if you're not, you mustn't.'

'Let's stop, shall we, darling? You must be feeling all rolly, anyway. You walk round the table as if it were "A" deck. Teach me picquet.'

This was much more fun. Indeed, to be sole instructor of the girl you love in a game you love is almost the extreme of happiness. When she went to bed, he kissed her good-night as he would have kissed his niece. Did she think of it as just his old-fashioned chivalry towards a woman alone with him in his own house? Or did she know that from now on he hoped no more of her? For all her sophistication she is a child where love is concerned, he thought. She doesn't know that I am off the waiting-list.

But he lay awake through the night, trying to keep the thought of her, where she lay sleeping, out of his mind, and telling himself that perhaps, one day, and telling himself that never, for now it was all over; and all through the night the room swayed beneath him, as unsure, as unsolid as his own resolution.

He had breakfast alone with *The Times*, contented to think that there were no papers like the English papers, wondering how he had lived without them for all these months. He had gone round the stables and the garden, talked to a dozen men and horses and dogs, before Chloe joined him on the terrace.

'Good morning, darling.'

'Good morning, my dear. Slept well?'

'Wonderful.' Niece and uncle kissed. 'What about you?'

'Oh, all right. Got good strong shoes?'

'The perfect country girl.' She pulled her tweed skirt tight against her knees, and looked down at herself.

'They'll do. Everything's a bit damp, but the sun will be through by the time we get to the sea. Jane, come and say good morning.'

A cocker bitch, as shyly excited as a Victorian girl at her first dance, wriggled into view and swam round her, head to tail.

'Jane darling, you remember your Auntie Chloe?' She knelt down and Jane snuggled against her, looking at Everard as if saying 'This is what you want me to do, isn't it, this is a friend?'

'Go on, Jane. Rabbits!'

Jane fell down the steps in her excitement, zig-zagged, head to ground along the yew walk, looked back to make sure they were coming, barked happily twice, and was waiting for them impatiently at the gate. As soon as it was open she was away, to be engulfed in a moment in the mist.

'This is Jane's happy hunting-ground,' said Everard, as he closed the gate behind them.

'Has she ever caught a rabbit?'

'No. There is an awful moment waiting for her when she catches up with one, and it stops and looks at her, and says "Yes? You were saying?" and Jane will say "You —er, I—er, what—er" and the rabbit will raise its eyebrows, and Jane will slink back and never be the same dog again. I love the early days of autumn. One seems to be closer to autumn than to any other season. You can feel it, and smell it.'

'You can hear it. Listen.'

They stood there, shut in by the mist, in a little solitary world of nothingness. A wood on their right ran down the hill and vanished. Silence. Save only for the drip of the trees, which in some strange way made the universe more still.

'It's what Judgment Day will be like,' said Chloe; 'would be, if I were God. Mysterious, expectant, but not frightening.'

'Yes. Just that. Shall I tell you the two most magical lines in all poetry?'

'Tell me.'

'I'd rather you said them. The first two lines of the Ode to Autumn.'

'Season of mists?' began Chloe, a little surprised.

'No, not that one, a better one—by a worse poet. Hood.' 'Sorry, darling. Don't know it.'

'All right, here you are. But first, listen. I don't mean to me, to— everything. Everything that you can hear and see and smell. To—it.' Involuntarily he held up his hand. 'Listen!' . . . And then, slowly:

*'I saw old Autumn in the misty morn*
*Stand shadowless like Silence, listening*
*To silence.'*

Only the mist and the silence and the drip of the trees. Yet not saddening; in some strange way beautiful. Chloe let out her breath in a great sigh of regret for some unfulfilment.

'It's magic,' said Everard, as they walked on, 'the way words can mean something greater than their meaning, can give you the whole of experience in a flash. There are lines which make me happy just to think of them, however lonely I am; as if I were part of all that beauty, and that that was enough. As if I had written them—and what else mattered.'

'Tell me some more,' said Chloe, her mind, it seemed, far away.

'Have you ever been at sea in an open boat in bad weather— when "Through scudding drifts the rainy Hyades Vext the dim sea"? Can't you hear the rain hissing down, can't you feel the loneliness of it? Vext the dim sea—I say it to myself, and there I am. That's magic.'

'Whose?'

'Tennyson. Ulysses. You can have Quebec.'

'Thank you, darling, I don't think I want it.'

What *did* she want, thought Everard. Rest, content, happiness: all the things which he wanted to give her, which he knew that he could give her if she would let him, but which, he seemed to know now, she would never be able to accept from him. It's a muddle of a world, but I like living in it. I even like being unhappy, it's all part of the muddle, part of the plan, I suppose you must call it. I like being outside my unhappiness and looking at it. What a muddle I've made of my life. How interesting to look at it, and think what a muddle I've made of it.

The mist rose, stretching itself, rising and thinning out so that for a moment there was a veiled silver sun in front of them, and then it was gone; and above them suddenly was a little irregular shape of blue, and then that too was gone, and the sun, pale lemon now, showed again for an instant in the south. It was as though the day could not decide, and was saying, 'Shall I? Shan't I?—Yes, no' —and even while it was still uncertain, the business was done for it, and the whole sky was blue, and the sun shone down on them, and the morning had never been anything but fair. Below them was the sea, rustling gently to itself on a sun-lit beach.

'Oh, Everard!' She clutched at his arm. 'You've got all this. It's so lovely. You can do without me.'

'You would make it more lovely, darling.'

'I wouldn't, I wouldn't. You don't know me. I'm no good to anybody.'

'Well, *I* like you,' he said, with a smile, half rueful, half mocking.

'Keep it at that, darling. If you will, I won't let you down.'

'Very well, my dear.'

If you don't know what to say, don't say it, was one of his rules, if you don't know what to do, don't do it. Do nothing, say nothing, you would only be wrong. In a few days we shall be having supper at the Savoy, and she will be the gay, unfathomed Chloe whom I have known so long, and never known. This is for a moment perhaps, the real Chloe, the stranger. There is nothing which I can say to her.

She let go his arm, and said brightly, the old Chloe now: 'It's Wil's first night on the tenth. I told somebody I was going with you. Is that right, darling?'

'Of course. I'll get tickets.'

'You needn't. He's sure to send them to you. Or to me.'

'I'd rather buy them. What would you like, stalls or box?'

'Box, sweetie. I like looking at the critics. They're so solemn and ugly.'

'And being looked at?'

'Well, darling, if that does happen, what can we do about it?'

'Box. Would you like anybody else? Who's' the latest? I'll inspect him for you, and tell you what a mistake you're making.'

Chloe looked at him with raised eyebrows.

'I don't follow the conversation, Sir H'Everard, if you'll excuse the remark, thinking only about an invite to a lady-friend, Mrs Clavering—'

'Kitty. Of course. But you must both promise to be good. No giggles.'

'A perfect lady like me and my friend, Mrs C., never giggles,' said Chloe with dignity. 'I won't say for hiccups, if after champagne, though always with a "Pardon!" and the hand over the mouth; but giggles is contrary to our nature.'

Everard laughed and took her arm again. This was the Chloe he knew.

# Chapter Fourteen

## 1

Mr Wilson Kelly was coming to London. His new play, which had opened so auspiciously at Culverhampton, and had broken all local records at Blackpool and Sunderland, was now definitely to have its great West End première at the Belvedere Theatre on November 10th. All the fashionable world (it was hoped) would be there . . .

In the resident manager's room, lent for the occasion, at the Opera House, Kidderminster, Mr Wilson Kelly was in conference. He sat at the head of the table with an inkwell and a pink blotting-pad in front of him. His dispatch-case was on the left of the pad, and a newly-sharpened pencil on the right; there were a few sheets of fools-cap on the pink blotting-paper; and any playgoer would have known at once that George Danvers (Wilson Kelly) was the Chairman of the Bella Vista Mining Company, on its way to declaring, or regretting its inability to declare, an important dividend. There should have been a glass of water somewhere, if the stage had been set properly, but the whole thing had been a little hurried, and the idea of Mr Kelly urgently demanding a glass of water at eleven o'clock in the morning may have seemed too unrealistic to be expected to produce any material result.

On the Chairman's right sat his Managing Director, Mr Pope Ferrier. Mr Ferrier had a bottle of beer in his lap, and another on the table in front of him. The blotting-pad had been pushed on one side, Mr Ferrier rightly feeling that he could provide all the absorption which events were likely to demand. On the Chairman's left was his private secretary, Mr Carol Higgs. Young Mr Higgs, hoping to be mistaken some day for old Mr Higgs, was supporting, and in some sort of communication with, a large, highly-varnished briar pipe, but six used matches on the blotting-pad showed that control was not yet established.

What Kelly called the agenda before the meeting was the re-naming of *Fortune's Wishbone*. Few dramatists, when they first put pen to paper, realize how much depends on the title of a play; few playgoers, when they read the first announcement of it, are aware of the struggle which has been going on behind the scenes between author and manager. From the moment when Shakespeare said impatiently to Burbage, 'Oh, call it *Twelfth Night*, or *What You Will*,' and Burbage called it *Twelfth Night, or What You Will*; or, possibly, from that earlier moment when the argument between Burbage and his Assistant Manager as to the difference in cash-value between the alternative titles *Benedick and Beatrice* and *Beatrice and Benedick* was suddenly closed by Shakespeare's contemptuous aside: 'Well, *I* call it much ado about nothing' —from some such moment authors began to develop an inferiority complex about their little comedies. They realized that managers would always be too much for them. To tragedies they can still be godfather; Shakespeare's implacable resistance to such titles as *The Ghost on the Battlements*, *One Fell Swoop* and *The Ungrateful* (?) *Daughter* has ensured this much. But romantic comedies are taken to the font by the Chairman of the Board.

The essentials of a good title are few. It must stimulate your curiosity and at the same time tell you something about the play. It must admit of one standard pronunciation, so that you need not be shy of recommending it to a friend, nor he be in a position to embarrass you by saying, '*What?*' It must be original. It must be short enough to be put easily and inexpensively into gas, and to leave room for Wilson Kelly's name in large print in the daily press announcements. Kelly explained all this to young Mr Higgs, who had arrived at the moment when his pipe was equally irresponsive to inspiration and expiration, and who was not, therefore, in a mood to dispute the matter.

Young Mr Higgs had called his play *Uncle Ambrose*. Wilson Kelly had a brother of that name who had been to Oxford in a small way, and was now a vicar in Lincolnshire. A little afraid, like so many actors, of being mistaken for a gentleman on the wrong grounds, he was accustomed to refer to 'my brother in the Church', or to recall some anecdote of the days when 'my brother was at Oxford', but without prejudice to a lifelong objection to the name, face, bearing and, indeed, whole existence of Ambrose. His first contribution, therefore, as collaborator with young Mr Higgs was to rechristen himself Uncle Dudley; and his second, since the euphony of the title was now lost, to rechristen the play *Fortune's Wishbone*.

'How does that strike you, Mr Higgs?' he had asked.

'Grand,' said Mr Higgs. 'What does it mean?'

'Oh, come, Mr Higgs, you know what a wishbone is. One associates it with the granting of a wish—that is to say, with the arrival of good fortune—in this case Uncle Dudley, with his influence on the fortunes of the family. You could give us something in the Second Act about the wishbone. Wishbone, of course, is used metaphorically.'

'I do see that,' said Mr Higgs with an encouraging nod.

'Fortune's Wishbone,' said Kelly lovingly. 'Unless you have any alternative suggestion, of course.'

'How about Wishbone's Fortune?' said young Mr. Higgs. 'It seems to give the meaning better.'

After the first surprised moment Kelly gave his mind to it seriously, and then announced, with some reason, that it depended which way you looked at it. Mr Higgs agreed; and the play was called *Fortune's Wishbone* . . .

'Well, that's how it is,' said the Chairman. 'Mr Higgs agrees now that *Fortune's Wishbone* doesn't quite give us all we want. Not for London. What do *you* say, John?'

'I always told you,' said Ferrier, 'that it was a damn, bloody, awful title.'

'Yes, yes, Mr Higgs sees that now. Any ideas, Mr Higgs?'

Mr Higgs had the wild idea of asking Wilson Kelly if he happened to have such a thing as a hairpin on him, but rejected it as tactless. He had no other idea at all.

'In that case,' said Kelly, 'a little idea that occurred to me—I thought that we might call it *Baa, Baa, Black Sheep*, stressing the idea in the first act that Dudley had been the black sheep of the family. You could do that for me, Mr Higgs? It just means a line or two.'

'How do I get the baa-baa in?' said Mr Higgs, after considering the matter. He had now stopped smoking (so to put it) and looked more like an innocent child than ever.

Kelly was about to explain that the 'baa-baa' was just—well, it could be taken to be symbolic of—when Ferrier took the bottle from his mouth, and said 'Been done'.

'Ah! I'd forgotten. A pity, it seemed to me the perfect title. John? Give us something.'

Mr Ferrier suggested something with love in it—always popular. This was business, and he was taking it seriously.

'*A Man's Love*—that sort of thing? Very good, very good. I *had* made one or two other notes—' he opened his dispatch-case with the air of a man opening a dispatch-case, and produced a sheet of paper. 'Ah, yes, I just jotted them down, I see. *Silver Wings* and— er— what's this?' He heightened the suspense by polishing and putting on a pair of horn-rim spectacles with the art which conceals art, and read '*Golden Melody*'.

'Is that the Barcarolle?' said Ferrier doubtfully.

'No, no, John, nothing of that sort. The golden melody of love. Symbolical. Mr Higgs could give us something.'

Mr Higgs offered to leave it to Mr Burns, who had already given them the news that his love was like a melody that's sweetly played in tune. At this Wilson Kelly rose to his feet as if in a trance, and spoke as follows, pitching his voice to the back of the gallery: 'Love, as the poet Burns so truly said, is like a *melody*, a melody sweetly played in tune, a *golden* melody, my dear, that plucks at the heartstrings of young and old alike—ay, old, Betty my child, and travel-worn—well, if you say so, but old indeed in comparison with your blooming youth—'

'Not blooming,' said Ferrier, bringing Uncle Dudley back to the Board Room, 'you never know where you are with blooming. Same like bloody. Ambiguous.'

Wilson Kelly sat down abruptly, passed his hand over his head, and suggested that all that could safely be left to Mr Higgs, who would give them something.

'Then we all agree, do we, on *Golden Melody*? John? All right from your point of view?'

'Right enough.' He drained the second bottle and elaborated the theme. 'Bloody good, in fact. What does the author think?'

Realizing from the silence which followed that he was the author, Mr Higgs indicated complete agreement with Ferrier. Good from the box-office point of view, he told himself, and bloody from any other.

'Then we're all agreed,' said Kelly. He turned to the author and added: 'May it prove to be indeed a golden melody for both of us, Mr Higgs.'

Mr Higgs, having no other reason for hope, hoped so too.

# 2

Claude was coming to the first night—you must, you really must, darling—don't be silly, of course you must. My first play.

'Is Henry coming?'

'I haven't asked him. I shouldn't think so.'

'Oh, all right then. Get me a pretty girl, and I'll come.'

'Couldn't you bring Chloe?' asked Claudia, busying herself with her compact, so that she could see his face in the mirror without appearing to be interested.

'Chloe?' said Claude indifferently. 'Oh, she'll be going with Everard Hale, won't she? She always does.'

'Oh!' She thought for a moment, wondering how much or how little it meant, and decided to leave it. 'Oh, well, do come, darling. I shall be so proud of introducing you to everybody.'

'All right, I'm coming. If I can find somebody.'

Claudia put away her compact and said brightly, with an air of surprise at herself for thinking of it, '*That's* a good idea! I never thought of that! Why don't you go with Carol?'

'I will. Is she pretty?'

'Carol Higgs, darling. The author.'

'Oh, that man. Why should I? Or why should he, if it comes to that?'

'I just thought. It's just that he said he was going to sit by himself in the dress-circle and boo, because he says W.K. is really the author, and Carol—well, we both think it's terrible, and he doesn't want to sit in the author's box or anything like that, I mean take a call or anything, but of course he does want to see it and—and, well, me and— and all of us, and it would be rather fun if you went together, you'll think it's terrible, well, it is really, and you could laugh at it together, and then come round and see me, he'd show you the way. You'll like him, I think, he's rather nice, and he was up at Cambridge with you—oh, I told you.'

Claude looked at her with a cynical but friendly smile, and said 'Is this IT?'

She was having tea with him in the studio: 'quite like old times.' Of course it wasn't *quite* like old times, because he was now in her bedroom, and the bed behind the curtain was no longer there. She was staying in a hotel for a few nights while she looked for a little flat. To-night there was a dress-rehearsal: to get us used to the stage, she explained; and no doubt, also, to get Wilson Kelly used to what Mr Higgs had given him on the golden melody theme. It was simply thrilling to be back in the old place again, and what ages it was since they had flicked cherrystones out of the window— how young she had been then! But since this had been only a few months ago, it was not so surprising as she seemed to think it that the studio looked pretty much the same.

So Claude, contemplating her happy, eager little face, said 'Is this IT?'

Claudia's instinct was to blush and say, as she had so often said, 'Don't be silly'; but she had grown up in these last weeks, and she stopped the words as they were coming out, and said, self- consciously still, but bravely: 'I don't know, Claude. I think so. I'm so happy with him.'

'He's not fooling around?'

'No. Not in that way. I mean, he did sort of ask me to marry him before we left London. Of course that was a joke, and we both laughed, but—you know what I mean, if he doesn't really care for me, he'll just go on making jokes, that's all. I mean he won't—he's not like that horrible Ferrier.'

'Oh? Who's he?' There was a sudden awareness in his voice, as if mentally he were bracing himself on his toes.

'Press, and sort of—well, sort of business representative, in a sort of way. But he's only got one idea in his head as far as the company is concerned, I mean the girls.'

Because she had never known her mother, because Henry had never had any life outside the Civil Service, because Claude had always been so much older than his age, the relationship between brother and sister had never been an equal relationship, but rather that of elder brother to cherished baby sister; almost now, since Claudia was grown up, of middle-aged uncle to a favourite niece. Chloe must have known this by instinct, have felt it wise to give Kelly immediate warning. Claudia, seeing his face now, thought, 'I'm glad I never watched him fight. I'm glad he's on my side.' He said in that cold, passionless, detached voice more terrifying than threat or anger, even to her as onlooker: 'Has he happened to put his idea into practice when *you've* been about?'

'He hasn't come near *me*, thank goodness. I don't know why. I mean— Oh, well, perhaps I'm not his sort.'

His voice relaxed as he said, 'Oh, well, this fellow Higgs can look after you now. What does he get for this dud play? Enough to support you in the style to which Henry has been accustomed?'

'He gets 5 per cent all through. Of course it ought to be more, but W.K. calls himself part-author, and takes the rest.'

'Five per cent on what?'

'Gross, darling,' said Claudia, feeling very technical. 'What we play to. Capacity is about £2,000, and I suppose we could just stay on if we played to £800. But of course he writes other things, I mean

207

stories and things. What fun if he wrote a story and you illustrated it! I mean, you might collaborate.'

What extraordinary ideas women had! As if it mattered a damn to him who wrote the footling little stories which once—or twice—he had illustrated. As if it were going to help him if Higgs said to his next editor: 'As a matter of fact, a girl I'm keen on has a brother who draws quite well'; or help Higgs if he said, 'A friend of my sister's writes a bit, if you're looking for anybody like that.' Where's the 'fun', anyhow? And did she really think that illustrated stories in magazines were collaborations? 'Oh, well', he thought, 'I daresay I'm just as ignorant about the stage, if it comes to that.' He grunted, and said, 'Well, if the play runs for ten years and he makes a hundred a week all the time, he has my consent.'

He got up, looking for matches. She put her fingers to her lips and kissed them as acknowledgment; she said unnecessarily that of course he mustn't—of course he wouldn't—it would be too awful if Carol—and was still saying it when he came behind her, put a hand over her mouth, and kissed the back of her neck. 'I'm not quite a fool, darling. Where do I meet the man?'

'I shall see him to-night, I'll tell him to ring you up. He'll have tickets, so don't bother about that. What fun!'

'Let's hope so,' said Claude.

Anyhow, he would see Chloe again. Perhaps it would have been a mistake to be with another girl. Or perhaps not? Difficult to say. No, easy to say. It just didn't matter a damn to Chloe or to anybody but himself what he did.

# 3

Silvie was on her honeymoon.

Her Humby was a careful man. He was insured against everything, including (Barnaby gathered) marriage and appendicitis; he had put by 'something every week'; he was to get a rise at the end of the year; the Silvie Suspender was going on the market in a small way. The firm of Humberson and Humberson could thus afford the fortnight's honeymoon at Torquay which the doctor had ordered.

'I'm sorry, Mr Stainer, if it puts you out, but I couldn't let Humby go off to Torquay by himself, could I, so we'll have to get married on the Saturday and just go off together, and Humby says he doesn't want me to come back to you because we mustn't ever leave each other now.'

'You'll have to when he's at work again, won't you?'

'Yes, but I shall be in his house, Mr Stainer, and he'll sort of be there, and he'll know I'm there getting things ready for him and waiting for him. Oh, Mr Stainer, it doesn't seem as there *could* be such happiness as just being alone with Humby in our own house together.'

'Oh, Silvie, Silvie,' said Stainer, wagging a finger at her, 'you promised you would stay with me, until you had a baby. Where is the baby? Produce it.'

'Well, I will, Mr Stainer, as soon as we can, but you see, that was before, when I thought we were going to live with my uncle and auntie, but after what we went through we felt we just couldn't, oh I *am* sorry to be sort of letting you down, I've been so happy here, and you've all been so nice to me.'

When she brought Barnaby his tea that afternoon, he said, 'So you're leaving us, Silvie?'

'Yes, Mr Rush, Mr Stainer was so kind about it, I feel so ashamed after I'd said—'

'Nonsense. You're quite right, and I should have thought nothing of either of you if you'd come back.'

'Wouldn't you really, Mr Rush? Oh, well, that makes it better. There's your tea.' She put the cup down. 'Humby says husband and wife don't just come first with each other, they come first, second, third, and also ran.' She laughed happily, and then tried to look sad, as she said: 'Who'll be bringing you your tea next week, I wonder?'

The surprising answer was Miss Jill Morfrey.

It had been left to Barnaby to put it up to her. They were all a little frightened of Miss Morfrey in the office —even Stainer, who was supposed to be equally unafraid of wild bulls and a post-office girl. Her catalogue completed, she would be leaving on Wednesday. She had told Barnaby that she had nothing to do immediately, and seemed in no doubt that she could find something whenever she wanted to. He knew that she had trained as a secretary. So when on the Tuesday Stainer had said to him, 'Silvie's not coming back, I suppose you've heard, it's a damned nuisance, are you very busy just now?' and he had said, 'Fairly, why, did you want me to be your secretary?' and Stainer had said, 'My God, no, but you might ring up one of those schools, and ask them to send along half a dozen specimens, and pick one for me, temporary of course,' then Barnaby had said, 'What about Miss Morfrey?'

Stainer had stared at him.

'Yes, I don't want a librarian to index my letters and catalogue my tea, I want a—'

'She is a secretary too. Bit of everything.'

'Oh? You know her?'

'She had lunch with me the other day.'

'Trust you for taking the prettiest girl out to lunch. Would she want to do it?'

'She might.'

'I wish you'd put it up to her, and then send her along.'

'Right.'

'Do your best for me. Say that, if she wants a testimonial, Silvie will give me one. I'd get one from the Vicar, but he couldn't say more than I can say of his Church: Looks all right from the outside.' As Barnaby was at the door, he called out 'Oh, Rush! Make it clear that I want a secretary, not a governess.'

Barnaby laughed and said, 'She's not really as bad as that.'

'You'd know. I've only talked to her for five minutes, but I had an ingratiating smile all the time.'

Barnaby put his head into the store-room and said: 'I say, Miss Morfrey, come and talk to me for a moment in my room, we mustn't disturb Mrs Prance.'

She looked at him coolly.

'I'm afraid I'm busy just now. I have my work to do. Oh, by the way, I gave Mr Stainer the twopence for that telephone call, you'll be glad to hear.'

'What did he say?'

'He said, "My God."'

'Yes, well, if you *can* manage to forget all that for the moment, and come and see me when you're less busy, I shall be glad. It's work I want to talk about.'

He went back to his room, feeling annoyed with her. She was just like a child, carrying on with a silly little grievance and thinking that it gave her dignity. He wished now that he had never suggested her to Stainer.

She came to him a quarter of an hour later, shut the door behind her, and said 'Yes?' He pointed to a chair without looking up. 'Sit down, won't you,' he said, 'I shan't be a moment,' and finished typing his letter. 'Now we'll both be annoyed,' he thought.

'It's like this,' he explained in his business voice: 'Miss Silver, Mr Stainer's secretary, is leaving at the end of the week to get married. We hoped she would be coming back to us almost at once, but for various reasons she isn't. Knowing that you were fully qualified, I suggested that you might be willing to see us through for a week or so until somebody suitable could be found. Obviously if you and Mr Stainer suited each other, there would be no need to look for anybody else, but of course I don't know what your plans are about that. Stainer asked me to mention it to you, and if you were interested, he would see you and give you the details.'

'I see. Do I carry the tea round in the evenings?'

'Oh, has Silvie been bringing you tea?'

'Yes.'

'How nice of her. It isn't provided by the office, you know. We run it among ourselves.'

'Oh!' She blushed right up to the corners of her almond eyes; it was embarrassing to be in the presence of such humiliation. He kept his own eyes on his letter, saying, 'Silvie manages our little club for us.

Obviously we shall have to find somebody else. It's a shilling a week, and that gives us a comfortable margin for visitors. Like yourself.'

Still busy over his letter, he heard her say, 'I have been quicker than I expected, and I shall have finished the work I came for this afternoon. I shan't want any more tea, and I don't think I want to come back.'

'Right. I'll tell Stainer.' He looked up with the friendliest smile he could manage. 'Come and say goodbye to me before you go. I liked our lunch together.'

She almost ran out of the room. Damn the girl, he thought, why must she be so prickly, she's got the hell of a life in front of her. That blasted aunt again.

He was, as he had said, fairly busy. When Silvie brought his tea, he would ask her to ring up the secretary place, and have the candidates sent round in the morning. He dismissed all women from his mind, and went on with his work.

It was about half-past three when Miss Morfrey came in again. She had a hat on and carried her bag. He got up, smiling and saying, 'How nice of you.'

'I'm not going,' she said. 'I mean not for good. At least, not if Mr Stainer thinks I'll be all right.'

'Oh, splendid. That's grand.' He beamed at her.

'I'm afraid I was rather horrid just now,' she said bravely.

'We were neither of us very nice, considering how nice we can both be when we try. Let's go out somewhere and try again one day, shall we?'

'Yes, please. I should like it.'

'Good. Come along and see Stainer. He's a very nice fellow, terribly good at his job—which is always rather appealing, I think—and won't really know what you look like until you've been here a year or so. Not that you'll want to stay here all that time, of course.'

Prosser's went to the wedding in strength. Silvie was being married in her going-away dress; which, thought Barnaby absurdly, was just as well, because it allowed her legs to be seen, and assured Humby that he was getting the right bride. It also, he acknowledged, allowed her face to be seen, but it was legs which got Humby down. Uncle Jim led this radiant, divinely-legged creature up the aisle, and waited, breathing heavily, for the great moment when the clergyman asked (though he must have known by then) who was giving this woman away. Having discovered after a week's intensive study of the marriage-service that men in his position get nothing from the author, Uncle Jim had improvised a response which left no room for doubt: clearing his throat loudly twice, tapping himself on the chest, and then, with an inclination of the right eye to the clergyman's startled pair, blowing out his moustache in relief, and feeling (prematurely) for his pipe. A tug at the back of his coat from Auntie kept the proceedings from becoming too secular.

The wedding was in Kensington, which was where Humby lodged, and Stainer was giving a little party for the bride at the Palace Hotel. Uncle Jim, pipe in mouth, glass in hand, drew Barnaby on one side by his middle button and said in a hoarse voice, 'You a dowser by any chance?'

Not being sure at first hearing if he were one or not, Barnaby said that he wasn't.

'Believe in dowsing?' asked Uncle Jim, pointing at Barnaby with his pipe-stem.

Feeling still a little out of touch with the conversation, Barnaby thought it safest to say with a laugh, 'Well, what do you think?'

Uncle Jim put his pipe back in his mouth and gave Barnaby a friendly punch in the chest. 'Course you ain't. Stands to reason it's dead against nature. What's the relation between a sprig of wood in a man's hands and a spring o' water twenty feet under the ground? Can you answer me *that*?'

Barnaby said that he couldn't.

'If I've asked that question once, I've asked it a hundred times—a sprig o' wood and a spring o' water the way I put it—and nobody's answered it proper.'

'It does seem unanswerable,' agreed Barnaby.

'I won't say if a man walked over a gold mine with a magnet is his 'and, there might be reperflections; but wood's wood and water's water, and wood never drew water nor water wood. You seen a dowser at work?'

'Never, I'm afraid.'

'Just a trick. 'E knows where it is before'and.' He took the pipe from his mouth, stared round the room with his protruding blue eyes, and said, 'There's a lot of trickery going about.'

'There is indeed.'

'Ar. Lyn looked well.'

It took a little time for Barnaby to identify Lyn with Silvie. He agreed enthusiastically.

'Nice young chap she's marrying. 'E agrees with me about this dowsing as they call it. I put it to 'im soon as I saw 'im. And 'e's inventive, mind you. Up to all that sort of camboodlery. 'Ere's your very good 'ealth, Mr—er.'

'Thanks. Same to you. And Silvie—I mean Lyn—Lynette, and Humby—Spencer— Oh, damn—The happy pair!'

'That's right.' He drank, said 'Dowsing!' with great contempt, and took his opinion of it to the next unoccupied guest. It seemed to be on his mind.

Silvie came up to him, saying, 'You *must* meet Auntie, Mr Rush,' and Auntie, smiles and tears, a little grey wisp of a woman, said, 'Lyn will never forget what you did for her, Mr Rush, nor will I, nor will Spencer, we shall miss her terribly, but it's always the way, isn't it, when they grow up.' Barnaby agreed; wondered if anybody had ever been told that she wouldn't be losing a niece but gaining a nephew; and said, alternatively, that everybody loved—er—Lyn, and that it was lovely to see them so happy together. 'And that's the great thing, isn't it, Mrs Silver?'

Auntie nodded. 'He's a good young man,' she said. 'I shouldn't have liked it if he hadn't been.'

Bride and bridegroom were catching the 3.20, and left the party while it was still warming up; but not before Barnaby had kissed the bride good-bye.

'And remember, you've promised to let me come and see you in your new house.'

'Oh, Mr Rush, will you really?'

Latitudes of Mrs Willoughby Prance suddenly blotted out the bride. Silvie was smacked on the back, and a hearty voice said, 'Well, good luck, Humberson, old chap. All the best.' It can't be natural, thought Barnaby. She must have gone into it carefully and decided that she would say it. Humberson! It meant nothing. He wondered if it would be helpful to tell Uncle Jim that Mrs Prance was a well-known dowser.

So on Monday afternoon Jill brought him his tea. Silvie must have coached her, for she knew how he liked it.

'How's it going?' he asked.

'All right. It's quite ordinary.'

'A thought has just occurred to me. I've been given two seats for Wilson Kelly's first night. On Wednesday. What I should like is for you to come with me, if you think it would amuse you. I haven't been to a first night for months.'

'I've never been.'

'Oh, well, you must go once to see how you like it.'

'You really want to take me?'

'Undoubtedly.'

'I should love it. Thank you very much.'

'Good. It's eight o'clock, so we shan't have much time for dinner. I'd suggest a drink, only you don't. Let's have supper afterwards instead, shall we?'

'Could it be some cheap place, and we each pay our own?'

'If you like. I'll try and think of somewhere. We shall both be looking extremely lovely, so it mustn't be too cheap. Shall I call for you, or meet you there?'

'I'll be at the theatre at five minutes to eight.'

'Right. The Belvedere. Stalls, fifth row. I'll give you your ticket to-morrow, in case we lose each other.'

The tickets were from Chloe. She had rung up on Thursday, can-celling their lunch; giving the sort of reason which seems, on these occasions, wholly reasonable to a woman but inadequate to the man, leaving him with the conviction, undoubtedly well-founded, that she has preferred to lunch with somebody else. On the Saturday he had had a loving, apologetic letter from her, enclosing the tickets as a consolation prize, and saying, 'Do come, darling, and then I shall be sure of seeing you.' He knew —who didn't?—that she had been a friend of Kelly's, guessed that he had given her the tickets, guessed that she was going with Everard. So, being still ruffled over his cancelled lunch, he decided to take Jill with him. If it made her jealous, all the better.

# 4

'All right, old girl, then I'll call for you on Wednesday. You wouldn't care to go to a first-night, I suppose?'

'Whose is it, darling?'

'Wilson Kelly. Fella with a long nose. I met him once. Crashing bore, I thought him, but that's not to say he can't act.'

'Oh, I *adore* Wilson Kelly! Oh, *do* let's!'

'Right. I'll be along at 7.30. We'll have a couple of rousers, and then push on to supper somewhere afterwards.'

'Lovely, darling. And you *will* introduce me to him, won't you? Because I simply *adore* him.'

'He's about ninety, you know. Fella with a long nose. Still, I suppose he can act. Right, old girl. I'll fix it.'

# Chapter Fifteen

## 1

The Belvedere had given up making history, and was now condemned to live on it. In the days when theatres were few, and mostly in control each of its own actor-manager-proprietor, the Belvedere was famous. Old actors in clubs still talked of its first nights, which had deepened the tragedy of Spion Kop or heightened the glory of Mafeking, to young actors who had heard of neither of these places, nor of the plays by which (apparently) they should be remembered. Vaguely they had supposed that all old plays were called Sweet Lavender or Colleen Bawn, and all actor-managers Sir Henry. They cared, as the old actors often pointed out to them, nothing for the traditions of the stage. They played golf, a game inimical to the art of acting. Probably they had never even heard of The Notorious Mrs Ebbsmith. They hadn't. Who was Mrs Ebbsmith?

Since those great days (and how easily old days become great days) the glory of the Belvedere had departed. It was now one of six theatres in the hands of a syndicate. When approached humbly for the loan of one of its five theatres, the managing director would end his depressing narrative of their commitments with the words: 'Of course you *could* have the Belvedere, old man'; and in reply to the unspoken comment would remind his hearer reproachfully of the famous 400-night run of *Hearts Are Trumps* in '98. 'Besides,' he would add, 'if you've got the play, old man, you know as well as I do, you can put it on in a mission-hall at Wapping Old Stairs, and people will come.' Convinced, as always, that he had got the play, the suppliant then made terms for a lease of the Belvedere, terms higher than he would expect to pay for a mission-hall in Wapping, certainly, but not unreasonable in view of the number of bank-accounts the rent would pull up at before reaching the actual owner of the theatre. And since, as consideration from the front row of any dress circle makes clear, most of the heads at a first night are of Boer War vintage, one could hope at least that the Belvedere would give its latest victim the fashionable opening for which it had always been famous. And that was something.

'In fact, Mr Higgs,' said Wilson Kelly, 'since we can't at the moment have possession of the Haymarket, I would as lief be at the Belvedere as anywhere. Curiously enough, it is the theatre at which I made my first appearance on the London stage.'

Remembering the seven provincial towns at which Kelly had first met his beloved wife, Mr Higgs did not think it was as curious as all that, but he admitted that it was interesting.

'You might mention it in your speech,' he suggested solemnly, 'as a rather romantic coincidence.'

'Well, that will be as it comes, and of course there may be no occasion for it. I find, Mr Higgs, that it is always better to leave these things to the inspiration of the moment; one generally thinks of something. You are quite decided not to take a call yourself?'

'Quite. You'll do it so much better, both as author and manager.'

'Very well, I shall tell them that you are not in the house; but I hope none the less that you will arrange to be there.'

'Oh, I shall be there all right, tucked away at the back.'

'Then I shall be very much obliged, Mr Higgs, if you will be so kind as to keep a stern eye on me, and tell me afterwards if I stray in this or that scene from your conception of the character. It is difficult to get a candid opinion from those whom one employs in the theatre, and the critics, of course, with no previous knowledge of the play or of what was in the author's mind, are of little assistance, kind though they are to those of us who have established our credentials.

For myself, if I can satisfy my author, that is all that I ask. Then I know that I am right.'

Young Mr Higgs assured him earnestly that he could not imagine *Uncle Dudley* played anyhow else or by anybody else, that for him *Uncle Dudley* was Wilson Kelly and Wilson Kelly *Uncle Dudley*, and it was impossible to distinguish between them. Having said this, he took a taxi to Berkeley Square, and ordered flowers for all the women in the cast as a tribute from a part-author, and an extra basket of exotic growth as a love-offering from Bunny. To which, later, he added a large box of chocolates.

As he dressed, he was wishing that he were to be alone at the theatre. Funny how women never liked a man to be alone. His aunts had always been like that. And Gwynneth up at Cambridge. And that ghastly Lorimer girl he'd been such a fool about. All of them just the same: a sort of jealousy, a hatred of uncertainty: 'I don't care who you're with as long as I know *who* you're with'— and of course in his aunts' case and Claudia's a real anxiety lest he should be lonely. Good lord, it was much more lonely with anybody but the right person than it was alone. What was there lonely about being alone, when you had the whole world to think about, or the one person to think about? That would make rather a good line in a play: I don't care who you're with as long as I know *who* you're with. Ought I to keep a note-book? Samuel Butler did. Well, if it's worth remembering, I shall remember it. He felt rather proud of noticing this about women, and told himself that he must always notice things. Well, I do, he thought, I know all about that crowd at the theatre. Damn this Claude, he'll spoil our little supper together, I suppose we're bound to have him. What about Ruby? Better be four than three, only I suppose she'll be booked. Sure to. Oh, well, I suppose I've got to meet the brother some time, and we can have supper just as easily to-morrow. If this blasted play runs as long as that.

His tie in his hands, his chin held up in front of the glass as he began to make the knot, he stopped suddenly, stared at himself in amazement at himself, and dashed downstairs to the telephone. For a moment he hesitated between two numbers; then dialled . . .

'Belvedere stage door,' said a voice.

'Hallo, Rogers, this is Carol Higgs speaking.'

'Good evening, sir. And I'll take the opportunity of wishing you once more the best of luck.'

'Thanks very much. I say, has Miss Lancing come in yet?'

'Yes, sir. The newer they are to it, the earlier they come.'

Carol laughed and said, 'Ask her if she could speak to me for a moment.'

'Right, sir. Hold on.'

He waited. It was a long way up to Claudia's dressing-room. I mustn't forget to tip Rogers, he thought. My God, I'm going to spend a lot to-night.

'Hallo, darling,' said Claudia. 'Oh, darling, I've just got your lovely flowers, and— Oh, you really *are*—'

'Yes, aren't I? Never mind that for a moment. Are you alone, or is Rogers there? Just say yes or no—are you alone?'

'No.'

'Well now, listen, and don't say anything until I have finished. This is absolutely urgent and deadly serious, really a matter of life and death . . . Are you there?'

'Yes, but you told me not to say anything.'

'Oh, well, I don't mind your breathing. Now listen. Here it is. I love you like nobody's business. You are the sun and the moon and the stars and the Milky Way and the sea and the sky and the hills and an anti-cyclone off Iceland, and everything that's lovely in the world. Will you marry me? Just say yes or no, and we'll have the apologies afterward. After all, why should you? Still, you've got to. Will you marry me? Yes or no?'

He could hear her breathing now . . . then a small voice said, 'Just say it again, darling, in case I didn't get it right.'

'Will Claudia Lancing marry Mr Higgs?'

'Yes.'

'Darling, darling, darling, darling, darling! Listen, sweetheart, don't think I was afraid to propose to you *vis à vis*, it was just that I was wondering what to talk to your brother about, and I suddenly thought that it would be nice if I could tell him that he was my brother too. Darling, I love you. Love, as Mr Kelly has observed, is like a melody, a melody sweetly played in tune, a golden melody, my dear, that plucks at the heartstrings of young and old alike. Wait till you see my heartstrings, they'd surprise you, not a feather left. Good-bye, angel! I shan't come round till the end in case we get too excited, and I know you're going to be the success of the evening. If you love me very, *very* much, say "Good-bye and good luck, Mr Higgs", and then I'll go back and finish tying my tie.'

'Good-bye and good luck, Mr Higgs.'

'Thank you and bless you. Angel!'

As he brushed his hair, he thought: 'If only it had been my own play, what a night this would have been.'

Claude, also tying his tie, wished that he were not going to the play with Higgs. To see a play with your sister in it, probably forgetting the words and making a damned fool of herself, was bad enough, but to see it so in company of the author was hell. All this about Higgs thinking his own play bloody wasn't good enough; just self-defence when he found that other people thought so. What did he want to write a bloody play for, anyway? He won't like it if I agree with him, and if I try to buck him up, he'll be condescending about it, and say that it's very nice of me, and he knows quite well it's tripe. So what do I say? And instead of being in the stalls, close to Chloe, perhaps even next to her, I shall be stuck up in the dress circle, and see no more than the top of her head. Damn Claudia. Why couldn't she let us make our own arrangements?

Carol, waiting for him at the Berkeley, jumped up eagerly as soon as he came in.

'Hallo, I knew it was you, do you like champagne cocktails as much as I do, otherwise I shall have to drink two? Well, I'm going to anyway, of course.'

'So am I, if I may,' said Claude. Life seemed a little brighter suddenly. This man had the right ideas.

'Good. We haven't much time, and I didn't want to spend any of it snapping my fingers at the backs of waiters, and then trying to pretend I hadn't. Here we are.'

They sat down. Claude picked up his glass and said, 'May we drink to the play?'

'Well, don't let's commit ourselves just yet. Let's drink to Claudia for a first one.'

They both said 'Claudia!' and drank.

'This is the best drink there is,' said Claude.

'Easily,' said Carol.

'Is she all right?' asked Claude. 'I mean at her job?'

'She's heavenly. You'll see. It's a tiny part, of course, but it gives you the one moment of fresh air in the whole evening. Everybody else is dead. They all died about thirty-five years ago. It's that sort of play. I've ordered two more of those, I hope they're coming. Perhaps I'd better begin snapping my fingers now, and then by Christmas—'

Claude caught a waiter's eye, and the waiter was there.

'I ordered two more champagne cocktails,' said Carol, and then to Claude: 'How well you do it. It's really the whole art of life, calling a waiter without calling attention to yourself. You must give me lessons.'

Claude began to like Mr Higgs.

'Just let's get it clear,' he said. 'Are you the author, or aren't you?'

'Part author. You'll see it on the programme. I have a collaborator with whom I do not see eye to eye. Shall we discuss it in terms of your own art? If you had painted your masterpiece—let's say "Hannibal crossing the Alps" —and I got my little paintbox out and turned Hannibal into John Stuart Mill on Monday, and made three of the elephants balance on cannon-balls on Tuesday, you'd realize on Wednesday that, if you couldn't stop me, the only way to prevent yourself going mad was to paint Ella Wheeler Wilcox and some swans into the foreground and have a really good laugh.'

Claude allowed himself a smile.

'Yes, I see. Of course one might disown the picture altogether. I don't mean in a highbrow sort of way, but as bad for one's Alpine reputation.'

'There was a reason why I didn't.' He picked up his second glass and said, 'Shall we drink to Claudia again?'

'Claudia!' they said together.

'You're quite right,' said Carol. 'This is the best drink there is.'

'Easily,' said Claude.

'You see,' said Carol, putting down his empty glass, 'I gave myself the privilege of falling in love with your sister the first time I saw her at rehearsal. So obviously I couldn't wash my hands of the play, and walk into the night. On the contrary, by staying on I've had the happiest two months of my life. I mean up-to-date. For at 7.15 p.m. this evening— Oh, good, here come the second ones I ordered before, no, quite all right, we want them badly, that makes six—' He gave the waiter a £5note, and went on: 'At 7.15 p.m. I became your brother-in-law. A new glass for this. This is historic. Claudia!'

'Claudia!' said her brother and drank. 'Somehow,' he added, 'this one seems even better than the last.'

'Infinitely. I'm so glad that you agree. Of course when I say that I became your brother-in-law at 7.15 p.m., I meant *in posse*. You can't do it *in esse* after 3 p.m., I believe.'

'It's a damned shame,' said Claude, 'not being able to do it *in esse* after 3 p.m.' He emptied his glass, and went back to the second one.

'Four p.m. summer-time,' said Carol. 'We must be fair. Did the waiter give me my change?'

'You put it in your pocket. I saw you.'

'Did I remunerate him?'

'You gave him ten shillings. Why,' said Claude, speaking slowly so as not to lose any of the letters, 'why did you give him what practically amounts to a prince's ransom?'

'Because, Claude, old man—may I call you Claude, old man?'

'Certainly, Higgs, certainly.'

'My other name, in case you care to avail yourself of it, is Carol.'

'I know what you mean, I used to sing you.'

'That was me. Little did you think, when sniffling in the snow, that one day Good King Wenceslas would practically be your uncle.'

'I admit that I little did think, but I deny *in toto* that I sniffled.'

'For the sake of your sister, I withdraw sniffling.'

'*In toto?*'

'In absolute *toto*. Shall we now drop in at the Belvedere, Claude-old-man, and see what is going on there?'

'We will, Carol-old-man.'

They arrived safely and cheerfully, and dropped in.

# 2

The circles were full, the stalls were filling. There was a cheerful bustle of conversation, against whose surge the 'Specially Augmented Orchestra', or, as it was more generally called, the Bellamy Quartette, opposed 'The Merry Peasant' with its heads only occasionally above water. Programme waved to programme, and the wavers turned to their neighbours to explain who they were waving to. Suddenly there was a stir at the back of the Royal Box; all eyes in the circles were fixed on it, as Chloe and Kitty manifested themselves to the expectant audience, leaving Everard at the door to gather in chocolates. Each moved to her chair as if it had been planned and rehearsed in detail, each took her seat, as it were in slow time, giving, with that gentle sweep of the arm which makes the dress one with the body, a lesson to the young in the gracious art of sitting down. They turned and smiled and spoke to each other; one might indeed have been watching royalty. Then they looked down on the stalls, divinely aware that the stalls were looking up at them.

She saw Barnaby, and gave him her loving smile which he knew so well. She saw Miss Norval next to him, the clergyman's daughter, and flashed another smile back at him, the mocking smile which was as much part of her as the other. She saw Percy and Maisie, and her smile was (was it not?) a little absentminded this time, as if the rest of her were still with Barnaby and that girl. She acknowledged other friends in the stalls, received their acknowledgments, murmured to Everard who was now between her and Kitty. Her eyes came up to the dress circle; indifferently; none of her friends would be there . . .

*Claude!* And Claude, seeing her face light up, thanked Heaven comprehensively for Claudia and Carol and the three cocktails, and the fact that he was sitting here, level with her, almost within reach of her, instead of right down there in the suburbs. She made a little movement with her hand which seemed to say come in and talk to me at the interval, and the three cocktails told him that he would do exactly that, whether she had invited him or not.

'Chloe Marr,' he said self-consciously to Carol. Even though the augmented orchestra was now playing Three Dances from Henry VIII, he felt completely master of the world.

'Which?' said Carol.

'The one at this end.'

Carol turned to the end of the row, and saw a stout mottled woman forcing her way out of a green satin dress loaded to the plimsoll line.

'Are we looking at the same end?' he asked, surprised.

'The box, idiot.'

'Ah!' He studied Chloe with interest. 'So that's Chloe. Introduce me afterwards, and I'll tell you what's wrong with her.'

'What do you mean, what's wrong with her?'

'There must be something, or she'd have got married long ago.'

'Why? She just happens never to have fallen in love.'

'That,' said Carol, 'may be what's wrong with her. Mr Higgs, the great authority on love, will tell you.'

Barnaby was thinking, 'She's more beautiful than ever, but I mustn't be a fool about it, she's just something beautiful like blue-bells in a wood, or *Primavera*, or the Ode to a Nightingale, they are yours but you don't own them, and they don't break your heart.' He looked at Jill and thought, 'It will be fun having supper with her, but I'm not going to have any nonsense about champagne. I could drink a whole bottle now. I'd no idea she was so pretty.' He said in a low voice, 'Have I told you how terribly pretty you look to-night?'

'No,' said Jill. 'Nor has anybody else.'

'Never?'

'Never.'

'Then you either go out with the blind or the dumb. Which?'

'I generally go by myself. My uncle—you know the one I mean—pretends he's in love with me, but he always leaves out that part.'

'That's no way to go on. Cut him out of your life at once.'

She smiled to herself, picked up her programme from her lap, and read it through for the third time.

Percy nudged Maisie, shaking her programme out of her hand, and said, 'Look, old girl, there's Chloe.' They both waved.

'Who's that with her?'

'A bloke called Hale. And that's Kitty Kelso, married a fella called Clavering who has something to do with something or other, she was Kitty Kelso, before your time a bit, she was in *Silk Stockings*.'

'I expect she is now,' said Maisie archly.

'What? Oh, no, that was ages ago, she's chucked the stage now, got two kids.' Maisie looked a little disappointed, and Percy, sensing that something was wrong, gave his mind to it. A sudden loud laugh announced that it had not been in vain. 'Oh, I see what you mean. Damn good, old girl. Damn funny. I must tell old George that. Yes, I expect you're about right.' He put a large hand on her leg. 'And I know somebody else in silk stockings, what?' He pulled up the knob of her suspender in a fold of her dress and let it snap back. Maisie gave a little yelp and said, 'Darling, you *mustn't*, not here,' and smiled at him with admiring, adoring eyes. Percy laughed and winked at her. To get back to respectability she said firmly, 'Now which are the critics, you promised to tell me.' There was always the taxi to look forward to.

Percy stretched up his head and switched it round the stalls.

'Roughly speaking and without notes,' he said, 'any ugly little god-help-us in a black tie, who looks as if he'd dropped in at a funeral between drinks. They generally park 'em on the gangways, so's they can get back to the bar quickly. Between you and I, old girl, there've been times when I've wished *I* was a critic.'

'Oh, darling, why aren't you? You would have been terribly good.'

'Well, you have to mix with such damn strange people. Look, there's one over there—scratching himself against the pillar.'

'Oh, *darling*, he's quite nice-looking.'

'Ah, then perhaps he isn't one.'

Percy attributed his dislike of dramatic critics to the fact that the bloody fellas couldn't dress properly in the evening; but, as he was to explain later to Claude when he got him up against the wall of Claudia's dressing-room, it went deeper than that. He had once put up the money for a damn fine show called *Bedroom Bertie*—well, when he said he put it up, it was really old George, George Chater, who found most of the doubloons, but Percy had put a monkey into the pot because he didn't want to be out of it when old George was in, and naturally when you have a sweet little girl like Babs on your knee, calling you her great big man and saying why couldn't you get her a teeny-weeny part in one of the new autumn shows—well, anyhow, he had gone out of his way to give a hand to one or two of these bloody fellas, taken 'em into the Ritz Bar and soused 'em well, and told 'em all about Babs, so's they'd know what they had to look out for, and mentioned what a damn fine fella old George was, and how the fella who'd knocked together the music came down to Woking and played it to them, had a haircut and all, you'd never have guessed he wasn't a gentleman—well, it wasn't losing the monkey or what a sensitive little girl like Babs naturally felt at being referred to as a pier-less beauty, p-i-e-r and intentional, mark you, not a misprint, it was the damn cold-blooded ingratitude of it which struck him so forcibly.

Maisie had picked up her programme, and was trying to commit it to memory before the lights went out. 'Zella, a gypsy girl,' she read aloud; 'Miss Claudia Lancing. Who's she?'

'What's that?' said Percy, coming back to the present. 'Here, let me look.' He took the programme from her. 'Well, I'm damned. That's the pretty little girl I told you about when I met this long-nosed fella in Chloe's flat. Claudia Lancing, that's right, and she's got a brother, Claude. Damn silly, I call it.'

'Oh, darling, you know *everybody*!' said proud Maisie. 'You will introduce me, won't you? You promised.'

The augmented orchestra came to the bottom of a page of *Merrie England,* turned over three pages by mistake and found to its surprise (or so it seemed) that it was playing the *Barcarolle.* The lights slowly dimmed; reluctantly the stalls hushed themselves at the request of the pit; and the curtain went up.

# 3

The curtain went down, and one could talk to one's neighbour in comfort, without being scowled at by the rude man in front; or one could go outside and line the stairs, hoping to be noticed by the noticeable on their slow progression to the bar. With the advantage of the dress circle Claude was the first into the Royal Box. Carol's refusal to come with him was accepted gratefully, for it gave him Chloe to himself, and spared her the embarrassing company of an author beyond congratulation. 'You must tell her my unhappy story,' said Carol, 'and then, when I see her behind— old, but unintentional joke, sorry—when I see her in Claudia's dressing-room, we can talk lightly and easily about the Barcarolle.' Claude grunted, and pushed his way out. Old though he was in many ways, his love was so young and innocent that the altogether physical Chloe never disclosed herself to his mind, and he felt Carol's 'joke' to be a desecration.

'Darling,' said the loved one, 'how nice to see you, and how nice you look. Everard, this is Claude Lancing, who you know by name, anyway.'

'Every way,' smiled Everard. 'Boxer, artist and friend of Chloe's.' He held out his hand, smiling again a little ruefully at the 'Sir' with which Claude greeted him. 'We both want to marry her,' he thought, 'and one of us calls the other "Sir". One of us must be wrong.'

'And Mrs Clavering. Kitty, come and be introduced— Claude Lancing. Ducky, wouldn't it be a nice idea if Claude and Claudia had supper with us?' And then to Claude, 'You could, couldn't you, darling?'

'You can no more resist that than I can,' said Everard. 'Do come.'

'Of course we'd love it, sir, thank you very much. At least, I should, but—' he hesitated.

'Miss Lancing is already committed? Couldn't he come along too, or would they prefer to be alone?'

'Oh, Claude, we *must* see him. Who is he?'

'Well, I'm sitting with him, I don't know if you noticed.'

'Oh, I thought that was your son,' said Kitty.

Claude allowed himself a smile, and said, 'My brother-in-law. They've just got engaged.'

'Darling, how exciting! Who is he?'

'Carol Higgs.'

Chloe said, 'Oh!' Everard said, 'Now where have I seen that name somewhere?' Kitty said, 'In the programme, silly,' and held it up to him. There was a moment's silence.

'Yes, I know what you're all thinking, but it isn't like that.' He explained the translation of Uncle Ambrose into Golden Melody. Chloe and Kitty looked at each other, and laughed. 'Dear Wil,' said Kitty. 'Isn't he Heaven?'

'That settles it,' said Chloe. 'I can't wait to meet him. And it will make us six, which is just right.'

'And I shall be sitting next to you', thought Claude. 'Don't have any more, don't spoil it.'

Barnaby had been wondering what to do, and had decided anyhow to leave it until the second interval. Since Chloe was in a sense his hostess, he ought to pay her his compliments. Having no reason for going behind, he would have to call upon her in her box. Should he take Jill with him or shouldn't he? Would she like to come? Would Chloe think he was ashamed of her, or self-conscious about her, if he didn't bring her? How silly to be bothered by this sort of thing. And how strange to realize suddenly that he had never been with Chloe in company since that first week-end.

'Enjoying it?' he said to Jill.

'Very much, thank you.'

She spoke so earnestly that he said, 'I didn't write it, you know, and I didn't even buy the tickets, so you can say anything you like about it.'

'I expect you think I'm a very critical sort of person, but I'm not really, I mean I don't want to be. And I've seen so little of the theatre that any play would seem exciting and rather wonderful. I really am enjoying it tremendously, so don't tell me it's very, very bad. Is it very, very bad?'

'You know, I'm rather like you. I can enjoy any play just because it's the theatre, and I don't think about whether it's good or bad until afterwards. I expect we shall both come to the conclusion at supper that it's not a very distinguished piece of work, but who cares? I'm hungry, and we're going to have supper together.'

'I'm getting hungry too.'

'Good. Now do say Yes or No, just as you feel. If you look up at the box on your left—'

'The one you waved to?'

'Oh, did you notice? Well, that's a very old friend of mine—'

'The lovely one?'

'Yes. Miss Marr. She's also an old friend of Wilson Kelly's and that's how I got the tickets from her. So I ought just to say thank you for them in the next interval. Would you like to come and meet her?'

'Are they all your friends in the box?'

'Oh, no. I think I know who they are, though. That's Everard Hale, the oldish one, he's an M.P. among other things, and that's Kitty Kelso, I used to see her on the stage, and I rather think the other must be a man called Lancing, Claude Lancing, I've heard Chloe talk about him, but I wouldn't really know. Well?'

'You go,' said Jill. 'I'll stay here. I shall be quite all right.'


As the first notes of Santa Lucia came through the matchboard and canvas of Mrs Langton's country house, and over the heads of the matchboard and canvas people who lived there, Chloe put her hand on Everard's arm and whispered, 'That's Claudia'; and when the singer revealed herself, and her very inmost self, to the audience, giving to each man and woman there all her youth and gay prettiness and joy of life, as a thank-offering for the happiness which had come to her, Everard put his hand for a moment on Chloe's and whispered, 'That's love.'

There was a reception going on outside the Royal Box when Barnaby got there. The guests had overflowed from the box into the passage and from the passage into the little withdrawing room. 'Good evening, Mr Rush,' said Chloe with what he thought of as her 'wicked' smile, 'I am so glad you could get here.' As they shook hands, she whispered 'Darling Barnaby', and gave him an unfathomable look. Love, reproach, apology, bitterness, pleading— any or all of these, it was gone in a moment; leaving him with the feeling that if he could have translated it, he would have understood her at last. She introduced him to Everard, and added, 'I was hoping you would bring your Miss Norval up to see us. She's looking very pretty to-night. What is her name, ducky? You can't go on hiding it.'

'Morfrey,' said Barnaby. 'No secret.'

Chloe frowned and shook her head.

'What's it short for?'

'Short for Jill Morfrey, or possibly Gillian Morfrey.'

'Oh, I see.'

'Any relation to Quentin Morfrey?' asked Everard.

They both looked at him in surprise.

'Daughter.'

'Darling, who's Quentin Morfrey?'

'Quite a well-known character in the Midlands. Sporting parson. I've hunted from his house once or twice. This would be the youngest daughter, I suppose.'

'Yes.'

'Do you mean you know her, Everard?'

'Well, we met once. I don't suppose she would remember it. She was in her bath. Splashing.'

'Oh, Barnaby, what a pity you didn't bring her, so that Everard could see what she's like when she's not splashing. Let's go into the box and look.'

As they glanced down at Jill, she pressed Everard's arm; and, interpreting this correctly, he said, 'It would be very delightful if you could both have supper with us. We have two or three other people coming. Do suggest it to Miss Morfrey, will you?'

'This is damned awkward,' thought Barnaby. 'In fact, it's impossible. You can't take a person out, and then hand her over to strangers to entertain. Damnit, I got the tickets free from Chloe, and now I'm to get the supper free from Hale, and I didn't even pay for her taxi to the theatre. And what are we doing while they go behind and talk to Kelly?'

'It's very kind of you, but I think, perhaps, as we've booked a table—'

It sounded silly. Chloe said at once, 'You can always cancel a table, darling.'

He looked at her, and held her eyes.

'I know,' he said, 'I've often had to do it. Often.' All the unhappiness of meetings stillborn, all the happiness of meetings consummated, swept through his mind. She seemed to know what he was thinking. She gave him that strange look again, and turned away, saying, 'Well, we'll wave to you, and you must bring Miss Morfrey over for a moment to see Everard again.' She seemed to take it for granted that they would be at the Savoy too. It was impossible to explain to her why they wouldn't be.

'Yes, please tell her that I should like to renew an acquaintance begun so unconventionally,' said Everard, as they followed out of the box.

'I will indeed. She's a little—not shy exactly, reserved. I don't think she would want to be thrown into a party of strangers suddenly. But it was terribly nice of you to suggest it, and for my own sake I wish very much—'

'Not at all. I understand entirely.'

'She's working at Prosser's at the moment—where I am. You could always get into touch with her there.'

'Ah, yes. I might do that. Thank you.'

So that's Barnaby, he thought. Chloe might have done a good deal worse. Have they quarrelled; or has he come to the same realization as I have? He has meant more to her than ever I have meant—but how little that means . . .

Barnaby went back to Jill.

# 4

The play was over. The curtain had risen and fallen, risen and fallen. Claudia had taken a call with Five Star Judy, and the gentle, continuous wave of applause had surged suddenly into an enthusiasm which Judy acknowledged as a particular and not unexpected tribute. Subsequent shouts of 'Lancing!' from the front row of the dress circle were no more successful in undeceiving her than they were in bringing Claudia back. The critics were scrambling to get out; the pit and gallery were still clapping methodically, reluctant to believe that the evening's entertainment was indeed over; the stalls and circles were feeling for their coats, and looking to see where their programmes had slipped to.

Then suddenly the curtain went up again, taking Wilson Kelly completely by surprise. In fact, he had his back to the audience, and his violin under his chin, some of the company having said (one supposes), 'Do give us that lovely thing again, Mr Kelly, I was in my dressing-room, and couldn't hear it properly.' So, the play over, the audience, presumably, on its way out, Mr Kelly picked up his violin . . .

There was a sudden, shattering laugh from the front row of the dress circle.

# Chapter Sixteen

## 1

Christmas was here before you knew it—or so everybody told everybody else.

As a special tribute to the season there was an entirely new Children's Play at the Belvedere Theatre, with, luckily, all the old ingredients. Owing, it seemed, to a long-standing engagement which it had been impossible to break, Wilson Kelly had been forced to withdraw his successful romantic comedy, *Golden Melody*, while it was still playing to capacity. What was the Metropolis' loss, however, was the provinces' gain, for Mr Kelly was now making an extended tour of the more important towns with his full London company. In the spring he would return to London with a new comedy which he was writing in conjunction with a distinguished man of affairs, whose name for the present must remain a close secret.

This was what Mr Pope Ferrier told Our Theatrical Correspondent, and what Our Theatrical Correspondent received with an indifferent 'Quite, old man—what's yours again?' and passed on to his readers. No doubt some of them believed it.

Claudia did not believe it. Whatever else in it might be true, it was not true to speak of the 'full' London company. The talented young actress who played *Zella* was staying in London. She had decided to leave the stage.

The choice between a Woman's Love and Her Career, which has used up so many thousand feet of celluloid, had not exercised her long. Between her art on the one side and, on the other, the mending of her husband's socks after dinner while he read his new play aloud to her, Claudia hesitated for a moment only; a moment's waiting for the flash of inspiration which revealed her as the producer of that new play. She would be known far and wide as a Great Producer, and famous dramatists from all over the world would beg her to produce their plays, and she would say, 'I'm sorry, but I only produce my husband's plays.' Well, she might make an exception for Shaw, if he wrote anything as good as *St Joan* again, but he was probably getting too old for that. 'Produced by Claudia Lancing'; and, of course, the gossip writers would remind people that she was really Mrs Carol Higgs, and only produced her husband's plays. What fun it would be!

And, if it hadn't been for Chloe, she would still be at the Academy, having tea with Herbert Potter! (She might give Herbert a very small part in Carol's next play.) Darling Chloe! Darling Carol!

On Sunday Carol took her to the tall house in Portman Square, where he lived with The Aunts.

There were four of them. Aunt Harry and Aunt Jo were twins. Aunt Jo was the elder by five minutes, but for sixty-five years Aunt Harry had disputed this; and since no third party was now living who had been within sight or sound of their arrival, and since the first-comer had long discarded whatever sign of priority had been affixed to her at the time, it was difficult for Aunt Jo to say more in reply than, 'Now, Harry, you *know* that's not true.' Aunt Harry's original theory had been that the doctor had found her under the first gooseberry bush he had come to, and had put her in his bag, and had then found Aunt Jo a few minutes later under another bush. So naturally when he came to the house and opened the bag, Aunt Jo was on top and came out first, and everybody supposed that she was the elder. It seemed a logical explanation of the way these mistakes arise, and there were moments when Aunt Jo was shaken. Later, when the facts of life had seeped through to them, Aunt Harry shifted her ground. With a lack of logic equally unanswerable, she claimed that the monthly nurse had risen up in the dead of night and changed the ribbons which identified them. 'Harry, you *know* that's not true,' Jo had said weakly, and Harry had answered, 'How do I know? Everybody knows that nurses are *always* being bribed to change babies. Because of Succeeding to Estates. Why, you've only got to look at us to see that I'm much, much older.'—'You mean fatter,' said Jo; 'and anyhow, five minutes couldn't make all that difference.' Harry said darkly that it wasn't just the five minutes, it was Everything.

They were now seventy. Aunt Harry's conviction that she was the elder was no less assured; but there were times when the truth presented itself to her in a new form: when it was she who had always been recognized as the elder, and Jo who had put about this ridiculous story of babies changed at birth. This left Aunt Jo more shaken than ever. She felt that she was being robbed of something, but didn't know what. In fact, seniority mattered little. They ran the house together: Aunt Harry, as the more masterful, controlling and dismissing the servants; Jo, as the more methodical, controlling and balancing the accounts. When frontier skirmishes threatened, they appealed to Aunt Amy.

They all loved Aunt Amy, for she had been the pretty one. There had been a day, and none of them could ever forget it, her 21st birthday, when a young gentleman in the Diplomatic Service had seemed to be on the edge of proposing for her hand. He had been put next to her at the family dinner-party that night, and the rest of them had made a point of chattering eagerly among themselves and away from the about-to-be-happy pair, leaving the lovers isolated in a sea of talk, to murmur unheard whatever it is which lovers say when they are alone. Suddenly one of those strange unconcerted silences stilled the family chatter . . . and out of the void rang the high, clear voice of Amy.

'Tell me, Mr Sowerbutt,' it said in bell-like tones, 'do you believe in the Immaculate Conception?'

Mr Sowerbutt lost all his diplomacy, and turned bright scarlet. Amy looked at him in surprise, looked at the horrified faces all round her, and went as white as her napkin. The family hurried back into a vociferation of chatter, in its eagerness to pretend that there had never been a silence, that the awful words had never been said. Harry on Mr Sowerbutt's left asked him if he had ever done any diplomacy in Broadstairs, insisted loudly that there was no place like Broadstairs for diplomacy. A Mr Stenning on Amy's right stammered to her of a curious affair he had read about the other day, really most bewildering, but perhaps he should explain first that he was in the wholesale cloth business. As soon as it was decent, the ladies ascended to the drawing-room, Amy, at a sign from her mother, continuing up the staircase to bed. In the dining-room, Mr Sowerbutt was accorded the privileges of an invalid, entitled to have all the vintage port which he wanted, and not to be asked any difficult questions.

It was never properly explained to the Head of the Family: Grandfather Higgs, as we must call him. As subjects for conversation, Sex and Religion were equally shocking to Grandfather Higgs. This appalling and blasphemous combination of the two, introduced at a dinner-table by a young woman, who should have no conception— that is to say, no understanding of what—of such things—well, he simply could not conceive—that is, understand how a daughter of his—did she realize that she was practically asking a guest at his house, in the most unladylike way conceive— con—imaginable, asking him *if he were a Christian*?

'I wasn't, Papa,' sobbed Amy. 'It doesn't mean that at all.'

'Doesn't mean what?'

'D-doesn't mean what you think it means.'

'And what, pray, do you think that I think it means?'

This might have gone on for a long time, had not Grandmother Higgs taken her husband on one side, and whispered in his ear.

'Who said so?' growled Grandfather Higgs resentfully.

'Amy says she read it in a book, a religious book which Mr Manley gave her for her birthday. After all, dear, he did christen and confirm her, he wouldn't choose an unpleasant book—she just happened to glance at it that afternoon, and was so surprised, and couldn't help wondering if everybody else knew—'

'My point, Emily, is simply this. Here is something, we need not go into details, which everybody believes. Why insult—'

'They don't!' cried Amy. '*I* don't!'

'*You* don't?' said Grandfather Higgs, aghast. 'Do you mean to tell me that a daughter of mine—'

'*Romish* doctrine,' warned Grandmother Higgs behind her hand.

'Just what I was saying,' said Grandfather Higgs alertly. 'Either this young man is a Roman Catholic, or he isn't. I suppose you will grant me that?'

'Yes, dear,' said Emily.

'Very well. If he *is*, then it is an insult to ask him if he believes what all Catholics believe. If he *isn't*, then it's an insult to suggest that he believes what no Protestant believes. In either case an insult.' He clutched his beard in his hand and summed the matter up. 'A blasphemous insult, with a nasty savour of sex about it.'

That was the end of Aunt Amy's romance. She should have consoled herself with religion, but somehow failed to do this; perhaps she felt that it was responsible for enough already. From that day she withdrew into herself. She was not unhappy, for she was now an object of interest, and that has never made a woman unhappy. Her parents watched her with misgiving, her sisters waited in half-admiring, half-fearful expectation, all wondering 'what Amy would say next'. She found it easier to say nothing. When the others talked, she would smile mysteriously to herself, as Mona Lisa smiled . . .

Now she knitted. When she was appealed to by her sisters, she laid her knitting on her lap, took off her spectacles, and said with pleasant diffidence, 'Well, dear, you know what *I* think.' One realized that one was in the presence of a profound but unorthodox philosophy, which made its self-evident contribution to any symposium. Unfortunately it was too late to ask her what that philosophy was; the question should have come thirty years ago. So nobody ever did know what she thought, and each side could claim her as an ally.

Auntie Bibs was the youngest. She was the only one called Auntie; perhaps because she was the only one called Bibs. From some common ancestor she and Carol had inherited that fresh complexion, that innocent look, that slightly tilted nose. Her abundant, snow-white hair cascaded round her still youthful face in a glory which befitted her genius. She was the youngest of the sisters and the most greatly endowed. She was, it was believed, a Poetess.

As a poetess, Auntie Bibs was in the direct line from Shelley, and almost any other poet. Indeed, faint far-away echoes of her literary forbears still seemed to linger between her lines—as the *Willesden Gazette* once cautiously put it. It might have been said of her: *Nihil tetigit quod non ornavit,* had critical opinion been more responsive to her art. Here, as an example of it at its most mature, is a poem entitled (for some reason)—

## EPITHALAMIUM

*The lark now leaves his wintry nest*
*To join the feathered cherubim!*
*His music soothes my saddened breast,*
*I feel new life in every limb!*
*His profuse strain I hear him sing*
*With unpremeditated art!*
*O Grave! O Death! where is thy sting*
*When careless rapture fills my heart!*

She was not a plagiarist, it was just that poetry was in her blood. Her prose style was, in a sense, more original. An occasional page of Reflections or Word Pictures would find its way between the poems, each reflection or picture protected from its neighbours by some pretty colophon of mermaids, or wild duck in flight.

## REFLECTION

*Wise men condemn action without thought. But only a fool*
*would substitute thought without action!*
Simple, yes; but one cannot remember that it has ever been said before.

## WORD PICTURE

*A baby cloud floated happily across the deep azure*
*of the sky, shadowing the mighty majesty of the*

*Sun! Then with an innocent laugh it flitted on, and*
*the Sun shone forth again with redoubled splendour!*

As the *Willesden Gazette* said, any of us might notice these common phenomena, but it takes a poet to give them full expression.

Auntie Bibs published her works in slender green volumes at her own expense, over the name Genevieve la Touche, which she felt to be more euphonious than Bibs Higgs; as no doubt it is. Gradually she had come to believe that la Touche had a separate identity from her own, being, as it were, a spirit which took possession of her from time to time, and then returned to Mount Olympus. For this reason she was able to be completely natural and unaffected as Auntie Bibs; indeed, almost in the mood sometimes to joke with Carol about the intruding Genevieve. Carol thought her a darling. Crackers, but a darling. She was his favourite among The Aunts.

# 2

So when on this Sunday afternoon over the tea-table Carol announced to the family that he proposed to change his name, it was Auntie Bibs who immediately approved. The others assumed that it was one of Carol's jokes. Even Claudia felt vaguely that it was not quite English.

'Very wise, dear,' said the poetess. 'You will find that it makes a wonderful difference. It gives one's art a freedom to which it can never aspire under one's own name.' She closed her eyes and murmured tentatively, 'My freedom, 'tis of thee!' It seemed as if inspiration had come upon her again. 'Freedom that never was on land or sea!' The poem began to shape itself.

'Darling, but why?' interrupted Claudia.

'Well, pretty, you can't want to be Mrs Higgs.'

'Mrs Carol Higgs,' she corrected. 'Of course I do.' Why, the name had been in every column of *The Times* (except Deaths) for the last ten days. Mrs Carol Higgs had been among those present at luncheon parties, had been delivered of twins, had presented a bouquet to the

Queen, and, in brackets, had joined Claudia Lancing in producing play after play for her husband. How could she be anything but Mrs Carol Higgs? It seemed so funny now.

'Darling, you'd much rather be Mrs Carol Congreve or Mrs Carol Sheridan. Of course you would. Come on, let's choose a really exciting one. What about Carol de la Touche?' He winked across the table at Genevieve, who came back to earth and shook her head at him smilingly.

'What *is* all this nonsense, Carol?' demanded Aunt Harry sharply. She sat at the top of the table behind the silver monogrammed tray. As head of the family it should have been her right, but Jo always spoilt it for her when visitors were present by saying, 'Harry, will *you* pour out?' On this occasion she had added to Claudia: 'I always get Harry to pour out for me. She's stronger than I am—naturally,' and Harry could think of no more dignified reprisal than the slipping of a lump of sugar into her sister's tea. Now, however, she could assert herself as The Eldest Living Higgs, and protect the family honour. 'Are you saying that our name is not good enough for you? Your own father's name?'

'If it's good enough for you, Aunt Harry, it's good enough for me. Ah, but am I good enough for it?'

'I think you are getting on very nicely,' said Aunt Jo. 'We all enjoyed your little play very—*Tchah*!'

'What is it, Jo? Don't say I put sugar in your tea by mistake.' Jo was certainly not going to say it. 'Oh dear, no,' she laughed.

'You could hardly do anything quite so silly as that. Is *your* tea as you like it, dear?'

'Perfectly, thank you,' said Claudia.

'It just tasted a little odd to me for the moment, and I wondered—' She closed her eyes, and heroically sipped again. 'Ah, yes, delicious. You were saying, Carol?'

'Well, you see, my next little play is going to be quite a different sort of little play.'

'Variety,' murmured Bibs. 'The spice of life. The many-formed.' She seemed to be feeling for something.

'Yes, dear, but the public doesn't care about the many-formed. Nor do the critics. They like to know where they are with you. Carol Higgs, the man who wrote—' He turned to Claudia: 'What was it called?'

'Oh, Carol, *darling*!' laughed Claudia. He really hated the play, didn't he? She knew now that it wasn't a good play, but he *had* written most of it, and he oughtn't to feel so bitter about it. I suppose, she thought, it's like choosing a new dress, and then loathing yourself in it, and wanting to give it away.

'You mean,' said Aunt Harry, 'that you would just take a *nom de plume*? Like your aunt. You would still be Carol Higgs in the ordinary way.'

'Oh, rather. A well-dressed man calling himself Carol Higgs.'

'You could keep the Carol, dear, couldn't you?' said Jo. 'I don't like to think of you giving it *all* up.'

Carol, spreading honey on a buttered bun, waved his knife in the direction of Bibs.

'Oh, but she had never been called Barbara. She was Bibs from a baby. What *do you* think, Amy?'

Amy, who had been wearing her Mona Lisa smile, put down her cup of tea and said, 'Me? Oh, well, I am afraid I take rather the modern view.' Nobody liked to ask her what this was, and Claudia said, 'Of course, you *could* call yourself Lewis Carol,' and laughed to show that she wasn't serious. Amy nodded at her, saying, 'I think Claudia and I understand, don't we, Claudia?' Claudia, who had been uncertain up to now, decided that she understood. She nodded back to Aunt Amy with authority, as one artist interpreting another. Very soon she would be a wife interpreting a husband.

'I think you are very wise, darling,' she said to Carol. 'Now let's be serious. What name shall we have?' She looked round brightly at the company. 'I've got it! What's your second name? Fancy my not knowing!'

It was clear to her at once that she had said the wrong thing. Aunt Jo flushed slightly. Aunt Harry's mouth hardened. Aunt Amy gave her enigmatic smile, as if here she were on her own ground. Only

Auntie Bibs remained impersonal. Her lips moved. The divine spirit had taken possession of her.

> '*What's in a name?* (it was saying). *The meanest flower that blows*
> *Will smell the same, though called by some a rose.*'

'That, beautiful,' said Carol, 'is the skeleton in the cupboard or Bluebeard's secret. I might whisper it to you one day, but—'

'You'll have to say it out loud in church.'

'So I shall. Oh, all right. Muggeridge. Say "Oh!" if you like, but don't say "What?"'

'Oh!' said Claudia.

'He was a bad man,' said Jo bravely.

Claudia waited for some development of the theme. There were so many ways of being bad. Did she mean— Aunt Amy, the authority on sex, recognizing that Claudia would soon be one, nodded to her. Yes. That was what they meant.

'But why *you*—'

'My godfather. He was a great friend of my father's. At one time.'

'He killed your father.'

'Aunt Harry!'

'And your mother.' 'Oh, well—'

'And now he has the impertinence to call himself Lord Sheppey.'

'Well, he had to take some name. He wouldn't want to be Lord Muggeridge.'

'I didn't know that they gave peerages to murderers and seducers.'

'Oh, rather. As long as they've got the cash.'

Aunt Jo caught Claudia's troubled eye, and said, 'I think, Harry, that Carol would prefer to tell our family history to dear Claudia in his own way.'

Aunt Harry sniffed. Aunt Amy, who had given up all for love, or had so persuaded herself, spoke gently.

'He must have been very fond of her. He never married.'

'That sort of man doesn't need to,' said Harry viciously.

Carol gave Claudia a look which meant 'I'm sorry for all this, darling, wait till we're alone', and said cheerfully, 'Well, anyway, Muggeridge and Shakespeare both being out, what's left? What about an anagram of Carol Higgs?' He took out a pencil and was busy for a moment. 'The best I can do is Charli Gogs. I couldn't be Charli Gogs, could I? We're so short of "e's," that's the trouble. If I put in a couple of "e's" I can get George Shilac. Hail to thee, blythe shilac. Shilac Holmes reached for his violin. You come to me and you say, "Shilac, I would have moneys of you."'

'John Preston,' said Bibs suddenly with her eyes shut.

They all looked at her.

'Why, darling? Any reason, or just inspiration?'

'It came,' said Bibs simply.

'It's as good as any other,' said Harry, speaking as head of the family.

'I like it,' said Claudia.

'Like it? It's marvellous. John Preston. Simple, dignified, and not obviously made up. John Preston Never had a vest on. When in Hants He also discarded his pants.'

They all laughed, and the skeleton went back into its cupboard.

# 3

'They're much older than you, aren't they?' said Claudia in the taxi. 'I mean as aunts.'

'Father was the baby of the family, twenty years younger than Harry. They brought him up. Then they brought me up.'

'What happened, darling? Or don't you want to tell me?'

'Of course I want to tell you.' He kissed her suddenly. 'I love you, darling. Don't *you* ever leave me . . . Father was everything to the aunts. Particularly to Jo and Harry. Particularly, I think, to Harry. He was the only baby any of them had ever had. And then they got another one. A girl this time. Mother. They weren't jealous of her, she was just another baby. Perhaps she didn't like that; or the way Father let himself be managed; or living in the house with them all. Anyway, she went off with this fellow when I was a year old. They went abroad and crashed in his car in France. I think they had all hoped she would still come back to them. Aunt Jo told me all about it when I went up to Cambridge, but of course I'd heard it all before. From Bibs and Amy. Aunt Harry tried to make out that he had deliberately killed her, and, when that was no good, that he was drunk. I don't see why he need have been. Father died a year later; Aunt Harry said of a broken heart. May have been. He just—died. So I never knew either of them, they mean nothing to me, and I can't be sentimental about them, or feel anything about this fellow Sheppey, as he is now. Then, of course, I became the baby of the family, but luckily not so badly. At least, I've managed to survive.'

'Oh, Carol, darling!' cried Claudia from a full heart. Anxiously she asked, 'Do you want *us* to live with them when we're married?'

'Good God, no!' said Carol.

# 4

There is hardly a woman who does not get some emotional satisfaction out of a wedding; a satisfaction independent of her acquaintance with the contracting parties. It is not entirely selfish. She may be reminded sentimentally of her own wedding-day, or savour happily the day which will come to her, this year, next year, some time. She may be criticizing, or even admiring, the bride's dress and the bridesmaids' hats. But deep down inside her, perhaps not fully realized by herself, is the satisfaction of her creative impulse. The world will go on. One more man has been beguiled into the business . . . Or there may be another reason for her emotion.

Claude and Chloe shared a hymn-sheet. Was it his fancy that her hand was trembling? There had been a pony, Peggy, lent to him to ride one holiday; there was a little bridge over the stream by Holt's Corner. At first she trembled whenever she came to it; tugged to get

245

her head round and gallop away from danger. He could see himself holding her there, leaning down to soothe her, telling her that there was nothing to fear. Gradually she had grown used to it. She didn't tremble now; to the hedger watching them over his shoulder their crossing was no different from that of any other pony on any other bridge; but Claude could always feel the difference: the awareness of Peggy as they made the approach, the inward trembling which told of her inward struggle to crush the memory of that bridge. Something had happened there once. He never found out what it was. He only knew that something had happened.

No, Chloe's hand was not trembling; it was not her hand. But something had happened once, something she could never forget. The clergyman's voice, the bridesmaids, the flowers, perhaps this very hymn they were singing together, they were all crying to her, reminding her, warning her. And he, somehow, was listening in.

She must have been to a hundred weddings. Does she always tell her secret to the person she is next to, or am I different? He remembered hearing Claudia's nurse say to the cook: 'He's sort of different, if you know what I mean. Gypsy-like. Must have got it from his poor mother. I tell you, he frightens me, he does really, Mrs Parsons.' He had been very proud of this, and had jumped out at her and frightened her. But that was not what she meant.

There was Henry, giving Claudia away. Sir Henry Lancing, K.C.B. Very important man once. Now retired. Father. Henry. A crashing bore. But damned good-looking. Only fair, not dark, not like us, not like Mother. 'Ah, she was a lovely one, Master Claude.' I suppose he *is* our father? He doesn't mean anything to us.

So little, indeed, that it had been assumed by Claudia that her brother would give her away. He did say halfheartedly, 'What about Henry? Rather his job, isn't it?' and Claudia had said, 'Oh, dear! I suppose it is. Then he'd want us to be married down there, wouldn't he? I can't do that.'

'If you're married down there, then you've got to have Henry. He can't be at the wedding and not give you away. Didn't you think of asking him?'

'Well, no. I mean, I haven't thought about him. We were going to be married at St Paul's—'

'Cathedral?'

'Portman Square, silly. Naturally I want all my friends to come. Who'd come to a country wedding at the end of January? Think of the poor old aunts. I say, Claude, we must ask him, mustn't we?'

'Have you organized this at all? Who's sending out invitations? Who's paying for the reception? God Almighty, woman, you didn't think *I* was?'

'Oh, Claude, I am a little fool. The aunts sort of took it for granted that they were, and I sort of—sort of—'

'Let them take it for granted that you were an orphan?'

'Well, yes . . . I told Carol,' she added proudly, as if this were an unusual concession on her part.

Sir Henry had come to London; now all London knew that the young Lancings were not wholly orphaned. He had called on The Aunts, charming them with his correct good looks, his gracious manner, his courtly acceptance of their desire to pay for the wedding reception. Almost as soon as he had heard, and mastered, the details of Carol's patrimony, he had waved all this aside as of trifling importance. What mattered was that their children should be happy together. Is it not so, Madam? Jo and Harry assured him that it was indeed so. Carried away by the thought of their loved one's happiness, Jo essayed a little reminiscence of Carol's first visit to the seaside at the age of three. It was a challenge which Sir Henry was not likely to pass by. He told them of his first visit to the Colonial Office at the age of twenty-two. Mr Joseph Chamberlain was already there; Rhodes and Milner were slipping in and out. It was a fascinating story, if they had heard it; but though they listened to it with an absorption to which it was quite unaccustomed, each of them was far away with her own thoughts. Jo was wondering which grandfather Carol's son, Claudia's son, would look like; she was following him from school to college, and so into the great world; perhaps he would be a famous singer . . . Harry had been caught by those old remembered names: the Jameson Raid, the Boer War, Little George playing at soldiers, big George frightening them all by saying that he would enlist in the Yeomanry . . . Amy wore the gentle smile of one who had had a passionate interlude with Cecil Rhodes, and could now look back on it without bitterness . . . Genevieve's eyes were shut. This in itself could still surprise, and might have annoyed, Sir Henry; but there was a purpose behind those tightly-closed eyelids and the murmuring mouth which told him that she was merely trying to visualize the dramatic scene which he was painting for them: the exact position on his table of the IN and OUT baskets. It was not so. She was composing. Later she wrote the well-known lines in her manuscript book, headed 'King and Country', with a question-mark after it, as if she were not quite sure.

*Some men are born to greatness; some,*
*Through craven awe of being great,*
*Have greatness thrust upon them! Come,*
*My Destiny! ere 'tis too late!*
*I also serve who only sit and wait . . .*

It had been a surprise to Wilson Kelly to learn that the golden melody of love had been playing round his own stage-door, but he had done his best with it. Paragraphs headed *Stage Romance* had informed the romantic that Wilson Kelly's latest play was breaking all records at the Belvedere. In reply to an unexpressed desire of the second-night audience for a speech, Mr Kelly had thanked them all for their gracious reception, and had told them how Love's wings had been hovering over the newest recruit to his company, their little nightingale Claudia Lancing, daughter of that distinguished servant of the State, Sir Henry Lancing, and betrothed but yesterday to Mr Carol Higgs, the brilliant young author with whom he had had the honour of collaborating in the play which they had just received so warmly. 'Claudia, my dear?' He led her on. The audience, glad to be able to applaud something, clapped her loudly; and, taking the brunt of the applause on his more manly shoulders, Mr Kelly bowed her and, after a suitable interval, himself, behind the curtains.

He was at the wedding. So were Herbert Potter and Dora, now engaged. Claudia was glad about this, though a little surprised that Herbert had so soon found comfort.

'Not so soon as you,' Claude had said, when his attention had been called to the fickleness of Mr Potter.

'I was never engaged to him,' said Claudia indignantly.

'Nor he to you, in that case.'

'No, but—he was fond of me. I know he was. A woman always knows.'

'Probably he thought that you were fond of him.'

'That's different.'

Things were always different for women, thought Claude. Do as you would be done by meant nothing to them in their relations with men. He took a quick look at Chloe; she gave him her loving glance in reply, and for the first time it did not move him. He realized that it meant no more than the smile of the girl behind the tobacconist's counter when he said Good morning. He heard Potter's voice thundering from the back of the church. That's what I ought to be doing, he thought. Having the sense to know when a thing's no good and beginning again. But not with women. To hell with all women. Why aren't I in Paris trying to learn my job? Paris—Spain— Algiers—the whole sunlit world to paint, and, waiting for me! No Claudia now, no Chloe. My God, I'm alone! I'm free!

# Chapter Seventeen

## 1

*Any more questions?* was on the bookstalls. Tired business men, stopping for a moment to snatch up an evening paper as they hurried to their platforms, saw the label above it, 'The Crossworder's Companion,' registered a passing interest, and went on their way. They took their corner seats. They nodded to the tired business faces opposite to them. They glanced at the headlines and the closing prices. Anything in the paper? Nothing in the paper. It went into a pocket for the wife; from the other pocket a morning's Times or Telegraph came out. Segments of the crossword still gaped at him; there was just time to finish them off.

Pluto in the sky. Six letters, last one 'S'. That was the fellow who was always hanging round Socrates. Like Boswell and Johnson. I wish they'd keep off these Greek fellows; we didn't all have a Classical education, thank God. Socrates too long, and why in the sky? . . . Oh no, damn it, that was *Plato*. Who the devil was Pluto? I know I've heard of him. There's plutocrats of course . . . The fellow who turned everything he touched into gold . . . There've been one or two like that in the City, and they ended in the dock . . . Oh, hell, that was Midas, wasn't it? But I've heard of Pluto somewhere . . . Pluto . . . of course! The Disney dog! Dog in the sky. Film star. Dog star. Damned good. But what's the *name* of the dog-star? That's what I want. Six letters. Why the devil doesn't one know *anything*?

Any more questions?

One of them might be: Why, when you decide to buy a copy a week later, do you find that the wife has bought you one for an extra birthday present?

Barnaby didn't answer that one; he accepted the fact gratefully. The book was selling. It was going to be an income of a sort. New editions from time to time. Two or three hundred a year. And in June he was to be a director. He could afford to marry: it was time he married.

Jill brought him his tea every afternoon. Lately he had found himself looking at his watch, and thinking that in five minutes she would bring him his tea. Her legs were good, but not so good as Silvie's; she didn't sit on his desk and swing them, but stood sturdily against the door, and talked to him from there. He always managed to hold her just as she got to the door; to say something which swung her round and stood her there against the shelves, in a strategic position from which to talk; as if still in some curious way, she was afraid of an attack on her integrity, her independence, and must keep in her own control the means of ending the conversation. Here; with her back to the door; her fingers feeling for the handle.

As she came to the door this afternoon, he said:

'Isn't it time we went to a theatre again? Or didn't you enjoy it enough last time?'

She turned round quickly.

'Didn't you think I thanked you enough?'

'Now, how did you guess that? I'm just insatiable in that way. I can't be thanked enough. I get terribly embarrassed, of course, with all this gratitude; keep buttoning and unbuttoning my coat; but it does something to me, and I have to have it.' He looked mockingly at her, and said 'Now laugh'.

'Why should I?'

'Just to be friendly. You know, you think So much about what people are doing to you that you never think about what you're doing to them.'

'What am I doing to you?'

'All sorts of things. I'll tell you when I've found out more definitely. Meanwhile, as I said just now, why don't we go to the Zoo together?'

She caught her breath, and said eagerly, 'I've never been to the Zoo!'

'You've never been—you've *never*—well, neither have I since I was about ten, but I know people who have. Why don't we go?'

'I should love it.'

'Right. Sunday afternoon? I can get tickets. I'm not saying that a winter afternoon is the ideal time for the Zoo, but the Crocodile House should be pretty warm. Look here, let's make it the morning, and we'll have lunch there. It gets dark so soon. You shall pay for the lunch, and I'll pay for the taxis.'

'That would be perfect.'

'Just let's get this settled before we part. You are twenty-one, and you have never seen a hippopotamus. Is that right?'

She smiled and nodded.

'Well, you'll be surprised. And don't say afterwards that you hadn't been warned.'

She laughed happily, and went out. I'm getting on, thought Barnaby, and was absurdly pleased with himself.

He stirred and sipped his tea, and nibbled his biscuit. I should miss her if she went now, he thought. There's something sort of—antiseptic about her. She's—well, apart from anything else, she's honest. It's refreshing, honesty in a woman. Independence. Even if it's rather knobbly independence. She's very young, of course. Good lord, she's fourteen years younger than I am—I wonder if that means anything to her.

He got up and looked at himself in the glass on the mantelpiece. I couldn't be younger than I look and be grown up, he thought, I won't say for beautiful. Is this the face that launched a thousand slips—and, when it had corrected the damn things, gave the world that futile book *Any More Questions?* It is. He went back to his desk.

He felt uncomfortable about Chloe. He had felt uncomfortable for many weeks. He had not seen her since that night at the Belvedere, but what could he do about it? Obviously he should write to her or ring her up, but every day which he let go by made the next day more difficult. She had no business to be so—so proprietary. There she is, he thought, going around with every kind of man since I've known her, and who am I to complain; but if I go out once with one other girl, she makes me feel that I'm disloyal to her. Why should all the disloyalty be on my side? Why should I owe her anything, when I've offered her everything, and she has refused it? The old feminine belief that she is a special case and has a right to a special allegiance.

Suppose that he asked her once more to marry him? She would refuse. All right, then he would say, 'So this is good-bye.' Oh, no, damn it, he couldn't say that, nobody did except in a Wilson Kelly play. But he would say that perhaps they ought to give up seeing each other any more, it would be better for both of them if—No, that was the trouble, not for both of them. The more men she had in love with her, the better for her, they gave her presents, they made dates which she kept or not as she pleased. Jam for her all the time, but not for the man. All right, then I'll say that *I* should be happier. 'It's no good. I can't go on like this.' (Wilson Kelly again.)

He tried to imagine the scene, and knew that one mournful look from Chloe, one meaningless promise in her eyes, would keep him. No, damn it, it wouldn't. It might have kept him once, but not now. The antiseptic was working. Loving words, loving looks, 'darlings' thrown off lightly in however lovely a voice . . . what a relief to be away from that—with Jill who would call no man darling until she meant it. And, with the entrance of Jill into the picture, Barnaby found himself pulled up suddenly by an astonishing thought. Suppose Chloe accepted me at last! My God, I never allowed for that!

He had never really seen himself as Chloe's husband, only as a lover seeking vainly to win her. Now he knew that, even if she would marry him, he could never marry her. Marriage with Chloe would be an endless torment of jealousy and frustration. A life in a silken web of cajolings and promises and excuses and falsehoods, a network of femininities from which he could never escape. No life for a man. An unhealthy, hot-house, distracting, unrestful life.

He finished his tea, lit his pipe, and went into Stainer's room.

'Do you want Mr Stainer?' said Jill. 'He's out.'

'I know. That's why I came. I just wanted to have a look at you.'

'Why? What do I look like?'

'So healthy. So fresh. So open-air. So—so—can't think of the other word. I must look it up in *Any More Questions*. Sorry.' He went out.

Jill took out her glass and looked at herself. She shook her head. He's crazy, she said, but I like him. He's nice to think about. As she typed, she thought about him.

So Barnaby didn't ring up Chloe, and on Sunday he took Jill to the Zoo.

# 2

Barnaby had spoken less than the literal truth when he said that he had not been to the Zoo since he was about ten; but he could have pleaded that this was in some sort true of all of us, since there was that about the Zoo which made one a boy again, whatever one's authentic age. It is impossible to assume a sophisticated attitude towards a hippopotamus. Self-invited attendants on its morning bath were, young and old, of one mind: And still they gazed, and still the wonder grew, That anything so ugly could be true. But none of them could feel contemptuous, none of them could feel superior. A hippopotamus is nobody's rival. The grown-up and the child feel the same single emotion. Wonder. Coo!

'Well?' said Barnaby.

'Well, of course I knew what it was like. I'd seen pictures of it.' 'But you didn't believe it was true. Well, now you know that it is.'

Jill was silent as they walked away, and then said suddenly, 'Do you know anything about Evolution?'

'Enough to explain it to a child who knows nothing about it. Like so many other things. That wouldn't do for you, I'm afraid.' 'The idea is, isn't it, that we are descended from monkeys, and the monkeys came from other animals, and so on, back to—to the first signs of animal life—'

'Sea-slugs, I believe, but don't take my word for it.'

'Yes. However *they* came.'

'That can be regarded as the major mystery of the world. How anything began. You don't worry about that too much, I hope?'

'No, what I was wondering was—things like hippopotamuses. Have they stopped, or are they working up to something?'

'Something in the City probably. But I see what you mean. Why has only one sort of local boy made good?'

Jill nodded eagerly.

'Yes! And then there's another thing—' She broke off and said earnestly, 'It's all very interesting, isn't it?'

'You dear, nice child,' thought Barnaby, looking at her with a smile. Aloud he said, 'You make it so. Go on.'

'Well, suppose monkeys turned out to be the only ones who could do it—for some reason which we don't know. Are they still doing it? And why not?'

'I shall have to give this my earnest attention. You mean that every stage of development from the monkey to the Piltdown Man, and the Piltdown Man to the Caveman, and the Caveman to the Talking Man, ought to be continually coming into circulation, so to speak?'

'Well, evolution can't stop suddenly, and it can't only be going on at the top end.'

'Wait a bit. Let's become concrete. That's a giraffe by the way, and if ever it achieves manhood it will be a poor lookout for its laundress.'

'I can look at it while you're talking,' said Jill. 'Go on.'

'Take a monkey in 50,000 B.C. who became a Caveman in 20,000 B.C. and a Talking Man in 10,000 B.C.—dates not guaranteed, and probably ought to be multiplied by ten. Then a monkey what was a monkey in 28,000 B.C. ought to be a Caveman to-day. If so, where?'

'Exactly. What's the answer?'

'Apart from the obvious answer, "Please, sir, it wasn't me", I can only suggest that Evolution, the Survival of the Fittest, and, as one says loosely, All That, is a natural thing. Natural Selection. As soon as

Man appeared, Nature took second place, and nothing has happened naturally any more.'

'That still doesn't explain why the hippopotamus didn't do anything before Man came on the scene.'

'He probably struggled up as far as a hippopotamus, looked at himself in the glass, and decided that he'd got there.'

Jill laughed suddenly and surprisingly. 'Because I'm happy,' she smiled, as if it were the only laughter a serious-minded person ought to allow herself.

'I hope you will always be happy,' said Barnaby seriously, 'because I don't think you've been terribly happy so far. But I hope that, happy or not, you will always find something to laugh about.

'I think that people laugh very easily at very silly things.'

'They do, bless them. You know, what one wants to realize is that the things one doesn't do oneself aren't necessarily wrong. Or silly.

'You think I'm very young, don't you?'

'*And* very pretty. Don't forget that, because it's important. But I think you haven't quite settled down yet.'

'Into what?' said Jill scornfully. 'Middle age?'

'Into youth. Your particular sort of youth. What you are. Now come into the Aquarium, and see how many old friends we can find in the tanks.'

They found Stainer at once. He goggled at them through the glass in a nice sort of way.

'Exaggerated, of course,' said Barnaby, 'but definitely Stainer. Stainer about to deliver himself of something important, and just a little afraid it may not go. How do you feel about it?'

Jill nodded and laughed, and then said seriously, 'He's nicer looking than that, though.'

'One tries very hard to be nicer-looking than a fish, and sometimes pulls it off—one hopes.' They moved slowly along. 'Do you know Marshall? There he is, whiskers and all. Class-conscious, but sound. Now *you* find somebody.

Little by little, she warmed to the game.

'Look, there's a man, sort of gardener-groom we had once! He broke his leg, and I had to read to him.'

'Couldn't he read with a broken leg?' asked Barnaby, a little surprised.

'He couldn't read, anyhow; I mean not quickly enough to remember what the beginning of the sentence had been about. We read a book called *Carrots, or Only a Little Boy.*'

'About carrots?'

'That was the name of the boy.'

'I hope you made that clear before you began.'

'I don't think it made much difference to him. It was the only book there, his wife had been given it as a prize when she was a little girl, he was very proud of her for that, and after she left him, he used to hold it in his hands every night, pretending to read it, and wanting to, but not being able to. So I think he wasn't really listening, but just lying there, remembering her as a child, and thinking of her reading this book, just as I was reading it now, and—and remembering everything.'

'She left him? When? How?'

'Well, I was about eleven, so this would be about ten years ago, and she had gone away with a soldier in the war.' Barnaby felt cheap suddenly. He caught hold of her hand, and said, 'I'm sorry.'

'Sorry?' said Jill, but she did not take her hand away.

'Being so bloody funny all the time you were talking. So smart. Such witty interruptions, back-chat comedian stuff. I'm really ashamed. I didn't know it was going to be that sort of story.'

'I suppose it was my fault really for telling you that sort of story, I mean when we were making jokes about likenesses, but I'd forgotten about him when I began, and then it all came back.'

'*I'm* doing the apologizing,' said Barnaby firmly. 'Forgiven?'

Jill became a shy schoolgirl suddenly, blushed and said, 'I—I—thank you, I mean yes, of course!'

He pressed her hand, let it go, and, taking her by the arm, led her across the floor saying, 'Come and look at these. They're really lovely, not all one colour, like us.'

He remembered with a pleasant shock of surprise that to-morrow she would be bringing him his tea . . . and the next day . . . and the next day . . .

# 3

There couldn't be such happiness as being alone with Humby in your own house. So Silvie had said, and now she knew that it was true. It was a little house, in a little road Caterham way which had started out from a bigger road with the idea of going somewhere, back to Caterham, perhaps, or more adventurously on and on to the sea; but it had stopped nowhere because (it was to be supposed) the builder couldn't borrow any more money, or was tired, or thought that perhaps after all it was a mistake to get so far away from a station. Silvie's was the last house, so that on one side it could be said to stand in its own spacious grounds of as many acres as you liked to call it; up to the line of hills, anyway, allowing for a few grand houses in between which might have been the stables. It really couldn't be nicer.

Naturally Silvie had wanted to be the one who lit the gas-ring in the morning for Humby's shaving-water, and naturally Humby had said that of course she shouldn't do anything of the sort, she would have breakfast in bed like the Princess she was, and naturally Silvie had laughed her gay laugh at that, and said that it was only a question of slipping down and lighting the ring, because of course they would get up together and have breakfast together downstairs, so what did it matter who was the one to slip down and light the ring?

'Our whole married life depends on it,' said Humby solemnly.

'All right, darling, we'll take it in turns.'

'We'd never remember whose turn it was. No, we'll toss up each morning, and the longer we live the fairer it will get, because these things always even themselves out.'

Silvie laughed and said that they'd never remember to take a penny to bed with them every night, but Humby was resourceful enough to meet a silly objection like that. So when it was time to get up, Silvie put her arms round him and said 'Ready, darling,' gurgling to herself, because it was a great joke like everything in life now, and Humby said fifty-six.

'It was twenty-three,' said Silvie, 'my age when I went to Prosser's. You're thirty-three out. Your turn.'

'Ready,' said Humby.

'Forty-eight.'

'Eighty-two. The age of an eighty-one-year-old man on his next birthday. I win.'

'Are you sure?'

'By a neck.' He kissed hers and said, 'Out you go.'

She jumped out of bed.

'I can't believe that those legs are really mine,' said Humby sleepily, and put out a hand for his glasses.

'They are, darling, every bit of them,' cried Silvie.

Woman-like, she chose always a number with which she had some personal association. This had made it more difficult for her to cheat; which she would have been prepared to do for the loved one's sake, even though Humby had made her promise that she wouldn't, a game not being a game if you don't play it properly. Another influence for good was a mysterious thing called The Law of Averages which he seemed to have on his side, ready to pounce on her if she went on cheating. Indeed, within a very few weeks they could trust each other absolutely, provided, of course, that Humby hadn't lost on the two previous mornings.

Humby bicycled to the station, wet or fine. At first Silvie came with him to make sure that he didn't lose his way, or get run over; but when she felt comfortable about this, she would wait until the shops were open before going down, basket on handlebars. The day couldn't be long enough for all she had to do, nor short enough to bring Humby home again. She was typing a book for a Prosser author, and there were other books waiting for her, she had all the work she could manage, and, as if that weren't enough, there was not only the house, but the garden to look after.

On one happy Saturday afternoon, when Humby was digging a bed for the excitingly-coloured packets of seeds which she had bought at Woolworth's, and Silvie was cleaning his bicycle as close to him as she could, the front-door bell rang.

'Now whoever's that?' said Silvie.

'The Duke of Norfolk come to borrow a postage-stamp,' said Humby.

'Well, I hope he won't stop to tea, there's ever so little of the cake left. Have I got any black on my face?'

When he had inspected it, kissed it, said 'Not now' and returned to his digging, Silvie, looking a little anxiously at her hands, went through the French windows of the dining-room into the passage, put Humby's hat and coat quickly into the cupboard under the stairs, and opened the door.

'Well!' she cried. 'You!'

'Me,' said Barnaby. 'May I lie down somewhere?'

'Oh, Mr Rush, have you walked all the way from the station?'

'That was nothing. It was walking all round Surrey which was so trying. Nobody seems to have heard much of Sycamore Avenue.'

'Oh, you ought to have let us know, and then Humby could have done you one of his maps. Oh, I *am* sorry. Oh come in, it *is* kind of you to come, I never thought you really would.' She called out 'Darling! Who do you think's here? Mr Rush!'

The men met in the dining-room, and Silvie, crying, 'I'll put the kettle on, sit down, Mr Rush, that's the best chair,' disappeared. It was a long disappearance, for there were hands to get nice, toast to make, a quick change into something a little less bicycle-conscious, and the assembling of a tray crowned with the special tea-service (Prossers) and the real silver tea-spoons (Humby's dad). And since nothing could be too good for Mr Rush and he himself had given them to her, and knew about these things, the change included the putting-on of a pair of those very special stockings which you could hardly believe were stockings at all. What luck she had done her legs that morning, thinking that, well, you never know.

'Don't let me interrupt you,' Barnaby had said. 'I can watch you from here and cheer you on.'

'Glad to stop,' said Humby, putting on his coat. 'That's the worst of being an amateur. You work too hard and get tired too quickly, and do much less that way. Cigarette?'

'Thanks. Making a Marathon into a lot of all-out quarter-miles, with long rests in between.'

'Yes, hopeless. That's why the man with nothing to do gets angry with the working man so often. He says to himself, "I could do twice as much in half the time," the time being ten minutes of his leisure which he wastes in watching work which is going on all day. Well, so he could do twice as much in five minutes—and then get into a taxi and go somewhere where he could put his feet up for half an hour.'

'All the same,' smiled Barnaby, 'I've seen working-men with their feet up.'

'Oh, there are slackers in every trade, I grant you. But I think that that's one of the reasons for antagonism between classes: the feeling that the working-man isn't working, because he's running a Marathon and not a quarter-mile.'

'You're probably right. I hadn't thought of it before. But I think another reason is that the working-man is for some extraordinary reason called the working-man, which makes him think that he is the only sort of man who works.'

'We know that that isn't true.'

'We know, but we forget. An argument is bound to lose its way if we keep talking about Red-Haired Men when we mean men with reddish hair who are under five-foot-six and live in Manchester.'

'Well, what would you call him? You're a writer, Mr Rush, give us a word.'

'You're an inventor, invent one. And for Heaven's sake don't think I'm a writer.'

'You know about words,' said Humby with a flicker behind his glasses.

'A little, thanks to you. The times I've cursed you and Silvie for starting us on that damned book.'

'Well, who are the proletariat? We hear a lot about them.'

'Now I *can* do that. From *proles*, Latin for offspring. They were the lowest class in Rome, with no property, so their only use to the state was children—man-power— spear-fodder.'

'What a way of looking at it! Do you wonder that there's bitterness?'

'But isn't it rather the way *you* look at it? That manpower, not the individual brain-worker, is the foundation of the state and has the greatest claim on it?'

Humby was silent for a little, and then said 'One ought to know more about the Romans. I suppose one can get it all in English?'

'Oh, yes. It's only just occurred to me that we owe you something for giving us the idea of *Any More Questions*. May I send you a book or two? It's just Prosser's line.'

When Silvie called out 'Door, darling!' and came in with the tray, it was lovely to find them so interested in each other, so comfortable together, Humby's good enough for anybody, she thought, even Mr Rush. It was a happy tea; and even when she and Mr Rush talked about Prosser's, because how could she not want to know everything, Humby never let you think that he was out of it.

'And how's Miss Morfrey getting on? Does she make your tea as you like it?'

'Thanks to you, Silvie. Perfect.'

'And does she suit Mr Stainer?'

'Seems to.'

'She's nice, you know, Mr Rush.'

'Oh, we're great friends.' He added, because it gave him an odd pleasure to say it, 'We went to the Zoo together the other day,' and then wished he hadn't said it, because it seemed to put Jill in a Zoo-companion class which Silvie had never been in. But Silvie, who had always known that Miss Morfrey was 'different', was the most unlikely person to take it to heart. If *she* had been different, she wouldn't have met Humby.

'Lyn's always wondering about you all, and how you can possibly get on without her.'

'As if that were true!' she cried to Barnaby. 'I mean thinking you can't get on without me. But of course I like hearing about you all. Why, if it hadn't been for Prosser's, I should never have met Humby.' She looked at her husband, he answered her look, and Barnaby felt that they were talking to each other in a language which he had not yet mastered.

'How did you meet?' He looked from one to the other. 'You can't leave it like that.'

'Do you mind, darling?' Evidently Humby didn't, for she went on: 'Humby was having lunch with a friend of his in the Botanical Gardens, it was a Saturday, and he'd brought lunch for the two of them, and Mr Stainer had asked if I'd mind taking a very important parcel to Regent's Park on my way home, well, it wasn't on my way home exactly,' she laughed at the absurdity of it, 'but of course I said I'd take it, so I went straight off before I had my lunch, and the flowers looked so pretty from a distance, and I'd always heard how lovely they were, so I went in, and there was Humby walking up and down by where you go in for the roses, with his little bag in his hand with the lunch, by himself because his friend hadn't turned up.'

'Girl friend,' said Humby.

'Yes, you see, it was his girl friend, and—and she hadn't come! We got talking, saying how lovely the roses were, and then he said he'd got lunch with him, only his friend hadn't come, only he let me think it was a man friend— you did, darling—and so we had lunch together.'

'What about the—the friend? Was she late, or did she just not come?'

'She was nearly an hour late when I saw Lyn,' said Humby. 'We lunched in another part of the gardens, so I didn't see her if she did come. In fact, I didn't see her again.'

'Humby thought he liked me better,' said Silvie proudly.

'He didn't think,' said Humby, 'he just knew that he'd been a fool the first time, and wasn't the second time.'

'Like Romeo,' said Barnaby.

'Romeo?' said Silvie in surprise. 'But I thought that Romeo and Juliet—'

'Even Romeo thought that he loved somebody else first.'

'Well, I never knew that! And then he met Juliet, and—'

'And Rosaline didn't exist any more.'

'Oh, *darling*!' said Silvie to Humby; and then to Barnaby, 'I *am* glad to know about that.' She laughed happily with them at herself, at her silliness, and said, 'Well, I am!'

# 4

Did he mind walking to the station, or would he like to have Humby's bicycle, and Humby would ride hers, and bring the two of them back, he was clever like that, there was almost nothing he couldn't do on a bicycle.

'A foot on each saddle?' smiled Barnaby.

'I expect so. Couldn't you, darling?'

'Not going uphill,' said Humby.

They all walked down together. Lights were beginning to point the little houses; in each a newly-married couple: in each some one to wave good-bye to in the morning, some one to come back to in the evening. Sitting in his train Barnaby felt a pleasant glow of happiness reflected from the happiness he had met that afternoon, and beneath it, a gentle melancholy that he was missing something which might have been his. 'I've been living on restaurant talk,' he thought, 'restaurant love-making; making it, not just the end of the day, but the purpose of the day. Oh, God, what a futile thing my life is. Just existence, with bits of tinsel hung on it to make it look as if it were worth something. What can I do with it now? What is left for me? Have children, and hope that they will be less futile, I suppose. Well, I *could* do that. If—'

'I shouldn't be surprised if he married that Miss Morfrey,' said Silvie as they walked up the hill together. 'You can always tell. She's nice.'

'I thought he was in love with that other girl.'

'*Was*, Mr Romeo Humberson, *was.*' She squeezed his arm. 'Now let's guess how many steps it is home, we've never done it from here. Seven hundred?'

'Twelve hundred and eighty-six,' said Humby firmly.

'All right, Mr Know Everything. One two eight six. Give me a kiss and then we'll start. I'll count the first hundred.'

They stopped, and he took her in his arms.

'My, that *was* a kiss!' gasped Silvie. 'I don't think we've ever— Now then, I'm counting.'

# Chapter Eighteen

## 1

The astonishing news that Aunt Essie was to be married had broken on and receded from the foreshore of Percy's mind for some days before it established itself firmly in the hinterland. He was the first, after Chloe, to be told; naturally, since he was the nearest relation and would himself be materially affected. But the affair smelt so damn peculiar and un-English that he was convinced that there was some unrevealed design at the back of it. Realising that a man of Wing's age who had played for Essex—and, mark you, a clergyman at that—and an old lady like Aunt Essie, practically Percy's mother, didn't go tying themselves up in knots at the age of ninety just for a little bit of fun, and rejecting his immediate idea that Chloe had arranged it all so as to spoil Maisie's week-end, Percy had had to look elsewhere for a solution. Money, obviously. The best that he could make of it was that one or other was hoping thus to dodge death duties or something.

The true explanation came later, when Miss Walsh offered to make over her house to him and Maisie.

'Dashed sporting of the old lady,' said Percy, 'and explains a lot. What about it, old girl? Don't think that we've got to go and live there at Aunt Essie's say-so.'

'Darling,' said Maisie anxiously, 'actually we're living in London, aren't we, I mean *actually*? Because of your work.'

'Well, that's the point. There's a house down Woking way, quite close to old George as it happens, and there's a damn good train service, and to cut a long story short, old George, that's George Chater, I've told you about him—'

'Yes, darling,' said Maisie.

'Well, he knows most of the directors, and if that gets about, and you do happen to be putting your feet up in a non-smoker and any of these Pacifists starts anything, well, they're damn civil to you—well, that's how it is, old girl. What it comes to, Woking with London practically on your doorstep and George Chater round the corner, or keep the flat on and have Aunt Essie's house for week-ends arid a bit of shooting with Bob Perriman up at the Hall.'

'Which would *you* like, darling?'

'Well, there it is. Mind you, I'm not saying that when you've been brought up in a place as a kid, and having lent a hand at one time or another with practically every inside lavatory in the village, not to mention the meat-safe at the Fox and Grapes which meant a first-class job of lockpicking, well, somehow or other you do get a sort of feeling for the old place.'

'Oh, you do, darling!' agreed Maisie, who hadn't got that sort of feeling yet for old George.

'Then you think we ought to take Bridglands off Aunt Essie's hands for her?'

Maisie most certainly did; and since it was now clear that Aunt Essie could only have been marrying old Wing at her time of life in order to provide Percy and Maisie with a house, it was nice to think that her self-sacrifice was not to be thrown away.

Miss Walsh had had a recurring dream since she had promised to marry Alfred. She was coming to an age when it was not always easy to distinguish between sleep and the half-sleep which precedes and follows it: between the thoughts for which she was in some degree responsible and those which came, unrelated and unbidden, into a mind beyond her control; so that sometimes it was difficult to be sure whether she had dreamed a thing, or wilfully imagined it, or even whether the thing had actually happened in some far corner of her memory. Perhaps this wasn't a dream, it was just something of which she had let herself become afraid, something which had started in her mind as a joke and slowly grown more real, more possible and more terrifying. They should have been married quietly at a Registry Office in London; so ridiculous at their age to parade in church before all their neighbours; but then Alfred would never have believed that God had joined them together. So he would have to publish his own banns of marriage. He would stand before them all, and say, 'I publish the banns of marriage between—' and everybody would sit up suddenly, fully awake now—who is it going to be?—'between Alfred John Winghampton'— and from the back of the church would come a long whistle of surprise—*Whew*!—'and Esmeralda Walsh'—a louder and a longer whistle, and then, most shattering of all, an utterly spontaneous 'My God!' No, she couldn't face it.

'So you see,' she explained to Chloe, 'I'm a cowardly old woman, and I've come to London for three weeks, and here I am. Say you don't think too badly of me.'

'Darling,' said Chloe, 'you were coming to London for your clothes anyhow, weren't you?'

'Of course I was,' said Essie, nodding to herself. 'Silly of me. I knew I had some reason for running away.'

'What did you tell Alfred?'

'Had to see my solicitor. I shall have to, of course. I wouldn't tell Alfred a lie.'

'And the marriage is the 27th. We shall be busy, darling, we shan't have too much time. Well now, where are you going for your honeymoon?'

'Alfred talked about the Holy Land, but we decided on the Vicarage instead. After four days at Torquay. Leaving the other for a real holiday in the spring. Chloe dear, do you ever think how silly some of the things are which we say quite naturally?'

'Darling, if I thought about that, I should never say anything.'

'I mean things like the Holy Land. When Alfred said it, it sounded just like a place you go to, but if you say over to yourself "I am going to the holy land", it sounds such an odd thing to say. And then there's Divinity. I remember when Percy was a small boy he got marks at school for something called Divinity.'

'Are you sure?'

'Oh, yes, he had a prize for Divinity. But how can you call knowledge of Jewish history "Divinity", Chloe? It seems so strange.'

'I must polish up my divinity,' murmured Chloe. 'Absolutely crazy.'

'And then think of writing "Xmas". Not that I would dream of writing it. But to save themselves the trouble of writing "Christ" people make a cross, because he died on the Cross; and I suppose, if he had been broken on the wheel, as he might have been if he had been an Englishman, they would write "Omas". It's so hideously vulgar, isn't it? Such an insult. Chloe dear, I get very strange thoughts into my head just now, I suppose it is because I am going to marry a clergyman.'

'Alfred is very broad-minded. He won't expect you to agree with him about everything. Why do I say that to *you*, Essie? You know him a hundred times better than I do.' 'That's what frightens me rather. I'm so afraid of putting ideas into his head which oughtn't to be there. Or, worse still, of finding that they were there all the time, and had had to be hidden.'

'Darling, you can't be a clergyman all these years, and not know all the answers.'

'No.' Miss Walsh was silent for a little. Then she gave herself a shake, and said, 'Now I'll tell you what I want, and then you'll think of all the other things.'

'Come into my bedroom,' said Chloe, getting up. 'That's the place to talk about clothes in.'

Miss Walsh was married at the end of October, for why should they wait who had waited so long; she was married in a hat, with one attendant, who was Chloe; and, since all Alfred's contemporaries were now elderly married men, it was Percy who attended the bridegroom. He knew all about it; having been, it seemed, best man some years before to a friend of his of the name of Chater. George Chater. He entertained the other guests with many interesting stories of that occasion.

# 2

Mrs Winghampton was happy. She had been married to Alfred for four months, and at times it seemed to her that she had lived at the Vicarage with him for all the forty years of his service there. It was silly of her to have been an old maid for so long, when she was not by nature an old maid. If she had had any sense at all, she would have proposed to Alfred fifteen years ago. Fifteen years! Why, she might almost have had a child of her own then, or would that have been dangerous? And would she have been a good mother? She decided that she would have been an indifferent mother, and that things were better as they were.

They were very good as they were. What had been frightening her, she realised now, was not the physical but the mental intimacy of married life. Alfred had always been so charming, so courtly to her, so—yes, it was a lovely word to-day, so old-fashioned. The leisured elaboration of his talk, the homage which he paid both to her and to himself by his feeling for style, had given a savour to his conversation which she had feared to lose. In the flow of catch phrases and household jokes which sprang so naturally from intimate contact, the careless 'dears' and 'darlings' and 'old boys', the thoughts so well anticipated that they needed only the beginnings of expression, how much of the scholar and gentleman she loved would be submerged?

She need not have feared. Alfred remained the courtly Alfred he had always been. There was no likelihood that he would ever become Alf.

But, as she had hinted to Chloe, there is a difference between Miss Walsh, listening in a mildly co-operative spirit to a well-known Sunday voice, her thoughts free to wander from God to garden and from garden to Lady Perriman's hat, and Mrs Winghampton taking intimate part in her husband's sermons both as shepherd and flock, half of herself up there in the pulpit with him, holding his hand, half of herself down here, each separate member of the congregation in turn, criticising him. She would find herself thinking 'Oh, Alfred, you *can't* believe that!' and 'Alfred dear, look! There's the Stratton boy just down from Cambridge. He wouldn't have come at all, only he didn't want to hurt his mother's feelings. What do you think he's thinking when you run away from your own argument? "All parsons are like that." He's intelligent. You *must* remember.' And then 'Alfred dearest! The little Conyers girl! Just behind me. You know about her, don't you? Her father beat her horribly and was sent to prison. She came down here to live with her aunt; you remember? *Don't* tell her that God is just like a father to us.' Sometimes she would look round guiltily, fearing, so urgent were her thoughts, that she had cried them aloud.

She wondered if all clergymen's wives went through the same experience, and then remembered that she was different from all other clergymen's wives, because they hadn't lived alone for years and years with all that time in which to think. It must be very difficult for clergymen, she thought now. They decide to take orders when they are twenty; either because their fathers want them to, and they must earn a living somehow, or (more often, she hoped) because they have an enthusiastic faith in all that they have been taught as children, and a burning desire to tell the world of the all-loving God in whom they believe. But, oh dear me, how many of us have had a belief in a person at twenty, and lost it at forty; how many of us have changed all our ideas as we grew and experienced and thought and learnt? How many Liberals at twenty have become Conservatives, how many Conservatives Liberals? How many early passions for an actor or actress, a poet, a composer, a hero, have seemed silly to us afterwards? How many young people brought up in orthodox families have lost their faith? But clergymen must never lose their schoolboy faith, must never change their schoolboy opinions, nor repent their early loves. What they thought and felt at twenty they must go on thinking and feeling for ever.

You can't be a clergyman for forty years without knowing all the answers, said Chloe. Could she talk to Alfred one day without disturbing his convictions? Well, that was the point, were they convictions?

I'll talk to him, she decided. I mustn't get in the way of thinking that we can't talk about things.

It was a Sunday night after supper. He stretched his long legs out to the flickering logs, sighed with happy tiredness, and said as he filled his pipe: 'The thought that, although we are sitting one on each side of the fire, I shall not be looking at my watch in a few minutes, and wondering where I have thrown my hat, still has power to bewilder me. I will not say that it is too good to be true, because goodness is the universal truth, but it leaves me in some doubt as to whether *I* am good enough for it to be true.'

Essie gave him a little smile and said, 'I shouldn't call you a really bad man, Alfred.'

'I endeavour not to be, my dear, and trust that the endeavour will not escape the notice of my parishioners.'

'Alfred,' said Essie casually, her eyes on her knitting, as if it were there that her interest lay, 'have you ever had any doubts as to the truth of what you preach?'

'Often, my dear, often.'

'What happens when a clergyman really begins to doubt?'

'I should say that he will follow one of three courses. One: he will resign his living; which will be a little hard on his family if he be a married man. Two: he will tell himself that Doubt is put into his mind by the Devil, and must be driven out. He may overcome the Devil by argument, of his own or another's inception, or he may run away from him; telling himself, in this event, that his reason is not to be exercised in what is clearly a matter of faith. In other words, he will stop thinking.'

At this it seemed that the Vicar had stopped talking. Essie waited, and then said gently: 'And the third way?'

The Vicar took the pipe out of his mouth and studied the ashes in the bowl.

'Is it a way, or is it just a retreat which I have found? To be convinced of the ultimate goodness of things, to be convinced that we are put into the world to take advantage of the beauty of the world and of the knowledge hidden there; to recognize that God is a mystery of Whom none can speak with assurance, but to believe that if we pray to Him He will help us to come closer to Him; to be sure that He is less concerned with the doctrine which comes from our mouths than with the desire which lies deep in our hearts; to be a friend to all in this parish, rich and poor, good and bad, of whatever creed; to help them by precept, and, in my humble way, by example, to love God, to love the beautiful world which He has made, to love the people whom He has put into it; and then, for his mercies are great, dear Essie, to tell myself that He will forgive me for making use for this purpose of the forms of a Church in which I do not now wholly believe.'

Essie put down her knitting and fell on her knees by his side.

'Oh, Alfred,' she said, taking his hand within hers, 'dear Alfred. My dear love.'

'We cannot praise God and reject the gifts which He has given us. Never be afraid, dearest, to make use of your mind. Nor must you ever be afraid of letting it lead you down a path where I cannot follow. Whatever you believe, I know that you are good, and this, I truly think, is all that matters.' He kissed her hand, and said, 'I am glad that you have found me out.'

'Yes, I have found you out,' said Essie, as she went back to her chair. 'I am glad too. Because I like what I have found.'

The Vicar leant forward and dropped another log on the fire.

'This morning,' he announced cheerfully, 'speaking for all of us, I said that we were miserable sinners. Speaking for myself, I shall now correct that. A sinner alas! yes. But *not* miserable. Very, very happy.'

# 3

Maisie was happy too. Maisie liked being married. She liked Percy to come into the bathroom and talk to her as she lay in the warm, scented water, and, when she stepped out, to take her on his knees and dry her, and then turn her over and, to the accompaniment of squeals of delighted protest, smack her bottom for her in an open-minded, open-handed way, as being generally good for discipline. She liked him to come into her bedroom when she sat at her dressing-table in her cami-knickers, and drop sixpennies down her front (though she preferred half-crowns); and, if this meant a certain amount of re-dressing, helped by Percy, well, she didn't mind that either. Not yet; though one could imagine that it would grow wearisome.

Percy, no doubt, saw himself as something of a sheikh and Maisie as his slave-girl. She was well content with this arrangement upstairs, but downstairs it was her tight little mouth which made it clear who was in command. She had won him, and she was going to keep him and exploit him. Percy, too, was content. It delighted him that the little woman knew which side their bread was buttered, saw through a brick wall as well as the next man, and, in short, had no flies on her. It added to his masculine pride in the little woman to pretend humorously to his friends that she kept him in his place and ruled him with a bloody rod of iron b'Jove; unaware for the most part that this was exactly what she did. She could hardly be said to love him; but her two younger sisters had married before her, he had £4,000 a year, a flat in town, and a nice house in the country, and they understood each other thoroughly; which meant that she understood Percy. It was almost an ideal marriage for both of them.

They came down for a week-end one Saturday morning at the end of March and found a letter from Essie waiting for them. Chloe was at the Vicarage, and would they come in to dinner that evening.

'You'd like it, old girl?' said Percy, handing her the letter.

Maisie took it, began to read, and said indignantly, 'Percy! It's *my* letter!' She picked up the envelope. 'Addressed to *me*!'

'Well, dammit, I knew it was from Aunt Essie, I ought to know her handwriting by now, considering she wrote to me every week when I was at school, and damned interesting letters for an old girl like that—'

'She couldn't have been very old when you were at school.'

'A good thirty if she was a day.'

Maisie, at twenty-five, saw his point, but didn't see what it had to do with opening her letters.

'My dear girl, she's *my* aunt, isn't she, what's the harm in it?'

'It's the principle of the thing. I don't mind *showing* you all my letters' (she made a mental reservation in the case of two possible correspondents), 'but they *are* mine, and—'

'That's all right, old girl, nothing to make a fuss about. Naturally if I see Percy Walsh on an envelope, in a handwriting I've known all my life, I take it for granted it's for me—

'Oh, well, if you thought it was yours—'

'Well, of course. Dammit, a fella doesn't go about opening another fella's letters.'

'Well, naturally I wouldn't *dream* of opening yours.' 'That's all right, old girl,' said Percy kindly.

Maisie accepted his forgiveness, confident that she had established her point. But she still didn't seem quite happy about something.

'I'd better 'phone after lunch,' she said, 'and say we'd love to. Percy, who *is* Chloe exactly?'

'How d'you mean? You've met her.'

'Well, has she got any relations?'

'Not that I know of, and none the worse for that.'

'What was her father? I suppose that's where her money comes from?'

'Fella called Marr.' He laughed loudly. 'Funny that. He ought to have been called Parr.'

'Yes, but what did he do? Was he Colonel Marr, or Doctor Marr, or what? I suppose he had money of his own.'

'You'd better ask her. Dammit, I don't even know what Wing's father was.'

'But she must have some *background*.' Maisie's own background was solid. It included a dentist father, usually referred to by Maisie as a doctor who, for some whim, had specialised in diseases of the jaw.

'Didn't notice it, I was looking at her foreground,' said Percy, achieving his second joke that day. Maisie still wasn't laughing, and he had to laugh alone, reminding himself to share it with old George on Monday.

'Well, but how did you meet her, darling?'

'I dunno. Sat next to her at dinner, I suppose. Yes, that's right, and then went and had tea with her, we played some bloody awful game jumping over each other—'

Maisie's eyebrows went up. She couldn't picture Percy jumping over anybody.

'—not chess, I know chess—'

'Oh, I see. Draughts?'

'Was that it? Damned unfair anyway, because I'd never played before and didn't know whether I was winning or losing—well, there it was, we got in the way of going around a bit, meaning nothing, of course, Chloe's not like that—'

'Not like what?'

An abortive attempt by Percy to give a delicate impersonal explanation made the matter quite clear.

'She's not religious, is she?' asked Maisie, who could think of no other reason for not being like that.

'Good lord, no. I mean she's never said anything to *me* about it. Of course, you can't get away from the fact that she clicked with old Wing as soon as they set eyes on each other. I say, that's rather an idea, old girl. I believe you've about hit it.' The idea seemed to please him. It explained what had always puzzled him, why Chloe had ignored all the opportunities which he had given her. 'Religious, that's it. Damn clever of you, old girl, to spot it like that.'

Maisie, too, was pleased. In public she might point out that Chloe was too big, too tall, for perfection; but privately she couldn't deny her beauty. Where Percy was concerned, every good-looking woman was a rival, save those who had renounced the world; and even most of these, according to that book by Botticelli or somebody which there'd been that row about at home, didn't seem to have renounced all of it. But that was in the Middle Ages, when religion was a thing everybody had to have. It was different to-day. If Chloe were really religious in a big way, then, however beautiful, she was neither a rival for the future nor a skeleton from the past. With a lighter heart Maisie went to ring up the Vicarage.

# 4

It was pleasant to sit in the sun again and watch the drift of daffodils under the trees, and know that all summer was in front of you.

'This,' said the Vicar, 'is part of the garden—indeed, the only part of the garden—which I can show you without shame. Now that Essie has taken it in hand, things will be different. 'She has already formed many plans to which I have said, "Yes, my dear, that would be delightful," but which will only reveal themselves fully to me at a later season. But this corner has looked after itself for many years, and grows ever more beautiful.'

'I always imagine a Vicarage garden as a rather untended place,' said Chloe, 'with beautiful old trees in it. Particularly a cedar and a copper beech. Don't disappoint me about that.'

'You need have no fears. You weren't brought up in a Vicarage?'

'No. I used to play in one. A long time ago.'

'And it had a copper beech?'

'Yes. It was the first one I had seen. I was very proud because I had been in a garden with a copper beech in it. I thought it was the only one in England.'

'You had a happy childhood, Chloe?'

'Until I was thirteen. Then I grew up rather quickly.'

The Vicar waited; but she seemed to have nothing more to say on that subject.

'You must come down in the summer, and see what Essie has made of the garden.'

'I may be going abroad quite soon,' said Chloe.

'But you will come back.'

'I don't know.'

There was another long silence, and then the Vicar said: 'You have made two people—I think I may say two people—so very happy, dear Chloe, that we should like to think that you also were going to be happy.'

'Dear Alfred.' She patted his hand. 'It *was* my doing, wasn't it?'

'Undoubtedly.'

'I'm glad. I'm proud. I shall always remember that. I shall bore St Peter with it, until he has to let me in.'

'Essie and I will come down to the Gate to welcome you,' smiled the Vicar, 'and to use such little influence as we may have.'

'Perhaps I shall be there first. You never know. I shall say that I'm waiting for some friends.'

'You're not afraid of death, Chloe?'

'Couldn't fear it less.'

'Whatever happens afterwards?'

'Whatever happens. If we are to believe what you preach, Alfred, it can't be very terrible.'

Has she, too, found me out, he thought.

'What I preach,' he said firmly, 'is that you must believe in God, repent your sins, and cast yourself on His infinite mercy.'

Chloe smiled at him a little mischievously.

'But isn't that what I am doing? Saying that it can't be very terrible.'

The lines round his mouth deepened as he said, 'It is perhaps a slightly uncanonical approach to the subject.'

'You would rather I believe that God was wicked and looked forward to giving me a Hell of a time, but that if I denied my belief and assured Him that He was good, it 'would be Heaven? Which of us is going to repent, I or God?'

'Chloe, Chloe,' he said, shaking his head at her. 'But it's a way of looking at it,' he thought.

'Sorry, Alfred. Do you mind talking about these things?'

'Not if it be in a spirit of reverence, my dear. Not if you are in the mood to talk about them.'

'Isn't "reverence" rather begging the question? Hasn't everybody his own idea of God? How can you reverence somebody else's idea which seems utterly false to you?'

'One speaks reverently, or at least not irreverently, to another person of his mother, even though one only reveres one's own mother.'

'Mothers!' said Chloe with what seemed to the Vicar extraordinary bitterness.

He looked at her in astonishment, and then looked away again. Here was a flash from Chloe's past, lighting her up for one revealing moment, and leaving her more hidden, so that now he wondered if he had indeed seen anything, or what it was that he had seen. Was it her own mother whom she was remembering; or, God forgive him for the thought, was it her own motherhood? He had no authority to ask. If he said nothing, if he waited quietly, perhaps she would tell him. He felt very close to her. With all the force of his wise and loving mind he was telling her that she could trust him, that it would help her if she trusted him.

Chloe explored her bag, produced a cigarette-case and a lighter, lit a cigarette, closed her bag again, blew a cloud of smoke in front of her eyes as if to veil herself, and began, it seemed, to speak.

'Hallo, Wing, old man! Hallo, old girl!'

Percy was waving to them. Percy and Maisie were coming across the grass. 'There you are, young Maisie, what did I tell you?' Percy was saying to her. 'Confessing.' Maisie agreed; accepting the interpretation without prejudice to a doubt whether penitents usually smoked in the confessional.

Six feet of Mr Winghampton rose up. One almost expected to see a long lean hand stretched out, and the earth riven beneath Percy's feet, leaving Maisie surprised but still efficient, alone. Mr Winghampton fought down the sudden hate he felt for Percy, telling himself that it was not hate, it was only anger, and that he did well to be angry; telling himself that a priest had no business to be angry, that Percy was in no way to blame for appearing at that one moment of all possible moments. He took out a handkerchief and patted his lips, feeling really shocked by himself, by his unjustifiable anger with an innocent man. God forgive me, he thought; and prayed that the moment might not be lost for ever.

Chloe stood beside him. She seemed neither to regret nor to welcome the interruption: as if, when she had been about to speak, she had forgotten that Alfred was there, and had been interrupted only in a memory which could be recalled or dismissed at will. She gave them both a welcoming smile.

'Something wrong with your telephone, old man,' said Percy, after greetings were over. 'Maisie rang up—'

'I rang Aunt Essie up as soon as we got in, but couldn't get an answer. Just to say we shall love to come to dinner to-night.'

'She's in the house,' said the Vicar, beginning to lead the way.

'No, we won't come in, old man, we shall be seeing you to-night.'

'I rang up again directly after lunch,' said Maisie, 'but couldn't get an answer.'

'Dear me!'

'I'll have a look at it to-night, see what I can do. Well, old girl, how's the world been treating you?'

'With its usual well-meaning hospitality,' smiled Chloe. 'You're looking very well, Maisie.'

'Well, actually, I haven't been too good—'

'Nothing in *your* line, old man,' laughed Percy, 'bit of tummy trouble.' His manner was one large confidential wink. 'We're just going down to the village, see you to-night.'

'And you will tell Aunt Essie how much we are looking forward to it, and about the telephone? I'm sorry we interrupted you and Chloe.'

'Well, now you can stop interrupting them,' said Percy, pulling at her. 'Cheerio.'

Alone with Chloe again, the Vicar made a tentative movement back to the seat; but she put her arm in his and said, 'Now show me that copper beech you promised me.' She was mistress of herself again, and the moment of revelation, he knew, had gone for ever.

# Chapter Nineteen

## 1

Barnaby and Jill were dining at the Moulin d'Or when the news came to them. It was June: Barnaby had bought a Star for the cricket scores as they walked up Shaftesbury Avenue, and had put it in his pocket to open later. They called each other Jill and Barnaby now, and on suitable occasions he was allowed to pay for her dinner. He was beginning to hope that perhaps one day he would be allowed to pay for more than that.

When they had given their orders, he put his hand to his pocket, drew it away, and said:

'I was in a restaurant once when a man and his wife came in, must have been his wife, and the man took out a paper and read it silently all through dinner, and then they went out. Rude, I call it.' He might have added: That was in another life when I used to go around with a girl called Chloe. We laughed at it together.

'All right,' said Jill, smiling at him, 'I get you. You can look at the cricket for two minutes.'

'I'll read it to you, just to show the place that we are together in this.'

He read, and they made appropriate comments.

'Anything else in the paper?'

'Not to matter at dinner-time.' He glanced at the front page, and said, 'Oh, an air-liner crash.'

'Where?'

'Holland. How little, how horribly little accidents matter if they don't concern you personally. Do you think that a real saint would grieve as much over an accident in China as over one in his own country, and as much if it happened to strangers as he would if it happened to his dearest friends? Ought one to?'

'Every moment dies a man, every moment one is born.'

'I know. You'd have no time for anything else. First lilies, and then napkin-rings, and then lilies again—Oh, there were two English people on the plane, that brings it a bit nearer home.'

'Have you ever flown, Barnaby?'

'Never. Wait a bit, there's something in the Stop Press. The names of the— Oh, my God!'

'What is it, darling?' asked Jill, alarmed. He didn't hear the darling, she re-assured herself quickly, he's not thinking of me, I hope it isn't anybody he knows, I mean really fond of.

Barnaby pulled himself together.

'It's nothing,' he said. 'Just somebody I used to know. Rather a shock seeing her name like that.' He put the paper back in his pocket, and took a long drink. This mustn't spoil our evening, he thought. I mustn't think about it till I get home. After all, it doesn't matter now.

'Would you rather I didn't talk, Barnaby? Or would you rather tell me about it? Or shall we talk about other things?'

'You darling,' he thought. He took the paper from his pocket saying, 'There you are.' She read: 'The names of the two British passengers are now given as Lord Sheppey and Miss Chloe Marr. All the occupants of the plane are known to have been killed.'

'That's the girl in the box that first evening we went out together?'

'Yes.' He saw her standing there, that unfathomable look of reproach, of hurt, of apology—what was it?—on her face. Six months ago! And he hadn't seen her since.

'Who is Lord Sheppey? Was he in the box that night? I suppose they were together in the plane?'

'I suppose so. He's some sort of hard-faced business man, you know the sort, public and political services. No, he wasn't in the box,

I've never met him. He wasn't a particular friend of hers, but she did know him, I believe. They might have met in the plane accidentally, of course. Probably did.'

'She looked lovely that night.'

'Yes, didn't she? I don't know how she'd have managed as an old woman. Not very well, perhaps.'

'Did you know she was in Holland?'

'No. I haven't seen her since that night, as it happens. She might have been anywhere.'

He realized again that it was six months since he had seen her. Why? I suppose each of us has waited for the other to ring up, and— there was Jill. There *is* Jill. So young and fresh and straight.

He used to be in love with her, thought Jill. But he hasn't seen her since that night we went out together. So perhaps— Oh, I *know* he's nice, I know I can trust him. He won't ever hurt me. Their hands crept towards each other . . .

I *mustn't* think about her, Barnaby kept telling himself. He knew that, if he thought about her, he would be thinking that the past was finished with now, wiped out; that no reproachful look could ever reach him now; that now there could be no awkward meeting; that never now could her loveliness come between him and Jill, tempting him to a moment's disloyalty. If he thought about her now, if he were utterly honest with himself, he would have to admit that he was glad that— Oh God, keep me from that final baseness. Poor Chloe! Poor lovely Chloe! How much of my life has been yours!

# 2

Carol and Claudia were having breakfast in their little house in Chelsea. Chelsea had always been Claudia's ambition. It was, she felt, artistic without being highbrow; also it was across the Park from the Aunts, which meant the other side of the world. Another advantage was that Claude was quite close, and now that he and Carol got on so well together, he would be dropping in on them in the evenings; and, while the men discussed all the latest movements, she would be darning her husband's socks, and putting in an occasional suggestive comment which would give them a new perspective. Unfortunately Claude had been somewhere in France for the last three months. She was reading a letter from him now; while Carol read the paper, as a good husband should.

'Good lord!' said Carol.

'What is it, darling? A lovely funny letter from Claude, you shall read it directly.'

'That friend of yours we had supper with, Chloe Marr—'

'Darling, what do you mean, she was at the wedding.'

'Was she? Believe it or not, I had eyes for only one girl at the wedding.'

'Darling!'

'Darling!'

'And she came to our party.'

'I was so busy shaking hands and saying "Sherry or champagne cocktail" to the same people over and over again— Yes, I do remember now. She was.'

'Why, what's happened to her?'

Carol remembered suddenly what had happened to her.

'Oh, darling, I'm a brute, forgive me! Why did I get talking like this? She's dead.'

'Dead?' cried Claudia, dropping her letter. '*Dead?*'

'Killed in an aeroplane crash.'

'*Chloe?* Are you sure? Does it say—it might have been another—'

'Miss Chloe Marr.'

'Chloe dead! Carol! Oh, Carol!' She went round to his chair, and fell on her knees and clung to him. If Chloe could die, Carol could die, anybody could die.

'Oh, sweetheart, were you so fond of her?'

'If it hadn't been for her, we should never have met each other.'

'We should,' said Carol stoutly.

'We couldn't *not* have met *some* time, could we? But we shouldn't have been in your play together, we shouldn't be married now. Oh, Chloe darling!' She began to cry quietly, and, as he tried to comfort her, said, 'There's Claude too. Oh, Carol, there's Claude!'

'He was in love with her, wasn't he?'

She nodded.

'I thought he was that night, though he doesn't give much away. Was she in love with him?' Claudia shook her head. 'Oh, well, that's something.'

'He'd be just as unhappy,' she sobbed.

'Not now. I mean he'd have been unhappy all the time. It's a horrible thing to say, but in a way it may be the best thing for him.'

'Yes. Lend me your hanky.' She took it from his breast pocket and dried her eyes. 'May I look?'

They looked at the paper together.

'Good lord!' said Carol again.

'Lord Sheppey?'

'Yes.'

'That's your godfather, darling?'

'Well, if you like to call him that. That's the man. Did you know she knew him?'

'No. But she seemed to know everybody. There's really no reason why she should have known him at all, is there? They might just have been in the same plane.'

'Yes, of course. Except—what would she be doing in Holland by herself?'

'She might have had an old mother there or something. We knew very little about her. I mean the family.'

She went back to her place and tried to get on with her letter. Carol picked up the paper, frowning, hoping for more light.

'What sort of man was he?' said Claudia suddenly, her mind still with Chloe.

'I never met him, darling, except at the font, when I was probably thinking of something else. I told you.'

'Yes, but the Aunts must have said something. Wasn't there ever a photograph?'

'I suppose so. In the Family Album. But Aunt Harry would have torn that up. The others talked sometimes.'

'What did they say?'

'Well, the general idea seemed to be that he was extremely repulsive in a perfectly fascinating way. Or the other way round, if you like. Amy said an odd thing once. She's a bit crackers, Amy, don't you think? Well, I suppose they all are. She said, "When he smiled, you felt that somebody really had come for you." I'm going to use that in a play one day. It gives a marvellous suggestion that, if you went with him, you'd be selling yourself to the devil.'

'That was a long time ago.'

'Oh, yes, he'd be fifty now.'

'Darling, do you think they *were* running away together?'

'Well, but why? Why not get married, if that's how they felt about it?'

'Perhaps he'd got a wife.'

'I looked him up in *Who's Who* once. Doesn't say so there, but that proves nothing. I suppose Chloe may have had a husband, for all you knew.'

'Oh, darling, how absurd!'

'Why?'

Claudia tried to think why. 'Of course,' she said, 'if you were writing a play, you *could* give her a husband hidden away somewhere, and make it seem plausible.'

'I certainly could. And give him a wife and make it equally plausible. And, good lord, if it comes to that, I could make them married to each other, hating it, agreeing to separate, and then, years after, being drawn together again in spite of themselves—I say,' he added eagerly, 'is that a play or is it?'

'Oh, darling, what a wonderful idea!' said Claudia. 'And then you could get that line in. You *must* do it! Promise me!'

'Well, it's something to start on anyway,' said Carol thoughtfully . . . John Preston began to give his mind to it.

# 3

'Well, he's dead, and about time too.'

'Harry! You oughtn't to say such things!'

'Don't be a fool, Jo, you're as glad as I am, only you're afraid to say so. And what's more, he's killed another woman.'

'Oh, Harry!'

'She was at the wedding,' put in Amy.

'Oh, my dear, so she was!'

'What wedding?'

'Ours, Harry, who else's? She was a friend of dear Claudia's.'

'Don't remember her.'

'Yes, it's all coming back to me. That tall, very lovely woman. And so gracious. I remember her telling me that she had never been to Bournemouth. But of course they may not have been together.'

'If she was very lovely, you may be quite sure they were together. That man would have been sniffing round her—'

'Harry!'

'Don't you think so, Amy?'

'Men are like that,' said Amy, with a smile which understood all, and forgave all.

'That man was.'

'Do you think they were going to get married? How strange that she should have come to our house. But then why not get married properly in England?'

'Married! Ha! I should like to know how many wives he'd got already.'

'Harry!'

'She may have been a poetess or an actress.'

'What *has* that got to do with it, Bibs?'

'Then she'd keep her maiden name.'

'You mean *she* might have been married, dear?'

'That sounds more like him. Taking a married woman away from her husband and killing her.' She held up the paper and said fiercely, 'Look at the great ugly devil! Grinning at the world.'

'Oh, is there a photograph in yours? There's none in this one. May I see?'

'*No!*' She tore the paper again and again, scattering the pieces round her. Then she put her head in her hands, and sobbed, 'Oh, Jo, Jo, it all comes back so horribly!'

'Darling Harry!' Jo was by her side. 'But we have our Carol now, and soon, pray God, dear Carol's baby.' 'But I'm so *old*! Older than any of you.'

'Harry,' said Jo gently, 'you know that's not true.' Bibs was far away. Two lines had come into her head.

*Toll for the dead, the dead that are no more!*
*For we still live . . . but they have gone before!*

Amy smiled at them all. They didn't understand.

# 4

I'm glad I got away from her before. I'm glad I did it myself, not leave it to this fellow or God to take her away from me. I was free a long time ago. Of course I went on thinking about her for a bit. Only yesterday, as it happened. Well, now I shan't. It's over. It was never really over before. Anything might have happened. One couldn't help imagining things . . .

*What* was the man's name? Lord something. Oh, here we are— Sheppey. Who's he? . . . James Muggeridge. My God, what a name. Who wouldn't want to be a peer with a name like that? Muggeridge. Sounds familiar. Where have I heard—Oh, of course. 'I, Carol Muggeridge, take thee, Claudia Mary'—wonder if he was any relation. Wonder if—dammit, that explains it! *That's* why she was trembling inside all through the service! I thought it was just the wedding, but it was the wedding *and* Muggeridge.

Had she been married to him years ago, and loathed it, and left him? But if the thought of it was so horrible, why did she go back to him? Oh, Chloe darling, these last few days, wondering what to do, trying to make up your mind! Well, you did make it up. It's the only way, you can't keep hanging about. I made up *my* mind. I'm glad I did . . .

Chloe. The most beautiful woman of the day, and I'm nobody yet, and she let me kiss her. Nothing can take that away. And of course we couldn't have got married anyway, she was much too old.

# 5

'Well, young Maisie, what have *you* been up to? Good, I could do with a drink.'

'Oh, hallo, Percy! You're back early, aren't you? Had a good day?'

'I don't know what you call a good day. Some bloody fella pushed into my taxi just as I was telling the driver where to go. Had the nerve to say he'd been there all the time and I hadn't noticed him. I said to the driver, "Was your flag up or wasn't it? My eyesight's as good as the next man's, and I know if a flag's upside down or not!" You won't believe it, but he said he was waiting for the lights to change before he put it down, because the other fella had only just got in, and this other fella said, "That's right!" It was a damn conspiracy. Well, I said to the fella—'

'Is that the evening paper?' She held out a hand.

'What? Oh, yes. Chloe's dead, by the way. I meant to have told you.'

'Percy! What do you mean? *Dead?*'

'Well, you'll see in the paper, old girl. I'm just telling you. Plane crash.'

Maisie snatched the paper from him. While she read, Percy mixed the drinks.

'Well!'

'Smells a bit funny, don't you think? Our Chloe! No wonder she was confessing to old Wing.'

'I thought you said she wasn't like that.'

'Like what. Here you are.'

'Thank you. You said she was religious.'

'Who did? Dammit, you don't even know that they were together, you don't know that they weren't going to get married, you don't know anything, and if it comes to that he might have been her uncle.' He emptied his glass and filled it again. He wasn't sure whether he was supposed to be attacking or defending Chloe, nor was he sure which he wanted to be.

'Well, who is he?'

'Sheppey? Higgs, Muggeridge and Higgs, Midland firm, but he'd had a finger in one or two pies in his time.'

'Shady?'

'Oh, lord, no,' said Percy, and, to be quite fair, added, 'Not to notice. I only met him once, mark you, so—'

'Oh, you *have* met him. At Miss Marr's flat?'

'Never saw them together there, or anywhere. It was a friend of old George's. George Chater. I was—'

Maisie said hurriedly, 'What was he like?' and on the improbable but alarming chance that he might misunderstand her, explained that she meant Lord Sheppey.

'Ugly little devil, if it's the man I'm thinking of.'

'How old?'

'Didn't ask him. About fifty from the cut of him.'

'How old was Chloe?'

'Twenty-eight.'

'You mean thirty-five, don't you?'

'Oh, nonsense, old girl, not a day more than thirty.'

'A man of fifty would be just about right for her. I suppose he had a wife.'

'Suppose so. If he hadn't at fifty, I should want to know what was the matter with him, not but what there's a damn lot of that about. According to old George, the stage—well, look at What's-is-name as an example—it's fairly riddled with it. Though what they can all see in it—'

'Well!' said Maisie again, still poring over every word of it.

So that was that. Good-bye, Miss Marr. Or Mrs Marr. Or Mistress Marr. They were getting a damned sight too fond of her at the Vicarage. Of *course* Percy had been to bed with her. Dozens of times. Well, you'd expect it if you married a man of his age, but you didn't want his pretty ladies hanging about him afterwards. Supposing Freddy turned up at the Vicarage, how much would Percy like it? Well, of course he didn't know anything about Freddy, and anyhow that was different . . .

She began to wonder where Freddy was now. It would be rather fun if . . .

A damn strange business altogether, thought Percy. Not quite English. Leaving all her old friends, and cutting off like that. Not like Chloe. A bit sinister, the whole thing. He'd miss her, dammit, they might have got together again later on. Not much sense of humour, of course, but with her looks that didn't matter so much. A pity.

He looked at his watch.

'About time for a bath, isn't it, old girl, if we're going to this show?'

'What? Oh! Yes.' She got up, and gave him her little-girl smile. 'You haven't kissed me yet, darling.'

'You'll get all of that you want in a moment, young Maisie,' said Percy fondly.

# 6

'Sweet, isn't she?' said Silvie, holding out the paper.

'All right. Who is it? Oh, the girl who got killed in that crash.'

'Poor thing. It doesn't say much about her. Well-known in London Society. I've seen her sometimes in *The Tatler*, dining with people, you know the way they do.'

'What else did she do?'

'Made some man happy, I expect,' said Silvie gently. 'Same as I do you. Or don't I?'

Humby went over to her where she lay on the sofa, and put his arms round her, and held her.

'You *swear* it will be all right, don't you?'

'What do you mean, you silly? Of course it will be all right. Why, it's nothing nowadays. Just like having your hair cut.' She laughed happily.

He went back to his chair and took up the paper again. Silvie returned to her knitting.

'I wonder what it's like,' she said, 'being as beautiful as that and going everywhere.'

'Hell, I should think.'

'Not all the time. Well, it's over for her now. Poor thing.'

'They don't show her legs,' said Humby. 'Just as well perhaps.'

'She'd have the finest silk all the time. Always. Wherever she went. That helps more than you think.'

'Still I'm glad I married *you*.'

'So am I, Humby.' She gave a sigh of utter content. 'Oh, so am I!'

# 7

'Help yourself, Mrs Maddick. There's plenty in the pot.'

'Thank you, Mrs Radipole. I always says there's nothing like a nice cup of tea.'

'Well, it's been a nasty shock for you, and well may you want it.'

'That it has.'

'Does she leave you anything, if I might ask?'

'Hundred pounds.'

'No! Well, I never!'

'A hundred pounds, Mrs Radipole. She told me herself the day she made the will.'

'When would that be like?'

'All but the two days before she went off. The lawyer came and we had the whisky out, and when he'd gone, "Ellen," she says, "I've made my will and I've left you a hundred pounds, darling"— very loving she was at times. Well, I didn't know *what* to say, I was so struck aback; I said, "I'm sure that's very kind of you, Miss Marr, you're not thinking of accidents, I hope, because dangerous those flying machines may be, but they're not as dangerous as some people's driving" and she said, "Meaning me, Ellen?" and laughed, and I said, "Well, I'd feel safer with you up there than on the ground, Miss Marr," and so I would, Mrs Radipole—terrible reckless driver she was. But there, it's all wiped out now and she's with the blessed angels.' She sniffed and blew her nose.

'It was a mercy of Providence, Mrs Maddick, she did make a will—just in time as you might say.'

'I always say that Providence knows best and it's not for us to question. But now you'll understand, dear, why I can't say anything against Miss Marr; though I'm not saying after all the time I've been with her—'

'Ah, you've been with her a long time.'

'Well, it wasn't more than the five years come August—

'Seemed longer, I wouldn't be surprised.'

'It did that. I had a lot to put up with.' She sniffed again.

'I'm sure you did, dear. These society beauties, there's no pleasing them.'

'Like children they are. First one thing and then another. Up and down. Hot and cold. Can't make up their minds.'

Did she—?' Mrs Radipole made a motion with her hand.

'No, I will say that for her, not secret that is. Nor anything else, though I'm not saying she wouldn't take something at night to make her sleep. Slept very bad she did.'

Mrs Radipole nodded.

'What I've always said, Mrs Maddick, you can't sleep if you've anything on your conscience. And all that rackety life dancing till goodness knows when. Stands to reason.' She brought up her chair a little closer: 'Did you know she was going off with this lord?'

'Not if you'd come and told me yourself, Mrs Radipole, I wouldn't have believed it. Sir Everard Hale Baronet, that I *could* have believed, or His Grace the Duke of St Ives, or even that Mr Walsh, though he hadn't been married above a few months—'

'Ah, you've seen some fine men in your time, Mrs Maddick.'

293

'All sorts we've had, but this Lord Sheppey, well now I'll tell you. He used to ring up regular, and no matter when he rang it was always the same, Miss Marr's in her bath, will you ring later, Miss Marr's just gone out, she'll ring you when she comes back; never had a word to say to him, and he'd be going on at her day and night.'

'Wore her down as you might say. He never come to the door?'

'I've never so much as set eyes on him. Of course, being yooman I can't say for what happened when I wasn't there. Not sleeping there I can't say for what happened at night.'

'Ah!' She came a little closer. 'Would you say she was loose in her habits?'

'I can't answer yes or no to that question, Mrs Radipole. Loose in her talk I won't deny, and if it was most of it talk it wouldn't surprise me.'

'Yooman nature is yooman nature, dear, and she wouldn't go fighting it all those years.'

Ellen said solemnly, 'She didn't, Mrs Radipole.'

'Ah! Now we're getting somewheres.'

'It's my belief, and there's ways of knowing, she'd had a baby.'

'That's right, and you'd see better than most, Mrs Maddick. Well, I can't say you surprise me. I said just now, you heard me yourself, yooman nature is yooman nature I said. Being before you came to her of course.'

'I can't say for when it was, only being before my time as you say, Mrs Radipole. And I'll tell you what I think. If you want to look for the man you don't want to look farther than that aeroplane.'

'Well, that *is* saying something, Mrs Maddick.'

'I've been thinking it over. The way I look at it, it came over him at last to do the right thing by her, but she wouldn't have no more of him, and who's to blame her, being left like that; and then she thought, there's the poor little boy without a name, and he'd be a lord himself if I married his father, and for his sake I'll sacrifice myself, if you understand me, Mrs Radipole.'

'Well, of course I don't know her as you do, dear, but I've seen her photographs and I've seen his, and the first thing I says is, "Fancy a

lovely girl like her going off with a horrible creature like him," and ¡
it's as you say, then it *would* be a sacrifice.'

'Well, now she's gone to her last home, and what's to happen to
the poor little boy, if it *is* a little boy, the dear Lord only knows. Still,
I daresay a way will be found if we leave it to Him.'

'That's what I always say meself, Mrs Maddick. If there's a way to
be found, He'll find it.'

Ellen nodded, and then began to cry weakly.

'She was so b-beautiful, and now she's all b-broken up, and she
left me a hundred pounds!'

'There, dear, I know how you feel and it does credit to you. Have
another nice cup of tea with a little something in it this time.' She got
up and went to the cupboard.

# 8

'Such a little while ago she sat here with me, looking at the daffodils,'
said the Vicar. There were no daffodils now, there was no Chloe.

Essie put a hand on his knee for a moment.

'You mustn't be unhappy, Alfred. All beautiful things have their
day. There is no pleasure in old age for them.'

'That is true, my dear, and Death must have come very suddenly.
She was not afraid of death, she told me.' Yet he sighed, and shook his
head, little comforted.

'You are thinking of that man?'

'Yes. I wish I need not.'

'Must we assume that they were together?'

'She said that she was going abroad, that she might not come
back. She could hardly have meant alone.'

'They may have been married long ago, and separated. She might
have gone back to her maiden name. Then they came together again.'

'Do you believe that, Essie?' he asked eagerly.

'I haven't tried. I suppose I could if I wished to. But I just don't
feel that it matters. I can't believe that the first thing which God said,

poor unhappy ghost came back to Him, was, "*Were* they
.n 1925?"'

.happy?' said the Vicar, deciding to overlook the rest.

Jon't tell me she was happy, Alfred, I shan't believe you. I should
that the whole of her gay life was an attempt to hide from herself
.ow unhappy she was.'

'She was happy as a child. "Until I was thirteen," he quoted, "and
then I grew up rather quickly." What did she mean by that, Essie?'

'It's the dangerous age, when you accept your nature or are at
odds with it, perhaps for the rest of your life.'

'Something may have happened to her then, you think? If Percy
had not come, I might have heard the whole story.'

'A story, yes. It would not necessarily have been true.'

'You think she would have lied to me?' said the Vicar, shocked
and troubled.

'Women have their own code. You must know that by now, dear.'

The Vicar sighed.

'One is reluctantly bound to admit,' he said, 'that it is a weakness
of your sex not to take the truth very seriously. Moreover, on one or
two occasions, notably in the case of Mrs— on one or two occasions,
as I was saying, I have observed an apparent lack of all honour which
has horrified me.'

'You need not have been horrified, Alfred. It is natural.'

'You are very wise, my dear. It is not too late for me to learn
from you.'

'When you were at school, wasn't it considered bad form to
cheat against another boy, but good form to cheat against a master?'

'Well,' said the Vicar, considering this a little reluctantly, 'I won't say
*good* form, but certainly it was not reprehended—save, naturally, by
the master.'

'Why was that? Have you ever thought?'

'I am not sure that I have, my dear, but I shall think now.' He was
silent for a little, pulling at his lower lip. Then he said: 'I suppose it is
that, regarding all masters as his natural enemies, the boy feels that

they have such great and, as it seems to him, unfair advantages on their side, that he is entitled to protect himself with whatever weapon he can put his hand upon.'

'Then if women have grown to feel like that to *their* would-be masters, who for centuries had all the advantages on their side, it might be charitable to find some excuse for them.'

His head in his hand, 'My duty,' mused the Vicar, 'is to be the first to uphold a strict moral code for everybody, and at the same time to be the first to think of an excuse for anybody who breaks it. I am not complaining. I merely say that that seems to be my duty.' He leant back and stroked his chin. 'It will occur to the independent mind that it would be simpler all round if I neglected to uphold the moral code in the first place. I don't know where that takes us.'

Essie was not listening.

'Chloe was a very beautiful woman,' she said. 'It was a pleasure to look at her, to listen to her, and, since she was unfailingly charming to us, to be in her company. I imagine that she was selfish as most young women are, untruthful as all women are, and possibly more unscrupulous than most. How far her unhappiness was her own fault we have no means of knowing. Indeed, we know nothing of her but what we saw and heard.'

'And loved,' said the Vicar gently. 'You're crying, Essie.'

'No,' said Essie, shaking away a tear, 'I won't be sentimental about her. The daffodils have gone, but they will come back. Chloe will not come back, and the world has lost a little of its beauty. That is all.'

The Vicar was silent, trying to catch at something in his mind. There was an unhappy woman he had known once—no, not Chloe, but, like Chloe, of a magical beauty, he had often wondered about her as a boy; she too had died, and somebody had said something about her which summed it all up. Who was she? Was she in this world, or in that world which often seemed so much more real, the imagination of the writer? Something somebody bad said . . .

It is coming, it will come to me directly . . .

'What is it, Alfred? ''

297

Yes, that was it. That was the end of the story. Softly he murmured the lines to himself:

*'But Lancelot mused a little space;*
*He said, "She has a lovely face;*
*God in His mercy lend her grace,*
*The Lady of Shalott."'*

# Chapter Twenty

Everard Hale and Kitty Clavering were having supper at the Savoy, at the table where he had sat so often with Chloe. It was early, for Kitty had to go on to a party, and the great room was nearly empty. The emptiness of the room was all round him. It would always be around him now.

'It was good of you to come at such short notice, Kitty,' he said. 'I wanted to tell you that I have just come back from saying good-bye to Chloe. There seemed to be no relations, so she was buried there. It would have made unnecessary talk if I had brought her back to England.'

'You mean you flew over to Holland?'

'Yes. I tried to get hold of you in case you would have liked to come with me, but you were out, and there wasn't much time. I put flowers on her grave for you, I thought you would like that.'

'Oh, Everard darling, thank you, that was lovely of you.'

'You and I were perhaps not her oldest, but I think her best, friends.'

'Don't make me cry, Everard. Not any more. I've loved a good many men in my time, or thought I did, but I'd sooner have spent the day with Chloe than with any of them. She's something out of my life, Everard. I suppose if one had a twin sister one might feel a little like that. I used to think of things to tell her. Oh, darling, we used to have the giggles together, and that means a lot to a woman.

Sounds silly now I say it. Oh, I've only just thought— what the twins will say when they know! I suppose I shall have to tell them one of those terribly unconvincing stories which are supposed to be good for them. Everard darling, I'm only chattering so that I shan't cry.'

'It will do us good to eat and drink first, and then I'll show you a letter which may make you smile, but which I want you to like.'

'Who from?'

'Wil.'

'Oh, dear!'

'Well, wait and see.' He raised his glass, and they drank a silent toast. He drank again, and said with a smile, 'I think that, on the whole, alcohol was a good invention.'

'I don't know *what* I should have done without it,' said Kitty.

When the coffee came, 'Another good invention,' he said, lighting her cigarette and his own cigar.

'What I can never quite grasp about the next world,' said Kitty, 'is how you get on without eating and drinking. And a lot of other things,' she added thoughtfully. As soon as she had said this, she told herself that she was a little fool, because Chloe was now in the next world, and it was just the sort of damned thing a silly person like herself *would* say. But Everard nodded, and said quite naturally, 'I've got my ideas about that. Perhaps I'll tell you if you'd like to hear them. But let's have a look at Wil first.' Everard was quite the nicest man she knew. 'I can't be such a little fool if he likes me,' she thought proudly.

*Grand Hotel,*
*Middleswick Midnight.*

My Dear Everard,

I heard the shocking news of poor Chloe's death as I was stepping on to the stage this evening. You can imagine what it meant to me. Fortunately I am an old trouper, older indeed than I care to think, with the motto 'The show must go on' well rooted in my bones. I think I can say that the house was not aware of any undercurrents in my playing, and indeed gave us a more than usually enthusiastic reception with no less than eight calls at the finish.

Poor dear, delightful, lovely Chloe! We have been friends, you and I, Everard, for many years, and I can speak to you of matters which I should not feel called upon to discuss with any other. It has come to my knowledge from time to time that Miss Marr's name had been, and indeed still was, associated with mine in the loose talk from which no public man is altogether immune. I wish to state emphatically that there has never been a jot or tittle of truth in the stories which have been put about. Miss Marr has never been more to me than a very dear friend; nor could the husband of so devoted a helpmeet as the much-lamented Helen Brightman have wished it otherwise. Moreover, I am firmly of opinion that, if the truth were known, dear Chloe's relationship with all her friends was of a similar character; and that Love, which plucks at the heartstrings of so many of us so insistently, had long ceased to touch her. Is it too fanciful to think that years ago she may have loved and lost, and, her poor heart broken, have vowed herself to chastity?

But I write to you, my dear Everard, less to parade my own grief than to sympathize deeply with yours. For I feel that you were her truest friend; understood her most fully, loved her most faithfully, and will find her passing most grievous to bear. Don't ask me why I know this; we artists have our own ways of reading the hearts of others. No relationship can be so close, so dear, so solidly founded as that between father and daughter, and it is as for a loved and lovely daughter, 'as truly mine as had she been mine own,' that you will mourn. May it be a comfort to you to know that an old friend to both of you understands and shares your sorrow.

Yours always truly,
Wil.

Everard watched Kitty's face as she read. First she smiled; then frowned; then looked bewildered. As soon as she had reached the end, she turned back and read it again.

'Darling, I don't quite know what to make of it,' she said. 'Why does he suddenly call her Miss Marr in the middle?'

'I think that that must be an extract from the letter which he was going to have written to the *Middleswick Gazette*, if he hadn't thought better of it.'

'Everard! He couldn't!'

'He only just couldn't. He did wonder about it.'

'It would be just like him, of course, but—' Once more she picked up the letter. 'Oh dear, why does he have to pretend, when he must know it deceives nobody?'

'Actors earn their living by pretending. I suppose it's difficult to get out of it.'

'Did you know Helen Brightman, darling?'

'Yes.'

'Hideous, a god-awful actress, and drank like a fish. So naturally he didn't want to go to bed with Chloe! And then he practically says, "She didn't love *me,* so obviously she couldn't have loved anybody."'

'I don't think he means to say any of those things. And now read the last paragraph again.'

She read it, and said, 'Yes, if he had only written that, it would have been a lovely letter.'

'That's what I thought. We'll forget about the rest; it's just the flourish of the actor-manager.'

She looked at him curiously.

'Is it true, darling? Is that how you thought of her?'

'Calm of mind, all passion spent? Lately, yes. Perhaps more than I realized all the time. You love your children, Kitty; you will never stop loving them. That's the only love which never changes, never dies.' He smoked for a little in silence, and then said casually, 'She made me her executor. If there is anything you want of hers, you are to have it.'

'Oh, Everard!' She took a handkerchief from her bag, and waited for the tears which she knew were coming. 'It is Chloe who says it, not you?'

'Yes. There are a Mr and Mrs Winghampton, a Vicar in Essex— do you know them?'

'No.'

'They also are to choose something, if they care to. And myself. Nobody else is mentioned, save Ellen, who gets a hundred pounds.'

'Oh, I'm glad. Ellen might come to me, if she would care to.'

'See her, will you; and choose what you want.'

Kitty nodded, dabbing at her eyes. 'I suppose I mustn't ask—'

Everard guessed what she wanted to know, and said that Chloe had had an annuity in some Insurance Company.

'Does that mean—'

'Anything or nothing.'

Kitty took out her compact and began to powder her nose. This always gave her a sense of privacy. She said to her mirror, and one can say anything in private to one's mirror: 'Did she ever tell *you* anything, Everard, I mean about herself? You know what I mean.' Lipstick in hand, she felt even more private. 'And who was that man?'

'Does it matter now? Each of us could make up a story about her, and it would be a different story. Each of us knew, and reacted to a different Chloe. That is the only Chloe we shall ever know.'

'I suppose there was a real Chloe that none of us knew.'

'Just as there is a "real" Kitty,' he smiled, 'and a "real" Everard? But is it the real one? That is what makes me wonder about the next world.'

'Oh, yes, you were going to tell me about that.' As soon as she had said it she thought how silly it sounded. As if any one could!

'We only see people from the outside—what they show to us. In the next world we shall see what they hide from us. Do we want to see it? And shall we recognize it when we do see it? Chloe was your dearest friend, and you had the giggles together. I imagine that two disembodied spirits don't have the giggles together, or, if they do, it is on a different plane, a plane of which neither of you has any experience. It is possible, of course, that your soul and Chloe's soul will meet and form a lasting friendship, but it won't be a continuation of your earthly friendship. That is what I cannot see: how the next world can be a continuation of this one; and if it is not a continuation, then it is nothing. It doesn't exist, because it doesn't matter. Any more than it matters whether or not I was a King in Babylon when you were a Christian slave. What is the good of telling a grief-stricken young husband that he will meet his adored wife in Heaven? He will meet somebody, but it won't be his adored wife, it will be a complete stranger; as he will be to her.'

'I suppose that's true. If you take away Chloe's beauty and her lovely voice and her quickness on to a joke, she might be a hundred other women.' She thought this over and added: 'Of course, there may be more jokes in Heaven than our Vicar seems to think.'

'Let us hope so. But take away everything we know a person by and what remains for us? Nothing. Have you ever noticed how little the modern novelists' habit of recording and analysing his characters' thoughts helps a reader to see the character? Well, of course, all novelists have done it. Look at *David Copperfield*. Every thought in David's mind is given us; we see him from inside; his soul is laid bare—and he simply doesn't exist. We know nothing of Mr Micawber, but what is seen from outside—and he is immortal.'

'So what, Everard? What's the answer?'

'I've wondered sometimes if Death is just an endless sleep with an endless dream; a dream based on what we have seen and known and done and thought in this world; so that each of us works out his own Heaven and Hell. In my dream, if it is a happy dream, as I trust it will be from time to time, my Chloe will be the Chloe whom I love, and my Jonathan will be the Jonathan whom I love, and when we are all three together, as I hope we shall often be, I shall be the Everard I was for him, and the Everard I am for her. Did Chloe love this or that man more than she loved me? Probably. But it won't matter. She will be having her own dream, and I shall never know that I am not in it.' He turned to her with a smile. 'In this way, Kitty, if you want to eat and drink in Heaven, you can; even though there is nothing to eat and drink there.'

'But don't you often have horrible dreams, Everard?'

'Not often, but sometimes. That will, literally, be Hell.'

'Nobody can control his dreams.'

'Your past can and does, down to every last second of thought in it.'

'Darling, it sounds terrifying.'

'Then let us hope that God will be merciful, and that we have been better men and women than we had supposed.' He looked at his watch and said, 'You will have to be going, Kitty.'

She looked at her own, said 'Gracious, yes,' and got up.

When she had gone, he came back to his table, poured himself another brandy, and lit a fresh cigar. The room had filled up. He sat there, alone in the brightness and the laughter, but in a curious way not unhappy.

'I must write to these Winghamptons,' he thought. The thought gave him pleasure. There must be something particular about them, if Chloe wished them to remember her; a country Vicar and his wife. Why not drive down to see them to-morrow? Yes, that would be a good thing to do. That would take him to dinner-time. He would dine in the House, and find somebody to talk to; there was a lot to talk about just now. It was time he made a speech again, he'd been very slack lately. And that girl, Jill Morfrey, he'd never looked her up as he'd meant to. 'He's forsaken me for your Miss Morfrey,' Chloe had said the other day. Well, perhaps she and Rush would like to come to Chanters together, with Kitty and the twins. The twins had never been, they'd love it. There were plenty of nice things to do, if one thought for a little. He would soon get into the way of it.

He rose and made his way through the tables, raising his hand to friends here and there. Write to Miss Morfrey and Rush and Kitty. Order the car for Much Hadingham to-morrow, but drive himself. Have lunch on the way down and get there in the middle afternoon, and then, if they all liked each other, he could stay to tea. He'd think of some more things later. But he mustn't think too far ahead. Just carry on from one thing to another until he could go no further . . . and so enter into that world of the imagination where nothing could die, and where Jonathan and Chloe would be waiting for him.

# Also Available

In his classic autobiography A. A Milne, with his characteristic self-deprecating humour, recalls a blissfully happy childhood in the company of his brothers, and writes with touching affection about the father he adored.

From Westminster School he won a scholarship to Cambridge University where he edited the university magazine, before going out into the world, determined to be a writer. He was assistant editor at *Punch* and went on to enjoy great success with his novels, plays and stories. And of course he is best remembered for his children's novels and verses featuring Winnie-the-Pooh and Christopher Robin.

This is both an account of how a writer was formed and a charming period piece on literary life – Milne met countless famous authors including H. G. Wells, J.M Barrie and Rudyard Kipling.

OUT NOW

# Also available

Gentle chaos sets in when the absent-minded Mr Pim calls in to see George Marden, bearing some innocent news…

George is a fine upstanding citizen and a stickler for doing the right thing. He has a devoted wife, Olivia, and is guardian to his somewhat flighty niece, Dinah.But his careful peace is broken when Mr Pim casually announces that he's recently seen an ex-convict from Australia, Telworthy.

The only thing is that the character sounds awfully like Olivia's first, and supposedly deceased, husband… and if he's really still alive, then Olivia is a bigamist.

OUT NOW

# **Also available**

How well can you ever know another person?

Happily married, Reginald and Sylvia seem to lead a perfect, and perfectly quiet, life. They have more than enough money and their own country house. But when success overtakes them, and allure of London life pulls Reginald in, they find parts of themselves they never knew. Where does their happiness really lie?

Reminiscent of Evelyn Waugh, this wry, intimate examination of a relationship is a gem of 1930s literature.

## OUT NOW

# Also available

Jenny Windell is obsessed with murder mysteries, so when she discovers her estranged aunt dead at her country home, the stage is set for her own investigation.

Worried that being the first at the scene of the crime will make her a suspect and ruin her inquiry, she flees. On the run, she befriends Derek Fenton, the dashing younger brother of acclaimed crime writer Archibald Fenton, and persuades him to join her in her attempts to solve the crime and outsmart dim-witted Inspector Marigold.

An affectionate send-up of the classic Golden Age murder mystery, this charming comedy is A. A. Milne at his most delightful.

OUT NOW

# Preview

A new collection of A. A. Milne's short stories and sketches for grown-ups. Collected in full for the first time, they are an epiphany, and show Milne's renowned charm, concision and whimsical flair in all their brilliance.

He paints memorable scenes, from a children's birthday party, to an accidental encounter with murder, and a case of blackmail – often with an unexpected twist. But he also deals in poignancy, from the girl who pulls the wool over her boyfriend's eyes, to a first dance and first disappointment or family reunion and domestic dissonance.

Beguiling and evocative, Milne's thought-provoking stories will make you see his works for children in a whole new light.

COMING SOON

# Preview

The Rabbits, as they call themselves, are Archie Mannering, his sister Myra, Samuel Simpson, Thomas of the Admiralty, Dahlia Blair and the narrator, with occasional guests. Their conversation is almost entirely frivolous, their activity vacillates between immensely energetic and happily lazy, and their social mores are surprisingly progressive.

Originally published as sketches in *Punch*, the Rabbits' escapades are a charming portrait of middle-class antics on the brink of being shattered by World War I, and fail entirely to take themselves seriously.

*So here they all are. Whatever their crimes, they assure you that they won't do it again* – A. A. Milne

COMING SOON

# About the Marvellous Milne Series

The Marvellous Milne series brings back to vivid life several of A. A. Milne's classic works for grownups.

Two collections – *The Complete Short Stories*, gathered together in full for the first time; and *The Rabbits* comic sketches, originally published in *Punch* and considered by many to be his most distinctive work – showcase Milne's talent as a short story writer.

Four carefully selected novels – *Four Days' Wonder, Mr Pim, Chloe Marr and Two People* – demonstrate his skill across comic genres, from the detective spoof to a timeless and gentle comedy of manners, considering everything from society's relationship with individuals, to intimate spousal relationships.

Alongside this showcase of Milne's talent is his classic memoirs *It's Too Late Now*, providing a detailed account of how his writing career was formed, as well as proving a charming period piece of the literary scene at the time.

**The full series –**
*It's Too Late Now*
*Mr Pim*
*Two People*
*Four Days' Wonder*
*Chloe Marr*
*The Complete Short Stories*
*The Rabbits*

# About the author

A. A. Milne (Alan Alexander) was born in London in 1882 and educated at Westminster School and Trinity College, Cambridge. In 1902 he was Editor of *Granta*, the University magazine, and moved back to London the following year to enter journalism. By 1906 he was Assistant Editor of *Punch*, where he published a series of short stories which now form the collection 'The Rabbits'.

At the beginning of the First World War he joined the Royal Warwickshire Regiment. While in the army in 1917 he started on a career writing plays and novels including *Mr. Pim Passes By, Two People, Four Days' Wonder* and an adaptation of Kenneth Grahame's *The Wind in the Willows* – *Toad of Toad Hall*. He married Dorothy de Selincourt in 1913 and in 1920 had a son, Christopher Robin.

By 1924 Milne was a highly successful playwright, and published the first of his four books for children, a set of poems called *When We Were Very Young*, which he wrote for his son. This was followed by the storybook *Winnie-the-Pooh* in 1926, more poems in *Now We Are Six* (1927) and further stories in *The House at Pooh Corner* (1928).

In addition to his now famous works, Milne wrote many novels, volumes of essays and light verse, works which attracted great success at the time. He continued to be a prolific writer until his death in 1956.

# Note from the Publisher

To receive updates on further releases in the Marvellous Milnes series – plus special offers and news of other humorous fiction series to make you smile – sign up now to the Farrago mailing list at farragobooks.com/sign-up